Havasu Heat

Havasu Heat

By

Peggy DePuydt

ISBN: 1-932993-32-0 (paperback)
ISBN 13: 978-1-932993-32-5
ISBN: 1-932993-33-9 (E-book)

Library of Congress Number
LCCN: 2006901702

Edit and Cover Design by Star Publish
Interior Design by Mystique Design & Editorial

A Star Publish Book
http://starpublish.com
Mesquite, Nevada U.S.A.

STAR

Published in 2006 by Star Publish

Printed in the United States of America

Dedication

This book rests dedicated to a special high school English/ Lit teacher, Dorrine Anderson of Gladstone, Michigan, who never flagged in her enthusiasm for writing endeavors. Dorrine is a graduate of Northern Michigan University in Marquette, Michigan, where she majored in English. She received her Masters Degree in Library Science and Media Services from Western Michigan University in Kalamazoo, Michigan.

The regret grows, however. She is now an institutionalized Alzheimer patient and will never know of this accolade. One asks why it is that a *thank you* is always *toolatetoolatetoolate.*

Acknowledgements

Doug Thomas, Wastewater Manager, Lake Havasu City Wastewater Treatment Plant, for tutoring a neophyte in the ABCs of managing a city's wastewater system.

Thailak Hernandez, Laboratory Manager/Chemist, a native Sri Lankan, for invaluable geographic instruction.

Lt. Casey Dreller for patience and guidance in the intricacies of narcotics.

Dick DePuydt, for his photography skills and hardline critiques on law enforcement *modus operandi*.

Today's News Herald, for the use of their archives.

Tom DePuydt, for expertise on munitions, and policies and procedures of law enforcement.

Barbara and Ken Bishman, for editing and encouragement.

Janet Elaine Smith, Publisher's Editor, for her thoroughness.

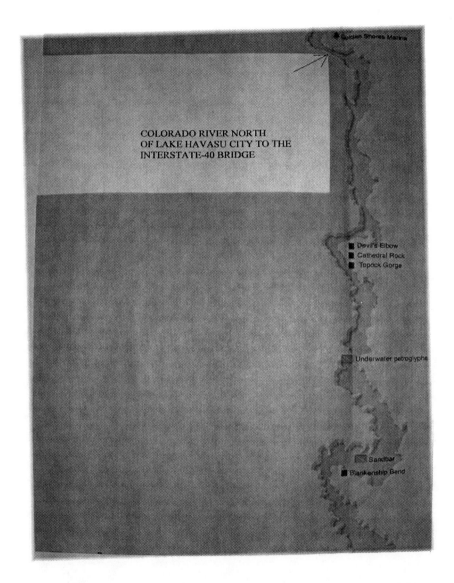

COLORADO RIVER NORTH
OF LAKE HAVASU CITY TO THE
INTERSTATE-40 BRIDGE

Golden Shores Marina

Devil's Elbow
Cathedral Rock
Topock Gorge

Underwater petroglyphs

Sandbar
Blankenship Bend

NORTHERN LOWER COLORADO RIVER VALLEY

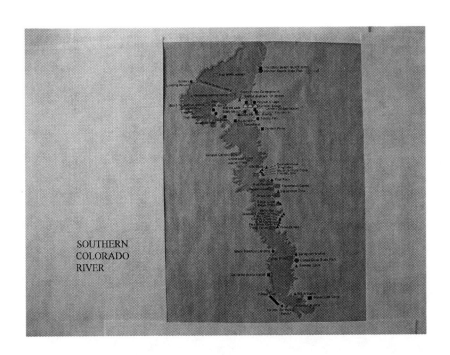

SOUTHERN
COLORADO
RIVER

SOUTHERN LOWER COLORADO RIVER VALLEY

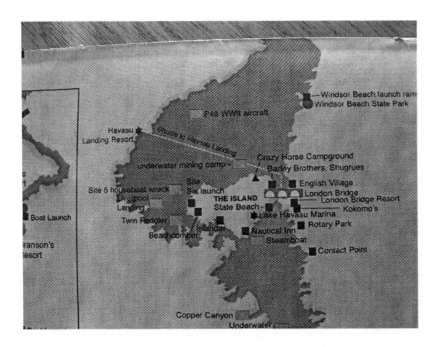

"The Island" or "Pittsburgh Point"

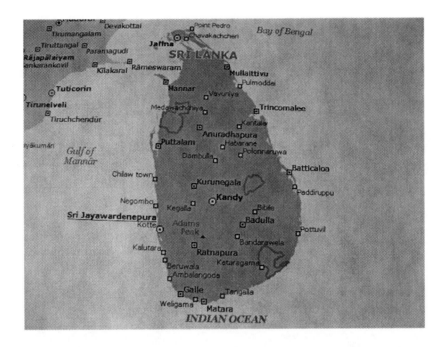

DEMOCRATIC SOCIALIST REPUBLIC OF SRI LANKA

PROLOGUE

"This is radio station KJJJ broadcasting from beautiful downtown Lake Havasu City this movin' along Monday afternoon, January 6, 1997."

Special Investigation Bureau agent Matthew Cameron Cruise marveled at the innocence of this Arizona day as he enjoyed his favorite country station while driving east on McCulloch Boulevard.

Standing six feet three inches tall, and weighing two-hundred and ten pounds, his quick mind was whip-smart. He never flinched from the chore of outwitting the narcs before they hit on the kids he instructed in the dangers of drug usage at Thunderbolt Middle School. The confidence of young people grew through the Drug Abuse Resistance Education (DARE) Program. Bending his great stature to meet the height of maturing youth gained him equality, an equality whereby trust built.

"Call me McCruise," he said laughing gently, revealing even white teeth, his intelligent eyes crinkling. M. C. Cruise morphed into McCruise.

McCruise's gaze swept the boulevard ahead to measure how far he lagged behind Laura in her maroon, ragtop Jeep. Moments ago, she finished preaching to the choir (third grade) as a DARE volunteer. McCruise and Laura enjoyed marriage for eight years. By any measure, she was his precious blonde-haired, blue-eyed, princess. At thirty years old, she was as beautiful and fresh as the day he chose her for himself, back when she was eighteen. She yet left him weak in the knees and proud of her!

His peripheral vision picked up an accelerating dump truck coming off Tempest Street. He held his breath. The truck's speed intensified as Laura approached the intersection. Slowly closing the distance between them, McCruise saw intense sunlight glinting off a pint container of Evian, which Laura waved in salute through the rear-view mirror, oblivious to the approaching truck.

It was the last thing Laura Anne Cruise ever did.

The impact hurled Laura's Jeep into the Tempest arroyo as the truck veered sharply west to disappear down McCulloch Boulevard into blinding late afternoon sun.

The ear-deafening explosion pitched the air with percussion from the imploded vehicle. Black smoke and fire encompassed the area. The ache in his ears turned sickening, while the smell of hot metal and gas curled around the deep wash. Stopping his Grand Cherokee, he quarreled with his feet to move, to stand, to take cover; his dark eyes glazed over with a fog of incredulity.

As he groped his way toward the disintegrated scene, he encountered stickiness, blood, but not his; he checked with blurred vision, confused. In a studied, clumsy gait, he moved toward the old vision of the car, the new vision of nothingness, the magenta-spattered rocks, and the nameless remains of Laura.

Laminated to her black face and severed hand in grotesque caricature was the melted Evian bottle. While her small Jeep smoldered, countless shards of glass danced in the sunshine—an ironic tribute to the holocaust.

With cold assertion, an aching grief rose in McCruise's stomach, his heart seizing up tightly for survival. Falling to his knees in broken disbelief, he rocked back and forth; a sound of agony, low and primeval, rose from him. "Oh, my God," each word echoed with his loss. As sirens sounded in the distance, he slipped into denial.

The gentle giant McCruise died within on that afternoon. A semblance of the same man who arose from his denial was in need of a confessor for his thoughts.

CHAPTER ONE

Monday, January 6, 1997, 7:30 p.m., Duluth, Minnesota

The drive from his Research and Development Lab strained long. Of glacial portent were the streets covered with impacted snow. Lake Superior, in an ugly mood, affected a shiver upon Fayne Norwood's fifty-five year old bones and a squint to his defining tan eyes.

The message light was summoning when he arrived at his home on Lake Shore Drive.

"Fayne, this is Sligh. Mission accomplished, but wrong target. Call me."

"Son—of—a—bitch." The words hung in the air.

A giant intimidating man, Fayne glided through his home with cat-like suppleness. His coat removed and hung up, he ran a hand through his slightly gray, sand-colored hair, picked up the cordless telephone from the secretary desk in the foyer and punched speed dial for Sligh.

Through the double-paned floor-to-ceiling windows, his tan eyes scanned the fierce whitecaps as they attacked the ice-packed shoreline.

"C'mon, Shoney, pick up the phone," he muttered impatiently. After four chimes, the answering machine kicked in with a beep.

"I'm out. Leave a message."

Fayne checked his watch. It was five-thirty in Lake Havasu City. Arizona stayed on Mountain Time year around giving Fayne a two-hour later difference in the winter and a whopping three-hour difference in the summer. All day, he had been stiffened with anxiety about this hit. The interferon, McCruise, needed to go down. One wild vigilante could put a helluva hole in Fayne's Colorado River enterprises.

"Christ, where are you Sligh Shoney?" His voice took on the characteristics of powerlessness, an emotion Norwood rarely entertained, the sense of it an effrontery to his superiority and infallibility. The timbre of his voice alone could cow an orator.

Pouring a snifter of cognac from the sideboard, Fayne swirled it as he speed dialed the King's Retreat in Lake Havasu. He'd have Shoney paged. After all, a hotel manager should be in-house where he belonged. Overcome with impatience, he informed the operator, "Sligh Shoney, please. This is Fayne Norwood." He listened to the monotonous ringing.

"He doesn't answer, Mr. Norwood. Would you like me to page him?"

"Yes. Thank you." *You goddamn idiot, Shoney. Take root where you're planted.* Fayne listened to the hollow sound of the page as it went out.

"No response, Mr. Norwood. Could I have him call you?"

"Yes. Immediately. I'm home." He thumbed the off button on the portable telephone.

"Damn!"

Fayne needed to impress upon Sligh the necessity to lay low. The wasted person served as sufficient warning to McCruise to back off. Further action perhaps would be unnecessary.

CHAPTER TWO

Sligh Shoney, the blond, blue-eyed Colorado River playboy, lolled back in his Jacuzzi, his eyes closed, allowing the bubbling jets to soothe his libido. A recreational drug user, his forty-five-year-old senses curried into a comfortable haze.

The confidence attaching itself to great wealth and power acted as an aphrodisiac. Surrounded by luxury, the bright red heart-shaped Jacuzzi was a playpen for his penthouse atop the King's Retreat—a four-story, five-star hotel holding court over a multi-million dollar chunk of real estate known as the Bridgewater Channel, a fabricated curtailment of the Colorado River.

Sligh was never sorry he had built these concealed quarters for his dallying. The remainder of the penthouse existed as a luxuriously appointed suite in which he could entertain legitimate visitors. Mr. Sligh Shoney, his chosen moniker, also welcomed illegitimate visitors. Both entities enjoyed gracious indulgence.

Sligh slowly opened his eyes and drank in the awesomeness of his newly assigned intern, Mallika Chilaw, a Sri Lankan beauty. A gem of dark walnut skin, huge depthless dark eyes, brilliant flashing teeth, she intrigued the hell out of him. A great restlessness consumed him to get her sufficiently receptive to his wishes.

Hearing the distant chiming of the telephone, Sligh chose not to respond. Matters of urgency could wait while he was gaining carnal knowledge of the conquest at hand.

Providing further privacy, his faithful bodyguard, Ricki Rodriguez, sat in the living room smoothing his heavy black mustache. A smile grew on his face with dreams of grandeur. At five-feet six inches, Ricki fancied himself six feet tall resultant of the assignment of Personal Assistant to Shoney.

Sligh knew wiry Ricki could hear the phone but he bowed to obedience. His instructions were not to answer. As shit flows downhill, those who worked for Ricki in their collarless white shirts and sunglasses bent to do Ricki's bidding.

Hearing the insistent paging, Sligh tuned it out.

"Mallika, you're beautiful," he smiled.

CHAPTER THREE

Tuesday, January 14, 1997, Lake Havasu City, Arizona, 9:30 a.m.

The day dawned bright and cool, the sun reaching over the mountains later this time of year. McCruise's bright red Grand Cherokee rolled silently west on McCulloch Boulevard.

Leaking through the silence, thoughts of Laura prevailed. If McCruise heard one more time 'Nothing you do will bring her back' he was going to puke. Bitterness rose like nausea while remembering her severed hand, her incinerated face. It was a nightmare of massive proportions, from which he couldn't shake loose.

Sure, she was dead. He was no longer in denial. However, he *could* do something. From the first inception of his plan, it was reality to McCruise. With police technology, he could gain an exclusive assignment to the hit-and-run investigation.

On the fifteen-minute drive from his home on Cherry Tree Way in the Mohave Mountains to the police department situated on the boulevard, McCruise was in the same mist of remorse he suffered since the holocaust. Hypnotically he stared at the splendor of Lake Havasu, the deep blue water spanning forty-five miles north and south separating Lake Havasu City from the Chemehuevi Mountains of California.

He sat tall in the car, but his eyes, normally warm with well-being, now revealed nothing. Nothing filtered through his terrifying thoughts but Laura's last moments. McCruise knew no time to smell danger or warn her. Involuntarily, he lurched against the steering wheel, the pain like a living entity.

He turned to the business of why he had become interested in the drug enforcement program in the Lake Havasu Area Consolidated Schools. Somehow, it all fit— the city lived off the economy of the lake, Cruise Liner Watercraft lived off the economy of the city, and the city regenerated itself with its youth. *First things first* read the McCruise mantra. Now, enter this: a heinous crime without retribution.

Working with the Chamber of Commerce, McCruise affected many city events that attracted thousands of visitors who used the motels, the restaurants, the pharmacies, and the shops. The International Budweiser Hydroplane Races last spring and the International Jet Ski Boating Association World Finals last fall were two of his latest accomplishments.

In a recent issue of *Havasu Connection*, a feature ran on Cruise Liner Watercraft, owned by his father, Coulter. *McCruise is a city pacesetter in business acumen, style, and panache. He consistently takes great pride in his hometown.*

Nonetheless, what has a man gained when he has lost his way, lost the light from his life? Night and day, the haunting memory flooded his thoughts. Why did he not sense the risks of drug cartel interference?

The thoughts smothered him.

He rode on an impassioned roller coaster since Laura's death, canceling even routine meetings, unable to function as an executive officer at the plant or a detective at the station. Even his devout Catholic faith was of no solace.

Tears stung behind his eyes. He would seek to avenge Laura's death—if need be, alone.

CHAPTER FOUR

McCruise activated his left turn directional signal for the exit onto the long bending driveway leading to the neatly landscaped grounds of the Lake Havasu City Police Department. A white mast held a trifecta of flags USA, Arizona, and United Kingdom. The flagpole stood proudly in an energized breeze, as if a beacon that all is well. Against a brilliant blue sky, the hoisting ropes tapped an arpeggio rhythm created by the rising and falling downriver wind.

Strange, it would seem to the uninformed, to see a British flag hanging so proudly and taking its place of respect in this far-western city. The motif of England burned indulgently throughout the city ever since the London Bridge saw purchase and shipment, stone by stone, to Lake Havasu in 1967. Impermeable, it spanned the Bridgewater Channel connecting the city with a grand island of premium real estate, much of it owned by the State Land Department, and held in trust.

While walking to the entrance of the new six-million-dollar brick building, McCruise saw himself reflected in the plate glass doors. He looked the same on the outside — light tan pinstriped suit, white shirt, bolo necktie and highly polished Justin boots. The irony hit him suddenly — executive on the outside, a washed up nothing on the inside. It reminded him of a shiny fire truck going up in smoke.

No one need show him through the two security doors that closed and locked behind him with soft authoritative clicks. Beyond a long hall came the stairs and elevator to the second floor, which housed the executive offices of the city attorney, police super ranks, and the Western Arizona State Regional Crime Lab.

The hit-and-run homicide was common knowledge to the readers of every newspaper in the state and every TV audience who watched the evening news in horror. The catastrophic case being unsolved was reason enough to assign him full-time to the mission he thought, but convincing Captain O'Shaughnessey was a horse of another color.

His father managed the boat works very well without him, indeed had done so for many years.

In addition, he mused, the department wasn't happy either. Having an unsolved crime of massive repercussions on their hands was not at the top of the list of *desirables*. A crime of such appalling threat could preclude tourists from considering Lake Havasu City and the London Bridge as a vacation destination.

The nameplate on the mahogany desk read "Captain Connor O'Shaughnessey, City of Lake Havasu." Character lived in his dark-complexioned determined face. Heavy eyebrows cantilevered over warm dark eyes, which were peering at McCruise. Circling O'Shaughnessey's otherwise bald head was a ring of Monk's hair, and deeply carved triplicate smile lines spread outward from his eyes. His tailored, pale fawn suit fit as smooth as silk across his broad shoulders.

O'Shaughnessy's huge hand slapped onto the chair arm as if to make a point. "You must know the seriousness of your proposal: full time on Laura's death or you quit and do it on your own. Don't you think you should give this further gelling time?"

"It's gelled."

Contemplative, O'Shaughnessey swept his fingers over his mustache. On the late side of fifty-five, he was a man's man in intelligence and stature, standing six-foot two, weight commensurate.

"There's a flip side, here, Mr. Cruise. Did you know you're among the suspects in the fatal crash?"

"Nooo—who would—how did?" McCruise felt an odd emptiness.

"You have a double indemnity clause in your wife's insurance policy."

"True, but that's because of her value to me." McCruise found the conversation inexplicable, perhaps even stupefying. Him? A suspect? Impulsive, and at times irrational in his frame of mind, his eyes bulged as he rose from the chair to do a nose-to-nose with the older man. Placing both hands on the desk, he leaned in. "That statement is over the top, and I suspect you know that." His jaw worked at self-discipline.

"You see, I can assure you of unbiasness in the investigation." McCruise leaned in closer, as if to make his words more meaningful. "I've pledged myself to it, pledged to solving Laura's death, to do it with cool detachment, and to put a better light on the city." He pointed his chin to the window that overlooked the metropolitan area.

"Such single-mindedness is unacceptable." O'Shaughnessey would nurture no naked hatreds on the force.

"Oh, I've been altruistic to the community and distributed my time and efforts equally, but I've entered into a pact between the devil and myself."

"A pact?" O'Shaughnessey's eyebrows rose.

"To avenge my wife's murder and save my two sons from a fate worse than death: narcotics." McCruise's eyes were unwavering with the delivery.

O'Shaughnessey tapped a pencil lightly on the desktop, as if the rhythm could put this young man's motives into perspective. Obviously, McCruise was neither negotiating nor listening, but simply suspended in the immobility of deep determination.

"Is this a decision reached since Laura's death, or have you thought for some time of seeking permission to work narcotics?"

"Since her murder. It's been eight days, fifteen hours and ten minutes." It sounded like a jail sentence to McCruise

He'd grown accustomed in the interim to feeling as if he were being torn apart; every passing minute he lost a piece of himself.

"Your desire to enter full-time into a single arena may be just a cover-up for the acid event, an avenue by which you may be able to cloud surfacing leads."

Was O'Shaughnessey needling him or simply baring thoughts that were processing? Did other people think along the same line? He fought the urge to slam out of the office, but he knew better. His temper was blurring his ability to think sensibly. He sat back, adjusting his left booted foot over his right knee, slowly thumping his index finger on the heel of his Justins.

"Why would I compromise my position at Cruise Liner Watercraft and my longevity with the Department? Surely not to cover up a crime I never committed." Unflinchingly, McCruise returned O'Shaughnessey's steady stare.

The captain brightened with new interest at the younger man's candidness. Leaning forward, he thumbed through McCruise's records. Thirty-four years old, height six-three, correct; weight, correct; black hair. He favored McCruise with a glance and added "curly hair, dark brown eyes." O'Shaughnessey penciled 'a confident mouth, health problems, none.' His shoulders rose.

O'Shaughnessey recalled the concern he felt when McCruise applied for the position of city police officer six years ago. ALETA—Arizona Law Enforcement Training Academy—was one of the toughest training centers in the Southwest. The institute made no allowances for age; most recruits were seven years younger. McCruise's body and mind would test to the breaking point.

O'Shaughnessey arose and walked to his window-on-the-world, clasping his hands behind his back, his mind running through a number of introspections.

"I'm sorry, McCruise," he said, turning around slowly. "Weighing everything, I can't qualify endorsing a personal vendetta. You've massaged your logic into making everything right for all the wrong reasons."

"Reasons that have been deemed wrong because of time and place have worked for many people." McCruise hung strong, although his insides were melting like wax. "Consider Lincoln's reasons for freeing the slaves when the odds were insurmountable, Jefferson's reasons for framing the constitution in a lawless land and Albert Einstein when he shook out the mysteries of the universe while skeptics denounced his theories." The stab of disappointment was acute; McCruise's chest grew cold, as if hit by a stun gun.

"All well and good, those analogies. The cost to the department, however, is more than seventeen thousand dollars to train a candidate for law enforcement in general, and not for law enforcement for one."

In addition, O'Shaughnessey considered the dollars the state kicked in for tuition, such money coming from a portion of traffic fines. Both his hands smoothed back the hair above his ears.

"Is there anything else you'd like to add?"

"Yes." McCruise never thought he would have to play the race card, but this was his last ace. "I have Afro-American ancestors. Although you see light skin, proof of heritage is in Mark and Luke; they bear strong semblance of their ancestry. As you know from your long association with the Cruises, they supposedly adopted a Caucasian in most respects. The department's requirements for affirmative action mandates would fall out of compliance should this officer quit the force. I'm the only minority you have."

McCruise's eyes were lasers of challenge, while his mouth was as dry as the Mohave Desert.

"Perhaps we need to talk over lunch," O'Shaughnessey grunted, his mouth controlling a grin.

CHAPTER FIVE

While driving to the Ramada Inn, where he would meet with the captain for lunch, McCruise digressed through roiling clouds of memory. Thoughts tossed and blown over the past week of loneliness flanked him.

With great clarity, he remembered having met Laura when she was a varsity cheerleader for the Lake Havasu Knights football team. He came home for the weekend from Arizona State University at Tempe. Electricity shot through him as he recalled her performance on the playing-field sidelines.

He could again feel the warmth and luster of the April night when he asked Laura to a movie at the English Village. He would just get her out of his blood and never see her again. He smiled with the recollection of his surprise to find that she was not the garden-variety eighteen-year-old. She was much more adult than many women he dated: adult and well adjusted.

How could this freckle-nosed child have him in a state of flux? He stood to slay dragons for her. It struck a severe blow to his self-imagery, to his constants. Her guileless characteristics were as natural as a newborn's; her happy smile set his blood on fire. Swedish blue eyes and long lashes tantalized him, while her crown of dazzling golden-blonde hair glinted in the sun like freshly panned nuggets. When humor struck, her eyes danced, her nose crinkled. She was unbelievably innocent looking and beautiful.

He kept her innocent by controlling his libido, rationalizing it even in irrational moments of need. The sacrifice paid off when at eighteen Laura succumbed to his advances.

"I won't hurt you," he said.

Nonetheless, he did, and found the warmth he knew was waiting there, and it was all his. He was not systemic, but neither was he regret-laden. He soothed her when she cried.

The years rolled by, years in which he and Laura shared the same bed, the same dinner table. They played and prayed together, her love the embodiment of everything good that lies within a human heart.

He attended her faithfully when the days of her gestation were fulfilled, stood by her side encouragingly when the pain of childbirth ebbed her energy to nothingness. When Mark and Luke were born, he wept.

The biggest surprise, however, was Mark. How strong Laura's tenacity through it all, with Mark exhibiting African-American traits. Did she stray? It was inexplicable to consider that she entertained an affair; they were so close, he would have known. Surely, he would have known. Paternity tests proved the child was his, creating a completely new world of mental explosions. He pressed to gather and harness bare facts in order to bring his world back into focus. McCruise and Laura cried with the conundrum and laughed with the release of knowing.

His father and mother, Coulter and Penny, dug deeper into the adoption agency, a slow and sluggish undertaking revealing little and comforting less.

Laura, as pure as the driven snow, turned stricken, her parents sympathetic throughout the entire investigation. Nevertheless, how they loved Mark—beautiful Mark with great brown eyes, a full mouth, fat cheeks, Laura's nose, and a mass of curly dark hair.

His whole insides melted when Laura breastfed the children, first Mark, and then Luke. With pride and protection, his chest swelled and his throat constricted. He would see to it they never wanted for anything. They were his: Laura, Mark, Luke, and Tucker the Terrible, a golden retriever with his coat of amber hair.

With the sudden reversal of fate, he found himself trying to spin a lifestyle affording him the happiness of getting up in the morning with purpose to his day—a day without indifference, a day without the fright and sudden dread of loss. The boys, however, needed his reinforcement—Tucker as well.

Maybe he would never find the nucleus of a new world. He was no longer young; he envisioned his life slipping away like water over the Parker Dam. He outlived days in this past week of hiding his head in the sand, then catapulting, carving ways and means to deal a new hand. He would finesse a new life in this synthetic society. He was a survivor, and he would not be a member of the Disinterested Bystanders Organization. Perhaps he would never love again as deeply as the first time, but he prayed that at some time he might experience a measure of peace.

CHAPTER SIX

At 11:30 AM, the Ramada Inn experienced a lull before the lunch crowd arrived, allowing the captain and McCruise a quiet table near the southwest exposure windows. From here, they overlooked Arizona State Highway 95 and the city's Community Center. To the north of the center, a condominium complex starting in the two hundred thousands grew, and the vast expanse of the Havasu blue lake back-dropped over all.

Connor jumped right in. "Sometimes the reality of a situation is a reversal of what one originally expects. Don't you want to change your mind—stay off the case?" A wry grin played at the corners of his mouth.

"It isn't exactly what I'd hoped my future would hold, but the choice is mine."

"It's not too late to reconsider."

"Not a chance."

"Good grief, McCruise," O'Shaughnessey shook his head. "Your presence on the murder investigation and the narc squad may not even jerk a difference in solving Laura's tragic death, which has turned over few leads so far. Dedicated hours to a single investigation can be a gray routine, even if you delve into narcotics trafficking at the same time," he discouraged.

McCruise nodded. At least he would know he was alive by the endurance he tested every day. He would be feeling *something*, which did not happen since the explosion of Laura's vehicle. His stomach contracted with the bitterness of the recall. Everyday he sandpapered himself with the thought that Laura would not have been as committed to DARE if he didn't set the precedent. He swallowed and emitted a groan. At times, in the tumult of the day, he laid his hands over his eyes for privacy with his personal nightmare.

A server approached, wearing a smile and carrying an order pad. Saving time, they ordered the daily special: tortillas with chicken, smothered with hot sauce and cheese.

"Heart food," Connor said, tongue-in-cheek. "You know, McCruise, you aren't the suspect I painted. It's our belief that *you* were the target of that truck. Do you really want to stick your neck out further—for another hit?"

"No, but..."

"Are your revenge motives weakening, Mr. Cruise?"

McCruise chose not to answer, silently sipping water. He wished the captain thought of him as having more substance than to fall apart over some hardships he may or may not encounter.

The Alice-type server hurried to their table with their plates, eager to please. Gibber jabbering incessantly, she refilled water glasses with a pitcher clinking with ice, and scurried away like a frightened field mouse overstaying its welcome.

"Are there any other negatives?" McCruise asked, his eyes downcast as he tackled his tortilla.

"Yes. On the streets, you'll find skuzz bags, individuals you would ordinarily give wide berth. These are individuals you will encounter, fearsome truck with evil pulsing through their veins."

McCruise inserted "cancel" into the thought. He'd experienced rigid physical training while playing football for ASU. Subsequently, the Arizona Cardinals considered him for a draft into the National Football League. Instead, McCruise opted to get his Masters Degree and use his business administration acumen in Cruise Liner Watercraft, his father's boat business. He was confident that he could handle himself mentally and physically.

"You may have to kill."

"Justifiable homicide." McCruise's jaw firmed.

"Nevertheless, a man can struggle with these torments."

"I need to do this. Desperately." McCruise breathed deeply, his dark eyes pleading. He felt a familiar lump in his throat, tried a smile that tuned out far left of arrogant, but far right to bitterness.

He shoved his plate aside, finding that he was not as hungry as he thought. The façade he was showing the captain far surpassed his burning stomach—the fear of failure. It was as if he were being shown a road too steep to climb, too rough to traverse, too long to endure, the pot of gold at the end too small.

Yet, for all the negativity, McCruise could not erase the picture of the unidentifiable remains of Laura outside the skeleton of her sporty Jeep. His heart sank. No one could feel the desperation and helplessness he suffered as he pursued the terror campaign. No one else could explain to Mark and Luke why their beloved mother left them in such a ruthless, shabby fashion. No one else could quiet Tucker's constant searching, tail dragging, and nose sniffing the floor. Vindication was the only escape from the horror.

Spiritually, he felt Laura's presence more than ever before; he felt her beside him, warm and undemanding, asking for peace, not for her, but for his tormented mind. A breath caught with the strong thought, which arose not willfully but without any conscious effort, causing a physiological change he could not shake. Was it sorrow, love at feeling her nearness, or hopelessness? He would suppress it. Nothing was going to deter his mission.

"You haven't changed your mind?"

McCruise lifted his eyes. "Not for a minute."

CHAPTER SEVEN

Saturday, May 3, 1997

Jacaranda Rose Remington pressed selection number eight on the Mariah Carey CD, *Hero*. The soft sounds of her new bright-red Corvette held a communion of the soul with the uplifting care words, 'A hero lies in you'. Interstate 25 South between Pueblo, Colorado and Albuquerque, New Mexico lay straight and benevolent before her. At twenty-five years old, she acknowledged she claimed a sore lack of heroes in her life.

Button-sized blue eyes viewed deserts and mountains. She marveled at how the early pioneers managed to maneuver their covered wagons over this foreboding, ancient land. Now it was her turn to venture west and number among twentieth century pioneers by those who would come hundreds of years after the present society disappeared. She sighed with the impact of how insignificant one life was in the total picture of time and space.

Jacquie dodged Duluth, Minnesota two days ago, driving the first night to Kingdom City, Missouri, and the next to Pueblo, Colorado. She knew she was pushing the mileage, but she wanted to spend modest time on the road. She would shoot for Gallup, New Mexico tonight. It amused her to think she could have flown to Lake Havasu City in only five hours. Frivolousness was not part of her lifestyle, however, and the car bulged tightly with all her earthly possessions.

Running her fingers through her short-cropped, Little Orphan Annie auburn hair, she hoped she would sleep better tonight, if she ever again would. Jacquie long ago stopped wishing it were yesterday once more. Although she was realistic enough to know Fayne Norwood cut all ties, and settled her with a payoff, that fact did not make it hurt less. From here on out, she would see to it that her feelings remained bolted to her brain. How does one wipe away three years of one's life and chalk it up to experience? She could hardly describe the invested years as a valued experience. War was an experience, too, but it was hardly valued.

Life at Norwood Research & Development after graduating college posed an exercise in naiveté. She could entitle it *The Seduction of Jacaranda Rose Remington* and find it a best seller. Fayne's flattering attention swept her psyche like a new broom. Graduating with her B.A., he arranged for her to have an administrative position in his suite of offices. She possessed only the barest understanding of what their life together would be like. After that, she was mesmerized. Magic dinners at his Lake Superior Mansion were leading to catastrophe. Nothing was free; she knew that.

Office gossip was rife with frenzied tales of his philandering. "He goes through women like Cracker Jacks, looking for the perfect prize. Commitment is a word he doesn't know." However, his muddy waters sucked her in like quicksand.

He never ceased to thrill her with his worldliness, bringing the seed of a girl into womanhood. His commanding airs compelled her youthfulness. Enclosed in the sheltering arms of an older man, she found a father substitute.

God only knew that her relationship with her deceased father, Charlie Remington, was always standoffish. He was all business—a cold fish. He had not denied her anything, but rather than a father figure, he was never more than a provider. She deduced that he squelched her love through simple disinterest, which she recently recognized as a form of negligence. What she missed in her father, she found in the warmth of Fayne Norwood.

Ejecting the Carey CD, she allowed herself to lull with the soft engine sound of the vehicle. She managed to shut out the intense sunshine on the highway ahead and replay Fayne, who turned out to be anything but a hero.

"You've made such a difference in my life," Fayne said. "I'd like to have you gift-wrapped—for me, from you—to keep forever." Cupping her chin, he turned her full mouth to his, a mouth as tempting as an August plum.

After capturing her innocence, he showered her with expensive gifts. The dazzle of diamonds leapt at her out of gift boxes. Flowers arrived for no occasion. Superb seating locations at Minneapolis stage plays were hers. At her disposal was foreign travel in his Dassault-Falcon private jet. She remembered the smell of cashmere and leather, and recalled the comfortable creak of his highly polished Italian leather shoes.

She owned it all—for a while.

She searched in her cooler, finding a can of diet soda with caffeine to keep her alert. Fayne was full of obscure puzzles. The more she learned of him, the more enigmas surfaced. Riddles of his life were unsolvable, but she chose to ignore them; her life was pat and secure. Clearly, her attachment to him sprung from some kind of cruel dedication, love of the good life, and hope for marriage and children. She knew, however, that he was powerfully rich beyond the normal earnings of a research and development lab.

She tucked her soda into the cold-drink holder and reached out to touch her briefcase, which held pictures and mementoes of better times. *Administrative Assistant*, a title she knew he concocted to make her feel important, a high-style position Fayne conjured up so he could flaunt his trophyesque sleep-in partner. She shuddered. The appointment, nonetheless, put her in a position in which she was privy to fuzzy phone calls, faxes, and e-mail, like puzzle pieces that never did jibe.

The muffled telephone conversations between Sligh Shoney and Fayne grew layers of gloom and shadows on her soul. Jacquie seized with an invading thought: Fayne would waste her in a minute if he thought there was enough substance to her to have found his business dealings less than legitimate. What *were* his business interests in Lake Havasu other than the defunct Golden Crest? If it weren't for money, Fayne Norwood wouldn't give the city a nod. She was too close to the picture not to view it in the full light of day. Were the blurry communiqués she'd stumbled upon from time to time part of the puzzle?

Traffic was heavy driving through Albuquerque to pick up Interstate 40 West. Her attention shifted to the large, green signs that read 'Gallup West Exit—2 Miles.'

Even with maneuvering in heavy traffic, an epiphany was unfolding. Something was wrong with this picture. Fayne must know that she held niggling suspicions of his various business ventures, but instead of keeping her in the style to which she'd grown accustomed, he dumped her, offering an English-style spirits and dining establishment on the Colorado River in Lake Havasu City, Arizona. He topped off the deal with the new Corvette and two-hundred-fifty thousand dollars to renovate the aging building, which sat closed for two years. The business needed to be up, running and profitable in one year or it would revert to Fayne, including the entirety of the renovated building.

What was in it for Norwood if, indeed, she made a success of the business? The thought startled her. Norwood didn't invest money without returns in sight—big returns. Therefore, did he project that she would never complete the renovating, thus reclaiming it for himself? In addition, he cancelled her from his life very gracefully. Comprehension washed over her in a deadened lull. As she negotiated the Interstate 40 exit and headed West into the intense late afternoon sun, her thoughts waxed her breathless and cold.

CHAPTER EIGHT

It was a real question around the halls of the Station: which came first, Lt. Anthony Valesano or Italian pasta? The consensus was common: all bets were on Valesano, an age-indeterminate man.

Commanding officer of the Special Investigation Bureau, it was Valesano's duty to not leave a stone unturned in the investigation of the Cruise murder, nearly six months old and yet unsolved. Valesano gritted his teeth with frustration. Shit flows downhill and he was catching a reservoir for not bringing this dilemma to closure, even with the addition of McCruise's special assignment.

Regardless of O'Shaughnessey's thoughts in respect to McCruise, Department Policy, and blah, blah, blah, Valesano waltzed around the edge of personally interrogating him. Just because McCruise served the department, it did not immunize him from a murder investigation. Anyway, casting aspersions on McCruise took the heat off himself.

Valesano arranged to meet McCruise privately, in a neutral corner, so to speak. The dining room at the King's Retreat was acceptable. It was most common to see two police officers meet there for coffee or to walk the esplanade along the Bridgewater Channel under the London Bridge. In a city declaring a population of 45,000 give or take tens of thousands of snowbirds and spring breakers, business owners recognized the two detectives, even though they were dressed inconspicuously in soft clothes.

McCruise, with a heavy-duty obligation to the department, agreed to confer with Valesano, who was his superior officer. He was surprised upon entering the coffee house fifteen minutes early to find that Valesano already arrived and was standing near the self-serve coffee urn. McCruise judged him about five-seven, slightly built, receding black hair worn slicked back, and a long-toothed smile that looked to McCruise like a split in a gourd. He reminded himself, however, of his commitment to being unbiased.

"Hey, McCruise. Nice you could come." Anthony Valesano's voice was wiry whenever anxiety struck him, as if the sounds were passing over a violin string. McCruise noted his dark eyes, set in a long, ruddy-complexioned face. For a man who was probably no more than forty-six-years old, his eyes showed age and his gestures were etched erratic. The *eyes* rolled toward a booth, indicating an invitation to sit. McCruise followed, observing the slight torso, the snappy George Jefferson step, messaging to all that Valesano was no one to underestimate.

"Your wife's death at the hands of terrorists—and believe me we are dealing with terrorists—rests heavily on me," he said as the two men slipped into a booth.

Valesano quieted, his eyes shifting herky-jerky. "I've read your recent daily reports, and reports submitted many days preceding your wife's accident, but I'm not satisfied. Did you leave anything out?"

"Leave anything out?"

"Yes. Maybe something you've recalled since you signed the statement?"

McCruise fought down a desire to go haywire. He knew interrogation as well as anyone, but this was bald-faced questioning by his boss! He placed his hands palm down on the seat of the booth, striving for control.

"Do you find these questions disturbing, McCruise?"

"I sure as hell do; they're getting old. This assignment culminated with one thought in mind: to be of assistance. You have my full cooperation."

Valesano knew McCruise owned a double indemnity clause in Laura's insurance policy, which paid off handsomely. He drilled McCruise with his eyes, his shoulders hitching in nervous response to stress. He also knew he was on shaky ground by interrogating an officer. If he was privy to incriminating evidence, he needed to put McCruise on Investigative Leave instead of hassling him. Nonetheless, he could not resist itching.

"Surprised at my inside information?"

"How do you know these things?"

"I know many things."

McCruise was affronted with these disclosures of a personal nature. How deeply did this ferret pilfer into his life? A zipped up and clean life — a life he lived with pride. Leadership sprung from every stride he took, leadership earning respect and affection. The same leadership in business prowess earned McCruise and Coulter Cruise last year a 2.3 million dollar net profit, their custom boats selling for upwards of eighty thousand dollars, with designer options running a purchaser greater than one hundred thousand.

McCruise's voice melded soft with warning. "Department Policy points to Hands Off until you have more than allegations. These questions fall just short of harassment."

"Your life is surrounded with questions; questions can affect the success or failure of your family's business and the success or failure of your police career."

McCruise was inclined to hate the Italian son-of-a-bitch, but chose not to lend any gotcha to his goading.

"Come. The esplanade is busy, and we can get lost in the crowd." Valesano rolled his eyes toward the vast, double doors leading to the three outdoor pools. The intimidating May sun was heading for mid-day, dripping sparkling light splashes onto the mirror-like surface of the pools and the ripples in the channel.

In silence, they walked past a line of wrinkled shops, restaurants and amphitheater, all patterned after streets in Dickens Eighteenth Century London. Defiantly old-world and differing from the Me-Too stylization of the city proper, the shops strung out along the mile-long channel. The Uptowners strived to maintain the English motif, but in a more modern fashion. A flower shop sported the name of Lady Di's Flowers. A golf course bore the sign Queen's Bay Links. Then there was Ye Olde Lamp Shop, English Pubs and Spirits, and Ye Olde English Candle Factory.

It was like being in another world, another time. McCruise glanced at the architecture of steeply pitched roofs, tall chimneys, and small-paned windows, cross-buck doors and wall exteriors, street vendors, and old English gas lanterns. There were costumed Bobby's on the esplanade, the sound of Big Ben chiming the quarter hour, the babble of muted voices, and a combination of tantalizing, drifting smells of popcorn, pizza, cotton candy, and burgers and fries.

Over all this stood majestically the London Bridge.

"Your demise, McCruise, was the thousands of dollars you pumped into the anti-drug programs in the school system and the signs erected in front of each school: This Is a Drug Free Zone. High Profile Enforcement. Valesano pointed his finger at McCruise as if it were a piece of loaded weaponry.

It would be so easy to just pop Valesano right between his rolling eyes. McCruise determined, however, to reject any hasty reactions, which when reached proved not worth the effort. Valesano was going to be jabbing him with evidence until the holocaust was resolved. The situation sat like a hitch in his side.

McCruise was going to wear the tag of suspect, and he knew what that meant. For his Master's Degree, he chose to write a thesis on prison management. He was aware of the inner workings of long-term jail sentences attached to persons who were unrighteously found guilty of sins they'd not committed, many times on incriminating evidence.

He did not like where this conversation was taking him. He also did not like himself now, because for one of the few times in his life he felt a lack of control in the direction his life was taking—a mindset he would not accept. It was up to someone else—Valesano—whether he worked preferable shifts, gained made promotions or received challenging assignments. For the rest of McCruise's career, Valesano would make it a point to hound him, to know what McCruise was doing every waking moment. Of course, the custom boat business entertained no desire for bad publicity, but even bad publicity garnered notice, and that was where Valesano would take this.

"Did your father approve of your special orders for sodium nitrate?"

"There were no orders, and if you've snooped into all the corners you've claimed to have covered, you'd know that." McCruise never experienced such digging and prodding, tearing the heart of a human being.

Valesano hitched his shoulders in a blatant gesture of skepticism.

Black crackels with yellow eyes chattered in the aging eucalyptus trees, the day heating up quickly. A Mission Linen Truck, parked in the alley, delivered fresh linens to the businesses that strung out along the esplanade. Nodding in recognition, a pair of bicycle cops rode by. Major remodeling was under way at the Golden Crest.

"Recognize this place?" Valesano locked his hands behind his back.

"Hardly."

"This is No. 35 English Village. Get used to seeing it. It's been vacant for two years and under surveillance for narcotic trafficking, but we can't get diddly on it. Until further notice, the Bridgewater Channel and the Golden Crest will be your assignment."

CHAPTER NINE

McCruise snapped a mental picture of the Golden Crest. It was very similar to the other village buildings, but ultimately more authentic. He viewed a one-story building built in the architecture seen in the depictions of Charles Dickens' Christmas Carol—mullion windows swung on sashes, heavy exterior doors suggested castle quality, multiple pitched roofs reached for the sky, stucco and crossbuck deco played out on the exterior walls.

Off the esplanade, McCruise and Valesano accessed No. 35 English Village through the west entrance, where renovation included a sizable deck, while the interior brightened from the dark, heavily beamed travelers-inn style to shades of white, with the kitchen amazingly modern. The bar, an inadequately small room, knew dismantling to allow for additional seating, yet holding its Hobbits Inn charm. It was difficult for McCruise to imagine the outcome of the project in its present state of entanglements of electrical lines, carpenter horses, and sawdust.

"So what do you think?" Valesano's voice interrupted McCruise's indulgent thoughts.

"Think?" Turning, McCruise viewed the man who resembled a bantam rooster in silhouette, his arms folded across his chest, leaning in the doorway. It mattered not what the man wore, he still looked like a scarecrow.

"Even in this barren state, can you imagine this being a stronghold for narcotic trafficking?"

McCruise grunted in dubiousness.

"Do you know, or have you connections with the family of the young woman who owns this place?"

McCruise studiedly moved his head back and forth, finding no need for words.

Valesano snorted. "Her name is Jacaranda, 'Jacquie,' Rose Remington."

Capturing their attention was a rustle on the newly laid deck.

"Ms. Remington," Valesano bowed courteously, if not genuinely. "Meet Mr. Cruise. You'll be seeing a lot of him about the premises in the months to come. The esplanade is his new assignment."

"You're the one, the one who..."

"Yes, that's correct," Valesano broke in.

"My deepest sympathy to you, Mr. Cruise." Jacquie's blue eyes showed pain.

"Thank you." McCruise's voice was barely audible. Would the memory never go away?

Valesano did the direction thing with his eyes, rolling toward the west entrance.

"It has been a pleasure to meet you, Ms. Remington." McCruise's own voice sounded flat to him, but it was obvious Ms. Remington was a ray of sunshine in an otherwise drearysome day. He stopped at the door for a second look at the overall layout of the interior, which gave the added attraction of Jacquie staring empathetically after him. She looked like royalty who realized herself in the middle of an extraordinarily chaotic situation. Sometimes the most trivial trailing could turn a case—and a man's intellect— around, he reminded himself.

The esplanade teemed with people. "So that's it, Mr. Cruise. The rest is up to you—you and Wally Denton, an officer of long tenure."

"We'll give it our best shot."

"See to it." Valesano's Italian eyes fixed on McCruise. "This city has suffered the bad publicity of terrorism, the area is flooded with drugs, drugs lead to prostitution, and armed robbery; the list goes on. There exists no intent to stand by and watch the situation worsen. Capiche?"

46

CHAPTER TEN

Tuesday, June 3, 1997. English Village

The Mohave Desert laid on a press of heat and more heat. A lazy puff of wind as dry as dust blew out of the west cooking McCruise's nostrils. The few clouds in the sky were trailing on a monotonous treadmill far into the mountainous horizon. High today 112, overnight lows in the 90's the weatherman predicted.

"Damn glad the holiday's behind us. What a smokin' Memorial Day Weekend! The thronged beauties, wearing strings of beads, were next door to nudity." Wally Denton strung out his words in the searing air.

"Nudity it was. Bare breasts earn one string of beads per showing."

"Yeah, and we'd have to walk on water to arrest them."

Wally took off his half-helmet, removing the chinstrap, and lifting it over his head—swiped his arm across his forehead. Astride his bike and dressed in summer issue uniform of navy shorts, white, golf-style shirt with epaulets onto which was clipped his radio, he looked like Godzilla on a unicycle.

McCruise responded with a soft fist to Wally's shoulder, observing him in all his wholesomeness—a large man of Norwegian ancestry. His electric-blue eyes squinted in a deeply lined face, as a plum dried to a raisin. Down his left cheek, from his forehead to his mouth, ran a profound scar, an unfortunate accident from high school days when a school door caught in the wind and sent large shards of glass flying. After years of maturity, the scar was entrenched, thus lending Wally a rugged appeal. A distinguishing space between Wally's two front teeth endowed him with country boy ingenuousness.

Standing next to him, McCruise wore identical dress, his name embroidered on the right side front. On the left was a gold badge emblazoned with blue: Lake Havasu City Police. The sleeve patch was impressive, reading the same message. Underneath was printed: Home of the London Bridge. Included on the patch were the American, Arizona, and British flags, like commanding falcons high above the London Bridge structure, which once traversed the Thames in London.

Having won the assignment to the narc squad, McCruise was amazed that O'Shaughnessey put Wally and him in uniform.

"Two officers are assigned at all times to the waterfront. If you two are sleuthing down there, you'll wear uniforms. Besides, what can be more subtle than the overt uniform? Ostensibly, it assigns you both in the right place, but only we know it's for the wrong reason." O'Shaughnessey's voice was full of *don't-test-me*.

Having Wally Denton for a partner was a big plus, an eighteen-year veteran who took the barbs of law enforcement without jading. Recognizably, however, his belly could stand some liposuction, which Wally called "Value Added."

To the west of them by a few feet flowed the Bridgewater Channel, separating the mainland from Pittsburgh Point commonly known as *The Island*. Approximately one hundred yards wide, the Channel arched east-southeast for one mile out of Lake Havasu, flowed under the London Bridge, then south-southwest, returning to the lake.

"Bike patrol is the goddamndest assignment I've ever tolerated!" Wally combed his fingers through his hair. "We've suspected that the narcotics movement resourced on the river. It makes me curious as to why O'Shaughnessey hasn't requested search warrants."

McCruise cracked a broad smile. "It appears he's not ready, but it's not half bad to be in the middle of everyone's playtime."

It was difficult for McCruise to believe that the city grew so much since 1971, when the bridge saw dedication. He shook his head. For slightly more than two and a half million dollars, Robert P. McCulloch, founder of Lake Havasu City, purchased the bridge. Shipping and erection brought the cost to an additional seven million. In slightly less than thirty years, the London Bridge blossomed to be Arizona's second largest tourist attraction—the first being the Grand Canyon, one of the Seven Wonders of the World.

McCruise realized that it did not take long before the shysters and the bandits tapped the thousands of easy hits in flux and flow through the city. The bigger the city, the bigger the problems. Because of its geographical location on the river, this city knows problems—narcotics trafficking being one of the biggest. McCruise's thoughts were troubled, even embarrassing sometimes, when he realized that for the first time in his life he needed someone outside the family to keep his sanity, to keep him afloat. His whole life was slowly sinking to the bottom as the London Bridge did when it could no longer withstand the forces of nature, sinking into the River Thames' clay bottom.

His family was very private. He'd never discussed his history with anyone: the loneliness he'd felt growing up as an only child, how he'd chased lizards with a fishing pole, line and loop to entrench the lightning little buzzards, but never caught any, how Coulter encouraged and praised him for his inventiveness, if not productiveness.

His eyes gravitated toward the Chemehuevi Mountains across the river, as if he were reaching for something tactile there. Throughout his youth, Penny sensed his lack of companionship and warmly opened the doors of their home for all the strays McCruise brought home, whether they termed friends or animals.

His childhood was privileged he realized, but still and all, excitement was in order when he graduated high school and awarded a football scholarship to Arizona State University in Tempe.

He promised himself that one day, when he was married, he would have a big family, but the dream died with the egregious twist in fate. He needed to find a theological answer for such an intrusion into his well-ordered life. It was pendulum-like and common to all living, evidently, that life swung rhythmically between bliss and bruise. Bruising consistently dominated the superior position, however, without a welcoming bridge by which to crossover to bliss.

McCruise listened to the pulsating slapping of the channel water on the dock pilings along the esplanade. With an elasticity known only to the human mind, McCruise's attention diverted to an adventure of aromas, the combination of buttered popcorn from a kiosk on the Esplanade, as well as the summoning smell of freshly brewed coffee.

"Did you see Sligh Shoney's Warlock and the Witch Craft boating in and out of the channel on the weekend? The scantily-clad tan goddesses standing at the wheels were a knockout." Wally combed his fingers through sun-baked hair. "How can a parasite like Shoney keep attracting such good looking women? What a piece of work!"

"Yeah," McCruise breathed, thumbing his helmet up onto his forehead, dark, curly hair dancing around the inner band. Flashing Wally a smile of agreement, his gentle eyes grew distant, thinking of his own goddess, Laura. How he missed her soft hands, her gentle words of encouragement...

He needed to funnel his energies elsewhere. The new owner of the Golden Crest, Jacaranda Rose Remington, was not bad at all. In fact, he'd found himself thinking about her all too often, the thoughts punctuating his mind as if they were a child's popped bubble gum. Jacquie-thoughts were getting him into deep-shit reveries.

Another day, another time, another place, and McCruise might have knocked himself out to pursue Jacquie. She was younger than he was, maybe considerably, her face angelic in its youthfulness, her blue eyes an entrapment. However, she was the kind of involvement that he neither wanted nor needed, especially in light of the fact that Valesano considered the Golden Crest a Colorado River iniquitous den.

Red flags flashed in McCruise's mind. This was one hell of an assignment—a contradiction of symbiotic characteristics, a building in common to both iniquity and morality. Supposedly, there existed an overwash of two entities here, the one politically correct and the second morally corrupt. Where did the one stop and the other start?

CHAPTER ELEVEN

The dual-purpose Golden Crest and the boats, Warlock and Witch Craft, sat as a part of the local scenario. McCruise mulled while walking to the popcorn kiosk and returning with a cone of popcorn to share with Wally. Tossing kernels into his mouth, he proceeded to throw handfuls into the Channel for the ducks, geese, and swans that were scurrying like a school of piranha to capture the white floaties.

Thoughtfully, Wally swayed back and forth for a minute. "Remember the two meth labs we raided a couple months ago when we arrested seven illegal Mexicans? My nose smelled a connection with Sligh Shoney, who employs Mexicans almost exclusively, but the guy keeps layers and layers of insulation around himself." Innate regulatory systems, past experiences, failures, and successes came together in Wally's appraisal.

"I wouldn't grieve over tagging the sonofabitch." McCruise clamped down on his teeth. "Can you imagine how big this operation may be? Allow your mind to wander far right to infinity."

Offering popcorn to Wally, he threw the remainder into the Channel creating another flutter of wings and underwater paddling, stirring waves against the pilings, and raising the aroma of moisture, mixed with heated piling tar.

"Shoney has the perfect setup for contacts," Wally mulled aloud. "Being the manager of the King's Retreat, which is part of the Gold Star Condominium International Conglomerate, puts him in a position of unquestioned power."

"Yeah, and imagine the size and scope of the multinational corporation. It sets on 110 acres right here on the Channel, and boasts 122 timeshares, a conference center, a golf course, three swimming pools, three lounges and two tennis courts. Frequented by global clientele, hundreds of people check in and out everyday without drawing any undue attention to them." McCruise's eyes blitzed Wally.

The image of Sligh Shoney—a polished Mr. All-American—loomed before McCruise. Black thoughts consumed him. When Shoney flashed his Olympiad smile, it never reached his eyes. They were like blue flint chips, hard and calculating. McCruise wanted a death for a death, but he struggled with the theory until his mind was reeling. The case against Shoney was flaccid; the stirrings of life in the case were missing.

Wally moved his bike to a park bench near Jacquie's Golden Crest, indicating with his head for McCruise to join him. Activating the kickstand, he gave McCruise a serious nod. "Something about the guy you can't trust." Wally stretched. A fanny pack holding a nine mm Sig Suer bothered an officer when he was on a bike all day.

"How old do you think he is?" McCruise sat on the bench.

"In his early forties, I'd say—imperious bastard. His headstrong arrogance is going to get him into deep shit one of these days."

McCruise entwined his fingers on the back of his head, tilting his bicycle helmet over his forehead. "I did some asking around. Contrary to how the boat appears, the Warlock and the Witch Craft are 28-foot Pickleforks, modified with two 450 hp engines and can move at speeds up to 110 mph. Seating anywhere from six to eight people, the boats easily pose as personal watercraft. However, we can't overlook the storage capacity under the front decks. They're perfect for trafficking—regular Trojan horses."

Abrupt as a wind sheer, frustration plunged through McCruise, uneasy with the thought that they both over looked the obvious. "Sometimes the two appear together, and other times they appear as singletons—mostly singletons." McCruise accented each word speculatively.

Wally toed up the bike's kickstand. "Let's discuss this up in the campus area."

The several acres behind the shops are abundant in shade, cast by elder acacia and eucalyptus trees. Serpentine sidewalks divide manicured lawns and invite idle-hour lingering, while park benches beckon relaxation.

"Christ, McCruise," Wally blurted, settling on the grass under a tree, his hands dangling over his knees. "What the hell's the difference, whether they appear together or separately?" Wally rubbed his nose.

"Look. In the first place, those craft are over the top of any other pleasure boat out here. You could navigate the Great Lakes with them. If you wanted to have the biggest and the best, that's fine. Nevertheless, why have *two* of the biggest and the best? Shoney can only pleasure himself with one at a time, which means that there is a reason for running the second one, especially like tandem tires." McCruise's eyebrows arched; frown lines creased his forehead. He negotiated dozens of deals for boats: boats for ferrying people, boats for pleasure, boats for law enforcement, nearly all of them custom, but he never contracted for watercraft as big and fortified as Shoney's navy.

Boat manufacturing is what he did for a living with his father, and did it well. Their combined efforts were why he was what he was, and where he was in the boat building business. The Cruise Liner Boat Manufacturing (CLBM) name extrapolated to Cadillac, and experienced prominence in the whole country, primarily because CLBM stayed on top with outstanding engineering and design.

Reconstructing in his mind the picture of Sligh's vast boats, Wally nodded. "As private watercraft, they look as if they were built to protect the King of Siam. Maybe riches greater than that of the King of Siam need protecting."

"True. Perhaps it is the armament needed for a monster mission." Nonetheless, the need of two such cost-prohibitive craft was highly questionable. The thoughts squirmed through his mind like summer maggots.

Standing, McCruise bent and picked a blade of fescue, putting a stem in his mouth, rolling it over his lips and biting it with his front teeth. "We need some reconnaissance pictures to study. Let's say every day for X period—where they go, at what speeds, what is their dockage time, etcetera. If this line of pursuit fails, it will not be for thinness of investigative evidence."

"Look." Wally said, pointing with his chin. "Speak of the devil. There goes Shoney over to the Golden Crest. He has an eerie way of moving, as if he really isn't there; loses himself in a swarm of people like a chameleon and simply never comes out, at least not noticeably." Wally's hands were flouncing a patch of shaded grass, as if gleaning coolness from Mother Earth.

"Jacquie's there with the carpenters." McCruise's eyes widened. For a moment, he could not characterize this unfamiliar need to protect. His lips curved downward, hard, with the sudden interpretation of the visit by Shoney a ruse to make a move on her. McCruise took no control over the hot bolt of jealousy grabbing him right in the gut. Silently, he cursed. Why did he feel this way? Jacquie's innocent face floated through his consciousness.

"McCruise, go back to the station and run these thoughts by O'Shaughnessey. He'll know whether it's shit or cheese. I'll hold down the fort." Wally's determination grew greater than ever to outfox the fox entering the Golden Crest's den.

55

CHAPTER TWELVE

McCruise waited in O'Shaughnessey's outer office, his spirits lighter with the epiphany he witnessed at the English Village. Perhaps Laura offered the illumination.

Sometimes he regretted opting for cremation. There was something tangible about a cemetery burial; visitation at the gravesite was available. There was closeness in the sighing wind, the soothing smell of honeysuckle, and the humming birds flitting in their blissful world.

Did other people know the torment of the fluctuating phases of grief: the shifting sand of purposefulness, the broad swings of lucidity and befuddlement, and the deep chasm between optimism and hopelessness?

"The captain will be a few minutes yet, McCruise," Sadie, the captain's watchdog secretary, advised. Her face was a trifle longish and her voice, thundering from heaven, put McCruise in mind of Moses on Mt. Sinai.

"Thanks, Sadie." McCruise sent rhythmic orders to two knuckles on the arm of his chair. It did not pay to ignore Sadie; she was a tough old bird. Her hair she wore pulled back in a Don't-Dick-With-Me chignon. With her eyes set a trifle too closely, she appeared to scrutinize people as if she was running interference for a Super Bowl wide receiver.

Hmm. Maybe she would have been helpful on the ASU football team.

"You smell as if you've been left on cook too long and got scorched in the process, McCruise." Sadie wrinkled her nose as if she encountered a dead pastrami sandwich sitting for three days in the desert.

"Love ya, Sadie," McCruise countered as O'Shaughnessey motioned for him to come in.

McCruise always liked walking into O'Shaughnessey's office on the second floor. The Berber under his feet responded receptively to his height and bulk. O'Shaughnessey's desk was a monster of oak and inlay, his chair a judgment seat. Behind his desk, on either side of a credenza, stood the American flag and the Arizona state flag. Two comfortable leather chairs rested in front of the desk; others sat against the wall, interfacing with Sadie's outer office.

Brightened by the shaded morning light lazily rounding on the large window facing the west, the walls consisted of off-white textured plaster. On the east wall hung a giant rendering in oil of the London Bridge, accompanied by scattered licenses, commendations, accolades, and awards.

McCruise was surprised to see Tony (the rooster) Valesano seated in front of the captain's desk, but McCruise stood to his full height before easing himself into the chair next to him.

On his armrest, O'Shaughnessey leaned an elbow and slipped his thumb under his chin. A deep fold developed under his eye, prompted by his index finger running up the side of his cheek. "What the hell took you off assignment in the middle of the day? It'd better be good."

Valesano blinked his opaque eyes and nodded in underwriting O'Shaughnessey's statement.

"It's speculative." McCruise knew the word was full of holes, but kept his voice inflexible.

Valesano's presence did not deter McCruise's admiration of the captain's rugged looks, his British conservatism, and his receding hairline. Dark, discerning eyes looked like two sweeping beacons resting under scraggly eyebrows.

McCruise felt a deep shudder at the formidable personnel interview he encountered with him last January.

It was a trap, a practiced trap, waiting for whoever was on the carpet to babble some dumb blurb and hang him.

"Cap?"

"Yeah."

"How the hell did you wind up sitting behind a law enforcement desk in Arizona?" McCruise swung an ankle over his knee and held his duty-shod foot. The pose Connor grew to anticipate, endearing the younger man to him.

"You're showing a measure of impertinence, McCruise." Valesano kept his hands cupped in his lap as if controlling them from some wild Italian gesture.

McCruise wondered if Valesano was always in a thorny mood, or if *his* presence triggered it.

"Questions are quite all right." O'Shaughnessey lifted a hand in objection. "It's not such a long story," he said, leaning back and relaxing. "I was educated to a civil engineer and lived in Nottingham, England. There stemmed employment to oversee the installation of the London Bridge when it arrived in Lake Havasu. Twenty-six years old at the time, I fell in love with this city." He scrubbed his face with his hand and sighed, shifting his gaze to the big window, as if rubbing his magic genie to scare up memories.

Swinging his eyes back to McCruise, his eyebrows shot up as he leaned forward, folding his hands on the desk. "Because of my zest for law and order, the position was offered to me by the city council upon the retirement of the previous captain. Not for a minute have I been sorry."

McCruise nodded again, still patting his ankle. "Like dominoes, everything fell into place." He enjoyed Connor's British accent, his arrogant smugness, and unwavering dedication. O'Shaughnessey's dry sense of humor and hard-ass discipline was legendary among the long blue line.

Testy preludes of small talk were not O'Shaughnessey's strong suit, however. Getting up from his desk, O'Shaughnessey looked like a wooden yardstick, the kind that unfolds three times, and then some. He sat on the edge of the desk, tapped a pencil gently in a slow, hypnotic tempo, waiting. Silently, his eyes interrogated McCruise.

58

For a few minutes, McCruise verbalized to O'Shaughnessey and the rooster a picture of the reconnaissance mission, his allegations, and his suppositions.

"That's it?" Valesano pulled a face of disbelief. "You've got to be out of your mind taking our time with such drivel. Owning two boats instead of one is suspect?" His voice turned acerbic, the violins screeching.

McCruise saw a fathomless pit in Valesano's eyes, a dead-end mirror.

After a hanging silence, Valesano spoke softly, the disciplined control of his voice just short of a hiss. "McCruise, perhaps one day you'll come up with some clues which are glaring and final. That's when we'll all be vindicated."

The captain and McCruise froze at the same time, their eyes meeting briefly as if to say *the lieutenant protests too much.*

Whatever the rationale, McCruise felt his law enforcement sixth sense slipping away like the tenacity of an old rubber band before enlightenment hit him again and gave him courage to go on.

"What I've brought in here is enough to laser attention."

O'Shaughnessey held up his hand in a halting manner, eyes passing between the two contenders. With the abruptness of a kindergartner tired of playing blocks, O'Shaughnessey changed venues. "Have you shot this month's marksmanship qualifications?"

"No," McCruise said studiedly. "One day turns into another and it completely escaped me." Where in hell was O'Shaughnessey taking this? To think both men would dismiss five months of surveillance and firsthand observation was unconscionable.

"I've qualified on the first day of the month, as recommended by department policy," Valesano said smugly. Rising, he leaned on the side of the captain's desk, palms down, staring hard at McCruise. "I think you have Dick Tracy delusions and Pinocchio imaginings, McCruise, or you're tired of carrying heavy guilt."

McCruise looked at Valesano, trying to map the man's craters and mountains as if he were from another planet.

"I've forgotten about qualifying, too," O'Shaughnessey interrupted. "So let's do it. What say you?" He added, winking conspiratorially at McCruise.

CHAPTER THIRTEEN

Radiant sunshine poured through the heavily tinted windowed walkway of the new police complex, yet there radiated no presence of solar heat. McCruise and O'Shaughnessey took the stairway to the first floor.

Angling left, they entered an interior hall, lined with courtyards, shower, locker, and workout rooms. Outside the back door, the sun dazzled their eyes to a squint as they crossed the parking lot for the short walk to the indoor firing range. Dancing on the pavement were myriads of heat inversions, distorting low-lying objects in the distance.

Connor switched on the lights, disclosing the long shooting range with upper torso targets at the far end and state-of-the-art virtual reality film.

Motioning to the table and chairs, Connor flipped coins into the soda machine.

"Name your preference."

"Diet cola."

"Okay. Let's cut to the chase." Connor popped a Mountain Dew, draped his suit jacket over the back of a chair, pulled it out, and sat near the table, crossing his long legs with a sigh of command. The press of his gray pinstripe suit was impeccable, white shirt crisp, silver, blue, and white tie conservative.

"We can talk more freely here; I have reason to believe there's a mole in the building." He took a long draft of his soda. "Valesano has the social graces of an elephant and the heart of a jackal if he smells something is wrong, and he smells you wrong as thunder in a snow storm."

"We'll find a way to turn him around." McCruise wished he felt as good about the conviction as he sounded.

He turned a straight-back chair around and straddled it. Over the next few minutes, he explained his theories and suggestions, with few interruptions. "It's been like looking up a dead dog's ass until this morning," McCruise concluded. He acknowledged Connor's mental tapes recording everything like some kind of a cockamamie machine.

"So you think the stuff is coming upriver via Shoney's personal watercrafts, stored in the Golden Crest, and distributed from there?" Connor's voice was crisp. "That's a helluva note. The wedding to Jacquie's mother is on the 28th. The invitations go out this week. Suspicions placed on the doorstep of the Golden Crest could wrap my life in a complicated situation."

"Well, congratulations on the upcoming marriage. Penny did mention it. Well, perhaps there's nothing whatsoever under that suspect rock, but..."

"And then, again, there may be." O'Shaughnessey turned, leaning his arms on the table, drawing circles with his pop can. "Son-of-a-bitch." His heavy eyebrows drew together. "Shoney is an artist at disassociation. He keeps thick peel-aways between himself and acts of a felonious nature; strange one, there." The crinkles around his eyes became deeper.

McCruise drilled the captain with bar-code scanner eyes, frowning. "As you know, I have two small boys: Mark, and Luke. I cringe at the thought of them hooked on drugs in the third grade, and that's next year for Mark; Luke enters first grade."

"It's happening right here, McCruise. The drugs ready availability has resulted in major law enforcement problems all over the county, covering a lot of territory—Mohave County being the fifth largest county in the USA—but we need to let out the rope before we tighten the noose." Connor's brown eyes were steaming. "We'd have to be blind not to connect Laura's death with the narcs."

McCruise's throat thickened with anxiety at the horror, revulsion and loss, his legs metamorphosing into sagging retreads. The grimness captured him with renewed pain, seeing and hearing again the heart-rending, metal-screeching incident in his mind. Why could life not be a series of small things on a string, like prayer beads, without heartbreaking interruptions?

Connor slipped him an empathetic glance, knowing he would act on this supposition. Due to McCruise and Wally's observations, he would set up twenty-four-hour surveillance tracking the movements of the two pleasure crafts.

Destinations needed documenting, frequency of trips counted, number of people registered, and signs of ordnance studied. One of his officers carried Navy Seal experience. Connor smoothed his mustache thoughtfully, while mentally throwing the logistics together.

"The determination is going to take time and patience. When the information has been collected, I'll call a meeting." Connor drained the last of his soda.

"A meeting?"

"Of the Drug Interdiction Task Force," Connor emphasized, clanking his empty soda can down on the table.

McCruise thought of the danger of any muscle applied against the cartel. How the Drug Free Area signs materialized at all coves and campsites on the Lower Colorado between Lake Havasu City and Parker, just before Laura's brutal demise.

He thought of the message Valesano sent, more so in his posture and eye contact than anything he said. *This is an explosive situation; some doors need remained closed,* he intimated.

The import of the warning was shouting at him, but McCruise's interior voice clamored for equity at all costs.

CHAPTER FOURTEEN

Jacquie saw what she thought was Mr. Touchdown USA standing in the backlight of the Crest's west door. Mesmerized, she stood staring as Mr. T approached wearing a teeth-set-together smile. Setting aside a towel she was folding, she accepted Sligh's extended hand, her face lighting with ingenuousness. Having seen Mr. Shoney many times in about the esplanade, she never experienced a moment to meet him.

Five foot eleven, great physique, hair the color of bleached sand, and vibrant blue eyes, Shoney carried the swagger and blazing confidence of a snake oil peddler. His pupils pinpointed and focused, maybe he simply was the owner of snake eyes.

"Hi. I'm Sligh Shoney." The apparition's teeth sparkled precluding Jacquie to see anything but his mouth, as if the snake was attacking.

"Of course, nice to know you." She felt minimized in his scrutiny, backing away. It was best, however, that she wing this visit. As part of her lifestyle in the Village, she would need Sligh's friendship and goodwill. Winning his respect was important. She smiled. On Sligh, it was lost in its wholesomeness, deflected like a bird hitting a window.

"Well, well, well, aren't you just what the Chamber of Commerce ordered for this place: beauty, brains, and bounty enough to do the retrofitting?" He said with a sprinkling of confection.

Breathing softly, he laid his hand on her shoulder, locking into her widened eyes. "Come out on the lake with me Sunday. I think you deserve a day off." His eyes shifted searchingly over her face.

"Well, I don't really know." Jacquie felt him fathoming her thoughts, looking for a facial flicker, as if testing for a quota of discomfort. His hand tightened and released on her shoulder with faux friendliness.

She would not allow herself intimidations, giving him a measure of power. She witnessed enough power ploys to last a lifetime.

"Ahoy in there. Jacquie?" Denton's big body lumbered down the hall.

"In here, Wally," she projected. As Wally came around the corner of the kitchen, a smile of relief lit her face. "Sligh Shoney, this is Wally Denton." She turned gratefully from Sligh's hand on her to make a graceful sweep of her arm.

Wally smiled wanly, extending his hand. "Yeah. Sure. I know Sligh."

Sligh stood there, mute and unresponsive.

"I guess you're going to prove me wrong and set this place right after all," Wally said, glancing around the interior. The Golden Crest's new deco emanated an instant message of expensiveness, snug and restful, and that which knew the meaning of the word cool, which umbrellaed a multitude of variables.

"Like it?"

"Yeah," he said, breathing the word out slowly. Smiling, he pushed his tongue into the single gap in his front teeth and chuckled.

Nervous comprehension was in the air. Jacquie's keen inner sense told her that Wally annoyed Sligh by interrupting, and Wally knew it, too, but carried on happily. A warm stream of satisfaction shot through the apprehensions roiling inside her. Wally and McCruise became her new best friends. Having best friends meant never having to fight through the fog of hidden agendas, double meanings, and transparent innuendoes. *Police*

Officers are cliquish, she acknowledged silently. Jacquie struggled to conceal a smile at the thought.

Sligh made his way hurriedly past them toward the front door. "See you Sunday around ten. I know you're over at the Queen's condominiums." Sligh's voice came trailing back as he walked away.

His tone and carriage wore the power of positive thinking personified. Jacquie quickly shifted her observations, making a decision. "Well, all right," she acquiesced. She would bank Sligh's comment on the bounty at her disposal to make renovations. What did he know about her means of underwriting the remodeling project?

"What the hell was that all about?" Wally asked.

"Oh, Sligh invited me on a tour of the lake, and then for lunch at Havasu Springs on Sunday." Jacquie's great Orphan Annie eyes grew, her eyebrows arched when she glanced up at Wally.

He squinted. "I would caution you, he's known as the biggest playboy on the Lower Colorado River."

"I thought the outing would be both educational and enjoyable." She shrugged palms up, in a helpless gesture.

"You're going to have to arm wrestle to stay platonic with him. He's slicker than a greased pig in August." *Righteous bastard!* Small, dark emotions played across Wally's face like wind shifts on the channel water.

As Wally exited, Jacquie held her breath and observed how he nearly became history by a touring golf cart driven by a Mexican from the King's Retreat who was wearing a white shirt and dark glasses. The tires squealed on the esplanade tarmac in a great show of precaution, after the fact. Was it really an accident? Would Sligh put a price on Wally's head for a single incident of frustrating interruption?

Tension built in Jacquie's neck.

CHAPTER FIFTEEN

Mallika Chilaw enjoyed her days off. She stared with interest through the condominium slide-bys overlooking the English Village. The village shops reflected golden sunshine glinting off the pseudo-eighteenth century small-paned windows. Buildings breathed the friendliness of a comfortable house slipper, while colorful crowds churned on the esplanade.

Turning, her long legs carried her down the hall and into the bedroom, where she stood before a mirrored closet before retrieving her bathing suit. She would take a swim before dinner. How lucky she was—young, out of college academia in just three years, a degree in hotel management waiting at the end of one year of internship.

A Sri Lankan by birth, she was a half-breed of a Caucasian mother and a Sri Lankan Tamil father from whom she inherited her walnut-colored skin, her bold black eyes and her flashing white teeth. American women aspired to obtaining Mallika's coloring by sun slathering or ray-booth romping. How she enjoyed wearing white—brevity whites. She rubbed her arms, feeling the silkiness of her skin.

A surging sense of achievement and self-satisfaction filled her. Experience at the King's Retreat complex would qualify her for at least assistant manager of a major hotel in Trincomalee—her home, the most beautiful port city in the world. The city hung in splendor on the northeast side of the Democratic Republic of Sri Lanka, a small island country lying to the southeast of India.

She adjusted the two-piece bathing suit, took a quick turn in the mirror to examine her tush, slipped into flip-flops, and tied her brief beach cover. Was it only ten days ago that she arrived in Lake Havasu City? She remembered the exaggerated warm welcome Sligh 'Ignatius' Shoney extended to her when he introduced himself. It was curiously admirable to find that he would play fun with his middle name, as if he were a saint. It put her at ease, however, so she prattled on like a child about herself, while he nodded and smiled, his eyes reflecting the pleasure he found in looking at her.

Increasingly, she observed how many trips he made to the Golden Crest. Sligh was suave as hell with women, herself not excluded. She found that he was frequently where *she* was at any given time, and not accidentally. *Keep your eye on the sparrow,* she admonished herself. *Allow yourself only a nubbin of distraction in the ensuing year.* Mallika's aspirations were queenly and not to be jerked aside for a moment's dalliance with sins of the flesh.

She was tall, five-feet ten, and felt throughout puberty that she poked and sprouted from her clothes like a July cornstalk. She remembered how gawky and ignorant she felt among the avant-garde American students at the University of Arizona/Tucson and how curious and impatient with the partiers and their frenzied enjoyment. *So much difference,* she thought, *between the pampered young women of privilege, and her Spartan rearing.* Such a huge, unfair, and eternally unbridgeable gulf lay between them. She would not succumb to their lifestyle.

A freedom fighter for the Tamil Tigers was her destiny. She would win back land in the north for her family. The City of Jaffna in northern Sri Lanka was a coveted prize for her long-suffering people. Mallika witnessed, suddenly, a delicious feeling of oneness, friendship, and security with the Tigers. She warmly relived the days before she left Sri Lanka. Suddenly, her homeland stood warm and vibrant again in her soul.

She rolled up her pool towel and absently thumped the soft cylinder against the side of her leg. Sometimes her thinking flubbed up on the most commonplace things. Was she ready to admit that Sligh was a womanizer? Did she care if he was setting Jacquie Remington up for the kill? The silent thought slid by, with a semaphore of warning. She found herself of two minds. Did she want to get involved with St. Ignatius? Perhaps she could use him as he intended to use her, intended to use Jacquie, as a conquest, a flight of fancy, and eventually toss each of them out like yesterday's newspaper. *Lie down with a dog and you'll get up with fleas,* she reminded herself. However, could she control her heart?

She opened a V-8, added ice, and stepped out onto her lanai, where the late afternoon sun burned sullenly through the shifting screen of heat undulations. Nevertheless, the air was sweet, turgid with the scent of early summer jasmine. She stared into the vegetable drink as if gypsy Sanskrit lay imbedded there as tea leaves to draw images of her future.

She added another question to the burgeoning list of Shoney mysteries. What degree of importance did the skinny Mexican toady play in Shoney's life? Waltzing around Shoney, building his image of importance, was this Ricki Rodriguez. You could look from here to next year and never notice the pissant in a crowd. He looked as if Shoney picked him out of Central Casting for the typical Mexican: fragile stature, janitor-broom mustache, and black-marble eyes. Rodriguez was a Mexican-was-a-Mexican-was-a-Mexican.

"Shoney's bloody sycophants," she said aloud. Wearing white shirts and dark glasses, they looked like movie desperadoes. The difference was that Rodriguez was smarmy, and it worked. Second thoughts told her that Rodriguez would do Shoney's bidding to the grave.

Her face grew glacial when she recalled the newspaper articles from two years ago. Soldered onto her hard drive were details she read while researching in *Today's News Herald*: 'Golden Crest Closes.' Did someone work bad juju on the Arizona Corporation, owners of the Golden Crest? How else could one account for such happenings as ruptured gas lines, broken windows, delayed deliveries of linens and foodstuffs? Evidence of skullduggery was slim-to-none, but the nuisance items built up like the proverbial straw.

The sabotage at the Golden Crest accomplished well, she concluded. Subsequent articles, anemic with leads not amounting to diddlysquat, dribbled away. While the Crest's daily trade ebbed, the King's Retreat's flowed. Unacceptable aesthetics such as boarded-over windows, Use Other Door Please and Out of Order signs did not help matters for the Crest.

Mallika's statistical reports while yet a student at the University informed her that more than a million tourists and snowbirds drop fifty million dollars a year in Havasu, so the visitors' pocketbooks were a commodity heavily sought after, at any price. Damn the inquisitor's designation thrust upon her by the Tamil! Sometimes it left her drained, trying to connect the dots.

When the Crest was on the ropes, Fayne Norwood of Norwood Research and Development of Duluth stepped in and picked it up for the price of a straight pin and ten jellybeans. Coursing through her like a prescriptive drug to heal ran the realization. She was finally clutching at an island of rock, after floundering on an overload of information. Norwood was beginning to fit into the inquisitor's puzzle.

Mallika set the V-8, rolling with condensation, onto a white wicker end table, her memory tapes on re-run. There was something mysterious about thought puzzles. One wrong piece set in place was justified to one's self, finding further things to substantiate the decision. Afterwards, additional thought patterns by their own merits needed justification. Turns out very often that a flawed piece needed tossing out and a new thought inserted and justified.

A grimace crossed Mallika's lovely face. She met Norwood when he was in town briefly over the Memorial Day Weekend. He owned the rugged good looks of Kirk Douglas in his gladiator role as Spartacus. When one added tan eyes and the ruthlessness of a Sinhalese greed monger, Norwood metamorphosed into a lethal combination.

She may have jumped the first hurdle. Norwood niched with Shoney's secretiveness. Her hand came up and flopped down restlessly. Shoney loose-tongued the story of how Norwood flaunted a three-year affair with Jacquie, broke it off, and offered the Crest as an appeasement for parting. The man was evidently reprehensible. Subterranean paths twisted through him eluding normal minds, and normal motivations. She needed to keep in mind that all the sincerity in Norwood could nest in the eyebrow of a hummingbird.

Now, take McCruise, who floated around the Bridgewater Channel Esplanade. *There* was a nice man. She hoped McCruise and Jacquie would experience some electricity and leave Shoney for her own demise. That eventuality ever occurring, however, was as obsolete as trading a Sri Lankan rupee for an American dollar. If she was anything, she was honest with herself.

Sligh seemed to know Jacquie backwards and forward. *After graduating from St. Scholastica College in Duluth, she went to work for Fayne. Her mother, Marvel, was a winter visitor in Havasu for years. Marvel and O'Shaughnessey, in the early seventies, were thicker than mourning doves on a palm frond. However, for some reason, while O'Shaughnessey was on a short trip to Nottingham, due to the death of his parents, Marvel up and married Charlie Remington. Charlie was an older man, who was C.E.O. of Global Paper, Inc., a paper mill in Duluth, which was a major contributor to Norwood Research & Development for human genetic research. When Norwood dumped Jacquie, he achieved both his feet on the ground with the R & D, and didn't need the Remingtons anymore.* Shoney shrugged the whole episode off as if it were trivial horseshit.

Gathering from conjecture, Mr. Cruise must have lived in a self-imposed hell for the past five months. Mental outlooks such as his left one wagging his tail in the mud like a turtle, bogging one down until he turned into something he was not.

Involuntarily, Mallika blinked from her reverie. The brilliant sun was beckoning her to the pool. Its dazzling brightness emphasized intermittent shadows, like the thought patterns of her puzzle pieces. How good it would be to get back to Sri Lanka.

CHAPTER SIXTEEN

Friday, July 25, 1997

McCruise parked the blue and white in the Village lot, under the protective branches of a slouching eucalyptus. He wore a duty belt carrying cuffs, baton and extra 180-grain, hydra-shock, semi-jacketed shells on the left, and pepper spray and gun on the right. Wally approached on a quad to pick him up. After complaining to Lt. Valesano about wearing out his ass on the bike, Wally won the motorized vehicle.

Today, McCruise set up under the bridge in the amphitheater, where the sounds of summer resonated. Pleasure watercraft purred in the *No Wake* channel. Loudspeakers announced Tiki Tours, and the Princess Paddle Wheel boat touted outings. Youngsters squealed while feeding ducks and carp in the channel, and foreign tongues lay heavily on the hot air. The sight blurred with the saturation of condominium pitchmen on golf carts bearing red and white striped ragtops.

The long days of summer lingered on high-cook, not a cloud appearing in the sky. McCruise's uniform was a sauna in the heat, and even the heavily tinted sunglasses didn't stop water-reflected rays from scorching his eyes and searing his brain. *This is your brain; this is your brain on Havasu heat.*

McCruise's thoughts strayed to Wally's account of Sligh and Jacquie's trip down the river. The pompous ass probably laid a heavy narrative on Jacquie in the form of a tour guide: *Tale of One City*. "Construction of the London Bridge in Lake Havasu began in September of 1968 and was completed in October 1971." Blah, blah, blah.

McCruise quickly analyzed his annoyance as that of the green monster. He'd rather Jacquie take the lake tour with him. *930 feet long and 49 feet wide, the London Bridge lay over land at the base of Pittsburgh Point. When completed, a channel saw dredging to allow Lake Havasu water to flow under the bridge and back out to the lake, creating an island.* At that point, McCruise would have seen the awesome expression in Jacquie's great blue eyes.

His glance shifted to the many indentations and chips of granite that shown blown away from the bridge piers. *German Luftwaffe machine guns made the deep scarring in the granite while attacking river barges during World War 11. When the planes strafed the river, the barges banked under the bridge for protection.* Again, he'd have watched her button eyes widen in amazement.

Radiating in the 12-mile distance across the lake were the Chemehuevi Mountains of California, unruffled, confident, reminding McCruise of the constants in his life— constants he prayed would be his for a long time: Mark, Luke, Coulter, Penny, his home, Tucker licking his face, the Cruise Watercraft Plant, the LHCPD. He was no longer able to endure a life robbed of everything he found wholesome and sacred.

"Hey." The voice jarred him from reverie. "Do you think the city pays you for sitting under the bridge, flattening your ass?" Wally made a broad semi-circle with his quad and stopped near McCruise.

"No," McCruise chuckled, as if a flat ass was a failing like flat feet. "Everyone I question is a dead end, even the cleaning crews, but they're wily little reprobates." McCruise stood and stretched.

"Well, let's have some popcorn and talk this over. In the long tradition of the boys in blue, I'd rather have doughnuts, but no one has the ingenuity to set up a doughnut stand in the Village." As was his habit, his tongue stuck behind the single gap in his front teeth.

Jabbing McCruise on the shoulder, he sighed. "No one's going to tap us on the shoulder and confess to running your wife off the road, or to moving drugs on the school campuses." With the worldliness of his eighteen years on the force, Wally geared forward with surety and swung the quad around, parking it near the channel water.

Moving to stand near Wally, McCruise didn't know whether to chow on popcorn or chew on his dilemma of the war against Shoney. In his frustration, he threw a handful of Orville Redenbacher into the channel for the ducks.

He mulled aloud. "With all these Mexicans on the King's Retreat payroll, don't you think they're indebted enough to do the bidding of the hierarchy—Sligh Shoney?"

Wally exercised his shoulders. "You damn right, they're involved. Just go slow. Have patience. It'll only take one breakthrough, one tangled tongue, a conversation overheard. It'll come." He affected an off-handed gesture with his fistful of popcorn resulting in the white stuff flying out into the channel, attracting the ducks and carp in flocks and schools, churning the water.

McCruise followed suit, throwing handfuls of popcorn to the moving mass. "I feel useless, like a shadow, with no substance." McCruise stared moodily into the dark channel waters.

"On some sizzling afternoon when all you want to do is get into some air conditioning, it'll break. Then it'll get hotter, and you won't be able to stop. The heat will turn to hell, and that's when you'll get your breakthrough. It's Murphy's Law." Wally toyed with popcorn in his hand, covering for the jaded tones of his voice.

McCruise glanced down at the water as Wally threw his head back, ready to toss popcorn into his mouth. Automatically, his hand came up and caught Wally's wrist, halting the action, staring down at an unbelievable holocaust.

The creatures fell to swarming and flipping, creating a rainbow of water droplets glistening in the morning sun, then nothing. Fish and ducks were rolling over, belly up, dying as if on command.

"Jesus H. Christ! It's the popcorn!" A flood of warmth and sweat enveloped McCruise with the realization. He could be lying on the esplanade as dead as the fish. What the hell? He looked to the popcorn kiosk.

It stood empty.

CHAPTER SEVENTEEN

"Come back here, you dirty double dealer!" The beckoning voice arose from the owner of the Golden Unicorn Shoppe on the north end of the village. A multitude of threats pitched at a fleeing figure.

McCruise and Wally responded, alert as bird dogs, twisting to view the far end of the village. A lean young man was running fleet-footed toward the London Bridge Shopping Center, then up the short embankment, his chambray shirt ballooning.

Wally slid onto the 500-cc quad, and channeled into dispatch. "Charlie One. Code 211. Request backup. London Bridge Road and Highway 95."

McCruise jumped onto the back of the quad for the chase, while Wally leaned into the handlebars as if his angled posture could close the gap faster.

As they slowed by the shop owner, his eyes bugged out, his face ashen. "He robbed..." His voice faded in the dry heated air as the quad accelerated and negotiated the incline to London Bridge Road.

Speeding across the vacant lot, the desert sand spewed from the perp's heels. On Marlboro Drive, a waiting car started ignition on the far side of the empty expanse.

McCruise could feel his heart hammering against his chest, measuring the ever-closing gap. The waiting car's passenger door flew open; the running man catapulted into the seat. Gearing down hard, the aging car stalled. A grating sound carried over the expanse of vacant land as the driver agonized the starter.

That's when McCruise heard several pops and saw orange flashes. Instinctively, he knew what it was. The desert flew by as Wally picked up speed on the flatter terrain, hitting chuckholes, tossing the men around as if riding a rodeo horse. McCruise stabilized himself with hands locked onto the back grip bars. From under his stiffened arms, sweat rolled down. In all his bravado, he'd never known such fear.

"Charlie One to Dispatch. Shots fired. Need backup." Wally was terse.

As the quad approached, the car's engine turned over and spun out, missing Wally and McCruise by inches. It took the curve onto Paseo del Sol and careened out of control, coming to an abrupt halt against the embankment of Arizona Highway 95, the engine dying out.

Wally gained the driver's side, his feet grinding heavily on the rock-strewn desert. With unspoken invitation, the driver stepped out, raising his hands over his dark head.

McCruise claimed the passenger—a ragtag, dark-skinned man, who on first glance, looked no older than fifteen, but closer inspection revealed dried apricot wrinkles from years of unprotected desert sun. His eyes were round and glassy. "You dumb shits got nothing better to do than to chase us poor Chicanos who don't do nothing. Nada."

"Where's the gun, you poor Chicano?"

"What gun? I ain't got no gun." Urine stain spread over the front of the perp's ragged cutoffs.

McCruise viewed from his peripherals that Wally straddled the driver face down on the ground, cuffing him. Sirens wailed in the distance.

"Don't play games with me," McCruise hissed under his breath, his stomach on fire with the acidity of stress.

"You ain't gonna find no gun, ever. *Yo ir a chingar a tu madre!*"

In an element in which McCruise never lived, experienced or imagined, he faced the evils of society. Only the gross, the truly vulgar, could abide in a sophisticated society and hang uninfluenced. It was, however, a society relinquishing no quarter to the lowly, who could never crawl fast or far enough to escape their irreversible beginnings.

The uttering McCruise heard caused him to shudder in disgust; the venom was pure puke. This piece of shit was going to fuck his mother? It wasn't as if he'd never heard the words before, but the guttural tones of delivery were worse than word impact: bombardistic, husky, cut-out-your-tongue abrasive.

McCruise spat. "You're an inch from getting your face stomped into burro dirt, poor Chicano."

"*Tu madre! Tu hermana.*"

His mother? His sister?

The sirens grew louder. In an automatic reaction, McCruise unconsciously reached for his S&W. No one referred to his mother in this manner, not ever! Dear Jesus! McCruise needed to repress a surmounting urge to crack the asshole across the head. He'd never thought himself capable of the rage boiling inside him. The Chicano tried to kill him! Instead, McCruise flipped him onto his belly in the desert dirt; tightened the plastic cuffs with a clip and flipped him over like a sand dollar at the beach.

"Now you can't prove I shot at you, shithead," the ragtag spit out, blowing his skinny mouth free of sand. "You gringos are all the same—pimps in uniform," he sneered, skinning his lips into a leer of sand-smudged white teeth in a dark face.

He forced a laugh. "*Hah! Yo ir a chingar a tu madre—y tu hermana.* This Mexican goes to jail; this Mexican gets out. They ain't safe."

That's all the Chicano got out. Looking for the sensor points in his neck—the carotids, and the fine bones—McCruise throttled the man. Staring down into the bulging eyes, the whites grew bigger and bigger. In the fog of ridding the world of scum, McCruise forgot his identity. In one moment lived all the hatred of yet unborn moments. There were no sirens; there were no patrol cars drawing near, nor weapons drawn. There was only him and this piece of filth. Squelching him forever mandated in McCruise's fury.

"Jesus! Take it easy, McCruise." Wally was all over him like a fresh hatch of gnats, ripping him from the kid. "Lighten up! Easy! Don't let 'em get to you. It'll eat your guts."

McCruise stood breathing deeply, leaning against the patrol car drawn up next to him. The two perpetrators bundled into yet another blue and white.

Frustration threatened to turn into tears. He wouldn't weep. He held back weeping since Laura died, and he'd promised never again. Never again, until he wept for joy when he caught the lowlife who cowardly plowed into Laura's little toy, her favorite vehicle.

He gripped with a despair he didn't want to discuss with himself—didn't want to go there, and didn't want to be analytical. It was frightening, what just happened to him. He went from a shining nickel badge to tarnished tin in the deterioration of a few minutes. Did he know himself? What kind of creature lived inside him since Laura died? No emotions lived inside him that he knew he should fear, not until this unfolding.

Wally eased beside him. "You can't listen to those provocative sons-a-bitches. They'll drive you wild, reduce you to an animal."

McCruise nodded, unable to speak; a sweeping surge of relief pervaded him.

"It's barbaric—police work. You can't treat it like your boat building business—a cultural plus. Shit! An incident like this could warp your soul if you stewed about it. A person could learn something about himself at times like this; you gain insight. Just let it go. Mother Nature thickens your skin as you move on." Wally's voice sounded as if he'd swallowed some desert himself. "Were you scared?"

"Siii." Why'd he mimic the Mex? Trying to whistle past the graveyard?

"I wasn't scared," Wally blew air up at his forehead with his bottom lip, "but don't check my pants legs."

McCruise's eyes widened with black humor shared by police officers in tight spots. Relieving the frightful tension, they shared a fit of laughter and watched the fading swirl of dust created by the departing squad cars that carried the two perps.

There existed no occasion in McCruise's life as terrorizing as when the bullets were flying. Laura's car exploding stirred fast and final, but this experience was foxhole fearsome.

One of these days he was going to find himself taking pendulum action against someone else again, someone who'd not known the breaks of McCruise's privileged life, someone who was quietly desperate. At that time, the proof of his makeup would present itself.

One of these days.

CHAPTER EIGHTEEN

Upon arrival at the station, it occurred to McCruise that rather than setting the world on fire he nearly set himself up for a roaring hot press, blaring police brutality to a poor unfortunate. His heart thudded wildly at the possible consequences. The importance of a senior officer on the watch was never more evident to him, nor was it ever more appreciated.

McCruise could hear Wally coming into the squad room with a Criminal Investigation Bureau detective.

"Did they find the gun? The money?" McCruise's breathing burned painfully.

"Not a blessed thing," Lt. Rynold said flatly. A man raised through the ranks, Rynold stood recognized for his common sense approach to daily arrests. His complexion was highly colored and he was wearing large-rimmed glasses; he often reminded McCruise of an owl—a wise old owl.

"A sample of two fish from the channel is being analyzed in the lab, however. As for the perps, you can listen to the tape if you wish, but these Mexican Nationalists are as street wise as a *puta*—a prostitute. They claim no knowledge of the robbery, know nothing of a gun, know nothing about the popcorn stand, which is a crock; they're a couple of bullshit artists. The shooter's name is Jaimie, pronounced '*Heimie*' he reminded. Last name, Hernandez, a single man,

23 years old and employed at the King's Retreat. He'll draw time in Florence with conviction. The driver is Carlos Paz, 17 years old. Paz is a two-time loser, gad-about stuff, public nuisance, burglary, donnybrooks. He'll sit behind bars at Adobe Mountain. But they'll both walk out of here by morning without evidence or identification."

McCruise's chest contracted with ice. "Impossible."

"Very possible."

"Without a gun, without money, without empty shell casings, we haven't a prayer for assault with a deadly weapon, but with the Golden Unicorn's identification, we'll have a clear charge of felony larceny."

"Can you identify the worker in the popcorn stand? Was it Jaimie?"

Wally and McCruise exchanged glances. Who in hell paid attention to Mexicans in a popcorn kiosk? They all looked alike. His stomach volunteered a coil.

"It's your word against theirs, and they're hanging together like tandem tires." Rynold snorted. "Stinkin' little mothers."

"Have you tried the *he said* routine on them?" Wally's eyes brightened.

"Not yet."

"Does that method really work?" McCruise grabbed at encouragement.

"Sometimes." Rynold's voice deepened as he left the room.

Wally straddled a chair next to McCruise in the small cubicle and spoke softly. "This is probably going to be the worst episode of your career as a police officer. It happens to all of us."

"Anyone who's dumbass enough to allow it to happen," McCruise said and swallowed. He couldn't fight the childish craving to feel oneself taller than, brighter than, and tougher than the moment, which thrust him into near insanity.

"No, a guy doesn't allow it to happen. It sprouts like a Chia Pet. From out of nowhere comes this survival instinct—survival on *your* terms, on *your* life's values."

McCruise nodded. Did he ever feel this frustrated? Maybe he'd never master the art and skills it took for law enforcement. The Academy never taught him the psychology of bottom feeding.

Wally re-visited his share of doubts—doubts about everything, especially his ability to learn. "Right after I joined the force here in Havasu, I was the cockiest kid on the block. Twelve years of law enforcement in the military totally tutored this guy. One night, on a domestic complaint, this crazed cokehead swung with a baseball bat, but missed. He missed only because something commanded to move. Bending just in time to have him knock the Smoky Bear right off the top of the head, he missed spilling brains by a fraction of an inch. Sprawling flat on the ass, with him still swinging the bat, the S & W swung upwards, full in his face.

"The hophead's face fell, blanching, his jaw hanging slack. He stood there like a goddamn statue trying to assimilate the no-win stance he was holding. He topped that with the audacity to drop the bat, saying with a look shouting loudly, 'You peg out this time, flatfoot.'

"I saw red. Bile rose upwards at how closely the moment moved to being a memory. Holstering the gun and jerking upright, the baton came out in the same motion. When the fog cleared, his nose bent broken, his front teeth shown absent, and he was on his way to the hospital with broken ribs. It wasn't this guy doing the skullduggery. Fury and exasperation lies deep within us all—a sort of judge and jury reclamation of what is right and good." Looking reflective, he ran his hand through his hair. "His attorney got him to plead guilty to simple assault, and he was out walking the streets again in sixty days. It made me mad as hell, but go figure."

"Yeah," McCruise said, choking, at once embarrassed over his reactions to Jaimie, yet resolved to loftier thinking.

Lt. Rynold returned. "We'll hold them both for I.D. from the Golden Unicorn proprietor. Every available man is shaking down the car and searching the vacant lot, but if those bullets hit nothing, they're probably lying at the bottom of the Channel."

"What about the casings?" Wally queried softly.

"None."

CHAPTER NINETEEN

The Golden Unicorn Shoppe owner arrived at the station, eager to identify the suspect, buying the department time on the greater charge of felonious assault with intent to do great bodily harm.

"It's leverage," Rynold acknowledged.

McCruise snorted, "There *is* a god."

McCruise could still see the smirk on the kid's face, hear the sniveling laugh, as he lay handcuffed and verbally abusive in the desert, diddling with McCruise's mind. His heart thrummed into his throat as the fury returned without warning.

"C'mere." Rynold motioned McCruise to follow to the mirrored, monitored interrogation rooms where Jaimie and Carlos sat answering questions in separate interrogation room.

"You're jerkin' me aroun', man," Carlos said, his anemic upper lip hair struggling for a wannabe mustache, his rachitis ribs those of a junkyard dog. "You can't pull that kinda stuff on me. I been aroun'."

They moved on to Jaimie's interrogation.

Opaque-eyed, black-haired Detective Passaro placed his jacket on a chair, and then paced around the room with his shoulder holster a stark contrast to his white shirt and navy necktie. "We're keeping things as simple as possible, Jaimie. Carlos said you enlisted his help in exchange for forty percent of the take."

"You're fulla shit, man! Carlos wouldn't say anything like that. He's too dumb to figure out what forty percent of a take is."

McCruise shrank with anticipation at this whelp getting off Scott-free on the weapons charge. "Let me at him; he knows I know the truth. Sometimes a fresh breeze turns the tide."

Rynold held up his hand in a gesture of 'wait-right-here,' and proceeded into the interrogation room, conferring quietly with Passaro. Together, they exited the room, leaving Jaimie cooling his heels.

McCruise entered.

Jaimie did a quick shoulder jerk.

"Did you know Carlos was a lot smarter than you?'

"You fulla shit, man. He's just a kid."

"He's smart enough to know he's a juvenile, and declared you influenced him, making him a sort of victim."

"*Alcahuete!*"

"Speaking of pimps, Carlos told me that you owned a whole harem of Mexican *putas,* no green card, collecting big-time for services rendered up in Laughlin, Nevada."

"*Yo ir a asesinar el sucio!*"

McCruise moderated his voice to conversational. "No, you don't have to kill him. Just tell the truth about what happened this morning. Truth is freedom. Freedom means you can continue to work at the King's Retreat."

"*Es ignorante!!*"

"No, not ignorant—informed." McCruise's eyes changed to a remote coldness. "Our computer knows more about you than your mother does!"

"Free, you say?"

"Free as a bird."

"Tell me another one, *policia sucio!*"

"You keep talking dirty," McCruise said, leaning closely, squeezing his fingers slowly into a fist, "and I'll clamp your nads until you've nothing left but crushed nuts."

Jaimie jerked his head away, emitting a small chuckle, which grew smaller and smaller, his eyes shifting back and forth over McCruise's deadly face.

85

"Okay. What's in it for old Jaimie, besides free? What's in it for you?"

"What's in it for you, besides free is nothing. What's in it for the department is a plant in the King's Retreat. You'll report to me anything wayward or remiss you observe there—the whole schmear, anything, and everything—and you'll walk."

"Sounds good to me, *hombre*," he said stoutly. "Free?"

"Free."

In naked desperation, Jaimie confessed. "Yeah, I robbed the store—to cover up the popcorn stand until the real person could dump and clean the drum. A fifty found its way into his hand. Man, gotta keep this job or see return to Mexico. This poor Mexican do like they say. Who needs the dumbass shop owner's money? Yeah, the gun is in storage spot, and the cut for Carlos is forty percent. There you have it," he said, a smile attempted but failed.

"Not so fast, Jaimie; it's not so easy. Who told you to jimmy the popcorn? Where is the gun, the money?"

"*Somos estupidos,*"he shouted, saliva forming in the corners of his mouth, immediately recanting at the frigid look on McCruise's face, his step stealthy and his fingers flexing.

Jaimie's answers were instantaneous. "Nobody never tells me nothing. The directions are in the time-clock slot everyday. The money and the shells and the gun are in the bottom of the glove box—the real bottom of the glove box," he snorted. "Cops can't see past their assholes..." His voice trailed off as McCruise stepped toward him, jaw firmed, and the ham of a hand reached for Jaimie's crotch.

"Look for a false bottom to the glove box," Jaimie stammered quickly. "Everything is there. So I'm free?'

"In the morning, Jaimie."

McCruise, struggling for denouement, weighed the interview against the caliber of the man. Was the confession forthcoming or mockingly contrived?

"In the morning."

CHAPTER TWENTY

The baking sunset was turning to a grateful dusk as McCruise left the station, and the quiet desperation of the day seeped away with the darkening of the sky. If he were lucky, the temperature would cool below triple digits after midnight.

Within minutes of leaving, bright lights flashed in McCruise's rearview mirror. Making the necessary adjustments to dim the reflection, he found himself musing about the fun Mark and Luke felt yesterday—a hundred years ago—splashing like penguins in the lake at Rotary Park.

Sometimes they were all that kept him going. Their youthfulness, their eagerness, and their enthusiasm made McCruise's throat swell, aching when he swallowed. In them, he saw a reflection of himself: large, dark brown eyes brimming with ingenuousness, fine-boned noses, full mouths, and fat cheeks. The only difference was their skin tone of bronze. Tucker knew no ethnic hang-ups, however, by sleeping at the foot of their beds every night. In fact, it was damned scary sometimes, knowing the pitfalls they'd face growing up in a white culture. It was scary as a single parent, but he'd not let them down.

The bright lights stayed uncomfortably near. McCruise accelerated, passed a plumbing truck, and pulled back into his lane.

Thank God for Coulter and Penny, living just up the mountain from him. They gave the boys a home when he was absent. Coulter stood tall with an athletic crew cut and All-American in ideals and philosophy. Penny, the coveted All-American wife with a short blonde pageboy and hazel eyes caused Coulter to melt, even after thirty-five years of marriage.

McCruise's neck crept with heebie jeebies, checking his rearview mirror, but the bright lights stayed behind the truck he passed moments ago.

Suddenly, he seized up by the desire to have Laura there to share these moments of reminiscing. It hurt so much his insides were fragmented and tossed. God, how he missed her—wherever she was, in an impossibly far-off place. Why did these sudden stabs of emptiness grab him like some man-eating jungle vine? It was like lightning striking twice.

The hair on his neck prickled, heightening his senses, his perception as keen as if he were receiving a FAX from Laura. A pulse beat in his neck.

McCruise left-signaled at Cherry Tree Drive when the bright lights passed the plumbing truck, sped abreast McCruise's red Cherokee and cut into the left front fender with a tearing, grating sound, pitching McCruise into the safety belt which held as tightly as a reined-in horse, lurching him forward, snapping him back. Deafening thunder split his ears, flashes of orange registered in his eyes as bullets danced around him.

The Cherokee careened to the far side of the street while a crib-bed pickup truck disappeared up McCulloch Boulevard ahead of McCruise. Dazed and shaken, no chance to catch license numbers, no chance to react except to breathe heavily, he numbed out, while his lungs quailed for panic-relieving air.

Out of nowhere, Valesano paced around the Cherokee. Emergency vehicle lights flashed in a humdrum cadence, a-red, a-blue, and a-white, on and on, until it hypnotized him. McCruise, shaken but rising out of his haze, was receiving oxygen, the Emergency Medical Technicians refusing to allow him to move until they restored normal heart rhythms, his physical checkup revealing cuts, abrasions, and a bullet-seared head over his left ear.

Lying dead in a mesquite bush was an unidentified man with a gunshot to the right eye and one through the neck. Next to him, in complete faithfulness, was a golden cocker spaniel, yet on its leash, in its last throes of agony, its back leg thrusting feebly. Three bullets pierced the dog's heart and back so symmetrically correct that they evidenced sweeping gunfire.

Cameras flashed. Neighborhood residents milled and shouted.

"What happened?"

"Who is that?"

"Oh, my God!"

Though his eyes were numb, Valesano's skinny frame moved with professionalism, checking the cordons, McCruise, the print men, McCruise, the photographers, McCruise. Valesano raised private questions; they could wait.

He experienced a dread, however. Did this smell of a Shoney-Norwood hit? Suppose he needed to accompany O'Shaughnessey to Coulter and Penny's house to tell them and the boys that their son and father were dead. His dark eyes bulged with the unforgiving thought. Desperation spiked in gridlock.

At what pivotal point would he draw the line of acceptance/rejection? He wished he could visually examine the folds and layers of his brain. Where did his commitment to Shoney and Norwood begin and end? For how much of this bedlam was he responsible? He was in up to his ass, that he knew, while Shoney and Norwood sat in high cotton. Valesano realized there would have been a third fatality in this chain of cartel domination: Matthew Cameron Cruise.

CHAPTER TWENTY-ONE

The English Village, Monday morning, July 28.

While the summer sun fried the parking lots soft, and cars reflected heat unbearable, last Friday's experiences threw McCruise into exhaustion. His ribs were raw and bruised, but not broken. Bearing many stitches on his forehead, over his ear, and on his forearms, he insisted he return to work as usual, albeit wiser.

The lieutenant and prosecutor approved the arrangement between himself and Jaimie. Carlos would add another line—that of accessory—to his growing list of offenses.

The terrifying incident at Cherry Tree Drive stirred with investigation by the Criminal Investigation Bureau. Not that there was relief in sight for McCruise; two attempts on his life in one day were more than messaging. Whose hot button was he nudging? He followed only one assignment: the waterfront. Was the truth more than speculation with the suspect naval- variety vessels suggestion? Hot as the day was, McCruise's hands were icy cold, yet sweat ran down his fingers.

The sound of pounding from the Golden Crest brought him back to reality. He knew Jacquie targeted Friday for opening. He followed the hubbub and found her standing on top of the kitchen grill, attempting to loosen the screen on the overhanging hood. A kitchen stepstool revealed her pathway.

His voice thundered angrily in the empty building. "What do you think you're doing, climbing around like some kind of chimpanzee? You could kill yourself..."

"Ooh," she said as she turned to look back at him; losing her slim footing, she fell in slow motion to what was certain disaster. Without thinking of his aching body, McCruise covered the distance between the doorway and the range in ever-broadening steps, catching her in his arms before she hit the harder-than-sin, Mexican tile floor.

Consequently, he knew he was the owner of ribs and stitches, taut, and unrelenting. The pain diminished, replaced by dreams, seeding and blossoming in his soul as she slowly sidled down the length of him. He clung to every moment of body contact. The warmth of her breasts dazed him. Her large blue eyes spoke volumes—spoke to him of fear and salvation, and joy at his presence. Those eyes did something to a man. It was definitely not good.

"McCruise! What a fright! What... what would have happened to me? On second thought," her voice grew annoyed, "you caused the fall." She closed her eyes and took a deep breath, the angry mood passing. "I'm sorry. That was a bitchy thing to say. Thank you." She tried to scare up a smile.

He wasn't prepared to deal with the sensations he'd felt as she smoothed her hands down his strongly muscled arms, his large hands, then glanced up at the height of him, the build of him. She was a whole legion of angels all braided into one. *Fight it, McCruise! You have neither the time nor the right to be looking at another woman.* The feelings lacked organization and forethought; they simply jumped out of nowhere, bedeviling him, interfering with his objectives in life.

"You take some friggin' chances." His eyebrows shot up in frustration.

He observed her tush's roundness as she headed across the kitchen, bent into the lower cupboard, fetching a coffeepot, running fresh water into it, measuring coffee.

91

McCruise folded his arms, leaning on the butcher block in the middle of the large kitchen. "You shouldn't be managing a—pub." His eyes skimmed over her.

He hated himself for this part of his job. Nevertheless, the words still rang in his ears from the captain. 'If the Crest remains vacant, it'll give us more latitude for investigation.'

He could feel Jacquie studying him.

"I can manage this place just fine, thank you." Her great blue orbs rolled as she set two mugs on the breakfast booth nestled in the corner.

McCruise crossed his feet at the ankles, mirth playing behind his soft brown eyes, at her confusion. "You need to drop this place like a hot potato. It's too much of a burden— for a woman." He flashed his best hundred-candlepower smile.

"So I'm an insignificant woman. Well, Mr. Cruise, this pitiful woman could work circles around you eight days a week and then some." She fussed with two Colorado-River-Points-of-Interest placemats.

"Exactly! That's how all women work—in circles." There shown a studied imperious smugness in his statement. Damn! What would he do if she really did give up on the renovation project? How would he explain his subterfuge after everything shook out? He wondered if ever she could get past looking at the uniform and seeing the man.

Gathering spoons, she came to stand closer to him, the silverware drawers sitting in the busy centralized work area. McCruise could see that a dart of annoyance nipped her with his 'circles' statement, but she obviously sought no debate. Would she risk a scene?

When a soft chime of happy laughter broke over her, she surprised McCruise. Blinking, he roused himself. He'd forgotten how good it felt to be close to a woman with whom he felt some communication. It made him desire to find Excalibur and do battle for this fair maiden, just as he'd wanted to slay dragons for Laura. *Don't go there, McCruise.*

How tiny Jacquie was; he faced thin air over her curly head of Irish auburn hair. He was as enraptured as a kindergartner at the glow of her magnetizing eyes, and the intensity and concern that reflected there. Numbered among her attributes were her ancestors, her voice velvety low, sexy. Her Upper Midwest dialect enchanted him. "In-ter-mit-tent-ly" she would say, pronouncing every syllable with cultured delivery.

He watched her tentatively reach out to him, withdraw her hand, and tuck it nervously into her back pocket protectively before busying herself clattering in the silverware drawer.

"What's the problem, Jacquie? Are you afraid to touch me?" His voice was formidable with imperious command. His eyes fixed on hers.

Jacquie took the posture of the bird vs snake syndrome. "No... No. Well, that is to say..." A stammer held sway. Her tone was tight, trying to hang onto a shred of dignity. In truth, she was as desolate as a child lost at family picnic was.

McCruise's voice was heavy but quiet as he grasped her upper arms tightly. "Did you ever wonder what it's like to kiss a cop?" Unhurriedly, he moved closer.

"Didn't give it a thought," she said as she breathed harder, turning, placing her hands backwards on the countertop.

Smiling, he stepped ever nearer until both his arms rested on either side of her, imprisoning her, daring her. What was he doing? Not the bruises from the attempt on his life, but the knocks he'd withstood for the last six months prompted his aggressiveness. He ached all over. His heart closed off his throat with seizing suddenness

"McCruise. Don't do this," she exclaimed in a suffocated rush. Her glance moved upward, her breath sweet on his face.

"Jacquie," he whispered, brushing curls from her forehead, her ears, his thumbs tracing the fine lines of her cheeks before he bent his head and kissed her gently on the mouth; he found it soft, supple, and sweet. McCruise's eyes, dark with emotion, saw registered on her countenance a mixture of wariness and wonder. His mouth came down on hers again, this time working, coaxing.

A low growl grew in his throat. "Jesus," he muttered under his breath, pulling away. Taking her face in his hands, his fingers reached back into her hair, held her head firmly while he slanted his mouth over hers once more, traveling to her nose, her eyes, her cheeks, and her shoulders. His breathing labored, he backed off. "Goddamn," he muttered. He needed to leave; his chest heaved.

Trembling, Jacquie leaned against the sturdy butcher block.

"So what's this, Ms. Remington? You're playing games. Tantalizing, experimenting, playing one man against the other until you find your Happy Meal?" He knew instantly how shallow the statement was. *He* was the one playing games. He stood envious of the time she'd spent with Shoney, and taking it out on her. Envy, he knew, was perhaps the third most powerful human drive, after hunger and sex.

"You egotistical—prig!" Her respiration was out of control, as well as her temper.

He walked over to the breakfast booth, picked up a coffee mug, found his hand trembling, and returned it to the tabletop.

Wearing a wry smile, he left without another word.

CHAPTER TWENTY-TWO

The King's Retreat, Monday afternoon, August 11, 1997

"Hello there," Jacquie peeked her head around Shoney's office door. "Your girl at the desk directed me in here," she said, apologetic for interrupting his busy day, her smile uncertain.

"Hel-lo! Come in." Rising, he inclined to her a preferential person look. "Grab a chair here," he said as he motioned to white-leather upholstered chairs in front of his desk. Jacquie felt sure that the over-sized oak desk, busy credenza, and one entire wall devoted to mirrors, reflected his narcissistic personality.

"Can I get you a soda, coffee, maybe a wine cooler?" He flashed her lots of white zoobies—his dental winner.

"A cooler sounds good." She sat back, smiling, crossing her legs, her white, cotton skirt falling modestly below her knees, her slim ankles moving gracefully over jeweled sandals.

Pressing the intercom, he said, "Mallika, please bring me two wine coolers and tall glasses. Thank you." He leaned back, pleasuring himself with Jacquie's presence.

"I'm interested in buying a suite at the King's Retreat, or sub-letting one," Jacquie said, raising her eyebrows in inquiry.

"We have timeshare units here, as well as privately owned condominiums. In fact, I can allow you to live in a timeshare at no cost until you have the Golden Crest retrofitted." He paused in subtle encouragement, knowing that eventually he'd call in his chits.

The mirrored wall opened. Mallika appeared with a tray of Gallo Coolers, as well as a bowl overflowing with fresh fruit and incredibly large Palm Springs dates.

"Thank you, Mallika. What a treasure you've been to me," Sligh spoke casually. "Oh, yes. I'll be out in the building for the next hour or so, showing Miss Remington some of our condominiums." His eye contact with Mallika shouted of intimacy.

Reminders of Connor's warnings swirled around Jacquie like an early morning ground fog. *He's smoke and mirrors — not to be trusted.* She was comforted that she enjoyed quality advisory time with Connor over the weekend in Duluth, where O'Shaughnessey and Marvel were married, much to her delight.

"Welcome to the Retreat," Mallika said, her smile radiant against her dark skin. "If I can be of assistance, please call. I'll be here and available every day for almost a year yet, serving my internship." She winked as she moved off, her long legs creating a soft hitch to her short dress, which swirled about her J. Lo butt.

Jacquie's eyes turned to Sligh. His offer of free lodging was as old and dried-up as dust. "We can narrow our tour to viewing available condominiums." She needed to keep aggression out of her voice, yet show no diffidence in her manner. Maintaining a buyer/seller mode mandated awareness of Sligh's alien values. "I would prefer about fifteen hundred square feet, Channel view, two bedrooms, two baths, and a lanai." She leaned her elbow on the chair arm, mulling, resting her cheek on her index finger. "I don't have anything in the way of furniture, which is a problem. Would you have a previously-owned condo for sale?" She lifted her glass, looking at him in askance over the rim.

Her blue eyes knocked Shoney right on his ass.

"Ahhh, for sale," he said unevenly. Sand-colored hair smoothed back as he ran a hand through it. "One comes to mind, situated on the third floor. It wraps around a corner. From there, you can see the full length of the Bridgewater Channel and its activities. It's quite spectacular." He shuffled through his directory of available units, not looking up. "It's furnished very nicely—a bit pricey, however, at $250,000."

Jacquie postured at the price, as if stricken.

"It's furnished—in spades," he added hurriedly.

Shifting uncomfortably, Jacquie took in a quick breath, overwhelmed with an avalanche of expenses. She attempted a smile, but the effort suffocated her. Taking a sip of wine, she screened the failed effort. "My expenses have been heavy in renovating the Crest. I'd be crunching numbers for a cash outlay so large."

He looked up quickly, phases of ingratiation shifting across his face.

Jacquie knew he was doing the arithmetic as to how much of the $250,000 Fayne had given her she had actually thrown into the old building. She was becoming increasingly aware that Sligh was privy to the arrangements; both he and Fayne knew the building inside, underside and outside.

How far would Sligh go to assure she never met the one-year parameter, which Fayne built into the agreement of sale? If she didn't turn the business into a productive entity in that period, she would sacrifice the entirety of the contract.

Why, therefore, was she knocking herself out to make it a smart place to visit, and to dine? Perhaps Norwood simply wanted a reputable person's name to be associated with the business—a buttoned-up filly such as herself. Ah, yes, but what were their interior motives? Learning Norwood was a disenchanting affair involving the constant reconstructing downward from her first perception. Before she sank too low into the bog of Norwood's murky waters, she needed to remind herself of the devastation wrought by hatred on the hater.

Jacquie went on. "I've already contacted an architect to design a seven thousand square foot enhancement for a micro- brewery, a two-story short order dining room in the brewery, a gift shop, and a receiving area. I'll use the existing square footage for fine cuisine dining." She paused, placing her index finger into the distinct dip in her upper lip. "The project is going to cost me big time, to the point of taking on a mortgage. It would be kind of you to allow me to buy the condominium for half down and the other half upon completion of the brewery." Her blue eyes grew clouded with anxiety as the proposal unfolded, her brows drawing to a definitive line.

Shoney sat motionless. A brewery! Sligh could feel the blood draining from his brain. He made an effort at smiling, and then took a deep breath, feeling suddenly clammy. Did he hear her correctly? A brewery, another dining room — and what else?

He was suddenly charged with a dilemma so rattling, he needed to muzzle it or shout it to the ceiling. His narcotics warehouse was about to become history, but over his dead body, and however many more bodies it required. *Whatever it takes!*

CHAPTER TWENTY-THREE

No-no-no-no-no-no! No brewery! His mind stretched across the incalculable time of six years of planning and organizing a well-oiled coalition, stretching half a country to Duluth, where the news would rock an empire. "You've lost me," Sligh managed. "When did this transpire? I know nothing of this idea." He was surprised his voice sounded as calm as it did, when his guts were clutching for a toehold to keep the shine on him that Jacquie thus far viewed.

"It's a recent development." She leaned forward with enthusiasm. "We should be able to break ground by October. It's the growing trend around the country—bigger than coffee houses." Smiling, she sank back and rested her arms on the chair.

Sligh could hardly speak. The leash on his emotions was taut. "Yes," he said, clearing his throat, coughing into his fisted hand. "I'm simply surprised I didn't already know. That's very enterprising of you, Jacquie," he added, with an attempt at graciousness.

How in the hell was she going to put up monster silos for a brewery adjacent to the area where the ingress/egress existed, under the Crest? Because of the building's close proximity to the water, the tonnage of silos required foundations of concrete-filled caissons sunk deeply within the ground, which would result in an infringement on the hidden chamber. Their cache fell exposed to discovery immediately. He needed to confer with Fayne by phone ASAP. October would come too soon! Sligh's head was spinning with calculations, sketchy schemes, and Plan B.

Preoccupying himself to cover up his intense frenzy, he opened a tall panel in the wall behind his desk, removing the condominium keys. His calculating mind ran on the Autobahn, as if it were on "cruise."

"The condominium I described to you is slightly smaller than specs." He turned around, smiling pleasantly. "What I'll do is purchase the condominium myself and sell it to you on a land contract for half down, a monthly payment, and the balance when the brewery is up, running, and profitable."

"It's a plan," Jacquie said, relieved.

Yes! She'd never see the business up and running profitably. His jaw worked around clenching teeth. In addition, she'd still owe him half. She'd pay.

****

The condominium was everything she'd ever dreamed of owning. Across the wide expanse of living room, she viewed the lanai through verticals of pale mauve, which covered two four-foot slidebys. The room spoke to her of quietude with its off-white walls and ceilings. She found pot shelves tucked into high recesses in the wall. Tastefully furnished with rich oak, the upholstery waltzed boldly with giant blossoms of jimson weed bugles in coral, mint and white.

Shedding warmth to both the living room and the den was a beehive fireplace, while above a Duncan Fife dining room table hung a chandelier, with dancing prisms blending rainbows into the day.

Off to the left of the entrance was a short hall past the dining room which led to a powder room, continuing farther to a "T" off which stemmed the two bedrooms, both facing the Channel and boasting their own lanai with slideby doors. The queen-size bed in the master bedroom stood garbed in a happiness bedspread of deep forest green and cranberry.

Jacquie's eyes fell delightedly on fully mirrored closet doors, leading to a generous walk-in closet. A vanity with mirror stretching clear to California graced the bathroom, and all interior doors smiled with wide louvers.

She loved it, every inch of it. The guest bedroom, done in lights and whites, cotton eyelet, lace, and mirrors, was fabulous. Sligh was so wonderful. Unexplainably, she wanted to cry, but she blinked the wetness off her lashes. "You've been more than generous to deal with, Sligh." For the moment, she could not characterize this unfamiliar melting of her defenses against him.

Standing close to her, he slipped his arm around her waist. Kindness softened his voice. "Its all yours, Jacquie." He smiled, giving her an intimate squeeze and then releasing her before she could object.

Looking ethereal in the reflected light off the lake, she enthused, "It'll be a pleasure living here." She extended her hand to him, which he grabbed by the wrist, drawing her into him, pressing his mouth onto her forehead. Again, he released her as quickly as he had swept her up to the full length of him, their groins touching.

Her cheeks colored, much to her frustration. He was following the pre-set pattern perfectly — the ice, the meltdown, the giving, then the taking.

Sligh held the perception of a fox, and he sensed her troubled thoughts, thus pressing for occupancy; confident tenancy would produce commitment, commitment would generate gratefulness, gratefulness would nurture in-kind considerations. His insides quivered with where his thoughts sojourned — thoughts of personal fulfillment, thoughts claiming eminent domain.

He sighed. "Shifting gears, how would you like to have dinner with me on Saturday night over the Labor Day weekend? The Retreat is sponsoring fireworks over the Channel." He flashed a Joe College smile.

"Sounds nice, Sligh."

Of course, she'd have dinner with him. He choked down a victory chuckle. After all, it was neighborly of him to go the extra mile for a new business owner in the Village. Moreover, what trouble could she get into in a public dining room? The invitation was a showcase of the compatibility of two, esplanade businesses.

101

CHAPTER TWENTY-FOUR

Thursday afternoon, August 28, 1997

As Jacquie moved into the condominium, dispirited second thoughts plagued her in regards to Connor's sage advice on Sligh. Surely a person like Sligh Shoney was not a distributor of lethal cocaine, thus, he suffered unfair assessment by herself as a cohort of Fayne's. Yet, she'd best gird herself against enticement into yet another net.

It was a mere six blocks from the Queen's Condominiums, where she lived in her mother's unit, to the King's Retreat. While accomplishing the mundane, she allowed her mind to luxuriate in the memory of McCruise and the boys last Sunday afternoon at Rotary Park Beach, bringing a smile to her busy hands as she unpacked.

****

The lake reflected the arrogant blue of the sky, countless shades of green growth, brown mountains, and gold sand, shimmering in the haze of Havasu heat. The clean smells of lake water, oleanders, and natal plum lay everywhere in the air. Lying on a blanket, Jacquie and McCruise watched Mark and Luke splashing in the water.

On his side, McCruise stretched out and devoured her with his eyes as she lay on her stomach. Virility glowed in his arms and chest, beneath the forest of dark hair curling down to the waist of his boxer swim trunks, disappeared and returned on his upper and lower legs like a flow of underwater kelp.

"Jacquie," he whispered.

Waves of emotion trickled through her as he said her name—soft, with barely concealed reverence.

"You came to Lake Havasu; you saw Lake Havasu and conquered my imagination." Feathering lightly, he traced the valleys and canyons of her back with one finger.

She almost dared not breathe while his words washed over her like fine velveteen, his voice ever closer. She turned her head away to obscure McCruise's reading of her thoughts.

"Not looking at me isn't going to make me disappear. Our response systems are in sync."

She knew she should move away, interrupt the hypnotic trance into which he'd lulled her, but she could not. A touch from him stirred smoldering coals never before ignited. She basked in the way she could turn quickly and catch him staring at her with approval and admiration, a look for which she'd have paid a million dollars from Fayne Norwood.

His closeness was akin to comfort food. He folded her shoulder in his large hand, and then fanned out long fingers, bewitching her back. Gently murmured thoughts flowed soothingly, playing her with a melody she felt deeply, and he rendered fatally, her muscles responding to the rhythm.

With a halting pressure of his hand, he rolled onto his back, closing his eyes under dark shades, the sun brutal. "I've pulled full-time duty for Labor Day weekend. Thousands of people will be milling around. Be careful." He looked at her, smiling, but facial lines reflected the concern he felt as he lifted his sunglasses.

She sat up, hugging her knees. Moving to sit near her, his hand touched her hair tentatively, fingers sliding into her curls, slipping down the nape of her neck, drawing her to him, whispering, "It's all right to touch me, Jacquie.

She wanted desperately to feel him all over, watch as he sucked in his breath. Fearful that she'd never let him go, she couldn't touch him. Besides, it wasn't proper to be carrying on so on a public beach—Laura, people, children, and all.

"You will some day," he whispered. "I'll show you how good it can be." He exhaled slowly, a remembering sigh. "How good it can be to trust someone completely and give of yourself totally. In time, I'll teach you, Jacquie, in proper time." He smiled deeply, his eyes warm and studying. "I can wait."

She simply rested her head on her knees, not responding, afraid to test her voice lest the words die on her tongue.

"Now." He patted her head as if she were a puppy. "I have an invitation you can't refuse." He chuckled deeply. "Mark, Luke, and I request the honor of your presence at McDonald's for burgers and fries." He held her hand, curling her small fingers into his.

"That is an invitation I can hardly refuse," she said laughingly. His goodness and humor swept her unexpectedly, like a cool breeze on this crackling day.

Whistling with his tongue behind his teeth, the boys came running through the sand. Good-naturedly shaking their heads, McCruise fluffed Mark's hair, then Luke's.

"What did you tell me your real name was, McCruise?" Jacquie asked curiously, pulling on her terry cloth cover-up, looking up the height of him. He seemed to go on forever when she wore sandals.

"Matthew Cameron Cruise at your service, Ma'am," his voice butler-affected as he motioned to the boys to gather up their beach gear.

"Matthew, Mark, and Luke... whatever happened to 'John'?" she asked before she could think of the impact of what she'd said. The words were out, spent, before she recalled the terrible death of Laura.

"I haven't created John yet," he responded, determined to rise above the incessant reminders of Laura's absence in his life. "Do you think I could enlist your help?" He laughed, never taking his eyes off her.

"Don't count on it, Mr. Cruise. I haven't given any thought to having a family." She stood, slipping her beach bag over her shoulder, never anticipating the flicker of hurt flashing before she averted his eyes.

Damn! She affixed to an inane talent for spitting out the wrong things. Probably the most debilitating thing a man can hear is a rejection to his procreativity. It left her feeling unsettled, making a small gesture of apology with her palms spread upward.

On the walk to the parking lot, five-year-old Luke scuffed along clearly preoccupied. "Dad?"

"Hmmm?"

"I saw you kiss Lady Jacquie at Mr. O'Shaughnessey's wedding to Jacquie's mother last week—and that's how ladies get babies, maybe, John..."

"Give it a rest, Luke."

****

The warmth of a day-at-the-beach memory did a slow dissolve as she reminded herself that McCruise was working this weekend. She sighed with relief, not wanting to see the hurt in his eyes if he found out that she accepted a dinner date with Sligh, and moved into his complex as well.

CHAPTER TWENTY-FIVE

For the first time in his police profession, Connor O'Shaughnessey questioned his sanity for such a career choice. The academy trained recruits from day one that the profession was dangerous—life threatening. He accepted it. His men accepted it. *Steel yourself to expect the unexpected. Respect your fellow officer on the job and in the funeral parlor. The sun will come up tomorrow and life will go on.*

These platitudes make sense until you walk upon the appalling scene of an officer down, innocent bystanders dead, flesh torn apart; bones protruding in bodies yet warm with the energized blood of past nourishment. It is the decisive moment when you aren't so tough after all. All the training in the world cannot cleanse the death of a fellow officer, for there, but for time and place, go you. O'Shaughnessey knew no loss of an officer on his watch, but the evil evidenced this year was appalling. McCruise's vehicle blown to hell, Denton and McCruise shot at in the vacant lot and McCruise a near miss at Cherry Tree Drive.

Rage of previously unknown dimensions swept over O'Shaughnessy. Laws may be drafted, legislation enacted, but evil cannot be erased from existence. It prevails like fleas in a bawdyhouse mattress.

****

"There you have it." Connor's eyes drifted over McCruise, Cleavus, Wally, and Valesano. His mind stalked about with gratitude at having Cleavus assigned to the Western Region Drug Enforcement Administration in Lake Havasu. Connor knew McCruise and Cleavus shared close ties at the academy, and they worked as inseparably as McCruise and Wally.

Cleavus Kolbe was one good-looking black man. Taller than McCruise, slim, wide-eyed and alert. Kolbe put O'Shaughnessey in mind of Will Smith, The Prince of Bel Air, his sense of humor superseding the darkest moments.

Connor sighed and sat back in his courtly chair. "Our surveillance operation at the King's Retreat for the Labor Day weekend will be called Wetland Watergate."

As a leader among men, he allowed himself to step into the sunshine of organized investigation. He'd zeroed in too closely not to believe the source of cocaine distribution lay at the Crest or nearby. In addition, he failed to believe the cartel didn't calculate the odds, and yet felt they owned the upper hand through bulldozer concepts. His mind full of hope, he yet laced the enthusiasm with prudence.

"It's become quite clear that the narcotics cartel and the recent rise in violence are not separate investigations; they'll both be handled by Valesano's Special Investigation Bureau."

O'Shaughnessey long since admitted to himself that there existed no love between him and the Director of the SIB, whom, Connor felt, was doing nothing to beef up the image of the Department. He stared for a long moment at Valesano, then again turned his attention to the three investigators.

"We need to keep Wetland Watergate under wraps from everyone. That includes your wives, girlfriends, parents, and pets."

O'Shaughnessey recalled the schematics he'd requisitioned of the entire King's Retreat. The drawings were hopelessly out-of-date, there being a multitude of changes made in the layout of the complex due to the changeover from hotel rooms to condominiums and time-shares.

"Mark these copies by registering architectural changes," he said, patting the stack of them on his desktop, "and I'll order new schematics drawn by our computer programmer." Connor scanned his trophy crew with pride, aware that the greater number of people involved in an undercover operation the greater the possibility of leaks and subterfuge.

"Are we going to have any work in the hellish outdoor heat?" Wally asked anxiously.

"Denton, you're in luck. For the next four days you may move in and out of any of the buildings in the Village, including the Retreat." Connor wore an amused grin.

"The gods have smiled upon me," Wally said, feigning relief.

Captains weren't supposed to have favorites, but sometimes his chemical nature ruled his mind waves. Wally was a department treasure.

"I'll have DEA personnel from Phoenix on the second and third floors, and Cleavus on the first floor. They'll attempt to work deals for drugs, and they may need backup. Keep your eyes peeled for any suspicious activity." Connor peered up from his glasses at McCruise, pinning him with his practiced laser-look.

"McCruise, avoid those giddy weekenders from hanging all over you." Again, there was the drilling glance.

McCruise mustered a salute by way of response.

O'Shaughnessey gathered the papers in front of him, organizing the corners, plumbing the edges until they were pulp-correct. He turned to Cleavus. "The first floor is a busy place; be analytical of people queuing. Curious characteristics show up there."

It would not surprise O'Shaughnessey one iota if a powerful drug cartel stood well connected with the complex. In fact, it would surprise the hell out of him if there *were* no connection. *Cunning bastards! They were no better than turkey buzzards.* He shivered with the thought. His eyes fell to the neatly stacked sheaf of papers on his desk, reached out, and placed his pencil holder on them as a paperweight. Was the action a Freudian reaction to gathering his people, securing them back into his once-orderly life?

"I won't be talking to you again before you get your details. Remember, failure is not acceptable. Your asses will be on the line next week if at least a few clues to this caustic matter don't turn over. Enough is enough." A heavy eyebrow cocked at Valesano.

Wordlessly, Valesano's scarecrow arms gestured upwards, eyes wide and rolling.

"Don't allow yourselves to become distracted from your reconnaissance." Connors vexatious mood was lifting. His teeth clamped at the cauldron his crew would stew in for the next four days. Oh, how he prayed for silence and peace! Not the silence of death, but the uplifting silence of a cleanly swept mind.

"Don't go for anyone's balls without backup. Ghosts of bad judgment haunt forever."

****

The door closed behind the SIB crew, leaving O'Shaughnessey alone with his thoughts. It was becoming a chore to ignore Valesano. The man was crass, rigid, and covetous of his own department. Valesano wore his resentment of high authority on his shoulder, like an epaulet waiting for someone to shake the fringes. Resenting O'Shaughnessey's appointment by the city council and the Chief of Police, a longstanding wedge lay between the two men.

It took practiced diplomacy to salvage anything decent and good out of an ordinary conversation with Valesano, but O'Shaughnessey learned long ago to travel the high road, leaving Valesano spinning his wheels for an archrival.

Noblesse oblige lay his motto from the day he took the oath of office. Raised in a law enforcement family, O'Shaughnessey was always proud of his father. A Constable in Nottingham, England, his father went without a number of luxuries to further O'Shaughnessey's education as an engineer. "So you can be better off than my generation," he declared. Connor stilled, warmed with the private memory.

Lake Havasu City being a rapidly sprawling city, Conner observed crimes grow more heinous, the hard crime statistics rising, the number of convictions decreasing in spite of no-stone-left-unturned investigations. The situation was wearying.

He'd go over the evidence himself: the carcass Jeep in which Laura met her early demise, the videos shot at the Cherry Tree Drive intersection where the elderly man and his dog lay dead. He mulled over the ballistics reports, the autopsy reports, and the still shots of the Warlock and Witch Craft. Maybe his horse would come in, what with uncovering earlier specifics gone unnoticed.

Maybe...

Christ, he wished he could have some time to go walking on the beach—just go walking—walking turned his mind-drum's abracadabra back into three plums instead of mashed banana.

CHAPTER TWENTY-SIX

Democratic Socialist Republic of Sri Lanka Consulate, Washington D.C.

Fayne Norwood's cab dropped him at 2148 Wyoming Avenue NW. The Consulate lights were shining as brightly as Times Square on New Year's Eve. And why not? The Southwest Asian Island Coalition for equality in trade with super nations was flexing its muscles. In addition to Sri Lanka, Taiwan and Thailand also showed representation.

Fayne researched heavily into Asian Island textiles, choosing a beige suit of lightweight cotton, rayon, and linen, under which he wore a crisp, short-sleeved white shirt and conservative necktie, featuring amber whorls that accentuated his tan eyes, a feature identifying him as singular among others.

Wisely, he chose, as travel companion, a beautiful woman, Mallika—intelligent, and a linguist in Orientalese such as Sinhala, the official language of Sri Lanka. She turned heads and won respect for Fayne as he drifted confidently among decision-making delegates.

Fayne, on stage, was unsurpassable. If one met him for the first time, it would be for all time, his attention riveting on only you, and his broad smile beguiling and persuasive. The Southwest Asian Island Coalition viewed Norwood as an individual who perhaps attended the wrong reception. Among the small dark race, he stood out as a giant, and perhaps represented a threat to their endeavors.

Historically, the Occident and the Orient never knew a meeting of minds. The ancient teachings of Buddhism, Hindu, and Islam lay historically confused and maligned by well-intended Christian pioneers. Barbaric western rites were considered distressing and unpalatable truths, superimposing themselves on peaceful Taoist philosophies.

Furtive western industrial conglomerates pilfered and sacked sacred temples, images, and grounds in the name of progress, building railroads, dams and the like. Banks and consulates, Christian churches, legal apparati such as courts and customs offices sprung up along the rivers and oceanside ports where the *nouveau riche* Westerners lived in spacious residences, manifesting their successes. More often than not, these arrangements culminated with Southwest Asian higherups who were devious and ruthless, many times playing their own people against the Western dollar.

Extreme unrest prevailed on the small island of Sri Lanka, which was only half the size of Alabama, until a Tamil rebel who detonated explosives strapped to his body accomplished the assassination of President Premadasa.

Tensions and questions relaxed, however, when Dingiri Banda Wijetung won election to the presidency of Sri Lanka in 1993. Wijetung now joined Fayne and Mallika in the round of introductions.

Sri Lanka was already producing large quantities of plantation crops, including textiles, processed agricultural products, and consumer goods. The processed agricultural products stimulated Fayne's interest, and spun so covertly for the past six years. He was ready to come out of the closet and get his cocaine legitimately. Fayne knew that Wijetung was impressed with the presence of Wall Street international bankers from New York City, as well as they with him.

International business pidgin was spoken, fostering links between the small island entities—a theme catchy and persuasive, a theme embroidered by altruistic, circulating Asians who spoke English as well as Sinhala.

If Southwest Asian Island Coalition governmental moneys could be filtered through the firm of Graspe, Grinne, and Barrett, they would be used to further such things as agricultural and reforestation expertise. Marketing promotion on the commodities trade tables anticipated reaching global scale to major trading partners, i.e. Egypt, Iraq, Saudi Arabia, U.S., U.K., Germany, Japan, Singapore, and India.

Since 1988, Fayne and the banking firm established themselves with the Sri Lankan government as a friendly marketing outlet for tea and trivial amounts of coca. Fayne, up to this point, did business by barter under the name of Norwood Research & Development. A gynecologist by degree, he established R & D's and provided staff at Colombo, Jaffna, Kandy, and Galle, thus distributing health care, as well as education.

His most lucrative donation was invitro fertilization service for the plantation owners who wanted to procreate outside the marriage bed, thus assuring continuing labor for their plantation, but wanted no part of the risk of venereal disease, which the Western Barbarians brought with them.

Prior to Norwood R & D's arrival on the scene, Sri Lankan women were often times frail, causing premature or aborted births, the infant mortality rate of new births at twenty per one thousand. With the onset of invitro, Fayne's practice saw a mother lode of candidates clamoring to participate in Norwood's programs, which provided pre-natal care, as well as good nutrition.

In return, Fayne realized *carte blanche* to tea exports—a smoke screen—and cocaine, which he marketed, ostensibly, for pharmaceutical medications as a local anesthetic especially for the eyes, nose, or throat.

Fayne handpicked the firm of Graspe, Grinne, and Barrett, with whom he was a heavy investor, so he could hold sway over marketing outlet decisions, the cocaine, refined from the raw coca plant, being his one and only interest, thus, he'd control the distribution and sales to all the super countries in the world. He'd become the most rigorous narcotics trader of all time.

Fayne would see to it that his very name struck fear in the hearts of all those who operated outside his domain. Fear of him, fear of Valesano, his champion of law and order in Lake Havasu, fear of Shoney, who knew no equal when it came to terrorism.

Indeed, convoluted insanity lurked behind Shoney's college boy smile. A life here, a life there meant nothing to him, but only escalated his libido. Take naïve Jacquie, for instance. It was possible to lead her around like a cow with a loop through its nose and was a real ploy in his adept hands. Fayne smiled twistedly.

At best, Norwood would have his hands full with negotiating a treaty with the Island Coalition for coca plant control, there harboring among the negotiators the bad taste of Western domination. It was always there lingering, clear, or muddy. In any event, the element of distrust hung heavily.

CHAPTER TWENTY-SEVEN

Labor Day Weekend, 1997

The sun set slowly and gloriously behind the mountains on a monsoon hot night, its glow spewing volcanic streaks for an hour longer, brilliantly orange, chartreuse, blue, turning to coral, then mauve as the hints of night pushed forward. Record numbers of people enjoyed the esplanade, dressed briefly, or less.

Visitors tied their boats into slips to view entertainment at the hottest nightspot in town: Kokomo's. The establishment loomed vast; it grew in tiers and various levels around the three swimming pools. Thatched umbrella tables were crowded. Misting systems cooled. Inside and outside bars were congested; live music pounded.

McCruise held a channel courtesy phone away from his ear in disbelief. "What the hell are you talking about, Jacquie? You bought a condominium at the King's Retreat?" An avalanche of questions swirled in his mind like dust motes in an abandoned barn. "When did this happen? Why would you want to move?" The words spilled out in a heated rush, as his heart turned to lead.

"When I overheard Cleavus Kolbe bugging Connor about a place to rent, I offered to move out of mother's condominium and buy a place of my own. The accommodation is very exceptional, but pricier than anticipated. Can you stop by to see it?" She paused.

"You bet I'll stop by to see it." *Goddamn right, I will!* "I'll be tied up all weekend, but I'll arrange to swing by tonight for a few minutes... say after ten?"

"Time's fine, McCruise. I'll make a point of being here."

The sound of her voice, smoky and feminine, caused him to calm himself. He recognized that she was becoming more than a mite of entrenchment in his life. It never entered his mind that she might buy a condominium, right in the middle of iniquitous stain, and Mr. Iniquitous himself living in the same building. She was driving him right up a tree of frustration, and the bark was rough.

Sligh Shoney was rapidly becoming a walking, talking, technical difficulty. McCruise figured that if he were God, he'd recall the dog. He knew that Shoney would use every opportunity to hit on Jacquie, and he wished to hell to see the asshole behind bars for years—plus tax. Although he strived to be dispassionate, it was almost impossible; he wanted her, badly. *Where your treasure is, there lay your heart.* One cannot find companionship with a ghost.

He'd send Jacquie flowers as a congratulatory gesture. Shoney probably already surprised her with something significant. The worm was the Duke of Delights.

McCruise recognized all the signs of seething as his finger traced the phone number of Lady Di's Floral. "The vine jasmine sounds nice—big, blossoming. Yes. Today, please." There. He had placed a foot in the door.

****

McCruise wished he could work the shift in disguise alongside the DEA incognitos, but admitted that recognition would come quickly. Penny told him a hundred times, however, "If wishes were horses, beggars would ride." Instead, he donned his uniform for business as usual at the Channel.

For a hasty analysis of its layout, he ducked onto the third floor. As many times as he walked through the King's Retreat, McCruise never really studied it. The third floor was a maze of halls, angles, elevator shafts, ice machines, soda, and snack vending devices that radiated red, blue, and white. The softly lighted hallways lay covered in carpeting, cushioning every footfall. Significant changes sprung necessary on the captain's schematic. McCruise found that the transition to time-shares and condominiums impressively finessed to please a materialistic public who demanded more every year of resorts in the way of amenities and incentives.

The third-floor walk from one end to the other was endless, with curves and juts, the building designed asymmetrically to accomplish stylization of a rambling English Inn.

He already determined that Jacquie's condominium was on the west end on the channel side of the hall, numbered 306. She described it as the only one that wrapped around the end of the building. Why did he not ask her? His frown fixated, realizing that he'd wanted to show indifference.

On the eastern end, he saw the condominium numbered 332, making his survey complete. With thirty to thirty-five condominiums on each floor, the situation was a very different kettle of fish than he'd anticipated. The DEA would need roller skates for this stakeout.

Candy striped, canopied terraces were interspersed off the middle of the halls, all overlooking the Channel. Misting systems hissed in the early evening; potted patio hibiscus smiled at the humidity afforded in an otherwise unfriendly atmosphere. Conversationally grouped were chaise lounges and small tables, inviting one to stay and chat for a while.

McCruise stood in silence, his stance retrospective, listening to the night sounds of the King's Retreat, and thinking it was like a great breathing, insensitive machine. He wished he could linger, but hastened outside to the Channel to retrieve his bicycle, which he'd locked to an uncomplaining bottle tree.

As an only child in a palatial home, he mastered the art of biding his time unworriedly. He sat astride his bike, sipping from a water bottle, near the steps leading up to the Retreat's pools. From the quietude, he found energy rejuvenated.

Four Sunset Beach stereotype girls, recently in from the lake, bounced by him and up the steps to wave to their friends above, who were playing in one of the free-form pools. Skimpy bathing suits and fishnet cover-ups seemed the uniform of the day. Not much remained covered up, however, McCruise observed.

"We're going to join you," they hollered, scurrying up the stairs, their flip-flops clacking on the stairs.

One of them, a petite, fragile-looking waif, waved her fingers shamelessly one at a time at McCruise. Upon leaving, her smile grew mischievous. He found it amusing. Obviously, they did too. He could hear them giggling as they disappeared from view. Kids, sexy kids, brave and buoyant in their out-of-town behavior.

Don't allow yourselves to become distracted.

Sex. He tried to remember who said that the only two things you could do badly and yet have fun were golf and sex. He reminded himself that he promised a round of golf Sunday with O'Shaughnessey, Cleavus, and Wally. Sex was an art denied him.

Several hours later, McCruise wheeled south on the walk toward Rotary Park. He jostled himself when he observed the Sunset Beach beauties leaving the elevator and exiting the west entrance. Their timeshare must locate on an upper floor, perhaps somewhere near Jacquie's. As they approached, he observed that they were wearing more clothes. Blondie clucked her tongue and blinked her baby blues, encouraging a platonic smile from him. The kid was alive with spirit.

****

Taking a breather on the steep stairway that led up to the parking lot near the amphitheater, McCruise saw Jacquie walking back to the Retreat from the Crest. God, she was beautiful! Her carriage was that of a duchess. Dressed in a short-sleeved wheat-colored suit, with a prairie grass shoulder bag, she was a creation. Her shoulders matched in dimension her full hips, which moved poetically to a measured meter. Her tiny waist nipped in, her legs moved gracefully, lean and curved as if sculptured, accenting the vacancy between her thighs.

He tormented himself with how soft she was and caught a rapid intake of breath as a surge of heat spread without warning through his body. A growing sense of approval from Laura-vibes swathed him.

McCruise knew Jacquie would be entering the building on the far west side, through large glass doors, which stood opposite a bank of elevators, where he saw the Sunset Beach beauties. Since the day he'd saved her from the vagaries of pitching herself precariously in the Crest's kitchen, he carried a vision: her fresh scent, her breathtakingly contoured face. What was it they said about saving someone's life? *Being responsible for*? Whatever! He wouldn't mind being responsible for her lovely countenance. Again, his approval rating from Laura intensified.

He shifted and sighed. Jacquie hit him like a narcotic on which he'd become dependent. If he were ever lucky enough to win her over, he'd never let her out of his sight, and never give her a concern.

He closed his eyes, with a wrenching pain gripping him unexpectedly at the thought of how quickly and grotesquely Laura knew extinction from his life—the chiffon texture of a relationship that was so easily torn.

CHAPTER TWENTY-EIGHT

At McCruise's soft tap at her door, Jacquie's short curls bobbed around the safety chain, as if defying gravity.

"It's me, McCruise."

To unleash the chain, she closed the door slightly, and then hurriedly opened it.

"So nice to see you" she said and laughed, deeply aware of the intensity of his bar-code-scanner eyes. "Thank you so much for the lovely planter of jasmine; its perfume hangs as if we lived in a rain forest."

"The pleasure was all mine; I came to check it out," he said, voice overtly aloof. There was a semblance of sincerity in his voice, however, which caused Jacquie to double clutch on a breath, he observed. Although he'd promised himself detachment, he felt drawn to her, like two bubbles of mercury.

"Can I get you a soda, coffee, juice?" She smiled.

"Coffee sounds right on, thanks," he said, folding himself onto the couch across the room from the fireplace. The jasmine fragrance from the lanai emanated a cloud of spicy fragrance.

Jacquie returned with a carafe of coffee, setting it on the coffee table while maintaining mileage between them.

Reluctantly, she lowered herself to the divan, nervously rubbing her hands together before pouring two cups of coffee and passing one to McCruise.

"I can't stay but for a few minutes, but O'Shaughnessey, your father, has promised me next weekend off if everything is quiet." McCruise smiled, remembering the intriguing story the captain told him at his wedding reception of his paternity to Jacquie, unbeknownst to O'Shaughnessey all these many years. His voice grew smaller and thinner with the telling.

Jacquie, too, learned heretofore unknown information at Connor's wedding reception: McCruise was a football hero for Arizona State University, held a Business Degree and an executive position with Cruise Liner Watercraft—a family business. Now a special investigator, she understood why. Resultantly, she viewed him in a more imperious light.

"Thought we could spend some quality time together, perhaps with Mark, Luke, and Tucker, too. He'll welcome you with a sloppy kiss." His voice drifted off with a soft wave of his hand.

Jacquie wanted to shout, *yes, yes, yes!*

She searched her soul for a kind way to tell McCruise that she was having dinner with Sligh tomorrow night. She knew instinctively that McCruise didn't like the man. Anyway, she needed to divert him from the smoldering look in his dark eyes.

"Sligh tells me the Retreat is sponsoring a fireworks display tomorrow night to celebrate the holiday, so he invited me to join him for dinner and the evening's fireworks display. He seems very interested in welcoming me to Lake Havasu." She pushed on, with her palms outspread.

"Dine...with...him..." Confusion and dread spread across McCruise's face. "Perhaps it would be best if I carried your key card. You don't know how an evening with Shoney will go down." Silently, he leaned his head onto the back of the couch.

"We've run surveillance on him with all due diligence," he said softly, his baritone voice resonating with the effort. He rolled his head toward her. McCruise's delivery turned soft as his gaze slipped over her face, her concern. "He is not a good person."

With magnetism unknown since Adam donned his loincloth in the presence of Eve, McCruise drew closer to her. Running a knuckle slowly down her cheek, he suddenly recalled scripture. *I preferred her to scepter and throne, and deemed riches nothing in comparison with her"* His thoughts ended above her mouth with a sound preceding angst.

His kiss was volatile.

Jacquie felt herself immersed in the pleasure of his possessive mouth, melting in the flames, listing into the cushions with his sheer size and weight, his kiss becoming more demanding, and his breathing harsh.

"McCruise," she whispered as he drew himself from her mouth to the soft curve of her neck, pulling back the lapels of her jacket so he could nuzzle her there.

"Don't say anything, Jacquie," he whispered over her throat, into her ear. His hand slipped down her arm.

"You're going to be my wife—mine. You can protest, or you can come along peaceably." His message lay quietly delivered. High-handed, yes, but he'd left no doubt about what he wanted and where he was going with this.

Her head told her to reject McCruise's advances, but her heart was molten with the same desires of seduction he was feeling. On her face, she felt his breath, his lips covering her mouth with dominance. She drew back. "We can't be doing this."

"Yes, we can." His voice grew throaty and unnatural. "We're going to be married."

Jacquie gasped.

"Humor me and say 'Yes'."

"McCruise, I've been hurt once already, and I know better than take a chance with someone who may not want me... for keeps," she breathed in barely a whisper.

"Oh, Jacquie, for keeps is what I want."

Her hands searched the Sierras of his back, strong, rigid with muscles beneath his cotton shirt. She was fully aware that she needed to show denial in situations such as this. When did her life become so complicated?

McCruise's mouth traveled down her suit jacket, sending urgent signals throughout her abdomen.

"McCruise..."

"Shhh, Jacquie."

Squiggling with protest, Jacquie sank her hands into his chest until she brought about awareness in him of what he was doing.

He sat up. "Christ, Jacquie!" he breathed. "Being with you is total therapy; having you would be healing. I'd be at peace." The forced restraint made him seek promises in deep susurrations and wild meanderings. His voice was soft in her ear, his breathing labored.

"You're not easy to control, and I, by nature, must control. Temporarily, a simple promise that you'll consider a serous relationship will do. Maybe we can work on the rest."

"I will give it serious thought."

The words were angelic to his cluttered mind.

McCruise's thoughts rushed to the Book of Wisdom again. *Beyond health and comeliness, I loved her...*

As he prepared to leave, McCruise's eyes grew firm. "I would give you a word of caution on Sligh's hospitality. He's about as altruistic as an alligator. Self-serving motives drive everything he does, and those are his *good* points. Don't be misled," he said quickly.

Lightly, working her head up with his thumb and forefinger under her chin, he murmured, "Look at me, Jacquie. My fondest wish is to have you all to myself." The words he breathed over her mouth, kissing her lightly. With a smile twitching at his lips, he said, "I'm coming back in the wee hours of the morning." The turmoil within him refused to settle.

His breath short and husky, he left. If the passkey she'd slipped into his right pocket meant what he thought it did.

It did.

****

He would never forget the moment when he returned. Jacquie stood in ultra pale green chiffon splendor, like a gossamer goddess. Her eyes were alight with teasing. A single dimple sank in her cheek. Beyond his wildest dreams, helplessly and irreversibly, McCruise filled with the warmth of enduring love. His mind scrambled with ambivalence. Could this be true? Would Laura approve? Was the time lapsation inappropriate? Was this a willow-the-wisp relationship spun from unreal cloth?

McCruise smiled at her, and despite his best intentions of being cool, all the tenderness he felt for her was in his eyes. Damn her! Damn her beauty! He realized that he was holding his breath, and he released it. How could anything but real love feel this wonderful? He wanted her. Damn her eyes! Her curly Irish mahogany hair sprang tousled from the bed. All the questions, the doubts, disappeared. Nonetheless, he must go easy. Looking at her, he ached.

She lifted her hand and laid it on his chest.

McCruise could feel his heartbeat pick up. He closed his eyes to study himself patiently and to gain his equilibrium— think clear thoughts. However, clear thoughts vanished like vapors in a man filled with vitality and maleness. His honest smile spread across his face when he saw the love in her eyes. She was not frightened, and she displayed in her warmth a share of understanding of his mental shifts.

"Come here," McCruise said, his voice self-assured. Unshakable. He smiled again at the collection of caprice expressions on her face. "I'm so glad that you're up and greeting me. The shift has been draining."

Folded in McCruise's arms, Jacquie sighed. "I'm so sorry, McCruise. A policeman's life is more wine-vinegar than rich Merlot." There was sweet warmth in her breath against McCruise's neck. Then she leaned back and laughed at her own analogy, and he'd bulged inside at the wonderful sound.

Tipping her chin in the palm of his hand, he pressed ever so lightly on her lips. The sampling was just too tantalizing. His tongue slid over her bottom lip, then between her parted lips.

The sun wouldn't be up for a couple of hours yet, but the air was redolent with the scent of jasmine from Jacquie's lanai. There were no flaws in the moment, only an excessive surge of joy. Carrying her to the bedroom, he laid her on the bed, her hair spread about her face, over the pillow. Standing above her, he removed his clothing slowly, while studying the near-apparition of everything he'd ever desired.

"McCruise, your body is beautiful, strong, and virile."

"Shush," he said and smiled. He watched her smile— there was that single dimple again—and felt something warm and sweet fill him.

Soon he would know the magic of his body lying against hers, her opening to him, welcoming him, yielding to him.

CHAPTER TWENTY-NINE

Warm and once more humid, the Saturday night sky was ablaze with fireworks. Thousands of holiday visitors, as well as many boats and shoppers, lined the Channel.

"Dinner was outstanding, Sligh," Jacquie said graciously as they moved onto the terrace of the Bridgeview Dining Room. "The salad was crisp, the linguine creamy, and the salmon with Dijon sauce was a diner's delight."

Upon only a subtle inclination of his head, the waiters hustled to set up an umbrella table out on a pool deck. Sligh flashed his best smile. "Anything for you, milady. Mallika made all the arrangements. So far, she's jumping through all the hoops." A smile twitched at the corners of his mouth. "These third world countries generate sycophants who strive to please."

Like magic, a newly linened table was awaiting them, Mallika blending quickly into the blur of partiers.

Her Irish skin misty, Jacquie looked freshly grown, but not picked. She was lovely in a sleeveless, cotton candy pink shell, with a matching circle skirt. Minimizing her waist was a tightly buttoned cummerbund.

The rockets flared with dazzling colors and resonant booms, while Sligh took Jacquie's hand and smoothed over the back of it. "Jacquie, I have a splendid offer for you," he said slowly.

She sank deeply into the subtle blue wells of his eyes.

"I'd like to buy the Golden Crest. The offer is fair market value plus twenty percent over and above. All expenses of transfer of title, as well as the accounting audit, I'll incur." His eyes held her gaze transfixed, but with calculated cunning which, in the past interpreted as *caring* by unaware women.

Jacquie wasn't sure she'd heard him right in the deep thudding explosions of the fireworks over the lake. "Buy The Crest?" She stammered. Separated by only a table's width physically, but by a world financially, he wanted to buy the Crest? Sirens of alarm shrilled through her mellowed mind. *He's altruistic as an alligator,* rang back to her.

His eyes were burning into hers; a gentle smile of largesse covered his lips. She knew he sensed victory.

Tenderly, he lifted and kissed the back of her hand. "It's an immense undertaking for you. This offer will take a load off your shoulders. I'm prepared to do this, since I'm already half in love with you."

Jacquie's balloon of expectations sagged and shriveled. He wanted to take her independence, her livelihood, her sense of accomplishment. He'd do it all with cold cash, exactly like Norwood. She felt empty, reading in his eyes the shouting success. Her hair bristled, stewing in the vacuum left by an electrical charge.

"You will *not* buy the Crest," she said, putting her voice in a silken envelope. Her hand withdrew smoothly in one twisting motion, while Sligh's reactionary jaw hung slack with her refusal. "It's not for sale—not now, not tomorrow. Not ever!" Never would she separate herself from the livelihood to sustain herself independently in this world. Her eyes snapped sparks.

Barely concealed was the disillusionment she experienced with the recognition of his objectives. All he wanted was her parcel of real estate on the Channel, and not the piece of personal comfort he claimed she gave him. He was as handsome as hell, but she was no longer Betty Coed. He'd not usurp the one thing to which she could cling for permanency in her life.

127

"No way, no how, Sligh. The Crest is not for sale," her piquant mouth firmed.

Raising his hand haltingly, he shook his head. "Okay. It's okay, Jacquie. The offer was artless of me," he said with a great show of sensitivity. "I want to take care of you, and I hoped you'd view it in such a light." His mouth opened in congeniality, while his eyes stayed as cold as last night's meatloaf.

Sligh never felt so dismissed. No woman ever did him this way. How dare she? Well, there was more than one way to beat a bitch. He'd contrive a new line of attack. He'd never failed at anything he wanted badly. Never!

"Jacquie," he went on, shedding her refusal like a snakeskin. "You're a very beautiful woman. You don't know how you haunt my days and nights."

Women never refuse me.

"I'm trying to be helpful."

Insipid bimbo!

"If I've insulted you or made you feel less than significant, please let me apologize."

Talk about a dime a dozen. Who does she think she is?

"Consider it a triviality; buying the Crest will never again be mentioned."

There is no need to mention a thing when markers fall due.

By the time Jacquie got back to her condominium, she was only fit for a warm bath and bed, yet, she struggled with Sligh, who insisted he see her safely inside her condominium. Suddenly, a Hippie-type, muscled, African-American man appeared out of nowhere and bumped into Sligh, sending him sprawling down the corridor while Jacquie made a safe entrance into her sanctuary—locking the door, securing the chain.

There was something between humor and goodwill in the kind man's eyes. There were only a few black people living in Lake Havasu, but Jacquie recalled how much Connor liked Cleavus Kolbe, the new DEA man who rented her mother's condominium in the Queen's. Hmmm.

CHAPTER THIRTY

"Portable 300," Dispatch squawked.

"Portable 300 here." McCruise spoke into his shoulder mic, which attached to the underside of his knit shirt.

"Check 911 call from timeshare 310 at the Retreat. Hysterical woman reports finding friend in bed, dead, illegible report. Sending backup: ambulance, emergency medical techs. Out."

"Copy here."

McCruise effectively chewed the distance to the west end of the inn. Nearing 310, he could hear sobbing and garbled voices of young women. One was sitting in the hall, her knees folded up to her chest, her head buried in her arms, shoulders heaving. Assessing the suite, a woman was hovering over another, who was lying disturbingly still on a bed.

Advancing to the bedside, an icicle stabbed his heart. There lay the petite waif who waved to him with her five fragile fingers. Her eyes were open wide, her mouth gaping in its last futile attempts for air, her pulse zip. Naked, she lay across the bedspread like a discarded doll.

He could hear the distant wail of sirens, and the *errnk-errnk* of the EMTs from Fire Station Number One on Lake Havasu Avenue. How close, yet so far away. "Not this time," he murmured, his throat constricting. "All the King's horses..."

"She's my sister," a young woman cried pitifully from the other side of the bed. "She's only fourteen years old. I promised my mother I'd care for her."

McCruise nodded as he perfunctorily checked the child. Undoubtedly raped, significant signs of more than once. Fragile in death, her budding breasts would never suckle a child; the thin thatch of blond hair in the triangle of her thighs was soft and pubescent. She'd never participate in the promise of womanhood—to know love and the joy of producing a replication of her.

There is a time for all things. A time to be born, a time to live, and a time to die ran through his mind torturingly.

He checked his watch—11:30 PM—the three girls coming home from a night on the town. He could smell beer and pizza. Funny how smells smother someone who isn't partying himself.

"We came in the door and found her like this," said the older sister. "She was tired. She didn't want to go with us after supper by the poolside. She was talking to a nice Mexican waiter who said he worked here at the hotel; he said he'd make sure she was all right, even seeing her to her room if necessary."

McCruise thought he was going to puke. "What was his name?"

"I don't know. We never asked," she wailed. "She isn't very strong. A birth defect—her heart. We thought she'd be all right by herself. What could have happened? Why would someone do this? She's dead, isn't she?"

Between the tears and half-coherent words mingled the traumatized crying of the other two girls, nearly drowning the raucousness of the approaching ambulance and Fire Department Emergency Medical Techs.

"Come with me," McCruise indicated, nodding toward the sitting room of the condominium. "She has professional help now."

The questioning went on until 2:00 AM. Wally and McCruise each interrogated all three women. *Yes, the waiter appeared slightly built, with a skinny mustache... smiled a lot... very polite... spoke with Spanish-riddled vocabulary.*

The parade of those involved with death never stopped: the medical people, house security, the coroner, O'Shaughnessey, and Valesano, his neck craning.

McCruise didn't know who was more impacted—the three girls or himself. His feet were as heavy as his heart, as if plodding through wet cement, his mind in a muddle. Was this his fault? The description fit Jaimie. If he didn't negotiate for a deal—if he'd choked the son-of-a-bitch at the site of capture in the desert near AZ-95. If-dog-rabbit.

Lake Havasu City. This is the place! The words to the Chamber of Commerce slogan screwed around his mind with bouncing energy, an ironic epiphany to the reality of the moment.

CHAPTER THIRTY-ONE

The shift ended none too soon for McCruise. He was quiet when he let himself into Jacquie's condominium, thankful that she didn't set the chain security.

While the stinging stream of shower water soothed anxieties from his muscled body, the sliding glass door smoothly opened. Swiping water from his eyes, he found Jacquie stepping in, resplendent in her nothings.

With fixation, he caressed her body by the sheer potency of his gaze. He wanted to record the look of surprise and pleasure on her face.

Slowly, he reached out, stroking her thick auburn curls, touching the glossy luster as if it were forbidden fruit. "Jacquie," the word swallowed in the delivery. It seemed to McCruise that she stopped breathing for a moment as a tremble ran through her.

"What a nice surprise you are, McCruise." The words were heavy on her breath.

Choking out of his closing throat words spilled, "I've waited all night to come."

His masculinity grew with the force and virility of a predator, a grid-field hero with fullback shoulders and running back hips. He circled her head, the nape of her neck with his hands, pulling her to him. With the warm water rushing over them, his mouth came down on hers, wet with insatiable hunger and strong desire to close out the night.

"What did I ever do before you came into my grief-stricken life, Jacquie?" he asked huskily, his eyes dark.

Jacquie shuddered like a new shoot in the wind; small sounds escaped from deep within her throat.

Running smoothly up and down his body, her hands feathered and possessed. A primitive need preened between them. He devoured her mouth, his kisses not gentle; they claimed and gnawed with ravenousness need, the need more primal than anything he ever experienced. This was what he needed, her yielding to a stronger power. Backing her against the shower wall, he easily lifted her into place on his hips, the soothing water bonding them.

McCruise's ecstasy was immeasurable. Breathing into her damp curls, he would keep her there for a while, still and quiet in their oneness.

When later he toweled her down and carried her into the bedroom, she was pink and glowing, her eyes bright, her hair clustering in damp curls over her temples and forehead. Laying her onto the bed, words he'd wanted to say all night rushed from him. "Ms. Remington, you're a beautiful woman—beautiful, tantalizing, intelligent, and mine." He traced a finger over her nose and mouth.

Reaching up for him, she purred, "Mmm."

Easing himself beside her, he pulled her to him, cradling her head. He'd previously called Our Lady of the Lake Parish. It took six months of counseling before they could be married, if he chose to do so. A feeling of walking on shaky ground never quite left him, however. He wrestled with the ambivalence of disasters resultant of hasty commitments, or proposing a civil ceremony until their counseling period be fulfilled. He cut a glance down to her left hand as if he could see the ring there already. Lifting her hand, he kissed her ring finger.

She turned her eyes up to him and saw the love he offered in all its honesty and without qualifications. She wanted to hear the words written in his eyes, but he'd not declared them.

He smiled a devastatingly powerful smile.

She settled for the warmth of it.

CHAPTER THIRTY-TWO

Sligh Ignatius Shoney wasn't born yesterday. This was the time to do it: Labor Day weekend, when there were more boaters than there were anglers. Of the two launch sites on Pittsburgh Point, the island across the London Bridge, Site Six was the farthest south and well into the open water of the lake. The long boardwalk extending out into the lake stood occupied by only a few diehards trying to snag a striper in the troubled waters, already at this early hour made turbulent by hundreds of boaters boasting supplies of beer and toilet paper.

Sligh was dressed in a pair of cut-off denim shorts, a muscle shirt, heavily tinted sunglasses, Nikes with no laces, and carried a rod, reel, and angler's creel slovenly slapped over his shoulder.

Walking to the end of the pier, he settled himself onto the decking, fussing with his equipment. Setting the creel between his legs, he reached in and retrieved the newly defunct AK-47 that knew action in the terrorizing McCruise accident. Broken down and wrapped in an innocuous oilcloth, the identifiable piece of ordnance slipped from beneath the oilcloth into the heavy currents of Lake Havasu, where it would ride the shifting sands at the bottom of the lake. In time, fungus and kelp would encompass the heat piece, and erosion would work metal metamorphosis.

Removing the cap of his coffee thermos with the pads of his fingers, he poured himself a cappuccino he'd picked up at the Retreat's dining room. He pulled a small cell phone from his creel and dialed Rodriguez, via Phoenix, forwarded to Rodriguez's cell phone in Lake Havasu; he allowed it to ring three times, and then hung up. With his legs dangling over the end of the pier, he put himself into memory transport mode.

He was in love with his name: Sligh Ignatius Shoney. It made him smile with irony, especially *Ignatius*: the Jesuit missionary, patron saint of education. While Sligh did not ignore his academic education, his derisive bitterness arrived early on the scene. A small-town kid from Ohio, he'd aspired to attend Kent State University, so he'd taken advantage of an open house to attract potential students.

The campus visit was May 4, 1970 just four days after President Richard M. Nixon appeared on national television to announce the invasion of Cambodia by the United States and the need to draft 150,000 more soldiers for an expansion of the Vietnam War effort.

At Kent State University, protesters launched a demonstration, which included setting fire to the ROTC Building, whereupon the governor of Ohio dispatched 900 National Guardsmen to the campus. During an altercation on the very day he arrived, twenty-eight guardsmen opened fire on a hedging crowd, killing four students and wounding nine.

Having developed a masochistic personality early on in life from an abusive father, Sligh found himself in the middle of the melee, tormenting the guardsmen and inviting retaliation. He rocked with savagery when he knelt near a dead student and rubbed ebbing blood unto himself, superimposing upon himself the pain of a non-existent gunshot.

Sligh found time to rabble-rouse at a similar incident, which took place ten days later, on May 14, at Jackson State University, an all-black school in Mississippi. During a student protest instigated by Shoney and his ilk, police and state highway patrol officers fired automatic weapons into a dormitory, killing two students and wounding nine others.

Unlike the Kent State episode, this incident evoked little national attention, embittering many blacks who felt that the killing of black students was less newsworthy than that of whites, disillusioning further Shoney, who turned into a sadist crusader.

Because of Sligh's impulsive spirit, vindictive followers nurturing unbridgeable differences accompanied him to other universities around the nation, where almost five hundred colleges shut down or reduced by protests against the involvement of the United States in Cambodia and Viet Nam.

In 1971, after only one year at Kent State, Sligh joined the Viet Nam War effort with an attitude of *can't beat'em, join'em*. St. Ignatius in sackcloth or a Jesuit monk in a cell, he would not become. One of 550,000 troops, he arrived in Nam at the time bombings were stepped up.

For two years he'd studied firsthand the unspeakable Viet Cong atrocities: the sharpened bamboo death traps along jungle pathways, captured soldiers buried alive upright in rice paddies, human feces spread over them, human compost, the napalm torching of entire villages. The marauding left an imprint on his mind for the rest of his life, compounding his masochistic tendencies.

Subsequently, Sligh obtained a degree in Hotel Management with a minor in Political Science, which taught him how to dance around issues, yet create an imagemeister of himself. Sligh could re-invent himself on a daily basis, if necessary, without buckling to anyone's demands.

The problem was which person was he? At his first exposure to public violence at Kent State, he trembled with the injustice of it all; it was his father beating him repeatedly, but on a grander scale—the big frogs eating the little frogs. He'd created a hero of himself and made magazine covers by assisting in the college protests throughout the country. For zealously battling the Viet Cong by exhibiting derring-do indifference for personal injury, an Oak Leaf Cluster Award was his.

That, however, was when he had sought causes. He no longer needed a cause. Killing was satisfaction, killing was easy, and killing was ecstasy. *"El morbido,"* Rodriguez would say. He admitted that counseling was in order, but from whom would he seek help? His pastor? What the hell? Who claimed a pastor, anyway? His parents? They were dead for a long time and non-caring when they lived. The Department of Social Services? What the hell? He, Sligh Ignatius Shoney, was not going to crawl like a desert tortoise into a shuttered room where he could pour out his problems to someone loonier than he was. No thanks! Fayne Norwood, perhaps, and then compromise his lucrative position? No thanks again.

"Yeah," he grunted, as a message came over the cell. A sleek smile washed over his face; his agate blue eyes glazed over. "No leads at the police department on the McCruise hit. Voyeurism cameras now were setup in Mallika Chilaw's condominium and Jacquie Remington's condominium. The underage young woman shot up with cocaine by Jaimie was dead and wouldn't any longer be a problem to him or the hotel. Before her body was cold, she was a victim of multiple sexual assaults, including sodomy." Sligh's whole body lurched with visual-aid thoughts cast by Rodriguez's description.

"Yes-s-s," he hissed aloud, wiping the sweat from his forehead.

Aside from the sexual deviations, Norwood was in Havasu for the Labor Day weekend. It was always another plus in Shoney's income ledger upon his arrival. Twenty percent of the narcotics take wasn't bad, not bad at all. He didn't have to do a thing but store and dispatch the stuff. The rest of the logistics were in Norwood's court. Forty thousand dollars in his personal coffers over the July 4th holiday shined not too shabbily when one considered that it was tax-free, and over and above his salary and expense account. He didn't care to calculate Norwood's take in Las Vegas—probably a couple of million.

He'd better check with Ricki and Jaimie on their run up the river this weekend. They made three drops so far, all on Friday. Three life preserver rings at the Novi Casino Marina just south of Laughlin, a drop of four at Herod's Beach, and a drop of only two at the Dam Site Casino tie-down. The pilgrims would probably ask for an additional drop tonight when the river was full of Labor Day weekend crazies and cops.

The lake sights and smells were everywhere: the old pilings, tarred ropes, watercraft fuel, and a saturation of sun and pricey boats. The weekend buzzed with subterfuge, possibilities, prospects, and *putas*.

A gluttonous smile crayoned Shoney's face.

CHAPTER THIRTY-THREE

The London Bridge West Golf Course was always McCruise's favorite, and a Sunday morning with Connor, Cleavus, and Wally was the best of times. The Mohave Desert sun was not timid today. It was ninety-four degrees already, and it held the promise of greater discomfort, yet the morning revived him.

After an abbreviated night's sleep, McCruise couldn't tell if he was walking or on horseback. The polarized emotions of the shattering image of the premature death of the young woman and the ecstasy of Jacquie clutched at his soul.

Wally braked the golf cart. All four players were on the green. "One more night to turn over something of substance," he mulled aloud. "So far, the only item uncovered in the young girl's death is a protective cover from a hypodermic needle." He sighed.

"We'll get further reports on dustings and DNA later," McCruise contributed.

"Our skins," Connor called, trying to psyche out Wally and McCruise.

It worked.

Connor and Cleavus took the hole.

Wheeling the cart around the course, Wally couldn't get his mind off seeing Fayne Norwood carrying a briefcase the night before on Wetland Watergate 200, while Wally was taking his quick once-over for the captain's new schematics.

Sharing his thoughts aloud with McCruise, he concluded. "It seemed strange to see someone carrying a business accessory down the hall on a Saturday night in a Timeshare/ condominium scenario, where fun-seekers are the order of the day." He turned to McCruise, his chest heaving somewhat with the fear that he may have overlooked cartel action.

Considering, however, that the entirety of the condominiums was booked full for the Labor Day weekend, plus thousands of transients in and out of the various bars, uncovering cartel activity would be a stroke of luck in the micro-time he spent on the second floor. Nonetheless, it was wiser to admit an oversight than not bring it to light.

"Everyone in town knows what Fayne Norwood looks like." Wally blazed on, Sunday morning quarterbacking chilling his blood. "He's been deeply entrenched in Lake Havasu business activities for years. His picture's been on national magazine covers. The TV news programs interview him every time a genetic breakthrough surfaces." Wally tapped his hand on the steering wheel. "I didn't want to stare, but Norwood nodded a princely acknowledgment." Something was niggling at his mind, but it kept slipping away. He studied the fairway ahead of him.

"Hmm." McCruise made a measuring sound.

Riding down the sixth fairway, McCruise was soothed by God's own spotlight, illuminating the mauve shadows of California mountain crests and valleys across the river. It brought a measure of peace to his beleaguered mind, followed by an overwhelming urge to laugh—at what, he didn't know. Sometimes there were purges in unwarranted laughter.

"Wally..." McCruise's voice was like water running quietly over smooth rocks.

"Hmmm." Wally turned, sensing electricity.

"I saw him, too." The words were *sotto voce*, as McCruise stared hypnotically at a rabbit standing frozen, its back to the sun, and the small veins in its ears a road map. "I saw him. I did the same thing you did,—met him in the hall, nodded, and blew him off as a given, considering the scenario," he confessed, his voice strangled. "I even thought it quite natural to observe him with a briefcase. The guy has tons of irons in the fire." He shrugged, feeling the color draining from his face. "Highly questionable, however," he turned to Wally, "is the kind of business he'd be conducting from the King's Retreat on a holiday weekend." McCruise begged himself to breathe.

Tee time on 12, par three, 145 yards. In surrealism, McCruise saw his cohorts leaning on their clubs, purple lantana bobbing, but his mood darkened. Trying to gain control of himself, he watched Wally choose a seven iron for a full swing, getting a nice loft on it. A swooping flock of pigeons flew directly in the line of trajectory. *Smack.* A pigeon faltered and fell, lying without movement. Wally's ball was short, falling into the water hazard in front of the green.

"You got a birdie, Wally!" Cleavus hollered, slapping his leg. "Did you know *Fish & Wildlife* have declared pigeons a protected bird?" He bellowed, "You're in deep shit!"

Effervescent laughter bubbled, releasing them from the unrelenting tension. Connor, called out in the middle of the night to supervise the handling of the crime scene, was equally as engaged in the horror and desolation. He felt deeply the exoneration of an all-out release of laughter.

McCruise frowned in surprise at the 19th hole to find he came in after the round with a forty-two on the front nine and forty-three on the back nine with two double bogies. They won the skins. "Connor and Cleavus buy the beer," McCruise added with a *coup de gras* air of victory. On the golf course, there was no Chief—no Indians.

They moved to the patio of the clubhouse for the 19th hole, and took a table at the far end for privacy. A roadrunner was busy tormenting some fresh hamburger the cook put out for him. Cocking his imperious aqua and coral head, he inspected the intruders. Deciding that they were insignificant peasants, the roadrunner went back to consuming his lunch.

Cleavus was contemplative as he listened to McCruise and Wally. "I didn't see Norwood, but I did see two curious old-salt types at the bar, comparing Merchant Marine stories, and laughing like hell. They were both massive chunks, wearing weathered complexions." Cleavus was beginning to doubt his cocksure acuity of which he prided himself. Every face at the table was studying him, alert, searching for seeds, which they could sow and reap.

"Something was skewed, however." Cleavus paused. "How many sailors have their wallets snake-chained to their belts, like bikers? It merely amused me to see two burly men go to such ends." His forehead creased with frown lines.

"Good God!" McCruise interjected. "I saw someone who looked like that when I visited Jacquie's condominium late last night. He was coming out of Norwood's unit, grinning from ear to ear, and crude laughter came from within; he seemed unlikely company for Norwood to keep. It's like finding burrs in a daisy patch."

"What's your read on this, Connor?"

Connor wasn't one bit reluctant to emphasize the importance of intuitiveness. "When you get a gut feeling, act on it." His hand came down hard on the table. "Compare notes." The palm of his hand flipped up. "Sniff trouble."

His dark eyes traveled the terrain of his men. "Sometimes the most inane observation can contain the information you're looking for. Norwood," he leaned his chair back and slipped his thumbs into his waistband, "was purposefully overt with confidence to throw off suspicion; his act is refined to perfection. You can believe he's not wasting his time in Lake Havasu, just celebrating the holiday. An aide from the hotel will provide a printout of the names and addresses of every Retreat guest over the weekend. It should prove to be very interesting." His chair came thudding down on all four legs.

"Within the sphere of investigations, objective criteria are well defined: who, what, when, why, where. Use them. You saw the subject where? Where did he go? What roused your curiosity? There's a bottom line there, always. Bad guys don't follow a Policy & Procedure Manual, and if you adhere stringently to Department Do's & Don'ts, you're going to get your combined asses in a sling or worse yet, sliced off." His eyes darted rapidly before he sighed, deflated.

His voice became gentler. "I stopped by the lab this morning before tee time. The popcorn analyzation proved to be stramonium, a derivative from the dried leaves of the desert jimson weed. The lab people discovered that the component added directly to the popcorn oil for greater permeation, and in addition, sprinkled over the finished product once it lay in the bin. It produces hallucinations, and in large doses, death." Connor pinned a meaningful glance on McCruise and Wally. "You both could have been dead within minutes." His words were no more than a soft breath when he concluded, "Someone wants you both out of the way, someone higher up than that toady, Jaimie."

CHAPTER THIRTY-FOUR

After the busy Labor Day Weekend, McCruise looked forward to the peace of the plant and helping Coulter on his few days off. Awakening to Tucker's kisses, he'd actually seen the sunrise this morning, the big, red, glorious, Arizona sunrise. It was there every morning for him to see, but *seeing* it and *viewing* it were different stories. He felt his body unscrew, as if it were in indescribable torque. Maybe this evening he'd have time to play the trumpet for Mark and Luke; they danced like pivoting prima donnas, their world having no edges. They especially liked "Rocky," from the inspirational movie of the same name.

The luxury of his vice-presidential office at the plant seductively drew him with its large oak desk, a chair in which be could lose himself, a credenza holding pictures of family in happier times, Laura's face beaming at him—just for him.

The walls stood lined with models of boats designed at Cruise Liner Boat Manufacturing, and guest chairs gathered in companionable quietude. A workout room and bathroom, including a shower, were off to the right.

McCruise knew Coulter designed the office for him before he graduated from Arizona State University. If Coulter ever feared McCruise would not join him at the plant, he never revealed it. It was a given that McCruise's real career was here, and McCruise never gave Coulter a second thought otherwise.

As McCruise left the office to check the timing on a line of wire harnesses, his cell phone chimed. "McCruise! Conner here. Need you over here." McCruise caught the demand in Connor's voice.

"Give me ten." He flipped his phone shut. Would his life ever be predictable again?

Arriving at the station, he took the steps two at a time up to the second floor.

McCruise's pleasure was perverse at rattling Sadie's chain. "Sadie! Here come dat man again and he be diggin' you, baby. You should wear yoh hair down moh often; you looks sixteen yeeahs ol'!" He winked at her, smiling broadly. A couple of good night's sleep and shared intimacies with Jacquie rejuvenated his devilish, dancing eyes.

"McCruise, you're the limit!" Sadie sparkled, pulling a Lily Tomlin mouth pucker.

He breathed a sigh of relief as he entered past the fierce dog guarding the gates of hell. What was its name again? It escaped him. Oh yes, Cerberus. He needed to remember the great alliteration: Sadie, the Cerberus Sentry. His long legs closed the distance into Connor's office, where he settled comfortably into his adopted chair.

Connor's deep gray suit glistened with every move. Draped to his wide shoulders, it afforded the relaxed allowance needed by athletes. McCruise wondered if Connor's closet contents were carved out of Marvel's touch and choice. The *haute couture* of a woman of Marvel's stature was simple arithmetic to him. Marvel never knew the department side of Connor, however; the strengths emanated to his men, the strengths he instilled in them, and the strengths he demanded of them.

McCruise fathomed that Connor was leashing his feelings, creating an appearance of chiseled handsomeness, and readily noticed the disparity between his disciplined eyes and the ruthlessness working at his jaws. O'Shaughnessey sat in his overgrown chair, leaned his head back, shut his eyes, worrying some question on his mind. When he opened his eyes, McCruise read, "drowning," which Connor tried to erase with a swipe at this mouth and mustache.

"I don't know how I can keep asking you for extra time. You've been a good steward." Connor inhaled deeply.

McCruise slid farther into his chair, placing one foot over the other knee. The posture comforted Connor. It meant that McCruise was ready for business.

"Sometimes the whole meaning of *illegal* loses its definition. It's too nice a word for the ceaseless horrors we're witnessing." He leaned forward, his eyes keen with concern.

"We have another murder—about two hours ago—at Jacquie's renovation site. A construction worker fell to his death. The scaffolding buckled like Tinker Toys, and it missed Cleavus by inches. Inches! It'd been weakened deliberately."

McCruise didn't think anything could compound what he'd witnessed Saturday night, but couldn't withhold a heaving breath.

Connor could see the temper of a chain saw cloaking this fine officer, but he pressed to unveil the sordidness of the accident before he lost control.

"I sent Cleavus there to snoop around. He's new on the job, new to the city. He's steeped with do's and don'ts, educated and a quick study, but hasn't kicked tires and looked under the hoods. We need you out on the job with him, Wally, too."

McCruise leaned easily forward. "Cleavus is doing a fine job. He was a pro when he came here, graduated from Quantico, Virginia, FBI Drug Enforcement Administration, following the Arizona Law Enforcement Academy. He never grabbed a chance to turn around before he was plunged into tragedy of proportions we've never seen in Havasu: terrorism, overdoses, addictions, deaths..." McCruise leaned farther forward as if to get closer to the problem, thus the solution.

"Yeah." Connor eased back, skimming both his hands over his ears, smoothing his monk's hair. "He's going to be an asset, but I envisioned him out shagging leads from pizza countermen, gaining local confidences. In a dominantly

Caucasian culture such as we have here, Cleavus needs testing and purchasing. My God, McCruise, he could've been killed outright!" Connor's voice broke and he put the heels of his hands up to his eyes to regain composure.

McCruise knew Connor's emotions were on a roller coaster. Like himself, Connor's family never sat involved in life-threatening situations, and Jacquie sat squarely situated like a frog on a lily pad in a hurricane. A living stage imaged before McCruise, more like a Shakespearean drama than real life. The fires burned uneasily inside him, a shifting heap of red coals.

"The man killed this morning was twenty-four years old, with a wife and three children. He doesn't have much but the insurance the contractor carried on him," Connor said.

McCruise stared with a dichotomy of disbelief and rancor. "Son-of-a-bitch," he breathed softly, a suffocating tightness in his throat.

"I sent Cleavus home. Wally is out there now." Connor went on, tapping a Department issue pencil against the desktop. "The alleged sabotage reports are scathing. It's starting all over again, a repetition of two years ago. Presently, we have four homicides: Laura's, the man at Cherry Tree Drive, the girl at the hotel and the latest, the construction worker. Jacquie is terribly upset."

"She saw it?" McCruise asked, appalled.

Connor nodded his assent. She heard the collapse of the metal, ran out, found the poor guy." Connor's eyes misted over.

"My God! What next?" McCruise slapped his forehead.

"She's tough, McCruise, an insidious dust storm never settling, but not made of steel. She was so badly shaken, Wally took her home and saw to it she was resting before he left."

"Has he called?" McCruise's eyes swept Connor's face in askance.

"Yes, he has. She told him she feels as if she's in a vise. She is, but not the vise she meant. We need to step up the investigation before more incidents happen, possibly even involving Jacquie."

"Very possibly Jacquie," McCruise groaned. "It's a constant worry of mine," he said dryly, hating himself for his lack of successes, lack of solutions.

Connor blinked, wrinkling his forehead into three defined geographies of planes and valleys. "I don't see any relief in sight. We'll soon be seen as a drug capital, and there's grievous decorum in such a title—and to think it's all cranked out by a narcotics warehouse right in the beehive of activity on the waterfront." He opened a desk drawer and pulled out a triple-folded document in a heavy paper sleeve. "Warrant." He handed it to McCruise. "Search Warrant."

"Okay," McCruise said, slapping his foot, his shoulders squaring. "I'll call Coulter and check it out. I guess he's getting used to it. Whattaguy."

Connor nodded several times in assent. "I'd like you to check on Jacquie's status at the condominium, and in addition, scour the Crest. There has to be something in there to lead us to more evidence. By the way, I informed Jacquie of our suspicions of Sligh Shoney. She's not totally convinced of his involvement in the narcotics trafficking. 'Perhaps an unsuspecting tie-in,' she said. She's a bit of a *show me* person."

Nervously, he brushed imaginary lint off his suit sleeve. "Also, the autopsy was performed this morning on the little angel who died Saturday at the King's *Retreat*. Enough cocaine shot into her veins to float a Sumo wrestler sky high. She put up a fight, however. The forensics people are analyzing fingernail contents, hair samples, sperm, DNA."

McCruise no longer viewed himself as a do-gooder or Mr. Proper, Right & Just. The imperfections he'd developed, he'd live with. Who ever said he was to be perfect? In the past year, he'd discovered he could hate, he could lust, and, yes, if need be, he could kill. "Son-of-a-bitching bastards! These people are worse than Ted Bundy; they're terrorists."

"You're right," Connor reflected uneasily, remembering our country's shifting phobias that reflected the trends of the decades. Bank robbers and car thieves dominated the fifties; black militants and antiwar radicals appeared in the sixties. Organized crime kingpins started showing up in the seventies, and America's war on drugs reflected in the FBI's Ten Most Wanted List frequented by druglords during the eighties. More recently, terrorists strong-armed their way onto the Ten Most Wanted list.

"The ramming of Laura's car was no less than a terrorist tactic. The rapid fire attack on your vehicle was no less than terrorism; the death of the young man this morning is by its nature, terrorism." Connor rested his case with a deep sigh.

McCruise grunted in agreement, opened the door and left. He ached with the renewed imagery of a broken car, broken glass, broken, irreversibly dead, Laura, all transpiring in minutes—seconds.

****

Curious, Connor mused, *how someone's presence can radiate a room with life to the point that their absence leaves a cloak of downer. Where do we get young men like McCruise?* He was as Connor viewed him: dark gray suit, white shirt, tie, and black shoes—executive. It seemed one of life's unexplainables that our society could produce dedicated men like McCruise, back to back with men like Sligh Shoney. Sometimes it mattered not who raised them.

Tumbling uninvited across his mind in photographic memory were the names of heavy hitters in varied industries that were on the guest register over the past weekend. Names surfaced such as Canadian Median giant *Porkilton Newspapers, Royal Dutch Oil* out of Amsterdam, The Netherlands, and *Regal Singapore* shipping lines. All were legitimate condominium owners at the King's Retreat, but here were names big enough for Norwood to deal with. All the suites were on the second and third floors. For what was Norwood dealing, and with whom? What was the tradeoff? Wherein did Norwood's protection lie? His thoughts raced and swirled like clustered clouds scurrying across the sky to vanish behind the Chemehuevi Mountains.

CHAPTER THIRTY-FIVE

Would she ever be able to forget this morning? Jacquie lay on her bed, propped up with pillows. *Click*, she turned on TV 45, whose cameras were set up in front of the Golden Crest, interviewing passersby, attempting to get a byte of comment from one of the detectives busy within the cordoned area. "I'm sure you do not need to be reminded that this is allegedly the fourth homicide in less than a year," the reporter shouted. "Far too many for a city of 45,000! Do you have any clues?" The reporter pressed on. "Will the department have a statement later in the day?"

The screen cut back to the studio, where the station owner, Dave White, was giving a running commentary on the previous deaths, old footage of the unspeakable incidents spewing again.

"TV 45 invites business and commerce in Lake Havasu to offer a reward for information leading to the arrest of the perpetrators. TV 45 will open the challenge with a $5,000 contribution, and maybe we can close the abominations of the past nine months and recapture our city."

Jacquie clicked off the set, watching the screen grow dark, and replaced the wet washcloth over her eyes. She could guess that at this very moment Sligh Shoney was telephoning Fayne with the news of the death. She'd overheard the same coded conversations dozens of times while she was in Norwood's employ. She could no longer view Shoney in patterns of light and shade, but in the darkness of hell.

How many times did she have carte blanche shopping excursions with banking fraternity wives while accompanying Fayne to New York City for meetings with his firm of International Bankers Graspe, Grinne, & Barrett? She'd tried to forget the whole thing once pensioned off by Norwood, but it sneaked into her psyche just the same from time to time, like a distantly ringing reminder. Rather than lose the lucrative Norwood account, the bankers would bend to his wishes at any cost.

****

Was Norwood's hand in the mishap at the Crest? If so, he never really intended for her to have it up, running and profitable in one year. He was God-like in his ultimate control of people and circumstances. Control was his forte, mercilessly and menacingly in control, far beyond anything she ever imagined. The man was repulsive, loathsome, and deadly, if not maniacal.

Was she captive in this situation? She could run, but how far? Norwood faced her with absolute ruin, should she betray him. How would she like the world to know she was an *insignificant* other in service to him? In addition, he could place her with him at every major deal he'd constructed in the last three years, even though she was not privy to his inner sanctums. Who would believe a simple-minded secretary as opposed to himself, a one-time nominee for the Nobel Peace Prize for Genetic Engineering? Mr. Nobel would likely have blown himself up with his own dynamite if he knew of a mad-scientist recipient of his coveted award.

Fayne discarded her like yesterday's French fries, salving the wounds with the Golden Crest. He obviously did not want her ever to finish the project. Why?

Unquestionably, things never stay the same forever, nor even for as long as we think they will.

CHAPTER THIRTY-SIX

McCruise's passkey gained him entrance to Jacquie's condominium with ease. Annoyed because the chain was unsecured, he wisely decided that he wouldn't rattle Jacquie about it today.

"Hellooo. It's only me, McCruise."

"In here, McCruise." Her voice unraveled like a small thread from a loosely knit fabric. He followed it down the hall to the left, the master bedroom. His disciplined bravado faded when there she laid atop the bedspread, clothed for work, a washcloth over her eyes. He took comfort in the fact that she couldn't see his face harden into hammered steel.

Nearing her, he found words as if he'd spaded them from the depths of the earth. "I'm so sorry, Jacquie, you saw that... that... unpleasantness this morning."

Her sagging soul hurt McCruise. The bed bent with his weight as he sat on the edge and gently pulled the washcloth from her eyes, observing her hands clutching at a shredded tissue.

Her attempt at a smile proved pitiful but brave, tugging at McCruise's heart. He plucked a fresh tissue from the box beside her bed, dabbed her eyes, her porcelain Irish skin.

His fingers traced her forehead, smoothing back the curls stuck there from shock-generated heat.

Reaching out to touch his face, she was like a drowning child, reaching for a knot in a rope. "I'm so glad you came, McCruise. It was awful, simply devastating." Her voice cracked.

His hand slipped up to cover hers on his cheek, bending into it, securing it. "Of course I'd come. Your father called me away from the plant and put me back on the case this morning—no days off."

Warmth sparkled in his eyes. "In addition, we're shedding the Armani suits for the armor of all-out warfare, if you care to help us." He made an all-encompassing gesture with his arm. "The goings-on have run the gamut from the malicious mischief practiced upon the previous owners to cocaine, felony assaults, rapes, and homicides. No more," he added.

She moved her head back and forth, as if shaking off the horror.

He felt her fingers ply his face for a touch of reality and security as she sank further into desolation. His heart ached for her. Where did this beautiful bystander fit into the human equation that was playing itself out on the river?

Unable any longer to be covert in his overwhelming anxiety, he groaned, lowering his head onto her chest. "Jacquie," he sighed, the agony in his voice gripping.

Her breath felt warm and welcome on his skin. It was as if she should always be there. The desire for her crawled over his skin, reaching reactive places, but he reminded himself of time and occasion.

Smoothing his face, his neckline above the collar, she ran her fingers through his thick hair. The touch was like an injection of license to the privacy of her life, an electrical shot of happiness.

"Jacquie, you distress me so. Let me offer you my protection, away from all this bullshit." His unexpected rush of words surprised him. He was annoyed with himself. Damn! She did it to him every time—stirred a tingle of warmth that curled through him like tantalized taste buds.

"McCruise." A soft breath escaped.

"Hmmm?"

"Would you be satisfied if I said that I will think about your fine offer, of the security of your home? When you're near, there moves a whole mix of emotion. I've felt protected, ecstatic, humored, angered..."

Before she could finish, his mouth was devouring hers; a deep swelling huskiness arose from his throat. A kiss that began as light, glancing, deepened with the invitation issued by her admissions.

His hand was under her waist, drawing her up to him, tightening, and his other hand stroking the back of her head, tangling in her curls, as if he could soothe away the morning's trauma. His kiss grew more possessive.

She lay entranced at the magic in his touch, the aggressiveness of him, the size of him, and the husbandry of him. She allowed her hands to slide slowly up his arms to his shoulders, back down, inside his suit jacket, caressing.

"McCruise," she whispered, "you're carrying a gun."

His tongue cut across her lips. "I'm not going to shoot you, Jacquie, at least not with my S&W," he teased.

Without any conscious effort, she relaxed. Her need to transcend violence with the stability of McCruise's love was overwhelming.

He moved his head back. "Damn," he said, his voice throaty, needy. "What you do to me, Jacquie, reduce me to an amoeba." His dark eyes moldering, he gazed at her— her magnetic eyes, her tiny nose, her warm mouth, his haven of silent communication.

The bedside phone jangled once, twice, three times.

"What the hell happened to you, McCruise?" Connor's voice was in rare form. Wind chimes, it was not. "Wally said you were not at the Crest. Is everything all right there?" He paused, sensing intrusion.

McCruise knew Connor could read him like a book. The man seemed to have an uncanny talent for capturing the essence of a situation without being drawn a picture. He could hear Connor chuckling as he clicked off the connection.

Pulling her to him by the wrists, McCruise kissed Jacquie's forehead. "I want you, Jacquie. Your neighborhood is perfect. I've evidenced how much, but I need you, too—need you for sustenance—a basic need, like food, and I need to know you're well and cared for. Get some rest and put your safety chain in place after I leave." Adjusting his holster, he shouldered his suit jacket to free-fall.

An otherwise fearsome morning she'd rather forget brightened by his quicksilver smile. Her faltering gesture of goodbye indicated that in her mind she stitched, ripped, and mended the fabric of their relationship. Would he love her as much if he knew what she suspected?

CHAPTER THIRTY-SEVEN

A searing, Mohave sun reflected on the river, plucking at McCruise's flesh, sucking for moisture as if enclosed within a dehydrator, the dome sealed tightly. With two hours remaining before mid-day on this Tuesday after Labor Day, this was not going to be a day for hot chocolate. The brutal desert sun knows no intimidation by a calendar that reads that September has arrived.

Valesano and his investigators milled around outside the Crest, Valesano's chicken neck pecking here and there, avoiding McCruise's eyes. The aggressive heat of an outdoor investigation produces unwelcome, heat-induced maladies just as sure as Ford produces heavy-duty pickup trucks. McCruise knew that Valesano would flee for an air-conditioned patrol car in a freeway minute.

Dodging the TV cameras, long booms, and hubbub, McCruise darted inside the building; the coolness of Wally and the interior was welcome. Something licked at his mind about the commercial kitchen. He leaned back against a cupboard, his thoughts troubled. Wally clanked around like a two-penny drum-and-bugle corp.

While flipping rocker panel switches near the door, McCruise found as quickly as a roadrunner kill what blackout meant: midnight black. His mouth contracted in a humorless chuckle. Unable to shake the aberration of a totally inside room, he mulled.

"There's something wrong here, Wally. We both know the outside of the building grows asymmetrically with nooks, crannies, indents, bumpouts, and is of impressive size. In contrast, look at the inside. It views cut-up with jut-outs, halls, sunken dining room, elevated dining room, with dark fencing around each. The holding bar and reception area are kitty compass from both dining rooms. The real question is why the kitchen is so far from both dining rooms. It's a planned maze so the interior size is unquestioned."

Wally took in the layout, following McCruise's eye odyssey. Sure, cut-up was the short description, but the building held with the architecture of old English Inns. He saw nothing awry.

"It would take a geometry guru to figure out the square footage. The kitchen is the only modern squared room in the building." *Modern*? "That's it! Go figure," Wally enthused. "This building is as old as hell—more than 25 years, but get a load of this room." A broad gesture said it all. "The tile's updated, the walls nicely textured, not an inch of unused space between the cupboards..."

Perhaps updates fell prescribed by the public health authorities, whatever, but something clearly didn't add up. Maybe it was faulty judgment, exaggerated by the power of suggestion, but...

"You're right, Wally. There must be some reason why the kitchen was updated before the place closed two years ago." He studiously sipped at coffee, his big hand circling the mug instead of holding it by the ear. His index finger tapped a rhythm on the side, while he observed the new oak floor, beveled oak cabinets, corian counters, and stainless-steel appliances. Maybe they'd never find the key to this kitchen's differential, but they'd bargain one wall against the other until they scared up some sensible symmetry. The whole place was an architectural desert, with a bit of 16th century deco, and a harum-scarum of upbeat 20th century plasticism.

"Let's take another look at the outside." McCruise gestured.

In the 117-degree heat, the black top around the building and on the esplanade was sticky in places. Sun glinted off windshields of cars and splintered into dazzling slivers against chrome wheels and hood ornaments. After what seemed like a hell of a long time, sweat pouring off them, they were back inside, having firmed their opinion that the outside dimensions of the building, albeit judgmental because of the country-inn architecture, were larger than the inside dimensions.

Approaching the large front window that faced the deck, McCruise leaned into it, bracing himself with his hands on the sill. He studied the crumpled scaffolding — the point of impact where the construction worker fell to his death, his skull cracked open. A cold shudder ran through him, in spite of the intense heat that was blistering the building. Remembering the harassment the previous owner endured two years ago, he found it dubious that this was simply inevitable construction collateral.

"Let it rest, McCruise." Wally could read nuances on McCruise's face as if he were transparent. "Besides, I need another pair of eyeballs to search this wonderful place." His tongue between his front teeth, he shot McCruise a look of indulgent amusement, jostling him from his mind's mileage.

McCruise registered on his hard drive the length of the hall, off which ran the restrooms and the kitchen on one side, the sunken dining room, elevated dining room, reception area, and holding bar on the apposite wall. An uncontrollable compulsion to holler beset him when his deductions came up shorter on the kitchen side of the building.

Wally, raising his eyebrows, approached. "Holy shit, I think you're right!" He was already at work, scrutinizing the width. With a shrug of his shoulders, the distance looked as if it jibed with the outside through mid-building. The opposite side of the building, however, in which sat the reception area and the holding bar, was dramatically shorter than the outside. "So what we've lost here is a room." McCruise's face ripped with a grin. Enthusiasm poured through him like magma down the mountain. "What we have here is a mystery spot, Wally."

"Yeah, I'll say. It's a mystery no one's discovered it before us!" Wally's excitement built. His Norwegian, blue eyes danced. Out of self-preservation, he started laughing. "We did it! We did it! Right under our goddamn noses and we finally found it." He slowed down, out of breath. If today were a vehicle, it would be a snowplow right out of his Upper Michigan roots. How grateful he would be for some Lake Superior breezes.

Wally was so predictable. McCruise knew he'd celebrate the finding, odious as it was. For some inexplicable reason, McCruise laughed, too. Releasing steam from overload valves, he concluded.

"This is it, Wally. We got 'em." Having set aside his suit jacket long ago, McCruise up-cuffed his shirt sleeves. "You start at this end and I'll start over there, rummaging in the cupboards; an entrance door has to be here somewhere." Motioning eagerly to the long row of cupboarding, his voice strangled with possibilities.

"No one ever told me I'd be crawling in cupboards as part of my job description," Wally grumbled. His voice muffled, coming from a bottom cupboard where he could hear the drip of the sink faucet echoing. It ticked at his ears, beating a steady *dan-ger, dan-ger, dan-ger* message. "They've probably planted trip wires in here and we'll blow ourselves into the next county."

"There you go again. You've been seeing too many Bruce Willis films," McCruise shouted over the din of the thumping and dripping.

"Nothing so far," McCruise sighed discouragingly. "Everything's clean as a whistle. There is no sign of secret passages or any ragtag stuff. Guess it only happens in *Romancing the Stone* and *Indiana Jones*." His voice flung in exasperation.

"How about this pantry?" Wally asked, completing his search.

McCruise glanced at the tall oak unit. "It's an efficiency pantry designed with a series of shelves that fold-out, fold-in, like those Chinese boxes we used to play with when we were kids. They fit inside one another—big, bigger, and biggest—or the other way around." He leaned on the butcher-block countertop; his lanky leanness sprawled over it like a daddy-long-legs spider, one elbow bent, the cup of his hand holding up his chin, turning his words fuzzy. The fingers of the other hand were drumming idly on the wood.

Wally opened wide the tall pantry doors, revealing shelves on the doors as well as a series of shelves inside. "I'll be damned!" He swung out the first set of shelves by means of a concave cutout in the middle of the door shelves about the size of his hand, only to find another set of shelves behind them with the same concave cutout. The right set of door shelves matched exactly the left set of door shelves, making the twin concave cutouts a full circle. "I'll be damned, again!" He said, pulling the shelves toward him.

As if he'd ingenuously detonated a 500-pounder, he drew a sharp breath. Did he imagine the back wall of the pantry to tremble slightly? Yes! Almost imperceptibly, the back panel wobbled. With deliberation, he drew his S & W from his holster and stepped back. "McCruise," he stage whispered.

Hackles rose on McCruise's neck with Wally's shouting whisper, his pall paling at the sight of Wally drawing his gun and backing away from the pantry. McCruise directed his glance to where Wally was looking. The back wall of the pantry showed a subtle flux. Straightening quietly, he drew his S & W, nodding almost imperceptibly.

Wally touched the panel, felt the feather-slight play in its stability, and then checked the wall on which it hung. It was grooved—*a pocket door.* Sliding the door sideways, he blinked at the blackness before him. Wally's Maglite sprang to life from a hand extended far from his body. Nothing stirred as he entered the dark room in a crouch, moving the light in quick takes. McCruise rolled in behind him.

"What the hell…" Wally eked out, his voice choked with adrenaline.

McCruise, brandishing his weapon from right to left, hated his vulnerability.

Silence.

The room was stacked with a long series of floor-to-ceiling shelving, containing a cache of cocaine delight. Wally's light passed over one-inch plastic bags, holding 1/16th gram, 1/8th and 1/4th grams. "Teeners" and "Eight Balls," shouted the labels. Kilo-sized amounts were in clear plastic bags, stacked individually. Vials of crack cocaine in the same quantities sat, color coded for quality. More boxes marked Zoom — thousands of Ecstasy pills. The room shouted muted money, millions of dollars worth.

Wally stage whispered, "When I was stationed in Italy with the Army, I lived in a trailer, which was fourteen feet by thirty-eight feet. This room is a dead ringer for the square footage of that trailer."

"At least," McCruise breathed.

They inventoried. A half bath to the right started a wall of base and wall cupboarding. A two-unit hot plate shared counter space with a utility sink and a countertop, utility refrigerator containing large fresh dates and bottled water. On the shelves above were stacked baggie supplies, tin foil, rolls of tape, plastic straws cut short, glass tubes, metal tubes, and razor blades. The quick-scan accounting took in a list in time, spanning only minutes.

"Voilà!" Wally breathed almost silently, cutting a glance at McCruise. "Look at this," he said and pointed at the door shelves on the pantry. "The rounded out hand grips for moving the shelves allows a guy to reach back and pull the pantry door closed by means of a round knob on the inside of the pantry door!"

"I think you'd better go back through the enchanted pantry door and call Cap, Wally. I'll mosey around..."

CHAPTER THIRTY-EIGHT

McCruise breathed softly in the air-conditioning. This inner room was the room that offended the whole Lower Colorado River Valley. It saw development for a clandestine purpose, like an Anne Rice netherworld creation, but holding more substance and no surface. Squeezed to the left, in the end wall, another pocket door evidenced itself. Should he investigate without Wally? What the hell! There was within him a flat certainty to move ahead. The formality of backup often dispirited him, not because he worried about taking a rubbing as a wuss, but because of what he'd always built into his values: the importance of being self-reliant.

On the other side of the pocket door was a blank wall — a close wall, not a yard away — *a staircase landing.* In one move, he entered, sliding the door closed behind him. The permeating smells were heady mixtures of the fusty and the pungent — pungent like Penny's tea canister. McCruise's overall inclination was to believe all was inert iodized metal, wood rot, wet sand, and acrid rubber.

His heart thumped wildly as he glued himself to the far wall. He would work the finesse. If there were no one down there, he'd look a hero; if not, he'd look a zero, but to build a dam, you start with one bucket of cement.

Strength lies in the instruments of strength. Did he have them? He evaluated it as if viewing a video: a body as agile as an out-of-practice defensive back, a mini Maglite, a S & W .40 in his shoulder holster, an extra clip, and emotionally illiterate at the moment. *That's it chum! Survive!*

The brief spray of light from the open door disclosed a short stairway leading down, open on the right; to the left there was a stairwell. Were there four steps? Five? He stopped, listening, hoping to hear even the faintest rustle. *Why didn't he wait for Wally?* He under-rated his need for guidance; he castigated himself. His stomach burned with the thought. Retreat was an option, but it would again make him a target.

Stepping back to the pocket-door wall, he eased himself down the first step, keeping his back to the wall. Goddamn, it was black! *Use one of your strengths, McCruise—the Maglite. Hold it as far away from your body as possible to draw attention away from your actual position.*

He breathed so shallowly his lungs stung when he activated the light. Down another step, when the whole room sprung alive with orange color, stinging his eyes as a shot rang out; the bullet tore through his shirtsleeve, searing his arm. The Maglite flew, landing with a brutal crack, withering and dying.

McCruise tumbled, cracking his head and his ribs on the fourth step, before he rolled limply to the floor. Something told him to keep rolling, charging him head-on into an unforgiving metal tank. He spun back, seeing brilliant flashes of colors behind his eyes. He was dead meat in this mindless scheme. All the essentials of a hare-brained foil were present: the unessential such as self-reliance and pride evaporated like water in his backyard birdbath.

Assessing his injures, he grasped his head, his ribs, and felt swelling starting—wet swelling. Trickling down his arm was the copper-penny taste of blood from the hole in his arm created by a gap in good judgment.

Slowly, he spun himself into a squat. Could he unsnap the fastener on his shoulder holster, or would the act sound like a bomb in the stillness of the room whose dimensions were a nebulous factor? McCruise's arms felt like licorice whips.

There was no doubt as to who stood better trained in jungle fighting, and it wasn't he. Was he strong enough to survive? McCruise knew self-defense, but how could he apply it against an unseen enemy? He'd not learned killer tactics, but control systems, and the vacuum between the two rendered him vulnerable to the "kill or be killed" school.

In a crouch, his body so still that any movement magnified ten times, his left foot traced for purchase and found flat, hard concrete. Thank God, Wally advised him to wear crepe-soled shoes, even keeping a pair in his closet at the plant. He kept his spine to the wall, leaning forward only slightly.

He extended his arms, spanned apart in front of him; his feet cooperated for a natural balance. *Stay against the wall, but move. Keep moving in the darkness and hope to encounter the unknown underground dweller—a Troll*, he thought.

McCruise's physical training instructor at the Academy ran McCruise's ass off to keep his brain on straight, filled him with survival memos: *Push for the edge, and give yourself the upper hand.* Why didn't he take out his gun before he entered the pocketed room? *Don't get careless or cocky. Murphy's Law will make a visit.*

Moving like a mercenary through the short jungle growth, McCruise's awareness heightened to the point of receiving signals as if by sonar. He listened so intently he heard the blood hammering in his ears, sounding powerful, like live surf. His weapon pulled smoothly from the holster, the flap opening muffled by his other hand. The pain in his arm, with no conscience for where it struck, was intense.

Just nine months ago, he'd not a care in the world. He'd lead an enviable life of privilege and prestige. He dined with zesty enjoyment on Laura's subtly flavored Swedish food served on fine china plates, and drank magnums of Napa Valley Merlot from bottles wrapped in colorful raffia shells. What a turn around to find himself in an unspeakable dungeon from which he may never return, from which he may never be found! He was hurting and dirty, even a suspect in the death of his wife.

His sightless defenses coalesced. He was in an underground storage room, and the Troll knew every square inch of it. Yeah, this was a corner, not a big room. He continued crouching to the left. What the hell—steel? Cold, grated steel, as far as his foot could reach out. Squatting closer to the floor, his sensitive fingers picked up a barely discernible horizontal slit, then more steel. There were two, two and a half-foot wide sections of finely grated horizontal steel. Two sections were over water, the gentle slipslop of water evident. There was only one place for egress: the Bridgewater Channel.

As a kid, he remembered coming down to the Village with Coulter to measure boathouses that established under buildings. Those were halcyon days. Coulter's words were his words; Coulter's dreams his dreams, Coulter's God his God. A feeling of warm security encapsulated him, but McCruise put away the green boulevards of his youth. Hoping his second-guessing was in line, McCruise continued left. The mental psychobabble was draining. His muscles ached; his mouth tasted like liquid leather.

Another corner, and then he froze.

CHAPTER THIRTY-NINE

Where was the Troll? The room was small, a boathouse, probably 14 X 30 feet, filled in with cement except for the grating, and used for—what? He knew! *Trafficking!* His breath caught in an open mouth.

Sweat rolled off McCruise, annoying obtrusive sweat. He wanted to swipe his forehead, knuckle under his eyes, but all would make sounds, soft sounds, and interpretive sounds. The further he ventured into the middle of this small room, the more vulnerable he was to closing the gap between himself and the Troll who damn sure wanted him one way: dead. His stomach convulsed.

A slow exhale metered between his teeth. Could he do this? Mentally he encouraged the synapses to rejuvenate his vitals: survival, survival, screaming survival. Survival, the academy taught him. *They'd like to cut off your balls and dangle them on the station door.* One stretch of his aching back or his cramped legs was going to isolate his whereabouts. *Prevail; this is the triumphing attribute in a two-man war.*

McCruise knew that if he tried one move, pinpointing his location, he'd be yesterday's headline. He was amazed at the sightless interpretive powers of his body, contouring around oxygen tanks and wet suits as if they were curves in the road. How long was he down here? Time was interminable in the dark.

Was the Troll moving in the same circular motion as he was? With an eruption as loud as a volcano in the quiet room, McCruise drew a hit of scuba gear. It was an old tactic; throw something for a decoy to bring out the stalked, enticing the stalker to move in. He closed his eyes tightly, waiting for the brilliant flash, the violence of a shot ringing out, pain in his side, in his shoulder. None. Adrenaline flooded his body; he fought for control. No sound came from him, no movement. His whole body coiled for the spring, his arms extended.

Disorientation was complete. It would be no asset for him to analyze. This confrontation would have but one winner. The Troll would throw again until he could locate him. McCruise was sure of it.

He did.

The propitious impacts, their descent to the floor, told McCruise that the Troll was also on the move and was at the bottom of the stairwell, across the room, unless he'd psyched himself to go in the opposite direction. In that instance, they'd meet head on, soon. He was mystified, not accustomed to second-guessing minds that did nothing but outsmart the law while the law outsmarted them.

His physical stamina tested to the point of exhaustion. If endurance were the winner, he'd probably lose. What would happen if he simply crouch-walked across the expanse of this underground prison and hoped for the best? He did, and waited. He challenged the darkness. After reaching what he thought was the middle of the room, he stayed hunkered down, feeling the air, sniffing for scents.

Another brilliant flash: a roar. Instinctively, McCruise got off a shot. The room settled, as dark and soft as silence. Okay, he'd missed his target, but the Troll was over there, in the corner below the stairwell, and he knew where McCruise was, too. He gritted his teeth, moved forward; he was tired of this cat-and-mouse game. He wanted to shout, to growl, to bite. Was he no longer human?

With an abruptness widening his eyes in the darkness, he was there. He didn't need to reach any farther. He could feel it—the radiation of energy, the rippling outward of survival instincts. He was feeling the tides of living energy.

The Troll.

The impact was nauseous. He grunted with the effort of in fighting, lucky-hammered the Troll's wrist, his gun thudding to the floor. It was the survivor struggling with the survivor.

He sucked in air.

McCruise took an impact to his wounded arm, which buckled as if he'd taken another shot. He fell, choked with pain. An unforgiving air tank tangled with his knees and unburdened him of his weapon. The Troll followed him to the floor, McCruise warding him off with a blind shot of his knee to the Troll's groin, garnering a guttural oomph.

"You're going to lose your jugular." The Troll's words spit out low and venomous.

Clutched in a bear hug, McCruise felt the hit-and-miss edge of a knife across his upper back, as if the Troll were attempting to slit open a shifting shipping carton. *The one who endures will be the winner.* Warm blood flowed—his blood—drawn by a hellish asshole. He sobbed, hearing himself sob.

He'd never be able to explain the punch of power ratcheting through him when flooded with the painful thought of his own demise. Struggling for control, McCruise's forearm came crashing down on the Troll's wrist, grasping it, twisting it with him to get behind the Troll's back, reached around his throat and hooked the Troll's muscled neck in the crook of his healthy arm.

In this manner, you apply pressure to the carotid artery and choke off the oxygen flow to the brain.

What, under other circumstances, would have seemed a base act of jungle fighting suddenly metabolized into a morally permissible war on evil. McCruise gritted his teeth in a haze of blind, primitive, self-preservation.

Not that way, McCruise, you dumb shit! Lift your elbow.

McCruise's elbow came up, lifting the Troll's chin. "Ai-yah" emitted from McCruise's mouth, discharging an energy overload.

That's good, McCruise. That's good. That's the way. Now squeeze.

McCruise grabbed the wrist of his fisted hand and pulled.

Hold it! A chokehold applied too long can cause brain damage.

Primal sounds. McCruise heard his own primal sounds—choking sobs.

You can really hurt somebody; maybe kill 'em.

There remained no more items on the menu.

The relaxing body of the Troll indicated he'd passed out. Revulsion gripped McCruise. Still, he couldn't stop. Seized with pent-up fear and anger without remorse, he choked harder, dispatching his faceless enemy to hell.

CHAPTER FORTY

"Where in the hell are you, McCruise?"

The lights blasted on from above, agonizing McCruise's eyes, and revealing Wally, drifting like a turkey buzzard on the thermals, frozen at the holocaust.

Looking down at the phantom, McCruise's eyes protested the sudden light, but widened at the sight of Jaimie lying at his feet. Bending with difficulty, McCruise checked for vital signs. Dead! His Golden Goose, dead!

He angered. He angered irrevocably, stiff with outrage. His tension and frustration were a howling epiphany. "Jaimie?" Raising tormented eyes to Wally, he ceded a groan, as if he were hardscrabble farming. "Jaimie?" He'd killed Jaimie? His ace in the hole? However, the man pulling Jaimie's strings was free, free, and still functioning, scheming, and devastating the lives of the young and the unaware.

Furious at the futility of Jaimie's death, he wanted to stomp on the inert body, take his gun butt and smash his teeth out, then take the offensive chunk of flesh and press him through a wood chipper. "Oh God," he groaned, collapsing like melting butter onto the grilled steel work, where he threw up. To what was he reduced? A killer among killers. Tears traced down his cheeks in weary hopelessness. May God forgive him.

Wally flew down the steps, two at a time, and hunkered down near McCruise, swearing under his breath like a shore-leave sailor, his eyes owlish with disbelief. "Christ, what you been smokin, McCruise? You look like a spavined horse. Besides, dying can ruin a guy's day, you know. You shoulda waited."

"A guy could get *killed* waiting for you, Denton."

"A guy could get killed keeping track of you. Roll over. You're bleeding."

"No shit. Where the hell you been?"

"I was so excited I needed to go to the can."

"Great timing."

Wally was shredding McCruise's shirt, assessing the depth of the knife wounds peppered on his back as if he took multiple shrapnel hits, checked his freely bleeding arm. "You'll live," he grumbled while taping the strips of the shirt around McCruise's chest and the deep flesh wound on the arm. "We can't have you bleeding all over this splendid place."

McCruise knew, however, that no one would ever be able to assess the hemorrhaging depth of his trauma, the tearing at his insides, the trembling he would endure in nightmares.

"How many times have I told you to change out of your good clothes when you work the waterfront?" Wally lectured with levity as he cast about for a cover-up for deadhead Jaimie, who was sightlessly staring up at him; eyes bulged out in anguished disbelief, his tongue lolling. A canvas tarp! Yes, he would cover the purple-blue grossness of death irrefutable within a dog-eared canvas tarp.

He continued his diatribe. "You crazy bastard; you coulda been killed."

"I'm too lean and mean to get killed."

The last time someone stood over him like this, it was the ALETA phy-ed instructor. "You'll never be an Arizona Law Enforcement Officer," he'd groaned. *Never!* Mentally, he thanked the man.

"Take a look at you." Wally's blue Norwegian eyes crinkled with relief, his voice struggling. "How are you going to explain to your mama how you tore your good pants and got blood all over your shirt?'

McCruise, flexing his shoulders to ease the sharp throbbing in his back, ribs, and arm, accepted Wally's assistance to his feet, glad to be alive with or without his good shirt and pants. Christ, his bones disjointed! He felt as if there were no bones in his body—a black hole entity. He possessed the vitality of a February groundhog that just saw his shadow.

Wally led McCruise to the stairs and sat down beside him.

"It's an old boat house," McCruise breathed.

"Yeah, and you smell like an old outhouse."

"Hmmph!" McCruise closed his eyes; too beat to think of a stabbing riposte.

"We need to get the hell out of here, McCruise."

"Yeah, and leave it as we found it. It's called 'letting out the rope'."

"We have a few problems. A body and three bullet holes in the wall."

"Jesus H. Christ, McCruise! You mean he shot at you as well as cut you up?"

McCruise nodded, indicated with his nose where the guns lay dormant in this battleground, where wits superseded weaponry. "He got off two shots. I got off one. Jaimie found cornered down here when we discovered the entrance through the pantry. He found nowhere to go, and couldn't venture opening the steel grates in the floor and swimming out into the channel in broad daylight."

"I'd go to the bank on your theory. Well, I don't need two dead men. Stay put. I'll call the captain from a private line upstairs—see what he advises. The cell phones can be too easily monitored, and who wants Chicken Valesano down here?"

Wally held the phone away from his ear while Connor dragged his name through the ragweed, calling him everything but an asshole, because, he said, that was part of man.

"And make it fast, before we spill the beans altogether, as well as the blood, you crazy, bald-faced imbeciles. You have a lot of explaining to do."

"We'll get right on it."

172

"Tell the emergency room team that McCruise slipped on the broken glass in front of the Crest and chopped up his back and his arm. They may not buy it, but hang with it. What's more, pack out a noticeable amount of coke so it looks as if Jaimie disappeared with a chance to sell for *his* profit, thus screwing Shoney. Move on it!"

"You got it."

Upon returning, Wally spoke to McCruise in a low, private tone. "I'll roll Jaimie in a tarp, carry it out to the patrol car, put him in the trunk, and come back. You okay?"

"No, but tell me, put him in the trunk, then what?"

"I'll come back and patch over the bullet holes best I can—compress the splinters, hang something in front of them, bucket up your blood, and take you to Good Sam."

"What'd O'Shaughnessey say about Jaimie?"

"If we call the coroner, the months of setting up this trap will fall by the wayside. The media will get their teeth into it and our investigation will turn out to be a tin-pot affair. However, *what* he said wasn't fit hearing for crawling creatures. Anyway, I'd rather ask forgiveness after the fact than get permission before."

CHAPTER FORTY-ONE

McCruise was shaking. "What we should do is dump him in the desert and let the coyotes have at him."

"Right on especially if we answered to no one."

"Wouldn't be the first time someone's done that." McCruise sighed. "So what's the direction we take?"

"We deliver him to the regional lab morgue and put him on ice; we'll do an autopsy later, identify him eventually as a Mexican Nationalist without a green card, and ship his body back to Mexico. He mixed in a drug deal gone bad and paid the ultimate price. Case closed."

"Where'd we find him?"

"North of town in Craggy Wash," Wally hummed, "where the coyotes howl and the wind blows free."

Eyes scalded with salt of sweat, McCruise studied the room. Three sides of the converted boat slip sported 1 X 4s nailed to the walls. On the boards were installed double farmer hooks on which hung a potpourri of changes of clothes, wet suit, scuba gear, and masks. Oxygen tanks lined the floor. Hanging on the wall were life preservers with pockets of Kapok hollowed out and zippers added. Life rings hung gaping, split in half horizontally, and hollow for concealing cocaine shipments. Lines of delineation buoys hung from hanger to hanger looking like take-apart pharmaceutical capsules.

"Doesn't this tell a helluva story?" Wally followed McCruise's gaze around the room.

"Their operation was so simple we overlooked it completely. They moved this junk on the river utilizing nautical devices we see every day. Who'd ever suspect?" He asked rhetorically, his voice heavy with the revelations. From somewhere in the dregs of McCruise's memory, he remembered learning that nothing was so difficult to achieve as simplicity.

McCruise, unplugged, wondered if he were running on high-energy Delco batteries, but stayed focused. "Coke. Lots." He spoke in monosyllables.

"You bet. All that remains to be done is catch them moving the stuff."

"They're not returning a dollar with inventory sitting here." How many times would McCruise have to put his life on the line? Being unaware of the undertow in which he floated, he came as close to sinking as he wanted to, ever. "Look at the genie button." McCruise inclined his head toward the end wall above the two steel grates. "The ingress and egress. By activating the red-eye, they have an immediate outlet to the channel, a few yards away."

Using a handkerchief to pick up Jaimie's gun, Wally tucked it into Jaimie's trousers.

"I'll add it to his possessions in the morgue and we'll send him off like a Pharaoh," Wally said, winking conspiratorially at McCruise.

McCruise chewed on his lip. "Jaimie must have entered the Crest for a twelve-hour shift before it opened at ten this morning. It has to be so. He couldn't come out until after 10:00 PM after the Crest closed or in the wee hours of the morning, when the esplanade is quiet, using the watery tunnel in the shoring for an exit."

"Well, he got paid overtime today," Wally clucked. With a bucket of water and baking soda from the upstairs supplies, Wally swabbed the porous concrete of blood and checked the walls for bullet holes, which he pressed with splinters and hung the gear over them. He rolled Jaimie up in the tarp, carrying him out as if he were taking evidence resultant from the morning accident.

McCruise gathered his suit jacket as he went through the restaurant kitchen; it seemed like an eternity since he'd left it there. Godddamn good thing he wore one to hide his bloody injuries! His muscles felt like rubber, and he stopped to rub them as he followed Wally.

After carrying out the trip to the hospital, where the tailors stitched and knotted, and while McCruise explained his phantasmal fall on broken glass from this morning's scaffolding incident, they delivered Jaimie to the morgue. Wally stayed upbeat, his leathery skin oblivious to the heat, as they returned to the Crest.

The air was hot and paper dry, intense and indolent, spreading out like maple syrup over the Channel. With less than an hour left before sunset, the western sky combusted into a brilliant coral, steadily deepening toward orange, as if the sun were hanging onto the Chemehuevi Mountains through sheer determination. The white stuccoed wall of the Crest took color from the rapture and appeared to be full of privileged righteousness. McCruise mentally assessed the mercury at 117°-120°. It occurred to him, in this heat, it was a toss up as to whether the coroner or the coyotes would have gotten to Jaimie's body first if they dumped him in the desert.

They'd been up and down the esplanade dozens of times and never noticed a sign of ingress. Now, standing in soft clothes, they paced.

"I must have room temperature I.Q. because I never figured on an underwater tunnel," Wally grumbled.

McCruise, his body aching all over, stood at the approximation of the access point to the old boathouse. "Yesss indeed, I can see it all clearly. You can auto control a genie button on a boat and the steel grates open vertically inside the old boathouse; unload right here—three, four yards—then go inside and home free. Return to the boat and beam the grates closed."

"We're not dealing with any Opies here," Wally concluded. "It took a stable of talent and know-how to rig up that warehouse."

"Misplaced talent, Wally. There is enough sadness and depression in that chamber to tear the heart out of every home on the Lower Colorado River, plus tax." He sighed.

With Arizona ranking second in the USA for trafficking in methamphetamines and cocaine, McCruise never thought that little Lake Havasu City would be a major player. "We can no longer expect to excel over the bad eggs by wearing a dignified suit and badge." McCruise was tired, and his eyes felt grazed. The heat illusions off the channel, combined with occasional dust devils, hammered at his temples.

Wally grunted. "That method worked when I proudly wore the blue and gold of my Boy Scout uniform as a kid, and later as a young man when I became an Eagle Scout. It worked when I was in the military. I thought that my small Michigan Upper Peninsula lumber-town upbringing insulated me against the mad dogs in the world. Now I need to abandon that thought. I know what abandonment is. My father left my little brother, Jeff, my mother, and me to fend for ourselves while I was yet a child."

McCruise studied Wally's sudden excursion into remembering.

"The hurt, I harbor forever. Nonetheless, remembering my mother having to go to the relief trucks for oranges, butter, and staples resulted in my determination to do better. My mother recounted to me many times how, after her night shift of tending bar, she returned home to count her tips and ration stamps to keep food on the table during and immediately after World War 11.

"I became a grown man before I realized what she sacrificed to keep a roof over our heads, but you know, I never remembered going hungry or being cold. She did what she must in her world, with her means.

"Now it's my turn. I'll do what is necessary to put out a fire."

"Yeah, it requires fire," McCruise said lamely. Hearing Wally's story left him feeling symbiotic, as if he was there, done that.

177

CHAPTER FORTY-TWO

Wednesday, September 6, 1997

Morning hadn't yet peeked full of poop over the mountains when McCruise's pager beeped, and Tucker came panting down the hall. On this, a sick day, he would ignore the beeper and take Tucker out. What's more, his arm and back carried countless sutures and he'd been only a stone's throw from becoming a mortuary inhabitant. Checking the number, however, he found it was O'Shaughnessey's.

"McCruise!" I'm calling a meeting of the Drug Interdiction Unit for eight-thirty. Be there."

Upon entering the bathroom, what he saw of himself in the mirror was rejectable. His face was drawn and pale, his eyes haunted. He wished he could scream to everyone of the nightmarish mortification he allowed himself to fall into yesterday. The anger of remorse flooded back, yet he wondered what subculture Jaimie swam in after he shed his dark glasses and white shirt at the end of a workday and put on home clothes. Did he have a home?

In his other life, when Laura occupied his days, his face was free of troubles; delight danced in his mirrored eyes. Currently, his six-foot-three-inch frame begged for a few pounds and alleviation from pain.

McCruise headed for the station by 8:00 AM. The temperature, already ninety-four degrees, only served to contribute to the sense of debilitation to which he awakened. His concern mounted as he peered apprehensively through the windshield of his new Jeep Cherokee. The sun was a silver overlay, and the sheen it shed was as malignant as snake venom. Even with sunglasses, he narrowed his eyes.

"Say hello, Sadie. Here come dat funny man again," McCruise recited in his favorite eunuch falsetto as he breezed into Connor's outer office.

Sadie, flustered, blew him off with a wave of her hand. If life were a ball of yarn, Sadie would entangle herself in it to hide her shyness, or write poetry to express her feelings.

It was then that McCruise noticed the *River City News* front page, featuring a picture of the death scene at the Golden Crest. The day flooded back upon him with staggering reality.

Remembering to close the door behind him, McCruise entered Connor's office, finding it a cool respite from the intense September sun. The room was large, the ceiling containing two skylights, which allowed the soft imbuement of filtered light. McCruise never tired of O'Shaughnessey's double-paned window of considerable dimensions on the left, overlooking the city and the lake, his massive desk, orderly credenza, state, and national flags sentries behind his desk.

Exhausted and concerned over yesterday's bloody fiasco, McCruise searched his mind. He wondered how many people filtered through this office, how many problems solved, how many reprimands meted out, and how many hearts broken. *None* of them could be suffering more pain than he felt.

Reining in his thoughts, he observed that there were four law enforcement agencies represented. Valesano's absence was glaring. Painfully, he folded his long frame into a soft leather chair near Wally and took his place among the prestigious assembly.

With law enforcement agencies being semi-military, McCruise could see and feel the respect meted to Connor by rank and age. Was the honor a source of panic to him?

Connor would never view even passing panic as an anxiety attack. Nonetheless, in specific circumstances and situations it resulted in intense self-examination. *A humbling experience,* he concluded.

"Gentlemen," Connor began as he slowly arose, a heavy respect in the word; his eyes traveled over the accumulated years of experience. "I've assembled multiple technologies here, so introductions are in order," he preempted, his smile becoming warmer. "Starting on my left is Cleavus Kolbe, our recently assigned DEA man."

Cleavus's face lit up with a winning grin. He nodded.

"McCruise Cruise and Wally Denton, Special Investigation Bureau Officers, our super sleuths who uncovered the clandestine cupboard." Wally and McCruise saluted flimsily, aware they were in the funks with the captain.

"Tom Trehan, Mohave County Sheriff."

Trehan smiled. Not with once-over first-glance did one digest Trehan, but with a second-take of his ice-blue eyes and nurtured muscles. Slim and wiry, he did not bear the packaging one normally associated with a sheriff, but he countenanced no guff.

"Chalmers David, San Bernardino County Sheriff."

Here was a sheriff's sheriff, thought McCruise. *Big, burly, affable, pink-cheeked, the Hollywood epitome of a southern state peace officer.* "Pleased to know you guys," he said chuckling, nodding to each one of them.

Toying with his left ear lobe, Connor lowered himself back into his chair. "Our SIB officers have uncovered a significant cache of cocaine, meth, and multiple other drugs here in Lake Havasu. I requested a computer-enhanced diagram drafted of the location, inset with particular locations of the warehousing, points of ingress and egress.

"My divers entered last night and came up under the steel grating, but the watery tunnel ingress can only be opened by a Genie from the inside or from a watercraft." Handing the diagrams to Cleavus, he indicated distribution with a nod of his head. The exactitude of the symmetry produced by the computer technician, using rough drawings and verbal descriptions rendered by McCruise and Wally, was amazing.

Sheriff David thumbed through the pages.

"I can't believe the extent of this operation," Trehan added, studying the schematics. His eyes lifted, grazing everyone in the room.

"We pick up plenty of this stuff over in San Bernardino; ready-for-use kind of stuff." David shook his head in frustration and swung his gaze to Cleavus for further information.

CHAPTER FORTY-THREE

Cleavus sat at the right tip of the horseshoe lineup of chairs in front of Connor's desk—long, lean and one handsome Afro-American. He exuded a crisp cool confidence. In this ninety-percent Caucasian city, Cleavus wore a sophisticated filter for social knocks, and he handled them well.

He closed his eyes for a moment, leaned his head back, gathering thoughts. "As you know, over the last few years there has been a tremendous increase in the number of people abusing cocaine. Once in the lungs, it's rapidly absorbed and circulated to the brain."

The group was attentive, nodding in acknowledgment.

"The preference of smoking the drug through a water pipe is, to a large degree, because of fear of contracting AIDS with the use of needles—no heroes here.

"Nonetheless, when coca paste, coca base or basuco is smoked, the user is inhaling high concentrations of lead, which, when absorbed into the body, are permanent. Again, no heroes." He delivered the statement with his palms flat out.

"Freebase is the most dangerous form of cocaine smoke, but the process of making freebase involves the use of explosive ether. Resultantly, the perpetrators need to explore other avenues.

"A speed bump in the road is all it amounts to for dealers and pushers. Deduced from what Wally and McCruise uncovered in the storage room, it appears that crack, rock, or ecstasy are the preferred means." He raised his eyebrows, confirming with McCruise and Wally. "What puzzles me is that the lab found traces of tea leaves in among the basic cocaine supply. The leaves now sit in tracking for variety and geographic likelihood.

"The only way to ingest crack is to smoke it." His fingertip ran slowly over his clean-shaven chin. "I've heard cocaine referred to as crack, rock, French fries, peewees, and zoom. Those names are crack mixed with methamphetamines. Crack markets in small plastic bags and sells in rock form. It's often carried in the seller's mouth, as it's not water soluble." His voice grew softer, but his eyes spoke with intensity.

"By 1986, the use of crack cocaine literally tidal waved in the USA, creating a virtual Johnstown Flood. I didn't want to lightly brush over any of this information, even though you're all on board in regards to this influence." He allowed his eyes to lock on each man for a moment.

"In most cities throughout the USA, crack sells for approximately ten to fifty dollars in quantities ranging from one-tenth of a gram to one-half a gram. The lowest prices are reported in New York, Providence, Rhode Island, and Detroit, where individual dosage units can be purchased for as little as five bucks."

His expression hardened with the futility of it all, as if they were fighting some kind of unending horseshit war. "In addition, we have the designer drugs such as ecstasy, which float in and out of the hands of young people as rapidly as airborne measles germs. It is expected that by the end of the year, 5.2 million pills will be seized nationally by law enforcement agencies."

The muffled ringing of telephones seeped in from the outer office. The hum of the air conditioner infiltrated the room like an ever-present welcome guest, while Cleavus passed out sheets of take-home information, including additional street names for coke, such as Snow, Lady, Nose Candy, Flake, Happy Dust, Yayo.

Pumped and rampant with narcotics knowledge, Cleavus was aware that the respondents already harvested and shucked the knowledge. "According to the list of paraphernalia given to me by Cruise and Denton, the warehouse they uncovered is quite remarkable—a supply source for anything desired—and all accomplished with charcoal air purifiers and covered by outdoor smells of cooking from the Crest. This all goes down amid thousands of passing tourists every day. It's like the old saying, 'If you want to hide something, keep it in plain sight.' Cleavus cut a glance to Connor, looking for signs of tension or restlessness.

However, Connor, resting his face on his hand, elbow propped on the chair's arm, only reflected burning, dark-eyed interest, one Daddy Warbuck eyebrow cocked. The furrows in his forehead plowed deeply into his non-existent hairline.

Cleavus's words held the trace of finality. "It's my guess this ring of suppliers has a multi-million dollar business in full bloom, serving all the southern Colorado River locations, as well as Las Vegas. They have all the accouterments necessary for processing, bagging, shipping, selling, and ingesting the narcotic. None of this information is conjecture. No descriptions are vague." His knuckled fist swept over his chin.

"According to Cruise and Denton, an estimated eight thousand ecstasy pills were found, in addition to the coke and its derivatives. Ecstasy is a hallucinogenic Hug Drug, manufactured in the Netherlands. It's the choice of young partygoers today. Popular at nightclubs, it comes in the form of a small pill and sells for about forty-five dollars per tablet. More than two million six hundred twenty-five thousand pills have surfaced nationwide so far this year. The arithmetic on the sales of ecstasy out of this warehouse alone is at least ten million plus dollars."

Connor closed his eyes, idly tapping a pencil on the desk. He sighed with the swamping evidence they'd presented. "What I propose is that we launch a full scale seizure of narcotics actually in transit up the river, but not until it *is* in transit up the river." He paused to canvas the questioning eyes meeting his.

There was a definite perceptible nodding.

"In this manner, we get the contents of the warehouse, as well as the movers and shakers." Connor's jaw firm, he tossed his security pencil lightly on the desk and parceled out his *pièce de résistance.*

CHAPTER FORTY-FOUR

O'Shaughnessey assigned the Mohave County Sheriff's Department to water surveillance from the channel north to Bullhead City. Peering over his half-glasses, he queried for affirmation.

"It'll be no problem." Trehan gave a two-fingered salute off his forehead, over which grew an abundance of blonde, blonde hair, as if it were a doll's wig.

Because the alternates, Nogales and Tucson corridors, were so closely scrutinized, Connor calculated the cocaine was coming over the border from Mexico at Elgodones, a stone's throw west of Yuma, then transferred to Black Meadow Landing, California, a sleepy little marina. Connor would need David's help on the river south of the lake between the canyons and as far south as the landing.

He sat on solid proof that the contraband transferred in ordinary nautical devices such as life preserver rings, buoys, and life jackets. The plan was simple. The packed devices from Mexico saw delivery downriver at the landing marina. Picked up by Shoney's Navy, the narcotics arrived safely in Lake Havasu.

Lights of concern danced in his eyes when he shared the information that there were four boats utilized for transport: two romping blue-and-white striped deck boats named *No Regrets* and *No Tears*, and bearing license numbers AZ 1432/

33 AT. A flamboyant maroon and yellow twenty-eight foot *Warlock*, altogether powerful as hell, AZ 1331 AW, and a rollicking aqua showboat by the name of *Witch Craft*, which was equally as powerful as the Warlock, but with license number AZ 2391.

Connor continued by shifting his attention to McCruise and Wally, smoothly pointing his prop pencil. "Denton and McCruise, you two will be re-assigned to Channel surveillance—nights, starting Friday."

It didn't abide well with Wally and McCruise when the captain called them by their surnames. O'Shaughnessey was in a snit.

"As soon as you see any of these crafts being loaded from the Crest, we'll implement our plan to curtail the shipment immediately before the 1-40 Bridge." Connor's voice caught at the *thought* of closure.

In a turnabout as nimble as a nighthawk, the captain turned to McCruise and Wally, his voice throaty. "Let me congratulate you both on a fine piece of work yesterday."

Tom Trehan, in true police tradition, led a round of applause.

McCruise's eyes connected with Wally, crinkled in amusement, but when he leaned back, a wince from the taut stitches shook him. They figured their minds were sizzled from the heat because they didn't discover the cache sooner. Then having uncovered it, they took such a chance.

Connor rose and went to the exhibit tripod and flipped the maps. "After studying the river terrain," he said, pointing to the map, "and to ensure the safety of all officers and private citizens, the bend immediately before the bridge will serve as a bottleneck for the narc boats. Neither can the perpetrators see law enforcement arrangements on the other side of that bend, nor will they have a place to escape with the bridge one-hundred percent protected."

Returning to his desk, he laid the palms of his hands on the top and leaned over, studying a work sheet. The room was quiet with the serenity confidence brings.

"We are a continuum group in this investigation; where one unit leaves off is indiscernible from where the next starts. Radio privacy, or lack thereof, will strongly affect the nature of our success. Use the Chase Channel when communicating with each other, and don't stay on for any length of time. If your message is lengthy, switch to LHCPD Channel, Mohave County Channel, and alternately to the San Bernardino Channel. In any event, keep it brief!"

Picking up his prop pencil again, he squarely met the gaze of their clear eyes, glowing with anticipation. Connor's organizational skills pulled everything together. "The project code name will be *Water Lily*. The LHCPD Channel and island surveillance is *Water Lily One*. Mohave County assignee is *Water Lily Two*, working the lake and river north of the Channel. The San Bernardino people come into play as *Water Lily Three*. No premature arrests will be allowed downriver, snafuing the upper river confiscation of goods and felons."

Connor, at the tripod again, flipped the sheets to the graphic of the I-40 Bridge. "Here's where a guy has to know his ass from sarsaparilla. We cannot make the arrests anywhere within the boundaries of Lake Havasu. Depending on the time, there could be as many as ten thousand people playing on the lake. They would be in jeopardy."

"By land, Mohave County patrol cars will be in place, creating barriers to escape in the event the narcs beach the boats. By river, the county patrol boats will appear from the Arizona side of the river. San Bernardino patrol boats will anchor on the west side of the river, under the bridge."

The plan went on. "From the San Bernardino patrol boats, the perpetrators will hear advice by loud speakers to bring their vessels to anchor at once. If this warning lies disregarded, a couple of canisters will fire to shake them up. If there is still no abeyance, consider them at war. All nighttime illumination will generate from the boats, or from SIB floods above the riverbank."

He sucked in his breath, his nostrils slimming, as if in finality he were delivering all the necessary ingredients for a successful stew, which heretofore was scarce. It would be a grueling schedule, but the magic of matching wits was a welcome challenge.

His gaze shifted. "Cleavus and I'll arrange to have a DEA copter on standby for us and Denton and McCruise, plus whatever other agents are assigned." *Tap, tap, tap* of the pencil

Cleavus nodded agreement, making a fold in his chin with his thumb and forefinger.

Leaning his head in his hands, Connor swiped across his ears. "All the stoppers will be pulled to move material out of the building—soon. They know the game plan has changed; the establishment of the brewery silos has dictated new rules. If that dog don't hunt, we'll meet back here next Tuesday."

Chairs slid back, hands shook in agreement, and notes compared.

Connor threw his tapper pencil on the desk in final dismissal.

"Best laid plans of mice and you-know-who," he breathed softly to himself.

CHAPTER FORTY-FIVE

Duluth, Minnesota

The Norwood Research and Development lay in an expansive sixty-thousand square foot extravaganza, situated on Interstate 35, south of Duluth, and set back within the confines of a one-quarter mile gated driveway lined with Italian cypress.

Norwood laid in place plans numbered A, B and C.

Plan A was to offer the Sri Lankans world marketing capabilities through the Wall Street International Banking Firm of GG&B, in exchange for the assignation of all government-owned coca plantation harvests and refining.

In case of non-compliance by the Sri Lankans, *Plan B* ran neck and neck in choice preference with Plan C. However, it was long-term and not suited to Norwood's mindset of speedy expedition. It would matter not if there were hundreds, perhaps thousands of Sri Lankan babies stillborn or spontaneously aborted before term in the Norwood Clinics in Colombo, Kandy, and Jaffna. An excessive amount of phenylalaline, a natural amino acid, injected over the period of gestation and the child would abort itself, due to a damaged nervous system, or born with a small deformed brain, and in some cases, a deformed heart.

Norwood would magically present a solution to their problems in exchange for the cocaine market. Workable? Probably. The arrangement was comparable to the deaths of the Holy Innocence or the appalling child's tale of the Pied Piper of Hamelin. Although the lead-time would be tediously long before pressure brought to bear on the powers-that-be, the plan was capable of effectuation at a moment's notice in all the cities where Norwood's Clinics reigned supreme.

Plan C was short term and even more sordid: sabotage the Wastewater Treatment Plants in the Sri Lankan Cities of Colombo, Jaffna and Kandy, killing thousands slowly, with disease, pestilence, and deadly chlorine gas.

It wouldn't take long before Sri Lanka, in gratitude for Norwood's forthcoming solutions, would bestow to Norwood the cocaine market. He would tout the commodity as theoretically pharmaceutical, while millions of dollars worth of cocaine reached street vendors and the profits invested in the Fortune Five Hundred by GG&B, a legitimate and reputable banking fraternity.

****

In the ambiguous atmosphere of the hallowed-hall, Conference Room of Norwood R & D sat the attendees. There were Bandaranaike of Sri Lanka and his associates, George Grinne from Graspe, Grinne, & Barrett, Mallika Chilaw, and Fayne Norwood.

Fayne sat at the head of the table, looking as if he'd just stepped from *George Magazine*, his tan eyes scrutinizing. Not as a toothless, corporate flunky did he view himself, but rather as a phenomenal Zion who was due all the reverence of God. As he read from a prepared document with enormous energy and determination, his eyes searched his audience, pinging off the attendees, picking up vibes. At times, he paused, resting his elbows on the table, making a pyramid with his hands, resting his chin on the tips of his fingers, emphasizing key words, and putting others into silk envelopes.

191

"In as much as the Sri Lankan bargaining team has found it unfeasible to use our Wall Street banking firm of GG&B for tapping the world market, I have a new proposal: the privatization of the municipal sewage systems of Sri Lanka. This project is waiting for underwriting by the firm of Global Earth Technologies, Inc., GETI. Every city in Sri Lanka shall see service by GETI eventually. All meters and maintenance of the system shall fall to the responsibility of GETI. No expenses of operation or installation will fall upon the national or city governments. No increases in sewage bills will be made for at least thirty years."

Norwood delivered every sentence as if his reference sheets were bulleted. The very self-importance of his words metered in a judicial beat.

"What a commendable objective," Mallika concurred.

Here lay *Plan C*, frosted over thickly with confection.

His armature in getting Mallika to the table was the enhancement of her training in management as intern at the King's Retreat. In reality, he needed her total understanding of the Sri Lankan culture, their dialect, and their values. If the Sri Lankans turned down this proposal, due in any part to her negativity, she lost, and knew it through intimidation. She lost face, she lost respect, she lost the peace, which comes with success, and she lost Shoney's admiration.

Mallika sat across from the Sri Lankan delegates, her dark eyes registering regal superiority and control. Democratic Socialist Republic Consulate Representative Singher Bandaranaike, son of a previous Prime Minister of the 1970s, sat with patience often shown by Orientals, as if they were tolerating fools. Charlie Grinne of GG & B tapped his index finger on the provided text.

Bandaranaike sniffed, heightening his dwarf-like frame. "I cannot find feasibility in shutting down our sewage facilities in lieu of new units."

"We are an under-developed country, Mr. Bandaranaike; our methods and treatment plants fall far short of what is to be expected in an internationally competitive market." Mallika Chilaw paused, her great eyes sucking in Mr. Bandaranaike's every facial nuance. "Our expenses far exceed our efficiency, and in many cases provide no services whatsoever."

Bandaranaike held himself rigid, his expression blank—almost scarily empty, as if he'd abandoned his willingness to negotiate, thus shutting down his mind mill. "This is true, but we enjoy our independence."

In his remote villages, citizens did not expect the best of everything. Sixty-six percent of them were yet burning agricultural residues and animal waste for domestic-use energy. He dealt with ruthless Westerners before, dictators in benevolent clothing. He knew a few Western subtleties himself, such as a load of horseshit disguised as something brilliant, but horseshit is horseshit; it didn't matter what other name stood assigned. He would not knuckle under to an ambitious American who intended to batten, thrive, and prosper at the expense of his compatriots.

Norwood ran his index finger down a sheet of his bound text. "Your independence is costing your government millions of dollars. Check the figures on page eleven. Your external debt was 7.9 billion dollars U.S. last year, nearly eighty-three percent of which was concessional terms. Your only concession to GETI is your raw coca exports and a very small amount of tea. You need to remember, also, that the United States Government classifies cocaine as a narcotic, for legal purposes. My research and development needs your coca source for pharmaceuticals."

Mallika cleared her throat. "This proposal will bring hope to our people who aspire to be counted as successful in the world marketplace, all the while costing you nothing." She poured fresh water from a pitcher, the ice adding punctuation to her statement as it plopped into her glass. With the diversion of the sound from the needling trend of her statement, she sighed.

The questions and answers bounced around the table, the meeting waxing tedious, and the minutes turning into hours. Fayne pushed a silent button and produced from thin air Sligh Shoney and Tony Valesano, who took chairs at the head of the table on the right and left of Norwood. They even appeared from the right and left side of the room, as if *Scotty* beamed them down. Valesano's chicken neck protruded from his white shirt, as if on a puppeteer's string. As he sat, the collar on his suit jacket slipped up to his ears. Repeatedly, he craned his neck, jerkily lifting his chin like a fowl finding feed in a furrow. His hand kept drifting up to where his hair laid slicked back over his ears, silently broadcasting that he felt out of his element, like a bicycle crushing through rush hour traffic.

Shoney, at ease, showed the Sri Lankan representatives an All-American candid with his short sandy-colored hair, vibrant blue eyes, and an on-again-off-again Finnegan electric smile. Wearing a non-committal gold-colored sport jacket and navy slacks, he conservatively selected a sparkling white Italian-stylized Bosche shirt and navy tie. An image of honesty and integrity, he was introduced around the table, Fayne adding Valesano as an also-ran.

"It's time for you to meet Sligh Shoney and Tony Valesano," Norwood drawled with quiet authority, addressing the group, the announcement more a gesture of courtesy fulfilled than formal introduction, yet as palatable as Palaza Pizza.

"They will act as intermediaries between Global Earth Technologies and," he nodded to Bandaranaike, "your Sri Lankan emissaries during the interim period of planning, organizing and implementing the new sewage systems."

Shoney and Valesano did a stint around the table, shaking hands, squeezing shoulders, and purveying plastic eagerness to be of assistance.

"How happy to make your acquaintance."

"Pleased to meet you, I'm sure."

Norwood set his teeth in a smile and radiated no compunction from his ice blue eyes. He held court, enjoying the impact of his late introductions, barely concealing the fact that these newcomers were men to contend with, not to befriend. It was a show of force to the Sri Lankans—a build up of military might, Howitzers in a yet-slingshot situation.

Grinne stood slowly. "Our offer stands until just after the end of the month; that's all," he said tacitly, his eyes moving around the table to his cohorts in silent confirmation. If he never said another word, there would be an understanding among them. He continued, laying the decision in the laps of the Sri Lankan negotiators. "It is a splendid opportunity for you to look like princes to your people. Whether or not you consider there is an advantage in it for your country remains subject to investigation on your part. Everything is relative. What we ask in return is your refined coca plant trade and five percent of your government-owned tea exports, for which we are prepared to pay market price." Grinne reshuffled his papers in preparation to leaving; confident he trapped his fish in a stewing pot, he smothered a smile.

Norwood pushed back his chair. "*And* we would gently encourage you to remove yourself from the Southwest Asian Coalition of Governments. With our help, you'll surface with greater autonomy, success, and living standards. Thailand and Taiwan will not be able to compete with your market share. When they abandon their harebrained legation parties and pushing papers, they'll want a union with Sri Lanka. Resultantly, it'll be your turn to call the shots, and call them you will, with a handsome profit for inventing the trade wheel."

"Yes," Grinne said stoutly. Shifting his attention to Bandaranaike, he went on. "All here are in compliance with the plan. When you set the wheels in motion with your government, we shall have an action procedure and policy in place. Thirty days you have."

"Thank you for coming," was the short dismissal by Norwood. "Thirty days," he repeated.

Bandaranaike and party bowed their way out of the conference room. "Thirty days it is."

CHAPTER FORTY-SIX

The Channel shimmered uncompromisingly in a heat screen, and the Havasu winds lay in the doldrums.

Jacquie responded to McCruise's phone call in the late afternoon, while sitting at a desk in her condominium, telephone hugged to her ear by means of her shoulder, leaving her hands free to shuffle Crest papers. "Sorry to hear about added surveillance, McCruise. I'll busy myself with the restaurant and the expansion, which is progressing, in spite of the terrible accident."

"Oh, and Sligh called. Because he has the paperwork completed for purchasing my unit, he invited me to his penthouse Saturday night for dinner and finalization of the title transfer." She sighed, laid the shuffled papers on her desk, and gripped the telephone in her hand. She would be glad to have the contract off her mind. Thus far, she lived in the condominium as a courtesy extended, and she wasn't fond of owing Sligh.

The silent simmer of McCruise's unspoken objections spoke loudly. Her heart rate picked up, aware at last of the predatory caste of Sligh and his ilk on the decent and the innocent. He consumed people with the attack system of a roadrunner on a baby quail.

His words came in short spurts. "I have feelings for you, and I've felt them returned. Come live with me, under my protection, and you will have no need of a unit. I make this offer with the intent of marriage."

She mustered her faculties enough to sound light. "I'm not ready to move up to the next plateau in our relationship, McCruise. Besides, the condominium is a super investment and a get-away for you." She embodied a trickle of excitement at the mere thought of a tryst with him.

"There's no objection to the get-away part," he said as softly as warm night air. "In any case, if you insist on staying there, don't go up to Sligh's penthouse. Execute the papers at your condominium or in a public dining room such as at the Retreat."

Jacquie felt the unspoken words in McCruise's receding voice, the terrible turn of events tying his tongue in knots.

"McCruise, your mind is working overtime." *McCruise and Connor are both rampantly prejudiced and over-protective.*

"Okay, counter his offer," McCruise suggested. "Invite him to have dinner with you, sign the papers, and show him to the door, in that order. Work with me here."

Jacquie heard clearly the brusqueness in his voice. "Okay, McCruise. It'll be colder than a well digger's lunch box when he has dinner with me Saturday night."

"Watch your back. I'll call whenever I can." His voice warmed.

In the time she spent with McCruise, she knew him to be honest and trusting. His passions swept over her like a riptide, but his mind slogged with over-marination in soaking Sligh so heavily in Fayne's shadow. She drummed her thumb on the desk, sliding the chair back.

She considered. Yeah, sure, she was thinking like Mallika, who just fell off the turnip truck and didn't consider subterfuge. Mallika, working intensively in America for the betterment of her people, would moan with malevolence were she informed of dark dealings. Her great brown eyes, which spoke for her soul, would fill with bitterness. Jacquie's spine crept with misgivings.

Why did she face these dilemmas—dilemmas other young women seemed to have escaped? Given the right set of circumstances, right time, right place, Sligh Shoney was probably no worse than most, and even better than some.

He was a Siamese to Norwood—a giant tactician dealing with ordinary men doing ordinary jobs. *Moreover, he crushed anyone standing in his way.* Jacquie's chin dropped; her eyes filled with tears, and she shivered with a tiny sob.

It wasn't her job to set the world straight, was it?

CHAPTER FORTY-SEVEN

The Mohave Desert twilight was showing off with the splendor of heat-generated undulating waves of varying colors: teal, pink, and salmon. The damp smell of the Bridgewater Channel blended with the floor planter of the jasmine McCruise sent.

Swimming upwards was crescendo laughter from Kokomo's while Sligh and Jacquie dined on her patio. Mallika made all the arrangements for baked chicken Oscar; the linens laid pure white, the napkins, and candles, coral. Into ivy-etched Waterford, wine glasses Sligh poured chilled Pinot Grigio. The print silk shirt he wore possessed soft hues of blue and beige, the lapels falling open to reveal soft gold hair curling to the neckline.

While Jacquie sipped on the zesty beverage, Sligh stared uncontrollably at the dampness of her lips. "I arranged all this especially for you." His gaze hung hungrily like an old Buddha about to claim the sacrificial virgin. "Mallika jumps at the chance to please me," he said, leaving the words hanging, their implications clear. *He needed to get more subservience out of Mallika; she needed to provide more mouth and less wide eyes while pleasuring him.* However, he need not entertain thoughts of Mallika's nubile sexual inadequacies at this moment. Devouring Jacquie with his eyes made his groin ache—so much so, that it was difficult to concentrate on the matter at hand.

"The buy/sell transactions with the east-coast owners went as planned. I bought from them; I'll sell to you." He spread his hands, thumbs up. "Most of the document is boilerplate. I'll accept your check for half, the other half to be paid in monthly installments until the Golden Crest accrues profits, and not before. Sligh delivers," he said, his throat bulging like a challenging lizard.

Transferring to Sligh was a cashier's check drawn on Jacquie's First of America account for one-hundred twenty-five thousand dollars. It was with a measure of pride that she did so, fulfilling her end of the transaction on time and without difficulty. She smiled deeply, her teeth looking like jewels in the dusky light.

Sligh's eyes darkened, regarding her with measured astuteness. "You look lovely. I hope you don't mind my saying so," he said, feigning subservience. Soft words of flattery encouraged a woman to be sensual and servile; he practiced this method of operation with every woman. It worked, leading to his gratification, feeding his hedonistic hunger.

The fact that he was unable to get Jacquie to agree to dinner at his penthouse oppressed him. The privacy afforded him there would be conducive to enjoying untested pleasures. The situation was not desperate, only serious.

"Are you uncomfortable, Jacquie?" He inquired solicitously as he poured more wine. "Is there someone already in your life since you've arrived in Havasu?"

She nodded, uncertain of where he was taking this.

"Would you care to tell me about it?" A small sigh escaped his lips.

"Yes, it's McCruise Cruise." She raised her eyes to his, steepling her fingers in front of her.

"Matthew Cruise. Yes, I know him," Sligh breathed out slowly, hooking an elbow around the back of his chair. "He and his father have a prosperous boat-building business, and Mathew parades around town playing cop. He must be a constant source of embarrassment to his father." *Good point of attack*, Sligh complimented himself.

"Oh, I don't think so. He has fine and noble objectives," she said, her statement void of uncertainties.

Unable to shake her faith in McCruise, he pulled his hand away and reached for the lanai telephone calling for a steward to remove their dinner settings and for Mallika to join them, to serve as Notary. He could dangle Jacquie's beauty in Mallika's face, maybe raise some fretful doubt over her status with him—her status as an intern. He sat, shot through with the thrill of torturing her. Wonking off while watching a roadrunner tease a lizard until it lay quite dead and de-energized was the highlight of any day.

"Here you are," he said, passing her the drafted text and pen upon arrival of the steward and Mallika. "Welcome to the King's Retreat. By far, you are my favorite tenant." His smile would have melted a kayak from ice in the Yukon. He was aware that his choice of words stiffened the Sri Lankan intern, who also carried tenancy in the building, as well as tenancy in his Penthouse. The exposure to Jacquie as competition was incentive enough for Mallika Chilaw to come around to seeing to his every whim—on demand.

"You can take my copy downstairs and put it into the safe, along with this check," Sligh instructed Mallika, dismissal in his voice as he capped his pen with a decisive snap. She retired regally, her head held high, her long legs and slim hips doing neat swaying things again.

Laying her legal document on an end table, Jacquie moved to a rattan-padded chair, Sligh blatantly noticing as she swung a refined ankle over the other.

Uncontrollable thrills pierced his groin, observing her becoming self-conscious under his intense scrutiny, her cheeks aflame. Whether the physical readings were from discomfiture, resentment, or anxiousness, he was hard-pressed to untangle, but he could not care less. Confusion was progress with a woman, especially a cultured woman. He wanted this woman more than any other female. Sligh's bed warmed with women as often as he chose to have company.

His eyes swept her with paralyzing clarity. "I'm glad to see you survived the unfortunate accident at the Crest," he said with practiced nonchalance, one eyebrow querying. "It is my personal opinion that the brouhaha attached to the incident was a bunch of hooey. Inexplicable things happen, very often through a moment's carelessness."

"It was an earth-shattering experience for me," she said, relieved to be in neutral territory. Her preference was to enjoy the awake and warm evening; a quarter moon hung overhead lazily.

"I understand," she said, "that the statistics on fatalities are calibrated on one death per million dollars of expenditure. Having said that, I should have no further incidents. The truth behind statistics is learned so much more quickly when number crunching becomes a reality." She looked to him for nurturing, but zilch was forthcoming.

Sligh reached for the Pinot Grigio bottle, putting a top on her already half-full glass. "You look ethereal in the evening light," he said, theatrically pulling down his mouth.

Jacquie raised an eyebrow. "You have a problem on this beautiful night, Sligh?"

"Yes, I have a problem." He sounded brusque. "It's been a blow to me to learn you're committed to someone else." He lifted her left hand, bending to kiss each finger, and then he drew a deep breath, histrionically smitten. "I always felt, in time, that I could gather you into my life, make you a part of it.

"You don't mean..." she couldn't put into words what she was thinking.

"I do mean. I want you. It's the biggest blow to my psyche in my whole lifetime—your rejection." He emanated rough energy, superimposing his weighty presence, the magnitude of his position.

He cupped her wrist brusquely. "Jacquie, I could offer you so much more than McCruise." The words rolled off his tongue as if they were mine-tailings. "His world is grossly finite. You and I could have world travel, an exquisite home at several locations, and all the toys. You would want for nothing, being my mistress."

Jacquie gasped with incredulity. If there were indicators of his mean proposal, they glided right by her.

Shoney wanted her to be his *mistress*?

CHAPTER FORTY-EIGHT

Mistress?

The quarter moon was no longer snoozing, but hiking high. The jasmine plant rustled in a soft breeze; crickets sounded in the bushes.

Shoney's mistress? Jacquie withdrew into herself, nibbling at her bottom lip. "Serving as your mistress is an intolerably abusive suggestion." She was silent for a moment, overtly struggling with anxiety and the social correctness in choosing her words.

"My proposal, as abusive as you think it is, is the one and only time I've made the offer to anyone." He leaned back, locking his hands behind his head, peddling his superior position.

Her words came with great effort. "It's a developing relationship that McCruise and I have. I'm the one who has a surfeit of decisions to explore—not him. If I'm lucky, he *will* be the man I marry." She moved her eyes directly to him. No hyperbole could inflate the hardness Jacquie drew from his blank, icy stare.

"Your offer is unacceptable, totally unanticipated, and crass. Thank you, but I am declining." Her throat worked at swallowing. "I won't be changing my mind," she added, managing a small smile, not wanting any invitation implied.

In a sudden move, Sligh stood in front of Jacquie, catching her by the upper arms and hauling her to her feet.

Smothering her into his arms, he bonded her body against the hard length of his own and hitched his mouth over hers, his breathing accelerated.

"I'll have you, Jacquie," his voice quivered. "No woman has ever turned me down. I'll buy you a gold Karmann Ghia, an emerald-studded coronet for your head, five times the diamonds in any ring McCruise may, or may not present to you." His lips moved roughly over her mouth as he talked.

She paled, her eyes growing in indignity, her hands intervening against his chest. "Please, Sligh, don't say anymore. You'll have regrets some day." *The man should be out looking for his mind.*

Sligh's arms tightened, undeterred. "I have untold resources, enough to live out our days in a style unimaginable. I can't get you off my goddamn mind." His hand fisted in the curls at the nape of her neck, holding her to him. Sliding the other hand slowly down her back and around her rib cage, he moved upward to possess her breast.

"Come," he said as he encircled her waist with his hands, lifting her bodily and carrying her into the living room as if she were a mannequin being removed from a shop window.

Her eyes widened in shattering reality. The metaphysical attachment experienced on previous exposures to Sligh quickly dissolved in the light of the cold certainty of his intentions.

Inside, he hauled her against a wall with demanding intensity. "I'm not waiting any longer, considering your rejection."

She stunned into frozen fear. How did she get into this? She turned her head aside to avoid his kisses.

Party sounds and gaiety from the busy esplanade reached her ears with uncanny irony—the jubilant weekend crowd a short distance away—and she brutally attacked within spitting distance of their mirth.

Sligh preened, reminding her of a roadrunner in heat, hissing and ruffling its feathers. The last thrust of his body against hers left no doubt that he could peck. He *intended* to leave no doubt. Slowly, he released the pressure he'd assessed her against the wall, allowing her to tumble toward the front of the fireplace.

With a resonating growl, he pulled her into his arms again. "I want to get to know you, tonight—all of you," he whispered, as he moved his tongue from her ear to her cheek.

"No, Sligh. This is not..."

He stopped her words with his mouth.

Holding both her hands behind her back with only one of his, he flaunted his sheer size and bulk at her. With his free hand, he allowed himself *carte blanche* to her by running his hand up her neck, to her chin, cupping her mouth to receive him, molding, and finally entering with the pressure he applied to her cheeks with his thumb and fingers, bruising, squeezing, and biting. Strained moans of pleasure emanated from the indulgent world into which he transported himself. His tongue was artillery; his teeth serrated sabers. Under her skirt, his hand ran up her thigh.

Squeaking and crying, Jacquie could not account for what she was doing. If this was a nightmare, it was a lulu. She froze with raw terror, an extreme emotion untarnished by any other. The fireplace tools were on a stand on the far end of the hearth. If she could turn him around and keep backing up toward them... maybe, just maybe... Slowly, she maneuvered Sligh to face the lanai as he groveled over her.

He breathed heavily, his eyes dark and deep in the icy blue. "I'll undress you any way I can," he said, his voice throaty and unrecognizable. "You can either cooperate or have your clothes torn off." His voice was a low rumble, catching on short breaths. "You're about to experience what love making is all about: my tongue on your neck, on your breast, on your belly, then..."

Sligh gasped, his voice choking.

****

His hand tore from her face; his head jerked back in one swift motion. A guttural cry of pain tore from within him. McCruise held him in an arm lock and fisted his hand in Sligh's hair in a come-along grip. Pushing him toward the door, through it, and out into the hall, McCruise rammed

Sligh's face smash-mouth into the wall on the other side of the hall.

Sligh screamed in pain as McCruise applied pressure to the arm lock.

"Listen and listen good, animal! Your mother should have castrated you at birth." McCruise roared, scrubbing Sligh's face back and forth against the textured plaster of the wall. "If you as much as look at her again, you're dead meat. You understand, fleabag?"

No reply.

"I can't hear you!" McCruise clutched Sligh's head back and slammed him, nose forward, into the wall with a sickening crack, blood spurting out against the paint. "Now you hear?" He gritted out between his teeth, his generous lips a thin line.

"Yes," Sligh barely whispered.

Pulling up on his arm in a quick flick, McCruise heard another repelling snap, resulting in Sligh sliding down the wall in a dead faint. In fierce fury, McCruise nuzzled his toe against Sligh's inert form, then thought better of it, shrugged his shoulders, and re-entered Jacquie's unit.

He found her profiled in fear, a statue, her mouth and ears bleeding, her fingers splayed over her face in terror.

McCruise dialed 911. "Send an ambulance and EMT's to the King's Retreat, third floor west. A man in the hall needs attention." His breath barely choked out the message.

Without need of words, McCruise lifted Jacquie in his arms. She sagged against him as he carried her into the bedroom, laying her gently on the bed. He wanted to snuggle into her and never separate again. Yet stiffened with fear, shivers of after-shock rivered through her. She wept uncontrollably, taking gulping breaths while McCruise bathed her face and neck with a cool washcloth.

He matched her deep breaths to keep from swearing in frustration. In view of the trials he experienced this week, he struck dumb. He checked the assault on her ears, her neck, and waxed bitter at the brutal bites. His heart hammered painfully with empathy. Was she going to be sick? He fought off his own nausea.

Assessing her strength, he steadied her, helping her out of a bloodstained suit. Standing before him, clad only in a lace bra, bikini panties, and a short slip, she was rich in gratitude for his presence. Inconsolable dry sobs poured forth as she pointed to a dresser drawer where McCruise found a white cotton nightgown with eyelet embroidery. He turned his back while pulling down her sheet and comforter, allowing her the dignity of cladding herself. Then, picking her up, he set her on the edge of the bed.

She settled her elbows on cotton-covered knees and lowered her head into her hands. Her shoulders slumped in disgrace. With a tremor of vulnerability in her voice that broke McCruise's heart, Jacquie said, "I owe you so much." Then only sobs and hiccups soiled the silence.

In the bathroom, McCruise quickly rummaged through her medicines. She should at least have Midol for her monthlies. Yes, she did—Ativan, too. He shook out one of each, which she swallowed gratefully, looking up at him with eyes like big blue pools, her lashes wet, and anguish showing from deep within.

The muscles around his mouth tightened as he pressed her back against a pillow stack, and pulled the sheet and comforter up over her.

The bedside lamp quickly darkened; he didn't want her to see the tears in his eyes. Rubbing his knuckles across her cheek, he whispered, "Don't answer the door for anyone," barely getting the words past the lump in his throat. "I'll lock the lanai doors on the way out. If you should need me, turn on the outside lights." His voice came from the aureole of her hair, his head buried deep within her shoulder. "I'll return around three when I get off duty. Sleep. I'll be watching." He bent to her, laying a kiss gently on her forehead.

McCruise knew Sligh worshiped three gods: control, greed, and power. The control god would seek retribution. The greed god would seek Jacquie again. The power god would struggle, at all costs, to stay top gun. Would his police acuity be enough to stave the tide?

His mind reeled with weight, while sirens wailed in the distance.

CHAPTER FORTY-NINE

The last of the night was wafting away as if it were a discarded, transparent snakeskin, and a hot pre-dawn wind pressed at McCruise's uniform. This night saw perception become reality in Jacquie's condominium. McCruise shook his head in disbelief at Sligh Shoney's gutsy aggressiveness, albeit being aware of his ruthlessness.

It was well after three a.m. before he returned to Jacquie's and sat near her bed. Observing her bruised face, welted neck, and swollen mouth, his knees jellied. Shoney was the offspring of a hermaphrodite who made love to himself and gave birth to a Satyr—half man and half beast.

Libido! The power it held over men was phenomenal. It was the impetus to drive even King's and princes to abandon their titles, their thrones, their fortunes, sometimes putting their lives at risk, all for the privilege of bedding the woman of their dreams, and Sligh was living proof. McCruise remembered Somerset Maugham's quote, "The love that lasts longest is the love that is never returned."

Shoney couldn't have what he wanted, which turned him into a raging basilisk. If he raped Jacquie, and accomplished what he'd set out to do, he'd see himself in shackles like a common criminal—in front of his four hundred employees, his hotel guests, and, in all likelihood spend years in prison—ten to fifteen, with a conviction. Some badass lawyer would probably plead the case down to simple assault and get Sligh off with probation. Lawyers! Not McCruise's favorites — turkey buzzards!

Watching Jacquie sleep, he questioned why he'd stuck his neck out for police work. It was unrewarding, demanded enormous courage, and held little dignity in the nineties. Even a solid arrest rarely resulted in an adequate conviction. What else would you expect of a world in which liberal professors taught anti-establishment ethics and everyone's views were right and valuable, regardless of reason or measure of hate.

He consoled himself, remembering the laws of economics: *Evolution would come after revolution.* Pendulums swing both ways. The way he'd handled Jacquie's assault was best at this time: *quid pro quo.* McCruise meted out the judgment, and Sligh walked.

His satisfaction slowly faded and his eyes stung as he gently caressed the gradients of Jacquie's face, feeling the puffiness, cuts, and bruises. Sighing softly, he found his grief and weariness going bone deep. Would he forever feel this sadness, which enveloped him at her inexperience with the experienced? His body sagged; tears stung his eyes. McCruise turned to counting his blessings. She'd known salvation from the fire.

Mark, seven, and Luke, five, his greatest gifts, safely slept at Coulter and Penny's, with Tucker snuggled at their feet. His beloved children. He leaned back in the chair, closed his eyes tightly, his lashes wet, and told himself he was getting soft. No, unpretentiously basic — home, hearth, and health.

Dawn seeped over the mountains before he allowed himself to leave, and he searched his mind as to where he was on the food chain at this point.

CHAPTER FIFTY

McCruise's answering machine at the plant was beckoning. Goddamn, couldn't he find a niche of peace? Yesterday was a comfortable, stress-free day with Mark and Luke while visiting Coulter and Penny. He'd even found time to play the trumpet for the kids. "Moon River" echoed over the mountains, while they danced as floppily as string puppets, with Tucker yipping around their ankles.

Now what?

"Meeting tomorrow, 1:00 PM, same place, and same people. *That dog did not hunt.* Confirm lunch at the Holiday Inn preceding the meeting, say 11:30. I'm home."

Of course, he would have lunch with the captain and go to the meeting. McCruise shook his head, sighing. Nothing moved over the weekend—*nada*. All he and Wally observed were the usual nuances of the night: soft lights, purr of boats, and plentiful partiers. The weeks since Laura's demise dragged on, dismal and distressful, and turned into many months.

Sometimes he thought he, in addition, was dead, but his eyes, frantically alive in the mirror, showed him a mind that was darting with determination. That was the important thing to remember; his mind remained unimpaired, and with it, he could dispatch waves and waves of retaliation. Many times, he felt possessed of the powers of pyschokineses. His mind became an electronic probe feeling others' failures, their successes, their half-lies, their heartaches, as if they spoke to him. Through the sheer willpower of his intense mission, the atomic structure of inanimate objects seemingly stirred within their depths, bending to his willpower.

CHAPTER FIFTY-ONE

By the time McCruise joined Connor for lunch at the Holiday Inn, the weekend disappointments cleared like a patch of blue in a tormented sky.

Connor, since reading McCruise's Friday night duty report regarding the assault on Jacquie, realized how wrapped up he'd been in this drug investigation and how he'd lost touch with his family.

"What the hell happened Friday night at the King's Retreat?" O'Shaughnessey adjusted his posture in the leather-upholstered booth in the dining room.

To hide the verge of internal combustion sweeping over him, McCruise sipped on his coffee. "To get us both on the same page, I think you need to know that I carry a passkey to Jacquie's condominium." He paused for confirmation, his eyes on fire.

Connor nodded. "Marvel told me." He stretched out his hand to McCruise. "Congratulations. You have good taste." His gaze beat a path to McCruise's eyes, nodding with encouragement.

Not often McCruise was abashed, but in the presence of Connor, he felt flattered. "Thank you. Marvel produced a beautiful daughter for you."

Connor talked around a held-back grin. "We are proud of her. It's a damn shame that I knew so little of her until she was a grown woman. Large chunks of her life are a haze in the gauze of my yesteryears. Now that she is mine, I intend to afford her my protection."

"Amen," McCruise said after a hesitating breath. "It seems Shoney wanted to get together with Jacquie to sign the Land Contract for the condominium." McCruise nudged himself to relax; he could feel tension building in his shoulder muscles. "So he took advantage of the situation Friday night to have dinner on Jacquie's lanai. From the second story walkway of the strip shops on the esplanade, I viewed every move. Shoney attacked her, packing her into the privacy of the living room."

Connor blinked, squinted in concentration.

"By the time I got up to Jacquie's condominium, Shoney seized her in a half-nelson, threatening to tear off her clothes. He was in such a zone; he didn't hear me come in the door." McCruise felt the command of the situation sweep over him again. "I applied the come-along hold, got him out into the hall—neutral territory so to speak—and let him have a piece of take-home information he'll never forget." He tapped his hand on the table three times with the last three words.

"Good Lord, McCruise, anything could have happened if you weren't watching." Connor leaned closer.

"Incredibly, yes. It would have broken your heart to see how she looked; there were bites on her ears, on her throat." He paused, leaned across the table, his elbows propped low. "Her lips were chewed so badly, they were bleeding." His eyes stung with tears, much to his chagrin, not wanting the captain to view his soft core.

Connor's jaw dropped, furtive annoyance hanging in his voice. "The man's a regular Hannibal Lector! Be forewarned, he'll never forget what you did. We could tag him with felonious assault, but should that be the case, we'd not be able to let out the rope on the narc charges. He's not gone without punishment, however; he's handicapped with a broken arm and a broken nose, and in the hospital. He told the investigators he was attacked by someone high on drugs."

They exchanged glances of pure proprietary pact just as the server appeared to take their order for prime rib sandwiches, then moved quickly away.

"Speaking of narc activity, this past weekend of non-activity is all the proof I need that the mole is alive and well in the department," Connor said with conviction. "What's at risk here are failed efforts; they have long-term implications and set precedents for future funding of operations." He folded his hands in front of him on the booth and cocked an eyebrow, affixing McCruise's attention with his candid concern. "I chill when someone mucks with my mind." He turned his head to the side, slapping his palm down on the table.

McCruise focused with deliberateness on Connor's department mole. Exhaling a long breath, he frowned.

"You don't think it's one of us—one of us sitting at the meetings?"

CHAPTER FIFTY-TWO

"A person at the meetings? Goddamn it, McCruise, I can't disregard any possibility!" Connor was on a slippery slope, taking him into Law Enforcement La-la Land if he didn't get a grip. "When you have to start distrusting your closest cohorts, you're up against it. It's a serious element in our problem solving."

McCruise folded his arms across his chest. "Look, no disrespect intended, but I fail to believe it's someone from our group." McCruise sat back, refusing to entertain any such thoughts. The planning group was divergent, that was a given, and the situation they faced was as sticky as crude oil, but all participants shared commonizing goals.

"Hey, I've no intent of conveying to you that I think I have the market cornered on fidelity and allegiance, but by necessity, all doors remain open. Let me run this by you." He leaned back comfortably. "We set up a bogus plan, a scam, and an action looking for reaction."

"What we do is advise our small group of a turnaround of our schedule. Operation Water Lily runs the reverse time frame of what we'd previously scheduled." Connor took out his wallet calendar. His index finger on the dates, he lifted his eyes. "We cease working weekends and setup week-day surveillance on Mondays through Thursdays. This will leave the weekends unmanned—supposedly."

McCruise leaned forward, with the attentiveness of a student.

"I'll use the ruse in this way: we don't stretch the department budgets severely with weekend overtime. It's a buyable excuse. City and county governments operate tightly."

"So if that's the ruse, what's the real story?" McCruise lassoed his mind into thinking law enforcement instead of prime rib sandwich, which sat before him, the Black Angus temptingly aromatic.

"Stick to the first advance." Connor paused, the deep furrows in his forehead playing tag.

It was as if this battle with Colorado River narcs was an all-out war. Somehow, McCruise guessed if he drew the bottom line, war would be the summation. There was not a doubt, not the slightest. It *was* war.

Connor's eyes smiled with glints of aggression. "So what the hell? I figure we've made an advance, unsuccessfully, but the enemy possessed the advantage as forewarned and forearmed. These next two weeks will be the feint. Given the nature of the people we're dealing with, I'm not so pigheaded as to think they won't view it as a feint. It's my guess they will. They'll test us. We'll allow them, by whatever means they decide." His forehead creased deeply, in triplicate.

"So what do you expect?" McCruise's eyes reflected a flash of interest, his table knife reflecting the sunlight of late morning spilling through slanted verticals.

Connor hesitated, taking a deep breath. "We need to see which way the cat jumps. If they want to take the offensive, we'll damn well be ready for them. Anyway, by that time they'll be led so far astray they'll feel smug with their offensive, and they'll make their move to haul the rich booty upriver to a new location or out of the area completely." Connor absently stirred his coffee.

"Time's on our side." McCruise spoke barely above a murmur. "You have the plays right. All we have to do is be patient and wait until they see those big silos delivered. With those in sight, they'll know they can no longer wait to move the stuff. Bulldozers are coming in—backhoes. Deep caissons will be inserted into the earth at the vicinity of the old boathouse." His voice advanced to a choke of excited certainty. "Silos for the brewery need a vast amount of underground support. The perpetrators will either save the warehouse contents by moving it, or get discovered and lose their entire investment." McCruise salivated at the thought of taking this bunch of animals to the stockyards.

"Exactly." Connor's dark eyes squinted, spilling tendrils of smilage into his invisible hairline. "So we stick to our original Water Lily plan: surveillance every weekend, covertly. However, the discussion at this afternoon's meeting will be as I proposed earlier: surveillance on weekdays. I've suspected for months that my office sat bugged; something was amiss. Electronics experts have come in from Phoenix on the Q-T, going over every corner with the eyes of a cat. Absolutely nothing was located. Yet these leaks are too much to be a fluke."

Connor shot an unshuttered gaze to McCruise. "Valesano won't be at the meeting; he's applied for a month off, no explanation. Personal, he says." A thick pause hung with weightiness. Both men sought the depths of the other with unspoken questions.

"I'm going to use terms this afternoon such as Pit Bull—that is, changing the operation name to Pit Bull—and refer to the traffickers as incompetent assholes." His tone lay soft, yet confidentially husky. "Those are fightin' words, the kind that get people pissed, thus get passed on. And somewhere, sometime, we're going to hear someone repeat them as a Freudian slip, and we've found our snitch." Connor's jaw was working, and it wasn't on finishing his sandwich.

They paused as the server poured fresh coffee, the rich Colombian fragrance circling the leather-appointed booth.

"How do you propose to let our group know everything you're saying is being recorded and that the genuine plan stays intact?" McCruise leaned forward.

"Strange one, there. I thought I'd have Sadie get out a written document for them to read while I'm talking my ass off about a bunch of drivel." Connor drummed his fingers on the table.

"Why don't you allow me to get out written notice on my secured computer? I'll make the copies myself. After the meeting, I'll collect all the docs and shred them. Accordingly, we'll know the information hasn't gone beyond the room, unless it *is* bugged." McCruise raised his expressive eyebrows, using his barcode beams.

"Do it—smashing idea," Connor beamed.

CHAPTER FIFTY-THREE

The fragrance of Cape Cod honeysuckle teased the heavy air of monsoon season as the two men moved out of the hotel through the large glass front doors. The September heat lingered like a lizard on a rock, waiting for a mishap cricket to skitter along.

McCruise's sixth sense flashed an idea, rendering his breathing quickened. "How long is Shoney going to be in the hospital?" He stood with both hands buried in his trouser pockets.

"Last I heard it'll be a couple more days. As I understand the story, he decided to have plastic surgery on his nose. His arm was set immediately, the same night, but it swelled so badly the doctors did it again on Sunday. The guys told me he'd be back on the job again by Thursday, albeit handicapped." Connor shuddered visibly with the thought, and then turned to walk along the narrow walk to the back parking lot, jiggling his car keys.

"Hold on a minute." McCruise reached out gently, laying his hand on Connor's shoulder in a show of camaraderie. "I don't know if this'll work, but I'd like to use the department's master key set and enter Shoney's penthouse for evidence of trafficking: paperwork, dollarization, dates, sources, and destinations. Wally and I could be in and out of there in no time, say tomorrow morning."

Connor stopped dead in his tracks, thrown mentally off balance by the unexpected proposal. His mouth opened. No words came out. Anguish crossed his face. Two squirrels scampered across the walkway, Yin and Yang of the desert kingdom, hunters, soul mates, hiders of all things coveted by small creatures. Wally and McCruise? Two of his best hunters sashaying around in a landscape, riddled with unknowns.

"You don't suppose—can't be sure," Connor took in oxygen.

"We've suspected for a long time."

"There've been so many ambiguities, but it would be nice to get something concrete on the bastard."

"Do it, Connor!" McCruise's voice grew thick with anticipation, so pumped with adrenaline that it must be leaking out his pores.

Connor could play hardball along with the best of them. "Goddamn it, you might make the grade yet for an Arizona Law Enforcement Officer. I think you've found Special Investigation a nail on which you can fasten your talents. I cannot, however, stop at the municipal court and convince Judge Andrews of reasonable justification for authorization to issue a search warrant for discovery. I'd need heavy indicators of the presence of incriminating evidence."

Connor knew Andrews was an amiable man—round-faced and judicial. Discerning eyes behind glasses created for him an aura of officiousness, but if one looked further, the humanity showed through the façade. Still in all...

Turmoil increased in McCruise's mind-maze. "Shoney told Jacquie he could offer her anything in the world. Because he owned unlimited resources, he could do more for her than I could. He leads an opulent lifestyle. I think he *does* have hidden sources of income so monumental it would knock us on our asses. He's making a pret-ty penny. There are plenty of indicators to suspect a man's high lifestyle without visible means of producing it."

Primal rage tore over McCruise, his brain making emotional adjustments to keep his cool. How easily Shoney could engineer the routing of cash circuitously until it landed pure and innocent as lilies in the field.

Connor shook his head in resignation. "Go for it, McCruise. I'll personally check out the master key set so it casts no aspersions on you, Wally, or the current investigation. You must keep in mind that any evidence uncovered by you and Wally will be inadmissible in the final analysis because it sources without due process. The court is seldom tolerant of shortcut methods by law enforcement." He shook his head. "What's more, I have no knowledge of this subterfuge. Understand?"

"None the less, the possibility of finding puzzle pieces in the penthouse is temptingly plausible."

"Yeah."

Their eyes locked in consent.

CHAPTER FIFTY-FOUR

Late that same afternoon, Jacquie sat alone in the gathering September twilight, a dim lamp on her desk, waylaying the inevitable onslaught of darkness. The western sun slanted through the tilted verticals onto the living room slidebys, directing fire-like stripes into the room. The pressures of the past pressed heavily on her mind as a frown gathered over her eyes with the sense that clarity lagged in the epidermal view of Fayne Norwood.

He was clairvoyant, Fayne told her. His angels told him what to do, and when. He was infallible. "I must be an archangel, an angel most powerful, one sent in the embodiment of a human, like Christ, to set the world straight, reign over it, be its benefactor." On September 29, the Christian Feast Day of Michael the Archangel, Michaelmas, Norwood celebrated his own birthday, disregarding his biological birth date under the Sagittarius sign.

Fayne assumed the distant steeliness of a mind deep within itself, the vacuum therein sucking on greatness—grandiose achievements, unprecedented plateaus, witnessed and experienced by no other human being. He was a Redeemer, with powers yet untapped. If Fayne was brutal in his endeavors, it was benevolent brutality.

Jacquie disturbingly perceived what was yet to come because she'd witnessed Norwood in all his chameleon personalities. She'd seen the enormity of this barbarity in the yards of wool pulled over her eyes.

Thoughts returned to the dark shadows of her condominium. Was she laying too much emphasis on what-ifs and yah-buts? What was wrong with Shoney working with Norwood? If it didn't interfere with his regular job, it was merely double dipping. In addition, Norwood R & D certainly claimed a market for the coca plants, for their own research, and for sale to pharmaceutical agencies all over the world as a legitimate enterprise. She was spooking herself into a pit.

Strange how Norwood never lost at anything. In contrast, the word 'never' was a mathematical fallacy. Never, never happens. Accordingly, perhaps his infallibity carried yeasty holes of doubt.

Her body sagged in overwhelming helplessness; her thoughts chilled by a sudden seizure of cold, as if a specter from the grave gravitated in from the lanai.

CHAPTER FIFTY-FIVE

The next day, under a canopy of smiling blue sky, the ninety-degree air was as still as stone; McCruise and Wally walked into the Retreat's west entrance.

They chose 8:00 AM to search Shoney's penthouse—the hour of new shifts starting. In addition, at this hour it wasn't as hot as Hades, making tempers short and time long. The heat in Havasu started building early in April and didn't let up for at least another month.

The State of Arizona Fire Marshall prohibits occupancy of any unit without two egress capabilities. McCruise knew he'd have a better chance of opening the door at the top of the stairwell than piddling his time in the public eye, searching for an elevator key for the penthouse.

Their footsteps resounded on the metal stairwell, putting McCruise in mind of climbing up-deck on a ship. The way became narrower, reaching a metal-sheeted door at the top. Wally tried the handle. Locked. Opening the locksmith kit, McCruise and Wally viewed layer upon layer of tooling.

"I've always been told a man needs a challenge, but this may be a task for the Manhattan Project," Wally mumbled, kneeling at the top step. "Whoa, there's no key hole, just a simple hole in the middle of the handle. A ratchet should do the trick, but be specific here, Denton, find the right one." Wally was glowing with excitement, processing his thoughts aloud.

Why did *Wally's Excellent Adventure* romp around in McCruise's mind? The thought made him smile dryly, but alerted him to the urgency of the situation.

"What the hell you think this is, Denton, a circus? Find the friggin' key!" The tendons in McCruise's neck intensified.

Wally wasn't dawdling, but his life experiences taught him to move slowly. A day is simply a bending of time to gravity. Tomorrow would always come, and yesterday would always be history. The best a man could be asked to do is make the decisions of the moment with the knowledge he has at hand, hoping for the best, praying he's on a roll.

Click. The ratchet tripped the lockset. McCruise wasn't sure if he was canned or frozen for a moment while the realization broke over him that the door was open and they could enter. He figured an alarm system to trigger; he was prepared to disengage it with immediate pressure on the doorframe, breaking the circuitry. Sweat broke out on his upper lip, and his emotional vista ran rampant.

Nothing!

McCruise shuddered, thanking God for some old-fashioned territorial justice. Entering soundlessly, McCruise and Wally found that immediately to the left was the elevator, facing a long Mexican tile hall. Rococo framed works of art hung from the walls. Air conditioning hummed.

"More of what your mouth waters for," Wally sighed as he read the industrial-strength signatures: Sargent, Monet, Prendergast, Audubon, Copley, all graced with down lights above the pictures. Ten feet down the hall, to the left, was the master suite—pristine, conservative. McCruise was disappointed. He expected to see something flamboyant and decorative—exotic maybe, depraved maybe, but not whitewashed.

Farther down the hall, they found themselves in an impeccably decorated living room with a corner fireplace made entirely of London Bridge granite. Eight-foot slidebys ran off the living room, dining room, and den in lineal order, accessing the lanai and the panoramic view of the blue lake and brown mountains. In one grazing scan, McCruise and Wally were able to take in the generous expansiveness of all three rooms. Off to the immediate right was a kitchen of a size and proportion one would allocate to a family. Again, McCruise was dumbstruck by the wholesomeness of the quarters.

Well-tended plants dispersed generously throughout the décor. Oak smiled with healthy richness. On either side of the fireplace hung exquisite jungle bird intarsias of extraordinary dimensions, at least four feet long and breasting to a foot and a half, easily. McCruise never saw such matched pieces of bleached oak so expertly blended. They must have cost an arm and a leg. There was no doubt the hard money Shoney was bringing in quickly converted into soft investments, ergo, art.

He choked up oppressively, applying rationale to the situation. How many kids hooked on coke so Shoney could buy priceless works of art such as these? Thousands? McCruise's stomach grew queasy. Here hung the braggadocio legacy Shoney wanted to share with Jacquie. *We-ell, love falls on hard times, Shoney. She's mine.* McCruise's temper flared with the primal possession of a mate.

Through an archway and into the den, McCruise breathed words, almost to himself. "Look at this, Wally. In Shoney's hurry to letch after Jacquie, he left his computer on. It's a shame to kill such a confident warrior spirit." He shot Wally a wry smile.

Quickly, McCruise draped himself in front of the computer and clicked on Shoney's e-mail, next on the IN Box. "Yes, here it is, twenty-three messages going all the way back to June. Shoney's so sure of this quagmire stronghold he doesn't even delete old messages. The last one's yesterday, 3:33 p.m." He gave Wally an unbelieving, quizzical gaze.

"Yesterday?" Wally fairly breathed the word, matching McCruise's excitement, ounce for ounce.

"Yeah, it's from *Charlie Chan.*"

Operation Pit Bull activated. Surveillance changed to Monday through Thursday. Weekends abandoned due to financial crunch. cc: Enn.

"Holy Mother of God. Right from the mouth of the captain to the nether world!" Wally sunk slowly into a Lazyboy recliner.

Sitting at the computer, McCruise quickly clicked "Select All," then "Print." The printer hummed, scrolling the ink packet into position on the bubble jet printer. Sheets of paper kicked out at great speed. "Nice equipment," McCruise commented.

"Let's see what he has on his Desk Top. Nothing out of the ordinary here. *Watercress.* What the hell would that mean?" He clicked twice on the mouse. The computer whirred into thought, its indicator light winking rapidly.

"WATERCRESS," the Header read. In neat rows and columns were dates of cocaine receipts, weights, conversion weights, market dates, expenses, splits, and hundreds of millions of market dollars, dating back to 1988.

"Here it is, Wally! This has to be it. Talk to me, meister machine. Talk to old McCruise." His voice was reaching fever pitch. He again clicked on "Select All," then "Print," his chest showing a rise and fall indicative of an adrenaline rush. "Bastard!" he said. "Dirty, Toxic-waste mutant."

Wally, looking over McCruise's shoulder, couldn't believe their good fortune.

"Life's going to be better here, Wally. This is the most bodacious stunt we've ever pulled, and we came up smelling like roses."

It was then that the soft chime of the elevator met their ears.

CHAPTER FIFTY-SIX

Iced over with a kick of fear, McCruise clicked "Minimize," cleared the computer screen, reached over, turned off the printer, and flipped the pages in the hopper upside-down.

Wally was already slipping through the slideby. Behind him scurried McCruise exiting silently onto the lanai, hugging the side of the building, his heart thudding with flight instincts. Shoney's patio went on forever, then around the corner of the penthouse, taking them out of sight. McCruise's head throbbed, making his skull seem too small.

Almost simultaneously, the living room slideby opened. Someone emerged onto the lanai, carrying a portable radio on which "The Ballad of the Guy Who Left Something Turned on at Home" was playing. The sound traveled to the parapet where it played out until the end, the visitor whistling along. "This is 102.7 K-Flag, KFLG, with stations in Bullhead City and Flagstaff. Your country connection in the west," the radio station I.D.'d

McCruise stared fixedly at a cloudless blue sky, hardly daring to breathe, the heat against the side of the building searing. Two commercial jetliners were racing east, leaving contrails of roiling white messages in their wake. It occurred to him that it might be the last thing he ever saw; bile crept up his throat.

The radio intruder continued whistling as he retreated into the penthouse. *Swish*, the slideby closed. McCruise allowed himself the luxury of a quick take at Wally, and wanted to hug him in relief. His shoulders sank expelling his deeply held breath.

Signaling for Wally to cover him, he slipped back to the den slideby, heard the flip top of a pop can opening. A loud "Ahhh" emitted from the phantom visitor; receding footsteps sounded down the Mexican tile in the long hall. The welcome chime of the elevator doors closing was music to his ears. McCruise's whole body relaxed; the rigidity with which he'd been holding himself disintegrated.

Waving an "all clear" to Wally, he headed back into the den, shaking his head at the vagaries of life—the dramatic change he'd witnessed from supreme exhilaration to heart-stopping fear. Not many things frightened him, but being dead did. He reminded himself that he needed to get out of this line of work and stick with boat building, but he didn't have time to get sappy.

A soft breeze blew the sheers at the slideby as Wally came in, rolling his eyes, moving to the hall immediately, and securing their position. McCruise flipped the printer back on and returned his computer screen to "Desktop" for further fishing.

Wally, the condominium secured, returned, adjusting his S & W under his arm.

With eyes flaming, McCruise said, "Look at this information, Wally. Shipments from Sri Lanka!" He jumped up from the computer and paced the carpet, his hand playing his thick short curls. "Sri Lanka?" His voice waxed small, and then cracked. There was an incessant scratching going on in his mind, as if skeletal fingers were probing the pages of his geographic gonads, waiting for production.

"What kind of a spin can we put on that?" Wally frowned as he bent into McCruise's screen. His voice came from somewhere within the depths of him, as if pulling up information from a long-inactive memory tape. "Sri Lanka is an extremely volatile country—lots of unrest. Lots of drugs too." He slowed way down, taking a deep breath, spinning quietly. "It's a small island country southeast of

India." The conviction in his voice growing, his eyes widened as he looked to McCruise standing with the heel of his hand on the wall.

"We may have a crack in the dam here," Wally said, his voice lowered. "Colombo is the capital of Sri Lanka. Colombo? Columbia? We've treed the wrong bear, McCruise. The cocaine isn't coming from *Columbia*, up through Mexico and into Arizona, but from *Colombo*, through the Port of San Diego, or the Port of Los Angeles, in innocuously small amounts, shipped in nautical accouterments." He gained in effusive conclusions as he continued. "The caustic smell of tarred rope, vulcanized rubber, and formaldehyde-treated kapok could very well cover up the smell of coke and get past busy port authorities." Staring at the floor, Wally scratched the back of his head. "From L.A. or San Diego, it's only a five-hour drive to the Colorado River. Son-of-a-bitch!"

McCruise's stomach churned with new sensations as the global impact of this operation settled around him like fine netting. He wanted to reach out and smack someone, kick in a window and hear a noisy cracking, the satisfying crunch of striking out. Instead, he ground down on a very large date he'd selected from a bowl near the computer.

Wally did a quick double take. "Dates! We found the same snacks in the hidden chamber. What'd I tell you about how things come together when you least expect it?"

"Dates may prove to be Shoney's downfall." McCruise again addressed the computer. "Damn! Here we have records going back nine years, when Shoney managed a hotel in San Diego. Look at the volume of shipments from Sri Lanka!" McCruise simply stared incredulously at the screen, viewing numbers; his mind paralyzed—phase two.

Wally pressed his hands to his hips, stalking the floor. "In Sri Lanka the rich are rich, rich, rich, and ruthless. The poor are poor, poor, poor, and restless. The Sri Lankans have the land to utilize for growing the coca plant, and Americans have the money to buy the euphoria it offers. Jesus H. Christ! What kind of a world are we living in, McCruise, when we trade kids for coke?" Wally's eyes hardened to steel, his jaw set tightly. He eased himself down onto the edge of the Lazyboy, cupping his chin with his hands, the deep scar line on his cheek wrinkled with the action.

Injustices were always a source of forage for Wally, who drew up his shoulders and let out a long sigh. "I love kids. Did I ever tell you I about my kid brother, Jeff, just two years younger than me? Jeff and me, we did everything together; we even slept together because there was only one bed. When he was twelve years old, the neighborhood bully punched him out on the sidewalk where he hit his head on the edge. Jeff lived, slipping in and out of consciousness, for two days. Before he died, in one of his lucid moments, he asked Ma and me if he was going to die; he didn't want to die, he said. I guess he really didn't die, because he still lives right here with me," Wally said, pointing to his heart.

"Karla and I have never found luck in that respect. We could still adopt, maybe, if we're not too old." He paused, his eyes staring straight ahead. "We should consider it." Having said that, he laughed. "Gotta talk to Karla tonight. I'd like to hear something around the house besides my number twelves echoing on the floors." He blinked his eyes in private consternation.

McCruise listened. There was a time to speak and a time to listen. The thought of having a child in his very own home was searing on slow cook in Wally's head, usurping his mind. His words were working, thinking aloud, his voice budding with conviction as he went along, as if his ideas were a photo metamorphosis of a flower seed, sprouting, stemming, and its petals opening in splendor.

When Wally's eyes turned back to McCruise, they were damp. He was taking in a mouthful of air.

It wasn't often McCruise got into Wally's closely guarded soul. At this moment, however, Wally was besotted with the hopes of having a child for whom he and Karla could provide—to supply his or her physiological needs, food, clothing, shelter.

As unlikely as the setting was, McCruise wondered what he'd have done without Wally after Laura's death. He'd pulled him through many bad times. Their relationship never fractured, and McCruise never knew anyone so refreshingly honest and dedicated. McCruise recognized that there was an intangible lifeline between him and Wally. He guarded it, protected it, never wanting it to sever. They'd developed a rapport in which communication was superfluous at times. They chain-thought to one another— no complaining, and no whining. They simply took things in stride—up to this moment, that is. This was one of their tougher chapters, getting into sentimentalities. He wished they could both, in unison, knock back a couple Coronas.

McCruise's mind clicked back to the reality of where they were—Shoney's Penthouse—and why they were there. "Yeah, sure, Denton." Was there a tremble in his voice? "You're old, all right, and an old goat. It won't be long and I'll be seeing your name on a jelly jar on the morning news programs. Your re-think of the baby idea for you and Karla is soul food. Go for it. You'd be prize parents."

Wally arose abruptly. "I'll check out the place again." His voice was unnecessarily loud with faux nonchalance.

CHAPTER FIFTY-SEVEN

As if regretting the insights he revealed of himself, Wally moved quickly. "I'm going to give the place a last once-over before we leave," he tossed over his shoulder as he headed through the dining room.

Suddenly, McCruise felt a little lonesome and half-dressed with Wally out of the den. *You're getting soft, McCruise,* he told himself. His hand dashed across his mouth, as if he could swipe away his strong sense of reliance on his partner.

"Hey, McCruise," Wally stage-whispered from down the hall. "Got a minute?"

"Yeah, sure." McCruise was standing there, hypnotically watching the papers spitting out of the printer as if they conjured up by silver dust and voodoo. He shrugged, feeling as stupid as hell, watching a mechanical process that did not need his attention. Sometimes a person feels that way — stupid as hell. He moved toward Wally's voice.

"Look at this." Wally was pointing to a life-size painting of the Blue Boy by Gainsborough. "This painting is as phony as my grandmother's teeth. Karla and I visited the Huntington Art Gallery in San Marino, and the real McCoy is hanging there in its original splendor. I always wondered how the kid ever got his business out in time to pee." Wally knuckled the zipperless contoured pants worn by the lad, when there was a soft *click-swish* as the painting converted to a door opening that led inward. McCruise suppressed his first impulse to follow the invitation of the open door.

Silence.

Nodding to one another, McCruise crouch-rolled into the room first, S&W drawn, followed closely by Wally, who covered the high ground stabilizing him on one knee. McCruise's eyes blinked as he caught movement everywhere, a weakness growing in the pit of his stomach.

Mirrors.

The whole room featured mirrored walls; the ceiling gleamed with mirrors over the bed. What the hell? Everywhere they turned, someone moved in the mirrors. It took a few minutes to settle the heavy heartbeat slamming into McCruise's chest, the overwhelming fear of being vastly out-numbered, measuring every breath, which might be his last. "Goddamn!" he breathed aloud. He really didn't have the makeup for police work.

It was as if they'd stepped through Alice's looking glass into another world. The room was ample—deep, probably sixteen feet. McCruise mixed fear with fetish. It was easily twenty-five feet long, and a large bathroom grew off to the left. To their right, against the far wall, was a round bed—a giant round bed covered in bright red velvet. The room's appointment for repose declared headboard posts, and yeah, footboard posts. All of them hung with thick, velvet-covered theater ropes and shackles.

McCruise walked over to the mirrored slideby closet to his immediate left, stood aside, and eased it open. Teddies, two-piece gossamer bathing suits, and layered diaphanous gowns with spaghetti straps hung neatly in anticipation of a warm body. Black leather chaps hung in readiness; black eye-masks sat on the shelf, as well as black leather whips. "So this is where he wanted to take Jacquie last Friday night. Bastard! I thought this place was too buttoned-up." McCruise's eyes were on fire, blazing with mental recordings of the aberrated environment. *Scum!*

Wally, bending over, going through the bedside table, found small, electronic fish that wriggled and jerked when activated. He didn't have to wonder how and where they utilized. Another drawer revealed electric vibrators—

dildoes of every size and color. There were condoms enough for twelve men, as well as lubricating jelly. Obviously, Shoney loved women. Wally returned his gun to his holster, a small smile building around his lips. "Bluebeard's brother," he clucked.

McCruise grunted in response, kicked at the bathroom door before entering, then fanned quickly with his S&W.

Nothing.

It was another ample room, complete with a bright red heart-shaped tub, champagne glasses on corner shelves, mirrors on the ceiling, and fluffy pink towels. Bottles of bath oil, body lotion, and cologne sat at easy access. The plumbing fixtures were polished gold, vanity sinks were bright red, and ceramic tiles were flamingo pink. Drawers in the vanity stood filled with ready-douches, packaged toothbrushes, the ones that came with their own tiny tube of toothpaste. Obviously, for Shoney, life existed below the belt.

Re-entering the bedroom, McCruise marveled at the extensive electronic equipment along the inside of the hallway wall: camcorder mounted on tripod, extra video tapes, forty-inch television, VCR, a sound system for acoustical seduction, not serenity. He took note of the absence of a telephone or clock.

"Neat, convoluted arrangement; cozy, very cozy," McCruise examined the wet bar: wines, champagnes, liquors, and liqueurs to please even the most discriminating taste: Johnny Walker, Madeira, Bordeaux Beaujolais, Meyer's rum, Drambuie, and Cutty Sark among others.

"So this is our big man's busy room." Wally's voice cropped to an incredulity whisper. "Ever see so many toys? I wonder if I could rent this room by the hour." Wally bent back, looking at himself in the ceiling mirrors, his knees shaking. "Shoney must have gotten more tail in this room than my Uncle Pat on his trap line in Michigan's Upper Peninsula." Going over to the closet, he plucked out a whip, trying it on the bed, snarling. "Ah, my pretty one," he said, his lips trying on a devil's leer.

McCruise watched the reflecting mirrors playing on Wally's antics. He cocked his head, taking a doubtful read on Wally's sanity. "Well, I wouldn't break my neck trying this stuff on Karla. My guess is it would be Karla ten, Wally zip. Looks to me as if Shoney enjoys one-night stands, especially if he thinks the woman is not willing, such as Jacquie. The cookie he wants is the cookie he can't get." He snorted a contemptible, heaving breath.

The elevator was their source of travel as they exited evidence in hand.

"Connor is not going to believe this," McCruise said, finally bursting with laughter.

"None of it," Wally agreed, his tongue pushing at the separation in his two front teeth. "I'm glad I didn't miss it. Do you think maybe I lived a misspent youth, and adulthood?"

"Nah," McCruise regarded him affectionately, "but I do think you and Karla should consider adoption."

"Think so? You care about things like that? I mean, like, for others?"

"Yeah, I care. I care a lot," McCruise said his voice small.

CHAPTER FIFTY-EIGHT

Tuesday, September 22, 1997, Colombo, Sri Lanka

Valesano felt more than accommodated to take a month's leave without pay in Sri Lanka.

The heated air was heavy and oppressive, but could Norwood have found any better time of the year to foul up the sewage system in Kandy, Jaffna, and Colombo? A city of well over a million, Colombo listed last for destruction.

Growing up in an ethnic community of Italians in Hurley, Wisconsin, Valesano altered, rather than grew. Hurley was a bustling, raucous village across the state line from Ironwood, Michigan, whose iron ore mines produced millions of tons of iron ore and moola paychecks for footloose miners, who found their way to Hurley and its hellish bawdyhouses and batteries of bars.

Valesano's upbringing was crude, allowing him anemic cultural exposure. When he landed in Lake Havasu on a spring break back in 1976, he figured he deserved every hour of this exotic adventure: boating, beer busting, and bathing. Voyeurism on the river gave him a new life.

Twenty-one years ago, Havasu was in its infancy and needed police recruits. He'd applied, and been accepted.

Given the stringency of today's Arizona Law Enforcement Academy, he wouldn't last two weeks, and he knew it. He'd not lasted at much, come to think of it.

As a child, he was always the brunt of brutal, verbal attacks, and shunted from one elementary classroom to the next and from one man to the next whom his mother brought home.

When Alex Haley's *Roots* published in 1976, Valesano knew dubbing as "Chicken George," after the squirrelly character in the novel. Coming to Havasu did not deter the slights or the cultural avoidance of his environmental upbringing. His bug eyes rolled, his chin jutted in and out, in and out. He'd never been able to lose his hard-consonant, clipped national tongue. Darting jerkily instead of moving smoothly earned him, in 1997, the name of "Chicken Tony." Wellll, he was not a chicken; he was not a *thing*!

Valesano would show the goddamn Lake Havasu Police Department. He'd earn handsomely for this stint in Sri Lanka. The captain could shove his lieutenant's stripes right up his righteous ass. No more "Yes Sir," "No Sir," or "Sir, if you please." He shuddered with the crawling and scraping and whoring he'd submitted himself to in his lifetime.

No-more-no-more-no-more.

He learned that the only way not to be a victim was to face up to an antagonist without ever showing fear. Easier said than done, he found. In Valesano's intense self-absorption, he cultivated disrespect for social norms and a tendency to project his own faults on other people. Resultantly, his mind massaged itself into a high degree of dishonesty and manipulation. Increasingly, he tended to see others strictly in terms of his own need. After all, he was an honest man, pushed to the brink to execute a cunning scheme in a devious world.

****

How simple it was to get a tour of the Sri Lankan Waste Water Treatment Plants, get an explanation of the mechanics of the system, and create havoc. Bandaranaike, in an effort to prove his plants acceptable, offered him *carte blanche* in writing.

238

"The system's idiosyncrasies will look like an oversight by a careless employee, especially an employee who has Tamil leanings," Norwood advised after the Duluth meeting. "I will provide history of such a person within the Waste Water Treatment Plant arena."

"How can it prove an impetus for a GETI contract if the Tamil sabotaged?" Valesano frowned. "Surely there is precedent of human error among the municipal employees."

Norwood placed his hands behind his back and paced after the hierarchy meeting with the Sri Lankans. Light filtered in through the Venetian blinds, slanting him in and out of shadows, his face changing with the light and shade, just as his mind changed from white to black in a nano-second.

"Ah, but therein lies the point." Norwood's lips thinned acrimoniously. "For how long will the Sri Lankan government put up with Tamil terrorists? Never! The governmental fuse is very short in that respect; retaliation by the Sinhalese is swift. If the malfunction were employee error, however, the Sri Lankan government may be more tolerant. The calamity of calamities, whichever the instance, would prove GETI could design, build, finance, operate, and protect the Sri Lankan sewage systems much more efficiently than the bungling locals, or those who were unable to filter out Tamil terrorists." Norwood warmed, feeling the self-imposed pull of destiny to his power.

If stifling the city of Kandy's system weren't enough of a blow, the city of Jaffna's sewage system would follow within one day, Colombo within one more day, leaving pockets of distressed souls. Norwood smiled thinly, with satisfaction turning full forward to Shoney and Valesano. "It's as simple as that and as complicated as that."

GETI ranked second in the world for sewer and waste water systems. With Norwood's stock placing him in a controlling position, he'd find no problem getting a majority vote on the privatization, thus eventual surtax profit off Sri Lanka's municipal sewage plants. In addition, he'd muscle a contract for all the government-owned coca exports.

****

Valesano slipped back to the present. Time to get moving. He'd meet Rani Adasa, maintenance supervisor, this afternoon for the grand tour. What a snap assignment! The sabotage played out at the right time, right place, a wrench in the works, and *voila*! Valesano felt overwhelmed, filled with excitement, yet the apprehension of danger was gut curling. Everything altered; his chin jutted forward, his shoulders weaved. He felt as if he were walking on shifting ground.

So he could escape the oppressive September heat and humidity, he wished the Municipal Sewage Plants were air-conditioned. Of course, there was no way to escape the stench of the drying beds or the heaving mass of suspended solids in the round aeration basins, which stayed in flux by a rotating bridge. Numerous submerged diffusers hung off the bridges, which delivered air to the sludge as the arm passed. It took about three minutes for the arm to make a complete rotation. The contrivance was eerily silent and powerful.

Upon reviewing the process, Valesano witnessed the sensation of macro millions of electric prickles creeping along his skin, up into his scalp.

CHAPTER FIFTY-NINE

Valesano became a familiar face, visiting the three marked Sri Lankan Wastewater Treatment Plants. His credentials, issued by the country's Board of Investment stood accepted on sight. Foreign investment was encouraged in Sri Lanka and tax concessions were available with the aim of stimulating growth in targeted areas, e.g. infrastructure, tourism, and non-traditional manufacturing exports. The BOI, currently employing close to 242,000 people, supervised these investments. Since 1990, the Colombo Stock Exchange opened to foreign ventures.

In addition, Valesano knew the assignment of a tour associate, Rani Adasa. Educated as a biochemist at Delft University of Technology in the Netherlands, Adasa's post graduate education, training, and research had been accomplished at the International Institute for Infrastructural, Hydraulic, and Environmental Engineering in Delft, The Netherlands.

Adasa was a squat, wide-headed man. Marinated in confidence, Adasa's vibes were unreadable—an annoying characteristic, which Valesano found commonizing among Asians. Disconcerting was Adasa's one roving eye; conversation was stuck on watching the eye. Having trouble controlling *his* bulging eyes gave Valesano quantitative trouble.

Adasa, however, knew the chemical composition of a particular biological substance from pine pitch to resin, and knew the operations of a Wastewater Treatment Plant from screening and aerating to sludge and scum removal—vital knowledge to Valesano—and he was taking no chances on compromising their thin relationship.

Especially interesting was the final process of killing the bacteria by the flow of the final effluent into a chlorine contact tank, where the chemical chlorine mixed to kill bacteria. Without this process, the bacteria would stay in the effluent and pose a health risk to those entities using effluents such as golf courses, parks, and rice paddies. What if the chlorine valve at the bottom of the tank happened to turn to "open," discharging chlorine gas and the contact tank stood denied the necessary, bacteria-killing chemical at the given electronic signal? What if the noxious gas seeped downhill, releasing deadly volumes of chlorine gas into the air environment?

"The answer is so easy," Adasa grinned. "It would be fatal."

Kandy, being the least sizable of the three targeted cities, with 200,000 plus population, would be the potential object of the chlorine leak, their first show of strength to the negotiating team from the Washington D. C. Consulate.

Whether the Sri Lanka plants needed it or not, Valesano, accompanied by Adasa, was to point out the advantages to Global Technologies takeover. They were to point up the concept of rehabilitation of the facilities. By effecting reduction of operational costs and elimination of the system's chronic compliance deficiencies such as unacceptable levels of odor and pollution of ground water, they were to be unrelentingly convincing. Valesano was to advise of critical facility equipment and assure the powers-that-be of Global Technology preventive maintenance and their implementation.

The tour of the four plants in Colombo yesterday was impressive. The city located them, strung out along the Gulf of Mannar, for a population of more than two million. Posing as a preventive and predictive maintenance engineer of GETI, he observed some educated tests. Valesano and Adasa stayed highly visible as consultants, their treks throughout the acreage regarded as a given.

The morning was warm and humid when Valesano, accompanied by Adasa, left the Hilton Hotel on Lotus Drive in Colombo, destinations: Kandy and Jaffna. He could hear the distant sound of the waves, moving rhythmically on shore from the Gulf of Mannar; a dog barked at a scolding old woman who leashed the animal too tightly. Valesano yearned for the yapping dog to take a bite out of the witch. *A bitch bites a bitch.* It humored him. It was strange how a good-looking morning could turn cranky in a matter of moments.

The fifty-mile drive west to Kandy was pleasant enough in the rented Mitsubishi, a vehicle widely seen in Sri Lanka, Japan being a major trade partner of Sri Lanka. It posed no problem at all to get a temporary operator's permit, but driving on the left side of the road was dyslexic to Valesano's motor operatives. The need to focus was imperative.

With only twenty-nine percent of Sri Lankan land being arable, Valesano stretched his neck at the rich and luxurious vegetation in this corridor. A great variety of flowers, trees, creepers, and flowering shrubs inhabited the roadside. Not being a student of flora, Valesano gazed deeply impressed by the beauty of this island. When the mists ahead of him rose to obscure the mountains, through the rearview mirror the process brought into prominence the luxuriant greenery of the palm-fringed shore he'd left behind, with its masses of foliage. Perhaps he'd come back here to live some day.

"We have rubber trees, palms, acacia, margosa, satinwood, Ceylon oak, tamarind, ebony, coral trees and banyans. Flowers and shrubs include the orchid and rhododendron. In addition, we have two great national parks, abounding in leopards, and elephants." Adasa recited as if informing a tour group.

Valesano needed to develop Asian unreadability. Goddamn Adasa could concentrate solely on him, looking into Valesano's eyes through Adasa's slowly dilating pupils and pull him out of himself, and it took an amazingly micro-space of time. There were times when Valesano felt helpless and immobilized during these mental extractions by Adasa.

The monsoon season refused to leave this year, and the air lay heavy over the land, yet Valesano garbed himself in Western wear—Dockers trousers, a light blue cotton shirt, and crisp tie; he was taking no chances on looking unprofessional. His identification, issued by the BOI, hung around his neck like a bolo tie.

The BOI already allowed four investment promotion zones to be created, and two industrial parks were about to open under their direction. It would be a piece of cake to nudge the BOI in the right direction. By allowing GETI the privatization of the country's wastewater treatment plants in trade for Sri Lanka's commercial cocaine product would soon become a given. Holocausts such as Valesano and Adasa intended to create would knuckle under even the most seasoned negotiators. An ache in their minds or in their stomachs was not part of the Valesano-Adasa team *modus operandi.*

Valesano's skinny ass squirmed on the car seat; there were few times in his life when he experienced such wide and immediate acceptance. After the plant visitation at Kandy, Valesano and Adasa boarded the train for Jaffna. As the bird flies, it was a one-hundred-mile jaunt, but the goddamn crowded train stopped at every hovel along the way. In addition, they backtracked about twenty miles, stopping at Peradeniya and Relgrakgasia Junctions, and then proceeded north to Kurunegala and Anuradhapura. The train swayed, jerked, was noisy and cantankerous with the singsong sound of Sinhalese, the querulous Tamil tongue, and incidental English tossed in like black confetti in an all-white freefall.

In the ancient city of Anuradhapura, where King's used to rule and Buddhist temples dominated the landscape, they were forced to rent a car by which they traveled north, through brilliantly engineered mountain passes. Where the railroad used to run the entire distance to Jaffna, there remained only a railroad bed, the tracks sabotaged and pulled up by the Tamil terrorists. Municipal employees, such as Adasa accompanied by Valesano, were able to go into Jaffna, but if a Sinhalese or Buddhist were to enter, it was certain death.

Some day, Valesano promised himself, he'd earmark time at the Peradeniya Botanical Gardens with its meandering paths through the fernery and the flower and spice gardens, where there were several fine specimens of the coca plant. Yes, the thought of the by-product of the innocent-looking coca plants made his skin ruck up on the back of his neck. How it could heighten and intensify one's feelings and clarify one's thoughts. There was always a plentiful supply of cocaine, powder, and crystals to mix with tobacco and smoke through a pipe, but Valesano preferred to inject himself with a hypodermic needle. How strong he felt in the high of the moment. How all seeing, and all-knowing. The experience was as if he were floating down one of the swiftly running rivulets, flowing back to the Mahaweli River and eventually out to sea. His thoughts put him in a Nirvana frame-of-mind for a few moments. If only he owned just one hypodermically injected dose of cocaine, it would make him feel so reassured, so in charge, in charge of the whole world.

The route to Jaffna, situated on the Palk Strait in far northern Sri Lanka, stirred with technical information from Rani Adasa, who spoke fluent English. Valesano pumped steadily for information through all the antagonizingly slow streets of Mankulam, the tedious bottleneck at Elephant Pass, before arriving at destination Jaffna.

Words rang repeatedly in Valesano's ears. "If no commitment by the end of the day from the BOI after the Kandy demise, we'll move on to Jaffna. It will get worse there." Shoney did not so much as clear his throat when he'd made the statement in Duluth. Instead, the terrible impact of his orders seemingly put him in the throes of passion.

Jaffna, Valesano found, was an easy target for total power outage at the wastewater treatment plant. Adasa explained that the energy source was hydroelectric power, city-provided and easily controlled by panel pummeling. Backup generators on the grounds proved to be unresponsive, due to Adasa's ability to disengage their accessibility beforehand. In the blackness after nightfall, the switches needed striking manually, since Jaffna's wastewater plant existed non-computerized.

The main switch, thrown and damaged at the fuse box point of entry, resulted in shutting everything down without the benefit of backup. Within a matter of minutes, sewer covers near the plant would start flooding over, and, depending upon the downtime, all over the city as the sewage backed up farther and farther away from the plant. It would take hours before the systems could be set right. By then, the damage would have curled to a finish. Done.

Adasa spewed hatred for the Sinhalese power mongers who stripped his Tamil family of its tea plantation near the Mahaweli Ganga near Kandy in the late 1970s, forcing his family north and northwest to Trincomalee, where their holdings increasingly marginalized. He witnessed the decay spreading across the tea plantations as the world markets for Sri Lanka tea minimized, resultant of governmental holdings surfacing less competitive than that of private owners. Sinhalese governmental ownership cut more corners and laid off generations of plantation workers; thousands of men struggled, humiliatingly, for even the most menial of jobs, and were compensated less and less for their back-breaking hours in the hot sun.

"Did you know President Premadasa was assassinated at a May Day political rally in 1993 when a Tamil rebel detonated explosives strapped to him?"

"Why would someone do something like that?" Valesano asked the short smileless guide.

"Because the week before, the country's leading Tamil figure was gunned down," the eye admitted, standing a little taller, with a stretch of his lips that passed as a smile.

CHAPTER SIXTY

Tuesday, September 29, 1997, Lake Havasu City

Burning breezes bent the bushes in Connor's yard, with no relief in sight from the heat. Indian Summer was non-existent in Lake Havasu; the dehydrated air sucked the moisture out of eyeballs, leaving a burning sensation.

After the bleak and bitter fall of his dramatic stratagem, Connor turned to feigning his enemy, but first, there mandated a meeting of the minds at Connor's home. By a fluke, McCruise and Wally arrived simultaneously at Connor's oatmeal-colored stucco home on Bison Drive. Xeriscape landscaping created a home for a twenty-foot tall saguaro, spindly yucca, blue agave, and golden barrel cacti. Casting cool shadows at the front door walkup was a graceful queen palm. The deep circular driveway in front stood populated with law enforcement vehicles; even Cleavus drove a department vehicle. Considered foot soldiers by the golden chevrons, McCruise and Wally were the only orphans on the team, driving their own cars.

Tastefully furnished, Connor's den exhibited symbols of pride, yet no ostentations, as if someone deliberately designed it for a Spartan five-star General, with a suppressed leaning to luxuries.

On the wall behind Connor's black walnut desk hung a palatial picture of the London Bridge with three giant flags unfurled in a down-river breeze: USA, British, and the state of Arizona. Floating under the bridge was a corked wine bottle, containing a rolled-up scroll bearing the dates of September 23, 1968 to October 10, 1971. Civil Engineer, Connor Michael O'Shaughnessey, titled it Reconstruction of the London Bridge.

McCruise knew pride, as he often did, in this multi-faceted man, who could make men feel like a success so they'd be successful.

Hands folded behind him, Connor stood at his desk. "Thank you for coming out of your way, but I feel more comfortable discussing sensitive material in my home for reasons which will unfold in a minute."

Clearing his throat, he continued. "I've assimilated a massive amount of evidence since talking to you last. Massive." The three crinkles on either side of his eyes were rippling with anticipation.

"It seems our clandestine alternate plan is neither being believed nor tested, as yet. All of our agencies are working according to Plan A, as they should. We have formidable evidence that on the same day of calling off, theoretically, Plan A, the word was out to Sligh Shoney." Connor walked to a flip-sheet tripod and explained the printout from Shoney's e-mail.

"Who's *Enn*?" Tom Trehan inquired, nodding his head to "cc Enn" on the screen.

Connor's eyes became remote, as if pulling venomous information from the deepest wells of his mind. "I'm wagering it's the big boss." He took his reading glasses off and rubbed them on a snowy handkerchief he retrieved from his back pocket, and then returned the glasses to rest on his nose.

"Shoney would need to borrow the brainpower to run the show as slickly as he has for several years." The words were sharp on his tongue. "He's simply the henchman for a hierarchy to whom he answers." The light of battle banked behind Connor's eyes with smoldering embers of revulsion.

Knowing nods of agreement sprang from the group.

Thrusting his hands deeply into his pockets, head bowed, he mulled aloud. "The Golden Crest will be installing the foundations for the silos of a micro-brewery on or about the first week of November, forcing the narcotics warehouse contents to be moved."

He spoke openly of this installation within the department, so whoever was leaking data surely scampered to Shoney with the information. In addition, Jacquie informed him that she advised Shoney of the excavating, which put the stamp of authenticity on the information seeping from the department. With his thumb and forefinger, he thoughtfully stroked the deep furrow between his eyebrows. *Unpleasant business, indeed,* he agreed with himself, *these cat-and-mouse games.*

"Do you expect an attempt at movement this weekend?" Trehan leaned forward, his eyes intent, his mannerism quiet.

"Yes, I do, but Shoney isn't going to show his hand by playing for big stakes up front." Connor looked troubled, his features seeming sculptured in statue stone. He dreamed dread by night, he breathed dread by day, and he kissed Marvel in fear of Dread Day.

"Shoney's surveillance around the Channel is shoddy, at best, as if his toadies view it as an onerous task. Resultantly, he'll test the players at the table. We'll watch. We'll record." His mind swam with possibilities of times, dates, destinations. His dark eyes danced with dangerousness; his demeanor broadcast a determination of spirit that was unbendable to underworld powers.

"There's been absolutely nothing moving downriver or at Black Meadow Landing," David said affirmatively, "so we know the supply side is definitely forewarned."

"Nothing upriver, either," Trehan said, crossing his legs.

Connor paced, his glasses swinging from the tips of his fingers. "It's been disconcerting mentally, but not in reality. Now there exists nothing to indicate anyone is out there waiting to make a bust. There is, however, a strong potential for the real thrust the weekend of October 25, during London Bridge Days. The perpetrators know that all police departments are overworked and understaffed at that time.

"What's more, they'll find the cheek to pull a penny-ante sneak some time before that date, possibly this weekend — the fourth or fifth." Connor's jaw was working again,

PEGGY DEPUYDT

savoring the sweet anticipation. It was enough satisfaction
to allow the thought of closure float around the edges of his
consciousness.

Framing his fingers on the desktop, Connor shifted gears.
"Further information shows that on previous transfers
upriver, the one constant arrival and departure flight out of
Bullhead City was made by a corporate jet, registered to
Norwood Research and Development out of Duluth; that
included super holiday weekends. On a hunch, I checked
the computer flight plans at McCarran Airport in Las Vegas,
which was no small job. The same jet flew in and out of
there on the identical dates." This was more than conjecture,
and provided Connor with plenty of provocation. He was
clearly pounding on salvation's door.

"The CEO of Norwood R & D Institute is none other
than Fayne Norwood, previous owner of the Golden Crest.
Is the plot thickening?" He asked with a great deal of
satisfaction.

CHAPTER SIXTY-ONE

Connor's gaze swept all five men, who stared at him as if in a heightened state of a supernatural revelation.

"I don't think it'll surprise you to find Norwood'll be in Lake Havasu for the Quit Rent Ceremony on Friday, October twenty-fourth. He'll be ready and willing to be part of the aplomb and ceremony of passing a Kachina Doll to British representatives in lieu of rent for the acre or so of land where the Crest sits. This acre was previously owned by the Arizona Corporation, of which Norwood was president." The sum of suppositions was like an angel's music, and Connor gave himself up to the haunting compositions reaching in and touching his soul.

The small coterie of men sat rigid and wordless as the word picture unfolded, their silence a positive reinforcement.

"Norwood's scheduled to stay all week after the twenty-fourth." Connor poured the verbal gambits as if he were following a recipe.

"You think it might be a coincidence?" The ever-doubting Trehan questioned.

"It could be. It wouldn't surprise the hell out of me; however, if the warehouse were emptied and moved upriver at that time." O'Shaughnessey's voice lowered to warning levels, making him sound dangerous. In all of his years of experience, he'd begun to rely on hunches, his gut making mental decisions. By the pound, measuring his men, analyzing departmental problems, he could weigh the statistics of his being right versus being wrong. Time and date estimates, decades of surmising all assimilated to his benefit.

Reaching out and tapping the exhibit sheet bearing the e-mail message to Shoney, "Operation Pit Bull," Connor waited a moment. "Enn. Do you think it might be plain old 'N' for 'Norwood' with the extra letters added as a red herring?" His eyes darted from man to man. "Perhaps, perhaps not, but a lot of things are adding up here. Predicated on an educated hunch, we'll play it that way." Connor arose and paced again, from one end of the desk to the other, like a caged animal, a powerful, muscle-pulling animal, eager for the primitive chase to which it was born. He'd stitched this narcotics-trafficking fabric, ripped the result, and stitched it again. Every time, the finished product looked the same. Trouble scrambled all over Shoney and Norwood.

Scratching his head, Trehan jumped in. "So you want us to continue with Operation Water Lily, Plan A, observe with no arrests until the major thrust is implemented." He scissored his lips, nodding.

"Uh-huh." Connor kept moving. "That's the cornerstone of this whole philosophy. It'll give them positive reinforcement by letting out the rope. It's a rickety old ruse, but damn, it works every time." His dark brown eyes seriously pinned Trehan.

"Sounds good to me," David said sagely. "I always did like Plan A. It's foolproof. There's no way for them to escape from that big curve in the river south of the I-40 Bridge." His eyes swept all cohorts, knowing they agreed.

"All systems are GO." Connor's face freshened with the aside from David. His face opened and the deep frown lines in his forehead moved back.

"It's going to be a glorious sight, the day when we bring them all in," Chalmers David admitted, thrumming his thumb on the arm of the chair.

Connor's chest convulsed with the enormity of it all. After studying Sligh's computer printouts, he knew the cocaine coming into Lake Havasu was highly refined and commercially grown in Sri Lanka, and not coming in from Mexico. All were Norwood's ineffable arrangements. He lowered his eyes, not feeling that departing this information now was necessary—need to know, etc.

His lips, nearly lost behind his salt and pepper mustache, smiled suddenly as he slapped the desk with his hand. He wasn't going to drown himself in the remorse of unanticipated setbacks. He came to terms with the crux of the matter, although it turned a bit of a challenge. His smile brightened the room with the same intensity as his serious revelations of moments ago. Things quickly became upbeat.

"McCruise, Wally, Cleavus. Stay loose," he said, using his finger to shoot *you, you,* and *you*, as if a sergeant assigning loo duty. "There's some department business we must go over. It won't take but a minute," he said, becoming more affable.

When the four of them were alone, Connor walked around to the front of the desk and sat on a corner, one leg swinging, his posture broadcasting *and-now-this.* "I went over the computer printouts of the historical tracings of this cocaine business."

He picked up a prop pencil and absently tapped it on the desk. "The printouts carry documentation that they operate with an inside man, the inside man being Shoney. His records show he has vested rights in every negotiation to the tune of twenty percent of the market price. We're talking hundreds of millions. For every ton of cocaine the perpetrators market on the river, their take is five hundred million; Shoney's cut is one hundred million. Nice work, if you can get it. His pockets are so deep that the money has established Squatters' Rights.

"The records are graphic testimony to the fact that for the sellers there are buyers, and traders from hell don't care to whom they sell." He took a deep breath and let it out slowly, spreading his hands in a gesture of hopelessness. Another dart of intense displeasure attacked his vitals.

"Norwood's record is impeccable. He glows in high esteem in medical circles, lectures globally on genetic engineering, and the travel provides him the necessary cover for bartering and transporting cocaine. He's put together a practically bullet-proof package." He tried to sound nonchalant, but failed, his concerns for the solution to their enigma prevailing. His present feelings ranged from apprehension to absolute fear.

To create a set of checks and balances, he would need to pit law enforcement professional skill against the professional skill of an organized narcotic cartel. His expression darkened, his temper-containing jaw muscle flexed.

Wally brightened. "If Norwood's going to be here for the week of London Bridge Days, we could stake out the hotel!" The smell of closure to this sordid affair was riding the wind, and smelling was five parts of tasting.

Connor nodded, scrubbing his hand over his face. "We can't avoid it, and it looks as if it's the same setup as last time for the whole week," he said, nodding. "The DEA will be in the hotel; McCruise and Wally will be on Channel patrol. I'll put on whatever men I can, because the squeeze is on, making the situation precarious. Desperate men take desperate measures. If they're aware that the warehouse has been discovered, they'll be armed and dangerous."

Turning to McCruise and Wally, he continued, flicking at a non-existent fleck on the knee of his trousers. "The perpetrators have little reason to believe we're onto their profitable program. All they know is snafu surveillance schedules. Therefore, I expect them to look down their nasty noses and run with confidence. Your assignments are going to be the same as last time: Watergate One, Two, and Three Hundred." He chuckled at his lead Iditarod dogs. Suddenly, Connor realized how mellowing it was to laugh. When a person spends months of his life chafing about the chanciness of an outcome that will affect thousands of people, he's not likely to be the department's Good Humor man. Trying to find the silver lining from day to day was like trying to swat away thick fog.

CHAPTER SIXTY-TWO

Sri Lanka, Wednesday, September 30

"A non-response from BOI after Jaffna means closure in Colombo," Shoney chuckled. Valesano, with little conscience for his fellow man, shuddered at the immensity of the horror in which he swam.

Shoney debriefed Valesano before leaving Havasu. "Gasoline poured into sewers upstream of the plant will be an awesome sight when struck by a match in the plant headworks." Lacking the feelings of a reptile, Shoney squirmed with excitement, Valesano's eyes widening even farther at the climactic sensations Shoney allowed himself.

Having returned to the Hilton in Colombo on Echelon Square, Valesano popped two Tums. He wondered how many he'd taken in the past week, and realized that he was operating by the seat of his pants on what-ifs. He preferred logistics to circumstances, but it mattered not; soon he'd be out of an island country that was only half as big as Alabama.

Once he and Adasa nested at the hotel, he wondered how Sri Lanka survived as a member of the Commonwealth of Nations, their national product ostensibly not measuring up, at least in Valesano's limited mentality, but that was something else that mattered not. He'd done everything asked of him, visiting all three wastewater treatment plants, and listening to complaints of the Sinhalese employees about the Tamils slowing Sri Lankan world progress with civil war and guerilla war tactics.

Venturing out onto his lanai, the heavily heated air rushed at him in suffocation. Quickly, he closed himself back into the suite, took out his American money and calculator so he could put to mind his expendable cash on hand. With the exchange rate at 61.15 rupees per U.S. dollar, Valesano would need a wheelbarrow to carry his money. He concealed a deep-seated fear of standing gypped, as he was all his life—gypped out of a happy childhood, gypped by social rejection. It was time to take care of Number One.

He was annoyed when the phone rang, his chin jutting out, his eyes dancing around the room. He'd be ready for anything. "Yeah."

"Tomorrow's D-Day, Tony." Shoney's voice held no cordiality, no solicitousness. "Be prepared to take action early tomorrow morning. You know what to do?"

"You're not talking to a fool, here. Of course I know what to do." His shoulders shifted herky-jerky.

Hearing only a long silence, Shoney laughed and added, "Have fun at the fair, old man." He wanted no misinterpretation of the messages, should someone be listening in or recording.

Valesano heard the click of the cutoff. He'd have fun at the fair, damaging valves, shutting down power, and pumping gas until all three cities were gas chambers, sludge pots, and firestorms.

A friendly Tamil biochemist employee took a liking to him.

CHAPTER SIXTY-THREE

The next day came two words from Shoney over the hollow-sounding telephone connection—"No treaty"—but it was enough to make Valesano's heart race with excitement.

He and Adasa left for Kandy by seven a.m., driving the same Mitsubishi they picked up at Kandy on their return trip from Jaffna. Arriving in time to cruise into the plant with the other employees, jostling and kibitzing, they blended like two of the regular personnel. BOI bolo tags identified them easily to employees who saw Valesano and Adasa scrutinizing the plant only a week ago. Wearing hardhats, carrying clipboards, micrometers, backpacks, and pagers, they achieved an aura of authoritative busyness.

The sign on the razor-wired enclosure read: "Authorized Personnel Only. Danger." With permitted access to the entire premises, Valesano and Adasa pulled gas masks from their backpacks—a precautionary measure, an observer would conclude. The valves at the bottom of two, two-thousand-pound chlorine tanks turned by means of a circular handle, to "Open."

As if testing, clipboards were registered and a hasty exit beaten from the *Authorized Personnel Only* enclosure, the gas masks stored in the backpacks. Adasa and Valesano were out of the city on the next train to Jaffna, having no concern or further need of the Mitsubishi. Behind them, the disagreeable poisonous gas gave off a seeping, suffocating odor, the same gas used effectively during World War 1 inflicting heavy casualties on both sides.

****

Valesano and Adasa sat in silence in a second rate hotel in Jaffna, the hours growing late. Blinking on and off, the hotel sign outside was beyond the annoyance of a Chinese water torture. The evening news telecast on government-owned television channels, *Rupavahini* Corporation and the Independent Television Network, a catastrophic debacle at the Kandy Wastewater Treatment Plant described.

Copious square miles of populated areas saw evacuation due to a chlorine leak at the Kandy Wastewater Treatment Plant. Seventy deaths register, with thousands more affected. Authorities are investigating the mishap... equipment old... outdated. At least fifty thousand people have left their homes, abandoning at once their jobs, their schools, and their residences. People are asking why this problem did not surface earlier and rectified. How soon would there surface even a greater number of fatalities? There has been no word as to when the evacuated area may know occupation once more.

Valesano and Adasa lurched when the phone rang.

"No treaty."

The Jaffna plant was as familiar as the Kandy plant. Access was equally as easy. They held written orders from the BOI, allowing inspections at hours of their choice. They chose to work overtime; start time was set for 6:00 PM. Backup generators were zilched early on. Busy employees checked generator indicators when time permitted. A dirty joke was more imminently entertained than the wearisome repetitiousness of taking ceaselessly unchanging dial readings. Suddenly, the whir and din of the plant slowed and converted to an eerie silence—total eerie silence.

An uproar of activity escalated, as systems were checked, power pulls adjusted to no avail. Adasa, in a last-minute coup, paid a Tamil Jaffna Light & Power employee to scamper up a transformer power pole and reduce the wattage to the Palk Strait Plant to an ineffectively low output.

The two inspectors arrived at the plant with the skeleton night shift, completed their tours, and disappeared in a Volvo provided by the friendly Tamil for the return trip to Colombo, via the direct route.

Spending Friday night back in the luxury of their Hilton accommodations, Adasa and Valesano again waited. They purchased one each of the three English language dailies: *The Daily News, The Island,* and *The Observer.* All were devoted to the disabled plants in Kandy and Jaffna.

In Kandy, the story has gone from bad to worse than bad. The death toll stands at seven-hundred-sixteen, with thousands more gravely ill.

Backup of live sewage is prevalent in Jaffna homes, streets, and places of business. An emergency session of the Jaffna Council for Human and Environmental Protection is convening to solve the ever-increasing problems. The International Red Cross is rushing antibiotics and typhoid vaccination supplies to both Kandy and Jaffna. Contaminated effluent is running rampant, as well as raw sewage. With only one doctor per 3,633 inhabitants in the entirety of Sri Lanka, the medical arena is hard-pressed to be of service, many with their hands tied due to the enormity of the situation. Many are relying on Ayurvedic remedies practiced traditionally for centuries on our island country.

Adasa wore a thin grin of satisfaction, and then lifted his shoulders with a grunt of mirth. Jaffna was probably his favorite place, but to get a pork roast, one needs to first slay the pig.

Valesano paced. Fear bred loneliness, and the loneliness intensified his fear. He'd goddamn well better be on a plane out of here at Bandaranaike International by tomorrow afternoon or he'd kick someone's ass. The airport was seventeen miles north of Colombo, but at least he could drive there and wouldn't have to take a damnable stinkin' train.

The million dollars he gained by taking on this assignment was his nest egg. In addition to expenses, he received $100,000 as seed money. Hereafter, $200,000 shuffled into a safety deposit box in Lake Havasu City for every successful juncture of his misadventure. When he returned to Havasu, he'd get the final installment of $300,000. Into the bargain, the department could take their job and shove it into the vacancy at the top of their legs. Moreover, McCruise would be out of his life forever and ever. Suckin' rich kid drawing a police officer's salary!

Nerves jangling, Valesano's hands trembled when the phone rang.

"No treaty." Shoney gave Valesano his got-the-last-laugh annoying chortle.

Colombo, like any large metro area, established sewer access sites, which staggered intermittently throughout the city. Although it was the weekend, Adasa obtained a set of blueprints of the sewer mainlines from his cohort revolutionist at the Public Works Department at City Hall. As luck would have it, Valesano found on the blueprint a thirty-inch sewer manhole cover. Its location sat just forty feet from the gasoline fill port at the Union 76 Convenience Mart Station at the corner of Main Street and Galle Road, just south of the Queen Elizabeth Quay. The sewer line ran directly to Plant Number One, which rested only a quarter of a mile away.

Early on this already stifling morning, a bulk delivery tanker, hi-jacked from a fast food establishment with the assistance and planning of Tamil guerillas, pulled up to the station to fill the underground gasoline storage tanks. It was a routine development, observed at least once a week. The less-than-mature attendant knew better things to do than check tanker deliveries and thus flipped it off as business-as-usual.

The tanker, filled with eight-hundred gallons of high-octane fuel, was all Valesano and Adasa required for action. Popping a manhole cover did not take the contrivance of a nuclear scientist. A short pry-bar concealed up Valesano's sleeve was used to lift the edge of the heavy cast iron cover. The lid pivoted at its center point without falling into the hole, as a coin set edgewise on the mouth of a Coke bottle. Down the hole quickly went the hose, and the flow of gasoline commenced.

In the early morning sunlight, Valesano and Adasa disappeared into a waiting dark-blue Volvo, while the tanker's entire contents flowed unnoticed into the sewer. They counted forty minutes before the lethal slug of fuel reached the plant, which was located south of the intersection of Galle Road and De Mel Mavata Highway. Here lay a splendid juncture for a wastewater plant because the topography allowed undirected effluent to be gravitated into the Gulf of Mannar.

Again, they trailed into the plant with the day shift. The subject matter for early-morning conversation dripped with problems from the Kandy and Jaffna plants. On every tongue was the Kandy catastrophe, where the death toll rose to 8,463. Public health officials have no idea how rampant typhoid might become in Jaffna.

Adasa shot a speaking glance to Valesano, understanding that they were to wear an air of somberness in keeping with bereavement by association, tipping their hardhats to fellow employees, adjusting their clipboards, and proceeding out to the multiple aeration basins, which stretched on for acres. Huge vats with protected, elevated walkways divided the basins whose aeration bridges circled monotonously, churning the sludge, and keeping it in flux.

The smell of gasoline permeated the already foul air as Adasa explained, "One of the first steps a wastewater treatment facility takes is to shake up the sewage, exposing it to air. As organic matter decays, it uses up oxygen. Aeration replenishes the oxygen. Bubbling oxygen through the water also keeps the organic material suspended while it forces grit, coffee grounds, sand, and other small, dense particles to settle out." The process created bubbling in the wastewater like a cauldron.

"This causes some of the dissolved gases, such as hydrogen sulfide that taste and smell bad, to be released from the water," Adasa went on in a surprisingly instructional tone.

Valesano counted the minutes he was willing to stand there. The whole place smelled like rotten eggs. Workers bumped around in the distance like butterflies, checking gauges, all too busy to notice two inspectors dawdling out in the stinking aeration basins.

Valesano dropped a match, which ignited the air before it even hit the sewage. A roaring *whoosh* ripped across the aeration basins, following the least resistant lines of the second section, or sedimentation tanks, ever seeking sufficient oxygen to maintain itself.

Adasa and Valesano watched from the protection of the overhead walkways in triumphant fascination as the flames shot out the end of the sedimentation tanks, then rose up as hungry tongues over the sludge, including grease, oils, plastics, and soap. The wind whomped down to replenish the oxygen supply. Slow-moving rakes skimmed the scum off the surface of the wastewater, feathering the flames. Billowing upwards in ever-increasing tendrils of black smoke, dragon fire headed into the chlorine tanks, which supported combustion just like oxygen, resulting in residual wastewater exploding.

No one would call Valesano "Chicken George" again. He'd take his rewards and live in South America, maybe even come back here again, an unidentified newcomer, whose visual image lent no attractiveness to inquisitive neighbors. Lulled by the thought and the imminent need to escape the inferno, Valesano's breath hissed between his clenched teeth as he caught the sun glinting off silver in Adasa's hand.

CHAPTER SIXTY-FOUR

A gun!

Valesano's mouth was moving, although words failed him. There appeared a white fleck on his lower lip; the cords in his neck sprang into prominence. He watched in dismay as Adasa's lips pressed together in mean-spirited enjoyment. As if in a time warp, icicles gripped Valesano's chest as realization sank in. A flood of adrenaline flashed and his eyes widened.

Two loud reports were not measurable in the din and boom of the roaring firestorm, as Adasa's powerful Lugar blew two holes in Valesano's chest. Valesano's eyes glittered with hatred, his arm lifted, his leg jerked forward as if to attack Adasa. Instead, Valesano thrust himself over the edge of the aeration tank, his body hitting the bubbling sludge where it suspended on the cushion of high-compression oxygen, forced in from the bottom of the tank. Sufficient air bubbles sought Valesano's clothing, causing Valesano to sink and then resurface as if he were Captain Ahab tied to Moby Dick, each time engulfed in the sucking flames, the slime, and the detritus of humanity.

Sweating, Adasa placed a handkerchief over his nose and scurried away from the confusion and the chaos that accompanies calamity. With the aeration tanks situated near the southernmost end of the Wastewater Treatment Plant, he ran into no problems exiting unnoticed.

His directions were clear. Return to the Volvo and drive to the domestic airport at Ratmalan and pick up the balance of payoff from a pre-rented locker. Air Lanka, the national carrier, would fly him to Bangkok, Thailand and another carrier to Taipei, China; at that point, he'd use Valesano's already confiscated ticket to South America, as instructed, and disappear forever with a new identity.

When the dust settled, there would be too much incriminating evidence of his involvement in the breakdown of the three plants. The hate filling him was enough food for survival. The Sinhalese, who usurped his family's holdings due to his father's allegiance to the Tamil Separatist Movement, now knew repayment for their rapaciousness. The fact that he impaired the Jaffna Plant, where his allegiances lay, hung like a dirty fog. It gelled as a compromise—a corrupt compromise implanted by Shoney, who used it as an art form, and found Adasa at a point in time when he was weak in the wallet. The thought was bitter vetch to Adasa. The loathsome memories swarmed over him, hovering like fine netting, waiting to obliterate psyche, sap the very life out of him.

He would be forever proud, nonetheless, of the fact that his cousin was the Tamil rebel who detonated explosives strapped to him and assassinated President Premadas in May of 1993. Any of Adasa's family would have done the same thing, many of them women who were ready and willing to repeat the suicidal mission.

Breathing a sigh of relief, Adasa eased into the driver's seat of the Volvo and checked his rearview mirror, where he looked into a dissolute American face with keening blue eyes, wearing the kind of smile that invited Adasa to smile back. The smile turned to horror in an instant.

"No!" Adasa shouted, looking at the barrel of a Beretta that loomed like a cannon. He reached to retrieve his Lugar when there was a sense shattering sound, then nothing— the back of his head blown off and his face nameless.

Shoney removed the airline ticket from Adasa's shirt, the paper warm from his body heat. *"Carpe diem,"* he breathed.

He'd try South America. A week or two on the Brazil beaches with Mallika Chilaw should handle his libido. First, however, he'd call Norwood and advise him of an assignment well handled.

CHAPTER SIXTY-FIVE

It was the first Saturday in October and Jacquie could
stand the stress no longer. Instead of working a busy
Saturday night at the Golden Crest, she clung to the familiar
surroundings of her condominium. Warm, dry air filtered
through the room from the open lanai slidebys. The sun
behind the mountains turned the sky to mauve, and the
electric, shimmering blue, which is often evident in far-west
paintings.

She clicked on the evening television news, finding Tom
Brokaw commentating on the tragic health problems faced
by the Sri Lankan Government, due, ostensibly, to Tamil
sabotaging of the wastewater treatment plants.

"Hospitals are overflowing with indicators of typhoid
fever: high fever, headache, coughing, intestinal
hemorrhaging, and rose-colored spots on the skin. The
death toll has climbed to 14,694."

For days, the news carried the abominable tragedy in
Sri Lanka. The Tamils arose and struck the country where
it hurt, badly. Three major cities suffered back-to-back
sewage problems. Drastic measures saw the implementation
of emergency crews working around the clock to restore a
reasonable measure of control.

Mallika, in ever-widening pride in assisting her
compatriots, divulged to Jacquie the wonderful offer Fayne
Norwood made to the Sri Lankan authorities while he was

in Duluth. "That helpful Mr. Shoney was there, too, and my cousin Adasa. There was even representation in attendance from the Lake Havasu City Police Department, Lt. Valesano."

With the ever-increasing volume of incapacitating news from Sri Lanka, however, Jacquie suffered the heart-rending experience of realization by association. Pictures of Cousin Adasa were prevalent on telecasts, his demise a justified ending for suspected deadly actions. A BOI identification picture of Valesano, Adasa's cohort, flashed frequently as Sri Lanka's "Most Wanted" person.

She shuddered. The shudder slicked pieces into place and she saw the picture clearly, with all its shade nuances and rolling terrain. By contrast, what previously lay plain and symmetrically black and white suddenly fine-tuned to texturized and colored with limitless subtlety.

Sligh Shoney was behind this, and Norwood behind him. She knew without a doubt that Norwood was flexing his muscles. If the BOI entertained the thought of upsetting the apple cart, they'd have Shoney to deal with. The situation held the stealth and intrigue of a super spy plot right out of a *New York Times* best-seller. It was bestial and appalling.

Norwood's edge of control for the cocaine market now began. She could imagine raising tan eyebrows over tan eyes, vaunting his grandstand play. Cocaine is addictive. Addiction means profits. The historical Norwood R & D merger with Global Earth Technologies and the Wall Street banking firm of Graspe, Grinne & Barrett would make hundreds of millions of dollars a year off children, many of whom would die of the addiction.

With privy knowledge of the Duluth session, Mallika unwittingly put Jacquie, her family, and McCruise at risk. Norwood would ask, "Did they know? Did Mallika tell them?" It would be immaterial. The knowledge was fatal, the purse too large. The killer already killed the killers. Norwood would not fail.

She finally understood something tonight, and the comprehension was with startling clarity. She couldn't live the rest of her life wearing blinders. She only had this life to live as her own. The acknowledgment compensated her for the chilly loneliness that encompassed her. Maybe she gained the first durable capsule of mature responsibility she ever knew.

She must talk to McCruise, but not here. The risk was too great. How did she become so deeply involved in Norwood's web now, after the umbilical cord cut and dried brittle?

"It was such a viable plan," Mallika divulged. "The Sri Lankans would get the crème de la crème of sewer systems as a tradeoff for a cub's percentage of their tea exports *and* a lion's share of their cocaine exports of which there was no shortfall."

These commodities needed marketing by some entity, sure as time eternal, and it would be Graspe, Grinne, and Barrett. The evidence was circling in her mind like vultures over carrion. She'd have to be hiding under a rock not to add the Sri Lankan situation to Norwood's laundry list of evil. Was the entirety of the cocaine he was importing going to legitimate uses, such as pharmaceuticals and research? Was he hardballing the Sri Lankans? Tamil sabotage was not the employable answer.

"Fayne gave my people until the end of the month to make a decision," Mallika related proudly. Jacquie heard the unbelievable words ringing in her ears. The timing was too overwhelming to be coincidental. Admittedly, she was in deep and serious doodoo, and needed help. The people into whose circle she melded were like creeping crocodiles.

****

"McCruise. I'm so glad you're home," Jacquie spoke into the telephone. She paused, her words stuck. "There's an art exhibit at the Community Center this evening. Would you like to meet me down there?"

"What the hell—now?"

"It's important."

After a long tunnel of silence, McCruise said, "Give me a half hour."

"Thanks, McCruise."

Jacquie studied every artistic submission hanging in the Community Center and started over again when McCruise appeared wearing well filled out Levis, a white knit Nike shirt, and Tony Lama boots. Her eyes searched the crowd relentlessly, not finding him. Here he was, towering over her, his eyes making contact, scanning as if he read her thoughts with the clarity of alien powers.

"What's your problem, Jacaranda Rose Remington?" He asked softly.

Something in his voice reminded her of a mesquite tree, dark against a desert indigo sky, imposing and immovable. Jacquie recoiled under his scrutiny. His law-enforcement scanning of her was purposeful, she supposed. Questioning was in order. McCruise was an influential figure within the department and carried great credibility. Did she see a change in his eyes, dancing between warmth and fear, balancing between love and disillusionment? Jacquie drew herself up. She wasn't some uncontrollable dolt who couldn't handle herself amongst the cultural right.

"I have the most unnerving suppositions to tell you. Norwood is at it again; he'll kill if he has to—kill millions if necessary." Jacquie's eyes were imploring McCruise.

"He knows everything I do, everywhere I go, and that goes for you, too, and the department. He has eyes all over." She was aware that her voice was riding the edge. McCruise's hand on her arm, leading her on from picture to picture, was the only comfort keeping her rational.

Jacquie's voice lowered with the reinforcement, almost to a whisper. "There is so much at risk here. The Sri Lankan debacle was created by Norwood."

She felt McCruise stiffen as he led her down the long corridor and out into the lazy breeze of the Mohave Desert night. Hot and dry, the air traveled in restless whispers among palms, acacias, and jacarandas.

His voice gentle, his eyes sad, he breathed. "Let's start at the beginning."

CHAPTER SIXTY-SIX

Friday, October 10, 1997

Facing yet another weekend of ten-hour night shifts on the river after three weeks of no-show by drug traffickers, McCruise wore dark clothing for night blending, the days becoming shorter by the second weekend of October. By 6:00 PM, the Mohave Desert stopped breathing fire as if its lungs sprung spent. Nights moderated into the high seventies.

In an unmarked watercraft, McCruise and Wally could ply the Bridgewater Channel and the Island and blend with the weekend waterway traffic. Backing out of the slip at city-owned Site Six launch site, the motor made smooth bubbling sounds. The smell of fuel, creosote-soaked docking, tarred rope, and floating kelp titillated their nostrils.

"Okay, we're out and on our way." McCruise maneuvered slowly while jet skis zoomed around the watercraft, looking for surging wake. All week he struggled to hang on to the simple pleasures of home and security, his whole life blasted open by Jacquie's ineffable revelation.

Surrounding the police patrol boat, the lake jumped and changed with a kaleidoscope of colorful water toys: jet skis, water skiers, powerboats, houseboats, even canoes, and kayaks. An entire segment of our culture was out for playtime, without remorse, without weighted worries, naïve with explainable joyousness.

This was how life should be. This was how life used to be. With regularity, Tucker woke McCruise and the boys by 6:00 AM. It was showers, making beds, preparing breakfast and then neatly off to Grandma Penny's, who sheltered and loved them all day until his return, with dependability, by 5:30 PM. His was a life of incredible routine, but not ever boring—never tedious. Calls from Mark and Luke came at any time of the day on his cell phone. He welcomed the interruptions.

With department networking, he privileged even greater means of communication, but nothing else was the same—nothing. Sitting here in the patrol boat with Wally, he knew Shoney's eyes were out there somewhere, watching and recording. Sharing Jacquie's confession with Connor and Wally that same night brought small comfort, except for the fact that someone else was aware of the magnanimity of the hellhole in which he floundered.

Connor launched an investigation with the FBI. The information being anemic, the effort was hushed until further developments and incriminations. Infiltration into the Sri Lanka Police Network stood deeply resented by the Asians, making progress slow and tedious.

"I don't think our lives are worth a snippet in the total scheme of things, McCruise." Wally twisted his handcuffs as if they reflected the snare in which they sat tangled. "Sitting on this information is explosive."

"Jacquie's life is at stake," McCruise blurted.

"Keeping the Havasu connection out of the media's hands is not a good idea." However, life's experiences showed Wally that everyone owed their allegiances to nine or ten different gods. "Wel-ll, what the hell, in for a penny, in for a pound," he said aloud, his voice softening with acquiescence.

McCruise swung a glance at Wally. "What a hell of a mess! Shoney has to know that Jacquie has conclusions of his intense involvement in the Sri Lankan Wastewater Plant's demise. He knows we know. It's explosive."

Wally said nothing.

McCruise did another quick study. "We're in it together, Wally, all the way."

"Straight ahead, Mr. Cruise; we're in it all the way for this shift, too. One day at a time." Wally clipped him with a soft punch to the shoulder and eased back.

"Got that right." McCruise knew Wally to be a police officer by profession, but a skeptic by nature, so the brass in his badge was firmer than his faith in partying boaters. The sound of Wally's voice when he got excited, the candidness of his emotions, McCruise liked with a phenomenal power. He turned slowly to face him, evaluating his irreplaceable worth. Even in sleep deprivation, Wally was the best cop on the walk, big muscles played at his shirtsleeves and chest. His strength of character etched clearly into his profile. You could carry on about someone's proprieties, about their benevolence, until smoke comes out your ears, but none compared to Wally's. Wally didn't just throw around words like responsibilities, church, home, and moral obligations. He *was* all of them.

****

By two 2:00 AM, the Channel barely crawled. Echoes of "Goodnight" from Kokomo's drifted over the smoothly running water as McCruise and Wally moored their boat into slippage across from the Golden Crest, got out, and silently crossed the grass campus of the slope leading up to the Island Mall. The temperature hung in at 79 degrees. They saw the glimmer of moths' wings circling walking-path lanterns, and the black swoop of hunting nighthawks against the sky. Flowing from the decorative gardens was the scent of oleander and white gardenias. Intermittent water features bubbled like angel laughter. A welcome respite from the Mohave heat and aridity of the day was the succulent richness of damp earth.

Infrared radio-metered night binoculars no bigger than opera glasses, but harboring enormous power, hung around McCruise's neck, part of the superior technology and materials offered by the DEA. He adjusted his shoulder holster so it didn't jam his rib cage, pulled up his knees, and allowed his long arms to dangle over his knees.

Blusters of warm breezes captured during the day from the sun circled McCruise and Wally like dust devils.

"How has Jacquie recovered from the Sligh attack?" Wally asked quietly.

"She's lucky. It's been a month and her face shows no scars or trauma."

"God only knows what's swirling around in her psyche, however." Wally stared over the multitude of shimmering silver mirrors that were dancing on the water in the filtering light of the moon, now riding high in the sky.

Hearing everything Wally said, McCruise's eyes and ears yet recorded normal night sounds: the groaning of the boats at their moorings, and an occasional car going over the London Bridge.

McCruise tilted a shoulder. "I've been disregarding the unrevealed traumas she's experienced: her abrupt separation from Norwood, shouldering the Golden Crest, handling Shoney and the Sri Lankan mess." He swallowed into a constricted throat, angered at his shortsightedness.

"Christ, McCruise, haven't we all been there?" Wally fiddled with a blade of rye that poked through the grass carpet. "Allow her to see some basic empathy time and again, *your* empathy." His eyes twinkled.

Slapping his drawn-up knees, McCruise blurted out, "Wally, you keep me straight." His past concerns sealed shut like a sepulcher. McCruise would never forget the special times he shared with his friend. He'd refine it and replay it for the rest of his life: the honesty he saw with such clarity, the mental depths he'd chosen to overlook for months, the reflections of the Midwest dialect never to be lost from his speech, the peace abounding within Wally's reservoirs. It could take a person from distress to levity within moments.

"Let's have coffee," McCruise said resolutely. Retrieving his thermos from the boat, he caught a peripheral motion across the quiet Channel.

Wally caught the same movements through his binoculars at his eyes.

McCruise thought the lenses on his binoculars were glitched. Heads moved around like magpies caught in a microburst, near the Golden Unicorn, which was located thirty yards north of the Golden Crest. Shoney's deck boat moored at a shoring post in front of the Golden Crest. Was that a brief glow of heat showing red picked up by the binoculars? A glow in the water showed for a heartbeat. Minutes passed. The watery glow appeared again. A man's silhouette clearly rose over the back railing of the deck boat.

McCruise and Wally heard low, powerful churning of the outboard motor and saw the deck boat move north, slowly up the Channel to pick up the magpies who flitted onto the boat, unaware of the source of the party-time coke, which Ricki transported from the warehouse to the deck boat.

A sudden quiet settled on the night, overshadowed with lazy clouds.

"Holy shades of shit!" Wally exhaled under his breath. "What a setup."

"No one, no one, no one would ever know the door was there—no one. What a setup! Right out of *Science Illustrated.*"

McCruise and Wally heard echoing murmurs from the deck boat. The craft moved farther north, the whole process taking mere minutes, like a capricious wind shear.

"How many people?" McCruise asked.

"Eight. Men and women." Wally's tone contained the electricity that fueled their stints together, generating common objectives, insights, enthusiasms and, most of all, results.

"It's the penny-ante gamble, exactly as Connor predicted. I'll be goddamned!" McCruise's night eyes narrowed, just as they did when he played defensive back for ASU.

Running lights on the deck boat dimmed. As the moon jumped from gauzy cloud to starry sky, figures in silhouette were easily discernible—four men, four women. With a defensive back's focus, McCruise determined that there was nothing delusional about this. It was party time, and indeed, the penny-ante move.

"It's good we can't make an arrest," McCruise rused. "The next time they make a move, it'll be with confidence."

"Baiting the trap. You can't take the police work out of police work."

"Speaking of police work, our shift is nearly up. I think I'll key in at Jacquie's tonight. Life's good there."

Wally reached out and tousled McCruise's hair.

CHAPTER SIXTY-SEVEN

Exactly a week later, the crinkles around McCruise's eyes were working in response to O'Shaughnessey's voice on the telephone.

"I'll assign Cleavus to work with Wally for tomorrow night, and tomorrow night only. That's it."

"Thanks, Connor. I ordered Jacquie an engagement ring from Crown Jewels a while ago, and this is the perfect time to present it to her. But..."

"No, no, no. If Jacquie wasn't my daughter you'd be out of luck, but rank has its privileges and all that stuff. Check in with me Sunday when you get back."

****

By the time Jacquie arrived home last Saturday night, McCruise was gone, the bed made, the condominium clueless he'd been there the night before. *The song is gone, but the melody lingers on, you and the night are gone, but the memory lingers on,* came to mind. McCruise moved his large hands over her with increasing excitement, leading her to the miracle wherein sensitive touching conveyed intricacies of soft tissue, hard muscle, and contrasting texture—giving rise to exquisite longings.

Images kept rising like a bright sun in her woeful world. He was a comfort and strong ally all week. The Sri Lanka devastation ceased with the incapacitation of the Colombo Wastewater Plant. Standing at 10,779, the death toll in Colombo saw no increase in two days. The light touching her face from the lanai showed a lonely woman pulled by the force of fear, anxiety, and exhaustion from sleepless nights.

At least she enjoyed a respite from Shoney, who reputedly just arrived back in town from a Brazilian vacation, accompanied by the lovely Mallika Chilaw. Jacquie saw him yesterday, looking macho and butch. Shoney, with his insufferable condescension, smugly kept eyes straight-ahead, as he'd met her on the esplanade.

Would she be the next one to disappear, as Valesano did? Via Mallika, she was privy to the arrangements for a barter trade with Sri Lanka, but she was not a sharer in the secrecy of the outcome. Neither did Norwood know of the information she'd garnered from his private office files while in his employ, albeit coded and generic. Thoughts that the man lived in a world of dark swirling mists caused Jacquie to shudder.

****

Jacquie answered the disturbing ringing of the telephone; extreme focusing was required to pull her from mulling.

"I have an invitation for you," McCruise said with enthusiasm. "England's Princess Anne will be in Phoenix to kick off the United Kingdom-Arizona Festival and attend the performance of Othello at the Herberger Theater Center tomorrow night. I thought the trip would keep you *compos mentis* in view of the situation we're facing here." He took a moment to chuckle for levity. "Interested?"

"Really, McCruise?" Jacquie's voice was a compendium of thrills and disbelief, as if a strong surge of Arctic Duluth air sucked her breath away.

"We can fly out of here tomorrow morning, stay at the Scottsdale Princess, loaf around the pool, and go to the Herberger Theatre for the seven-thirty performance."

"McCruise," she said quietly. "Thank you. Yes, of course I want to go." There was a pause in her voice. She would return at last from her nightmares to the illusory beauty of a tropical night, with blinking stars and a moon rising like an enormous silver fantasy from behind the Superstition Mountains.

McCruise clearly found himself victim to the velvet of her voice. He hung up, having been pleased to hear the devils of excitement prodding Jacquie's psyche. Maybe the two parallel lines of their relationship would bend and meet this weekend. Time was a precious commodity. Who knew what next week would bring, for both of them? In one sentient moment, McCruise experienced the awful burden descended on the petite, ingenuous shoulders of his beautiful woman.

****

Like an oasis in the desert, Sky Harbor International Airport in Phoenix was a heart stopper of restful beauty.

Jacquie's blue eyes—large, casting at will—breathed. "Look McCruise. The palms are growing right through the roof!" Her smile rifled him in the gut. He couldn't find a flaw in the woman, except maybe her independent mindsets sticking like bark to a tree: *no children, no interfering in her life's decisions.*

"I arranged for a car rental—a Jaguar." He laughed, flipping his carry-on bag over his shoulder and wrapping his other arm familiarly around her shoulder as they made their way down the concourse, where fringes of lantana in mutations of red and orange, yellow and purple smiled a welcome in scattered terra cotta pots.

Upon arrival at the Scottsdale Princess, McCruise watched Jacquie lose her breath at the sight and size of the complex—acres and acres of Five Star Hotel: campus, flower gardens, swimming pools, tennis courts, golf course, courtyards, splashing fountains, conference halls. Welcoming palms sighing and clicking in the lazy breeze surrounded it all like nurturing motherly love. The lobby was big enough for a banquet, and decorated in levels of soft vanilla, mauve, and mint. Glass, brass, and mirrors were tastefully in abundance.

The bellhop, who inserted a pass-card into one of two carved oak doors on the fourth floor suite, revealed to them an endless view overlooking a lush golf course. Opening onto the lanai, there were generous slidebys, and off to the right and left were identical great bedrooms, dressing rooms, and baths.

McCruise struggled to keep a straight face as she blinked speechlessly. She was the source of immense pride, and he shadowboxed constantly to fill her with a like pride for himself. He threw his carry-on bag onto a nearby chair, gathered her quickly into his arms, and kissed her deeply. She was his possession for twenty-four hours—all his. No one else existed—just them, with time to do anything they wished. Cares melted away, transporting them into the vastness of time that is endless for two people in love, alone.

Late that afternoon, Jacquie heard the pop of a champagne bottle. Putting the final additions on her ensemble, in the mirror she saw the look she wanted: a Gianni Versace silk and rayon blend, whiskey-colored evening dress, the bodice lightly quilted in rust. Sleeveless, the high jewel neckline framed her petite face. Lucid blue eyes stared out from under arched eyebrows, a hometown smile melding her mouth. As she turned in the mirror, she picked up the reflection of the A-line skirt moving gracefully. Now, she'd test Jungle Jim.

She could still smell the warmth of his passion, his aggressiveness that knew no let up all day, see the dark, sparkling desire in his eyes, feel the abandonment of his devouring kisses. The rush of an unexpected thrill ran through her. A small thick sound came from deep within her throat.

"*Voilà!*" She exclaimed. Pirouetting, she entered the sitting room where McCruise was busying himself over the sidebar with champagne and flutes.

He was regal, compelling, right off the cover of *Gentlemen's' Quarterly.* Short-cropped curling hair, deep brown eyes, generous mouth, Caesar nose, and shoulders as big as a mountain. The diamond studs in his shirt were stark, the black of the tuxedo a complement to his sun-bronzed coloring. The grosgrain lapels suited him much better than satin; a cummerbund accented his athletic physique. Powerfully stropped at the corners from years of exposure to the desert sun, his eyes narrowed.

Towering, he stood in trousers with black stripes down the side. He observed that she was trying to act only mildly impressed in an effort to control her excitement. A sharp rolling sting of passion ran through McCruise almost painfully. His eyes danced with the delight of her.

Mouth ajar, McCruise looked at his golden lady. "Christ, Jacquie! You look like pheasant under glass to a starving man. His voice carried tremors of emotion, his eyes a fever of pagan worship. "Those colors look as if you were born in them." He met her halfway across the room with a flute of champagne, bent, and kissed her lightly on the cheek, not wanting to spoil the image. The inexplicable attraction between them was palpable. This was the McCruise and Jacquie he wanted to see: the McCruise and Jacquie off work, on holiday.

"And you, sir, look as intimidating as hell—very arresting." She looked up at him shyly, her eyes saying that she loved him deeply. "You are all things to me, McCruise, everything. There is nothing else for you to conquer." She leaned her head on his chest, her desire spelled openly.

McCruise gently squeezed Jacquie's upper arm as a melted-wax softening spread over his disciplined face. Jacquie would always have something for him to vanquish with the minuscule something she kept withheld. She protected a hidden niche that he couldn't find, causing him to growl. He longed for the day when she would share the unfathomable something with him.

As McCruise led Jacquie to the slidebys and out onto the lanai, a soft breeze teased the palm fronds. October evenings were hurrying in earlier every day. Already, the deepening Arizona sky was filling with a myriad of diamonds as bright as those McCruise saw in his dreams, his dreams that danced around the edges of ever becoming reality. The outdoor pool showed tentacles of mist where the surface flirted with cooling temperatures. The moon, promising a bright harvest, peeked over the mountain like a sentry.

Whispering "Jacquie," so as not to break the magic spell of early evening, McCruise reached into his pocket and withdrew a black velvet box.

Quizzically, she lifted her eyes to his and found them warm, searching, as anticipatory as Luke's did. The box lid opened with a slow click, drawing a shallow intake of breath from her as there sprung to life a ring of gold, inset with a carat diamond, surrounded by another carat of cut rubies.

McCruise's face warmed with pride.

Speechless as a mime, Jacquie's lashes lifted, her blue eyes flooding.

McCruise removed the ring from the box and put it into his mouth. Withdrawing it, he meaningfully inserted it into her mouth. Extracting the ring from her tongue, he lifted her hand and slid it easily onto her finger.

"Oh, McCruise," she breathed. "It's awesome." Her fingertips ever so lightly brailed the fine lines, the warm, ice blue beauty of it, the warm, red setting of rubies. She questioned whether there was anything else in the world that could replace the magnitude of receiving an exquisite ring that said, "I love you," elevating a woman to being something very special.

McCruise's heart quivered against his ribs. His stomach warmed.

"You shouldn't have McCruise, but thank you. I've never owned anything lovelier than this. That is, unless it's you," she said softly, smiling up at him, her eyes tearing.

He knew he must turn away or he'd break down and cry with the honesty of his love for her, and he'd rather keep that to himself. At least for a while, the ring would have to spell "I love you."

CHAPTER SIXTY-EIGHT

The Herberger Theatre was a tangle of sight-seekers, eager to catch a glimpse of Princess Anne and her entourage. Paparazzi scurried to snap exclusive shots for network newscasts and syndicated publications. Microphone booms dangled crazily. Man-on-the-street interviews were underway.

People milled about the new bronze statues that commissioned and permanently installed on a circle of advantage. Dancing gracefully in the beauty of young bodies were the naked nymphs of artistry, their every muscle, fiber and feature struck in bronze splendor.

Resultant of the presence of the princess, there prevailed a hushed, honorary droning of voices. Expectant electricity hung in the air, anticipating an all-English cast for the performance of *Othello*, an English Shakespearean tale written in the first decade of the 1600s.

McCruise idly questioned Othello's love for Desdemona. "How could Othello ever cede to an evil lieutenant like Iago, who planted seeds of suspicion about Desdemona and Othello's new friend, Cassio?" It was a question without academia, casting McCruise into thoughtful silence again.

"Well, he did. It is a real question. Othello was a decent individual who brought about his own downfall through a tragic flaw: suspicion. I've never seen the stage play, but I caught the movie in '95, starring Laurence Fishburne and

Kenneth Branagh. I wish I could have seen it with you, McCruise."

McCruise watched her expression mutate to soft and sweet.

****

In the box with the princess and associates sat a handsome man, regally dressed, his tan eyes, tan hair, and cleft chin an imprint of identification as positive as DNA, his smile as bitter as Kirk Douglas's in the Gladiator—Fayne Alexander Norwood.

He was biding his time. Patience always paid off. Soon he'd be one of the richest men in the world. He needn't hurry. The Sri Lankan BOI bowed to the miraculous changes the GETI people promised.

Sri Lankan President, Mrs. Chandrika Bandaranaike Kumaratunga, a small woman with black hair that she wore severely pulled back and coifed with bone combs, confirmed the commodity exchange.

The Tamil terrorists severely crippled the economic and environmental well-being of the country, bringing it to its knees. The terrorists, however, were not going to take over her small island commonwealth if Mrs. Kumaratunga had anything to say about it, and she did. Her fellow citizens would have wastewater treatment plants second to none in the world. They would rebuild. American contractors and equipment were already moving in, replacing, retrofitting, and functionalizing existing plants.

Fayne knew Mrs. Kumaratunga weighed every element of the price she paid for the exchange. The New York banking firm of Graspe, Grinne, and Barrett asked of the Sri Lankans the right to their governmental holdings in coca plant plantations and refining processes, as well as a small amount of their green tea franchise. Fair enough, harvests were good, tea production was reaching a record, and prices for rubber and coconut were high.

Tourist numbers were rising and foreign investment continued to grow, with fourteen new enterprises in manufacturing and infrastructure scheduled for near opening. The Sri Lankan economy blossomed, not so much by the bartered products, but by Sri Lanka's main exports, which were textiles and clothing, tea, cut diamonds, petroleum products, gems and rubber products; coca plants were a small part of the island economy.

The only pain in the ass for President Bandaranaike Kumaratunga was ethnic Tamil conflict. Sligh Ignatius Shoney, under the direction of Fayne Alexander Norwood, would see to it that the uprisings continued if Sri Lankan cooperation ceased.

Fayne Alexander Norwood knew international trade, spoke five languages, and understood several Asian dialects. Born the son of a mining captain and raised in Hibbing, Minnesota, he'd learned early of the magnetism of, *What's in it for me?* A mining captain in the iron ore heyday of Hibbing was king. The mine owners gave their captains *carte blanche* for freewheeling skullduggery. Miners enjoyed hiring and feared firing at the whim of the captain. Miners realized Workers Compensation for sustained on-the-job injuries at the whim of the captain, who could make or break a report to the State of Minnesota Compensation Board.

Fayne grew up spending all his free hours in the iron ore mines, and at sixteen, he worked weekends for his father. The war was over and the good times of the fifties rolled. The first time he'd seen a miner smashed against a stope wall by a run-away ore cart, he'd thrown up. Three weeks later, the independently wealthy dead miner's wife, Maddy, was married to another miner who worked with the run-away cart. Fayne witnessed it all, and milked the felon miner for years. Being privy to work schedules, Fayne also milked honey from Maddy while her first husband was deep six, and her new husband six levels below the earth blasting iron ore out of the stopes.

The woman wasn't the prettiest in the world, but she was intelligent and from stock who founded the city of Hibbing back in 1878, when families such as Maddy's bought up acres by the forty, including mineral rights. She knew how to please a man. Moreover, never let it prevail that Fayne wasn't up to pleasing her, pleasuring her right into revealing privy knowledge of where there was to be new drilling for assays, assays that were already reputed to be minable to the tune of eighty-four percent iron ore.

Enjoying Fayne's amours immensely, she deeded Fayne with one-third mineral rights on acreage, which was diamond-drilled, showing proof of layer upon layer of iron ore. By 1960, Fayne was a wealthy man and took himself off to the College of William and Mary in Williamsburg, Virginia, with no intentions whatsoever of ever seeing Maddy again. Appeasement being appropriate, he reimbursed her a bare-bones amount for the deeded property by mail, not wanting any hysterical encounters.

Human genetics proved attractive to him, and enticed not with what was, but with what could be. His life of incalculable *what ifs* was staggering. One success followed another, with genetic engineering earning him a place in world history as a nominee for the Nobel Peace Prize.

Greed appeared while using invitro fertilization in Sri Lanka, where he established three R & D Centers to avoid burdensome American taxation and salaries. The Island's wealthy, infertile women needed him. Norwood anticipated years ago the advantages of Sri Lanka's cocaine production— a seed of an idea growing into humungous fungus. His heady successes lent credence to all his acclaim. He fared well, but he was no longer satisfied with the limitations of cocaine tradeoffs for successful births.

Greed permeated the American culture and soaked Norwood's intellectual sponge. He took his time, however, to set up the major thrust because he didn't want to spoil the joy of the kill. His GETI Offensive was the mother of all offensive tactics.

Fayne, pulling himself back to the present, was enjoying his lofty position-by-association with the princess. The United Kingdom, having historical ties to Sri Lanka since 1815, applauded the Norwood team for its altruistic and humane undertaking's in the small island nation. After the island (at the time, Ceylon) became fully independent and joined the Commonwealth of South Asian Nationals in 1948, the United Kingdom yet held immense economic interests in Sri Lanka. In 1956, talks with Britain ended in the return to Ceylon of the Katunayake Airfield and the Trincomalee

Naval Base. Sri Lanka negotiated great gains, but never completely shed the British cultural and political influence.

****

Norwood beamed thought themes at Jacquie as if, through telepathy, he could control her psyche—subdue her into submission to his righteous hierarchy, his ego as puffed out of proportion as his reputation.

Jacquie scanned the princess's loge, noting the Cadillac location on the mezzanine. Glancing farther at the peopled loge, her heart came to a jerking stop when the sweep of her gaze landed on Fayne.

His eyes brittle, he pulled his thumb across his mouth in zipper fashion, followed by a thumbs-up as if she were a willing cohort in his bizarre unconscionable exploits. There was dangerousness about him as if he'd pulled his forefinger across his neck in a slitting gesture.

She nodded, her whole body stiffening to stone. "McCruise, I'm suddenly sick." My God, what happened to the beautiful new world she'd promised herself in Havasu? She trembled like a wind-whipped ocotillo.

He squeezed her hand reassuringly. "You've just been too excited about our holiday." Giving her the smile of the vanquisher over the vanquished, he released the full strength of his charm, ever so slowly, anchoring her stability. He was her slice of life—as reliable as a tuning fork, dynamic and gentle.

Never, however, did *gentle* win a war.

CHAPTER SIXTY-NINE

Returning to the Scottsdale Princess, McCruise used valet parking. He could think of nothing but how much he wanted Jacquie again, but his thoughts drifted, due to her paleness, the rigidity of her body. It would be best if he didn't come off like a predator. His eyes locked onto hers— smoldering, ever assessing.

She reached for his hand, which he took willingly. In the elevator, he drew her close around the waist, his lips feathering her hair, conscious of the emotional adventure coursing through his veins with the heat of lust, yet with a soft gentleness that shook him. He'd held beautiful women in his arms before, taken them to bed, found comfort in them, but never felt obligated or apologetic about leaving the next morning—until Laura. Now, here lie a second chance at happiness, and Jacquie was the purchase he wanted gift-wrapped and taken home.

After opening the door of the suite, McCruise stood aside for her to pass through, smelling again fresh linen. It drove him nuts. He wanted her. If she stood near him too long, but she waxed wilted, her eyes dark. He watched her, breathed of her. This timeless place was their place in time, and time was irrelevant, only the moment mattered. The magic of making love was in its spontaneity and in its accessibility.

Although appearing to be in a weakened state, McCruise
suddenly saw with renewed wonder the way she looked at
him, as if seeing a flaming baked Alaska. He found it
amusing, since he viewed *her* as his favorite dessert.

"McCruise" she breathed, hesitating, as if in doubt of
her energy. Swooping her up, he swirled her in the air,
carried her to the bedroom, the freedom of lust curling
within him, making his blood swirl and eddy like mountain
runoff.

In frenzy, their clothes came off. He leaned over her on
the bed. He simply stayed there—naked, lean, and powerful.
She looked away, but not immediately. He heard her draw
in her breath sharply. Calmly. He was calm now,
comfortable, and confident in his own skin. He wasn't sure
how long he could chart her without exploding. "You drive
me crazy with need, Jacquie." He breathed deeply, moving
beside her on the bed.

Yet fighting fear, Jacquie clung to him. "I want to touch
you, McCruise," she murmured raking away from his
mouth.

The anticipation nearly did him in, sending him spiraling.
His chest thumped. He craved her with an all-consuming
need, the same craving he'd witnessed repeatedly with her.
The blood pulsing through his infrastructure made him
forget all rationale, her previous paleness, and enervation.

Comfortable possessiveness reflected in his eyes. "Set a
wedding date, Jacquie. I'll make you happy for the rest of
your days." The words tore from deep within his chest. He
would never be able to resist her, would always be her slave,
although he aggressed with dominance. He recognized that
it was a fool's ruse not to acknowledge her sway over him,
but she would never know it, damn it! A man needed to
walk away from lovemaking with some reserves.

He'd pushed himself as far was safe, the pressure was
urgent. The muscles in his stomach convulsed. He moved
over her, found her warm wetness and held himself there a
moment for control. There was no turning back.

She stirred, sibilant in her own world of ecstasy allowed
by the evolution of time and higher intelligence, yet enjoying
the primitiveness of mating.

He slowed to prolong the passion in his groin. He'd never exalted so high into possessing anyone. Her gasping pleasure moved him over the edge, into the land of exultant love where no one else exists and time stands unmarked. Aftershocks shot through him repeatedly, his body shuddering.

Life's better here rang confidently through McCruise's mind, laying a kiss on her forehead. "Marry me, Jacquie."

"Mmm." She snuggled into his neck, weak, the thoughts of Fayne flooding back, washing over her like evening tidal flow sucking at sand, consequently shrinking back for the next surge, and the next.

"I'm so tired," she offered without exaggeration, sighing into his neck in the softness of post-coital *joie de vivre*. "Let's order a snack sent up and sit on the lanai; we can watch the rest of the world go by."

A great sparkle of agreement danced in McCruise's warm brown eyes, but concern registered as he viewed her thin smile. "Sounds good to me, Lady Jacquie." His awareness of her heightened; a slow sweep of his eyes inventoried slight shadows under her eyes, her Irish skin lacking its normal vibrancy.

"You all right?" he asked, putting his arm around her shoulders protectively, adding an extra squeeze.

"Yes... yes..."

He could feel uncertainty seeping through her composure. His warm eyes searched her quiet face.

Jacquie showered and changed clothes while McCruise ordered up a hors d'oeuvre trolley, then joined him to relax on the lanai. Opening the door, he stepped out onto the lanai, and with a grand sweep of his arm, welcomed her to enter.

For an eternal moment, Jacquie hung in place by an overwhelming feeling of distance and detachment. Faltering unsteadily, she put her hand up, reaching out.

McCruise froze when she slipped slowly to the floor like a disembodied specter.

CHAPTER SEVENTY

"My God, Jacquie," he groaned. Carrying her inside to her suite, McCruise felt as if he were carrying a rag doll. She was down for the count, pale and ashen. Her pulse slipped down to the low fifties.

He dialed zero.

"I have an emergency in Suite 417. Make it right away," he said, his voice husky.

Carrying a dampened washcloth to the bed, he noted sweat beads on Jacquie's forehead. "C'mon, Jacquie, don't do this to me." Gently, he cupped her face in both hands.

A soft tap on the door sounded like a battering ram to McCruise's heightened senses. He smoothed his fingers through her curls, drawing outwards, tenderly watching as they sprung back to encircle her face before he took long strides to open the door.

His hair graying elegantly, a man of about Connor's age and height stood before him, dressed in a charcoal, pinstripe suit. Intelligent eyes observed McCruise from behind heavily rimmed glasses.

"I'm Dr. Brooker, resident physician for the complex this weekend. I understand you're having a problem." There was warmth in his eyes as he stood on ceremony, politely waiting for McCruise to respond, which added a plus to McCruise's quick-assessment.

"Yes. Come in. My, er, wife fainted. I have no idea what precipitated it, maybe something she ate?" He knew he was talking mumble-jumble, leading the doctor to Jacquie's suite where she laid on top the bedspread, moving slightly and making soft sounds.

"Oh, I'm sorry. My name is Cruise, McCruise Cruise." He extended his hand, which the doctor shook firmly as they advanced to the bedside. McCruise never felt less in charge as his gaze raked Jacquie's face with an assessment intended to produce a read-out.

He easily translated Brooker, his head slightly slanted, viewing the woman before him as a magazine cover model.

"Pulse is normalizing rapidly." The doctor spoke softly, leaning over the patient, his fingers on her wrist. "Eyes are re-focusing, breathing labored," he continued as if to himself. "Hello there, Mrs. Cruise. I'm Dr. Brooker," he said loudly.

McCruise stood near the bed meditatively, hands behind his back. His strong rugged jaw flexed with a clench of his teeth, making the fine lines of his nose more prevalent and his stance as imperious as a defensive back again.

"You hit a bit of a bad patch," Brooker conveyed, his voice exuding confidence.

Jacquie shifted her eyes foggily to McCruise. Instantly, the anxiety in her eyes disappeared as if she connected the McCruise-dot to the doctor-dot and found peace.

Brooker took out his stethoscope to listen to her lungs, concerned over her labored breathing—healthy heart, lungs clear. He sighed more easily. "Do you feel nauseated, Mrs. Cruise?" His eyebrows rose.

Jacquie nodded, as if a foggy distance shrouded her thoughts. Eyes fluttering, she was slipping back into oblivion.

Brooker's hand reached out to encompass her wrist, finding a slowing pulse again. He spoke loudly. "Mrs. Cruise, are you tired?" His voice hung sharp in the still evening air.

She nodded, and then her eyes closed. A blush crept into her cheeks. Dr. Brooker was aware of what went on in hotels when visitors were on holidays and getaway trysts—

strange happenings. She appeared worn out and showed all the observable signs.

McCruise stood on the other side of the bed, wavering, wanting to help, but feeling numb. He'd demanded too much of her, of her energy reserves. Reminding him of her small stature and lower stamina levels, he felt a compulsion to wrap her in his arms, keep her warm.

Dr. Brooker cleared his throat as silence hung in delicate balance. "Mrs. Cruise, when was your last monthly menses?" He asked with marked insight, and no compunction whatsoever.

She paled, an uneasiness playing on her countenance, her eyes becoming hollow and frantic, causing Brooker to check her wrists again. This woman lay webbed in something weighty, her silence speaking succinctly of dread anticipation.

Jacquie's eyes welled over with tears. When she calmed herself enough to speak coherently, her lashes lowered. Covering her face with her hands, she confessed, ever so quietly, "August 16th." She wept in palpable desolation.

Brooker coolly cut his glance to McCruise, his brow raised with a mixture of empathy and amusement. No one needed to tell him this was a tryst, and this young woman was terrified of her condition. Why she was terrified was none of his business, but she obviously needed some rest. He chose to hang with the ruse.

"Mr. Cruise, I'd say your wife is close to two months pregnant and needs to take it easy—needs more regular hours, needs a regimen of balanced diet and vitamin supplements." His eyes transmitted firmness, yet reassurance and respect.

McCruise reeled with the revelation, but realized that he stood raked over the coals with no declarable defenses. He'd won the Power Ball! Nonetheless, he couldn't share it with Brooker.

The sharpness leaving his voice, Dr. Brooker allowed sentiment to surface over professionalism. Managing his material back into his bag, he leaned over the bed. "Congratulations Mrs. Cruise." There was an intense amount of goodwill in the simple words. "And to you, sir," he said, rising and shaking McCruise's hand.

He picked up his bag and adjusted his glasses by the heavy rims. "I'm leaving you a sedative to take before bedtime, Mrs. Cruise. It'll assure you a peaceful night's sleep." He patted her hand.

"You'll feel better in the morning, I'm sure."

CHAPTER SEVENTY-ONE

McCruise spun, speechless, in a dichotomy of ecstasy and agony because Jacquie never shared this sacrosanct secret with him. He wasn't accustomed to dawdling in the dark about such things. *He* was in control. News such as this needed no concealment from someone you supposedly love.

Uh-huh. *That's* the unreachable niche. *That* was the reason for his parallel thoughts while caressing her breasts; they swelled as Laura's did with Mark and Luke. The realization grieved him. It was one thing to be a good lover; it was quite another thing to be a blind fool.

Walking back into her bedroom after showing the doctor out, McCruise found she'd not moved. Her hands clenched at her sides. Silently, he sat down next to her, took a taut fist, pried it open, and kissed inside the pocket, then kissed her fingers one by one.

"Jacquie," he whispered tightly, bending forward, holding her hand. "Do you know how happy I am?" His voice sounded like a swinging, weathered sign shifting in the wind. He was a Mt. Olympus god, a very privileged one. He felt the fulfillment of being a man, her husband, and his eyes showed dark with pride. He'd taken the ball over the goal line after intercepting a pass.

"Why didn't you tell me? I would have been more careful, considerate of your delicate condition. I did not have an idea you were pregnant with my baby, my son." His heart swelled in his chest. His eyes teared over. "In view of this, you'll want to settle under my roof and set a wedding date." He murmured the words over her, eyes intent, sweeping her face.

She hardened herself against the tremendous look of honest pride and possession that his eyes revealed. Silence was tactile as she stared upwards at a blank ceiling, as blank as she wanted her womb. *Why is it,* she wondered, *that things such as this only happen at the very worst of times, when it's terribly inconvenient.* She acknowledged a very sophomoric job of handling this whole situation.

Her voice thin, Jacquie laid it on the line. "There will be no child, McCruise. I'm going to have an abortion. That's why I haven't told you." Her hand in his shook in the telling. Her Havasu blues held his. "I'm sorry if the decision doesn't meet your expectations, but I've never deceived you about this. I don't want to have children." Her voice lacked energy, cold with a hint of bitterness. "It's unfortunate that I was caught in conditions disallowing proper measures for prevention, and I've been stonewalling the abortion. You might call the procrastination a denial. Unwanted pregnancies don't happen to informed women such as me."

She did not explain enough. Maybe there weren't enough words to deny a man his child. But it was her body, and she wasn't about to become an incubator for someone else's higher honor and glory, no matter how much she loved him—him and the brood of children he anticipated creating. She offered him a weak smile when she saw his fine face dumbfounded beyond recognition with disenchantment.

McCruise thought he was going to have to put a bag over his head to breathe. "What are you saying, woman? Have you lost your mind?" There was a pitched sharpness of incredulity in his tone, unhidden and unbidden. "You can't abort my child!" He stammered with indescribable bafflement. "I disallow it." His eyes shone fathomless, trying to waylay her strong message. He felt as if they were moving elliptically around each other in a private solar system, almost touching before she swung away again in her own off-center orbit.

"This is what I've wanted all along—my child, your child. Don't you see how beautiful he'll be? You're messing with the traditions of nature."

His breathing was raw. "I'll give you anything, Jacquie. Do you want me to transport Duluth to Lake Havasu and make it part of our city? I'll do it. Do you want me to lasso the Spaceship Mir and put it under the Christmas tree? I'll do that. But you can't abort our child." His voice cracked with the ambivalence of emotions sweeping through him; the delight of another child—the abortion of another child.

"No, McCruise. I'm very definite about this. There will be no child." Her chin came up firmly. Her eyes lost expression.

Shaking his head in total rejection, he rubbed the stiffness growing in the back of his neck. "There *will* be a child. You have no choice. It's my child. You shall carry it. You shall give birth and breast feed our son." He splayed his hands, fending off doubt. "It's mine." His eyes held hers with gravity.

Her teeth were becoming sore from unconsciously clenching them. The temper of her Irish ancestors came into play. "Have a second thought, McCruise. I'm the designated decision-maker in my life. It's not going to happen." She turned her head to him with firm validation.

McCruise flared. He'd known few times when he'd been more out of control. "You... you," he stammered, searching for adequate words. "You certainly know how to show a man some quirky twists."

He knifed both his hands through the air. "No baby, no marriage." His emotions tangled violently: insult, injury, anger, disillusionment, and fear. "You can't do this to me. It's outrageous to have a perfectly normal child torn from your body. It's sacrilegious and contradictory to... to womanhood. In addition, it's blight on my manhood." His baritone voice cracked. "I want no part of a woman who can't see her way to bringing children into the world."

He couldn't rationalize living the rest of his life with a creature of such wanton values, a woman who could take him to indescribable heights only to sink him into the dungeon of the devil incarnate. There grew a sandy lump in his throat; fright stole into his heart to meld with sorrow.

Jacquie was becoming disturbingly unhappy with his insistence on the one and only solution to this enigma: *bear the child.* Her eyes glittered with determination; she lifted her left hand, looking at two karats of diamonds and rubies. Did the gems mean this? To knuckle under to his every demand? She didn't think so. Yet, with her immediate decision, she swallowed against the jawbreaker in her throat.

"Have it your way," she snapped, taking off his ring and letting it slide between her fingers onto the nightstand as if she were sifting beach sand. "I don't particularly give a damn. I cannot in all good conscience accept such a valuable token of your love when I'm rejecting what you really want—a child." Her energy ebbing, she spoke softly. "I'm not a brood hen, and I don't ever intend to be." Her eyes swept his face, glowering in their intensity.

It must be this way. Norwood wove her so deeply ensconced in his plan to rule the world, she feared for McCruise's life, as well as her own. She needed to distance herself, for his protection. A child would clutter her life, which was in total chaos. The complexity of chaos she found disconcerting and frazzled like the snapping ends of an old rope.

It would be dishonorable to relegate McCruise to some shelf space in her life where she, at her convenience, could take him out for idle time. He was too wonderful, too manly, and too straight ever to realize how deeply she waded in demise of more than 20,000 people in Sri Lanka. How deeply she swam in the surge that Shoney was conscienceless and despicable, perhaps even insane. His inhumanity to humankind was as certain as sunrise.

Faintly, she heard McCruise curse garishly, his lips moving like a ventriloquist.

His cold fury stood heated, ready to implode. His ire at her unreasonableness devoured him. The woman was on the other side of the street from being what he wanted in a wife, darkly incomprehensible. He knew he must leave the room, knew he needed to make his exit before more was said. Besides, his whole body was shaking with disappointment at the duplicity of her character.

He sucked in his breath and felt as cold as stone as he bent over and picked up the yet-warm ring, rolling it in the palm of his hand, re-living the excitement he'd built into the presentation and her acceptance. How long ago? A hundred years? The ring he so proudly slipped onto her finger, sealed with their salivation. He took a deep breath, his curved lips becoming a thin line. Never did he think he could be so far off base in judging character. Jacquie was a woman of ineffable mystery. Abortion was downright reprehensible!

He carefully cloistered his expression to vacant as he left her there, striding from the room without pause.

CHAPTER SEVENTY-TWO

The jangling of the telephone was incessant, bolting McCruise upright. Where in the hell was he? In Phoenix! His sleepy hands wrestled with the bedside phone.

"McCruise?"

"Yeah," he said thickly, sleep clinging.

"Connor."

"What the hell..."

"Sorry to bother you, but."

"Yeah?"

"Wally was—we lost Wally tonight."

"Lost? Wally?"

"Yeah, shot to death."

"What the hell—Jesus, Jesus, Jesus, Connor. Shot?" McCruise was spiraling dizzily.

"On Channel Patrol with Cleavus." Connor's voice was flat.

Jump-start awake, McCruise tried to control the flip-flop spasm in his chest. It was inconceivable. "Good God, Connor," his voice cracked. "What kind of barbarism are we dealing with here?" Icy fingers tightened his rib cage as the full impact of the message hit him.

"What time did it happen?"

"Shortly after 10:00 PM."

"How?"

"A high-powered rifle."

"Goddamn!"

"He was shot about half way to Rotary Park, under the light of a street lamp."

McCruise sucked for breath.

"He took a direct hit to the head—never knew what hit him."

"Bastards!"

"More than."

"How's Cleavus?"

"Reduced to putty." Connor's anguish filtered through the line.

McCruise imagined Cleavus's expressive brown eyes silhouetted against the night by the overhead lighting. He began to sweat.

"What time's your flight tomorrow?" Connor continued

"We leave at eight-twenty, putting us back in Havasu about nine fifteen. I'll see you as soon as I deliver Jacquie to her condominium." McCruise's stomach burned with renewed angst of her threatened abortion.

"Bring her along. She can visit with Marvel while we speak in the den." Connor brightened somewhat.

"That's not such a good idea, Connor. We've been quarreling." It was difficult for McCruise to say the words. Words weren't enough.

"Well, that's absolutely desolate! These two days were for cementing your relationship, not relenting of it. I'm so sorry." He made a disgruntled sound. "First Wally, and now you say..."

"Yeah, nothing will ever be the same, and what'll I do without Wally? He's saved my ass a dozen times—become my second self."

"Take it easy, McCruise."

"Goddamn, life *can* get desolate."

"Yeah." He closed with barely perceptible delivery.

The loss hitting McCruise was immeasurable. In the stillness present to pre-dawn, he paced, checked on Jacquie, and found her looking innocently angelic in repose, his child snuggled in the warm cocoon of her belly. He thought he was going to be sick. His heart tugged as if someone shot a hole in it. Slowly, he ran his fingers through his thick hair, as if the act could keep his head on straight.

Returning to the lanai, he lowered himself onto a chaise, his whole life sagging, intolerably bent. Simultaneously, the early-morning sprinkler system activated. The *shusha-shusha* of the water spread through the air, then onto the lush grass; it was like a rhythmic orchestration of his thoughts.

Knitting his fingers behind his head, he stared unseeingly into the eerie dawn's illumination, silhouetting the Superstition Mountains. Worse than accepting Wally's death was his own failure to have been there. Through the best of times, through the worst of times, Wally was his anchor—*always* been there for him. His death was hanging tangibly, but irrationally; such evil endings only shouted in newspapers.

He filtered through information. Shot dead in Rotary Park—should have been *him*! The thought struck him like a hammer blow. His mouth grimaced into a straight line, almost disappearing. Who ever did it knew—knew that he and Wally worked the channel and suspected they knew too much.

He sat lost in a world he no longer understood or cared to understand. A police officer bartered his brain and body to a governmental agency; he took an oath to protect and preserve—preserve what? Being a law enforcement officer was akin to partaking in and planning one's own execution.

From somewhere far off in the night, Matthew Cameron Cruise heard going-away train whistles. The sound hung in the air endlessly, doing a slow fade, like his life. A wash of friendship crushed him. Wally'd bailed him out again, and he'd never see the day he and Karla adopted a baby. Wally would never hear the sound of little feet in his house. He'd never again visit in the evening and listen to McCruise's trumpet solos in which Wally soaked the notes to the exclusion of place or space. "Stardust" and "Sleepy Lagoon," old Harry James songs touched Wally's places of reverie.

Absently, he snapped a fingernail against a flower vase on the end table. Was it worth a life to maintain a banner city? He knew he must fight this feeling of wanting to trade a death for death. He scoffed. It was worse, even worse. He was thinking of exchanging the torture he was feeling with a similar torture for his torturer. McCruise's jaws locked on the bitter blade of grief.

He didn't feel this abandoned and alone since Laura died—fragmented in a burning hell. The image of the carnage returned to him repeatedly, at the strangest moments. Part of him would always sting as resultant of losing her. He'd been so close to finding heaven again with Jacquie, only to have it crumble in two minutes like a parchment dream. A snort escaped his mouth.

He was unable to bear her demands of no children and aborting the one on the way. And she never told him! He shuddered. A deep, primitive sound rolled from his throat. What an ass he'd been! A gullible ploy! She'd doled herself out in snippets and pieces. Unconsciously, he realized he was holding his breath as thoughts cascaded with great clarity. McCruise knew he'd leave Phoenix with his heart wrapped tighter than when he'd arrived, and wiser for the experience.

The pearlescent pink of morning leaked color into his life as if shedding promise. He'd get a grip. He could go to the bank on the fact that he was a textbook case if he could dig into people's souls and know of the deep scars they carried there. No one's immune. Except Wally. He gave his heart unconditionally to Karla, and she to him. He felt tears sting the back of his eyes. Not a crack of his emotions would show through again, except for Wally; his admiration for Wally would always surface.

During moments alone, he'd turn to his trumpet for solace. The golden instrument moved him through some bad times, blending his brain into oblivion. The haunting sounds produced imparted to him memories of companionship, dependability, warmth, and time passages.

McCruise felt a lump rooting in his throat. The tears burned and boiled over, unbidden. Giving them full rein, he wept with great sobs.

CHAPTER SEVENTY-THREE

It was mid-morning before McCruise arrived at O'Shaughnessey's home. Warm, dry air indicated that the Monsoon season was in the discard.

"C'mon in, McCruise. Welcome back from the frantic Phoenix freeways." The indentations around Connor's mouth waxed deeply engraved.

In the foyer, McCruise stood, wearing gloom and doom and a Ralph Lauren navy sport coat and light blue, open-collared ivy-league shirt. His eyes traveled to an oil reproduction of Rembrandt's *Seascape of the Apostles' Fishing Boat on a Turbulent Sea*, the froth flying in their faces. It reminded him of his own psyche, tossed in an inconsolable sea of doubt.

"Welcome back, McCruise." Cleavus's voice fell into the conversation from the doorway of the den. His voice was flat, his smile never reaching his eyes.

"Cleavus," McCruise breathed barely above a whisper, taking long strides to capture his hand, embrace him. His African-American black hair and black eyes were window-dressing for an opaque nightmare that read, "Closed for Business."

"Come, sit in the den." Connor's voice was gentle and modulated, gesturing for them to take the leather guest chairs in front of his desk. The commiserating tone of his voice was like a hand on the shoulder to both men.

"None of us knew much sleep, but I need to piece things together." Connor's voice was vibrant, yet anguished. "The forensics people found what was left of the bullet. I'm waiting for a call on caliber, make, and trajectory." He ran his thumb over his chin, looking down. "I wonder if we could impose upon you, Cleavus, to pull some ends together on events leading up to the shooting." There was no misinterpreting the thick grief in Connor's mien, easing Cleavus out of his silence.

Struggling as time stood still for an eternity, Cleavus's rugged profile strengthened; he moved his hands over the stubble of his unshaven chin.

"As you know, the Budweiser Mohave Unlimited Hydrofest Championships are being held here this weekend." The intensity in Cleavus's voice strained every word. "In honor of the event, the King's Retreat put on a fireworks display over Bridgewater Channel with sound decibels off the charts, so we decided it was a good time to check out Rotary Park and save our ears. It was about nine-thirty.

"Crowds estimated at twenty thousand were out along the lake and the channel, with boats moored all over the place," he said, making a sweeping gesture. "The fireworks burned more than its share of thunderous boomers, crackers, and orange sky bursts fluttering downward." His breath double-clutched with what yet was forthcoming.

"We were approaching the big curve in the sidewalk leading around the Queen's Bay Golf Course. I'm telling Wally a joke, when I hear *crack-splat*, a sound I'll never forget. Wally fell forward on the sidewalk without as much as a grunt, his hands twitching slightly, his foot jerking, and then he lay still. It was beyond comprehension." Cleavus shuddered. His lips softened, worked.

"Instinct split through me like ice shards. I did an instant pitch and roll into the shadows, pulling my weapon and panning from left to right. All was normal. A group of girls coming down the sidewalk started screaming. I picked myself up and holstered my gun. The girls screamed louder, staring at me as if I was the cop from hell. What the... I asked, feeling all over myself. I was, was... full of Wally's stuff. Spattered."

Cleavus's respiration picked up, re-living the moment with a choking sound. "I could hardly breathe." He spoke in an evocative tone. "My knees were rubber, my heart bursting out of my chest. My senses smelled the night, my own fear, blood, bone, tissue, mown grass from the golf course. Wally surrounded me like an early morning mist, as if I could gather it together and re-cell him." Choking on a sob, he went on. "It was as if I could change the structure of time and space and put Wally back together as he was a few minutes before." He pulled a handkerchief from his back pocket, swiped his eyes—eyes hardened like ice in a fjord.

"My stomach was coiled so tight, I danced around in a circle for thirty seconds, looking like an Indian shaman, all the while leaning my head into my mic shouting for backup. I wanted Wally's stuff off me. It was like a snake pit."

Connor nodded in encouragement.

"The EMT's were there in minutes, the fire engine belching throaty 'Yield' messages, while Wally's life-blood rolled down the sidewalk as if it were trying to stay between the lines." Cleavus's voice deepened at re-structuring the event.

The silence of the room thick, McCruise looked away, feeling his stomach kicking sour. This was battlefield stuff— gray-faced, open-mouthed devastation.

Cleavus leaned forward, resting his elbows on his widespread knees, cupping one hand within the other, holding himself together. "The booms, cracks, and falling orange sizzlers continued dazzling the night sky as if nothing happened, as if a life wasn't snuffed out in two seconds."

Raw emotion was electric, rampant in the room.

"I wanted to stomp and holler with the torment and tell everyone to go home, be still, and have some reverence." When his control broke, he hedged. Barren of control, tears rolled down his cheeks.

Why couldn't McCruise do something to ease Cleavus's pain? He sat stricken dry-mouthed by the telling, hence embarrassed. He'd not be able to navigate the distance; his knees were like pipe cleaners.

Squaring his shoulders, Cleavus's voice hardened. "I looked at my watch. Isn't that unconscionable?" His shoulders shook with a sob. "I looked at my goddamn watch!" His voice cracked. "It was nine fifty-four p.m. — so elementary." He shrugged, and then leaned back.

In the eight months McCruise worked closely with Cleavus, he'd recognized his strengths, his human foibles, but never did he see him so defeated. Anger and grief scoured his throat; bitterness crept into his mouth. McCruise found the strength to rise — rise as if he tacked together with spreader fasteners — and moved to Cleavus, where he massaged his shoulders, ever so slowly, himself teetering on the brink of a breakdown.

With a touch of empathy, Cleavus's shoulders shook. He wept as if every nerve in his body sprung loose like fibers from brittle cordage. The heat of Cleavus's ravagement McCruise felt through his shirt, ravaged as the Spanish moss-covered pines of Cleavus's Georgia youth.

"I can't take these offenses against humanity any longer." The words came out, slurred through swollen lips. The urgency of his plight reflected in his eyes, in his voice. The opaque shutters came down again with unspeakable finality. For survival, he retreated once more into an impenetrable hell.

Connor's mouth tightened balefully. These were his men — good men, dedicated men — sacrificed to mad dogs. An icy coldness glazed his eyes, feeling close to despair at the scandalous culture into which they lay ensnared. He'd received word yesterday of the positive identification of Valesano by Sri Lankan authorities. His body lay among those of dead animals trapped in the tubing leading to the clarifier at the Colombo Wastewater Treatment Plant. Things were adding up. Trouble was, it took months to get asses moving, puzzle pieces that fit together.

"Cleavus, I'm seeking an administrative leave from your superiors in Phoenix, time for your convalescence and counseling." His voice cracked with the difficulty of trying to stay relentlessly upbeat in the face of tragedy and dealing with waste-of-space assholes.

The shrill ringing of the telephone interrupted the silence in the room.

CHAPTER SEVENTY-FOUR

"Yeah." Connor grunted into the phone, listening. "It's the lab," he said quietly, holding his hand over the mouthpiece.

"You gotta be mucking my mind! What an egregious error on their part! What's the distance?" Pause. "Keep me posted." He hung up, his dark eyes intense with disgust.

His gaze rode steadily on the men. "We-ell, we've just spun some ballistic jurisprudence," each word ejecting articulately. "The bullet was hollow core, for ultimate damage. It appears it came from a Heckler and Koch, long-range rifle PSGI, .300 caliber. The lab techs tell me this particular rifle can accept a twenty-round magazine and is effective for a range of up to a half mile. The effort could have downed an elephant." He slapped his hand futilely on the desk repeatedly.

"The bullet entered Wally's brain and fragmented. The manner in which the bullet struck gives us information that it fired from a trajectory of at least forty/forty-five degrees, which puts the expert shooter on a plane of elevation not known in that landscape. Except... " he paused, his eyes traveling between Cleavus and McCruise.

"Except the King's Retreat!" Leaning forward as if propelled, Cleavus patently exploded, his eyes red-rimmed. He turned fully to face McCruise. "Remember the gun collection you told me about? The one you saw in Shoney's penthouse over the fireplace?" The words rushed out over puffed lips.

"Right. Wally and I wondered where he hunted big game."

"Why didn't you arrest Shoney that very day?" Cleavus said with difficulty, indentations on either side of his mouth, which was set in a grim look of incredulity.

The paralyzing words prompted McCruise to look away, knowing evidence of this genre was not, at that time, germane to their investigation. Being a student of human nature, McCruise knew Cleavus was drawing at straws with rhetoric peculiar to hindsight. Nonetheless, the utterance tore at McCruise's insides, leaving him hollow.

Like vapor in a rain forest, the discomfort level in the room was heavy. Outside, the morning sun streamed in through the window verticals, casting light on intermittent dust motes swimming in an everlasting tidal stream of flux.

Tears sprung from Cleavus, unabashed, as if someone opened the spill gates at Boulder Dam. "I'm sorry, but my mind is full of *what ifs*. Besides, the bullet was meant for *you*, McCruise." His breathing was ragged. "I'm so friggin' glad to see you sitting here, and so sad to have lost an officer, that I'm wound tight, gripped with guilt. Absolutely nothing I rationalize speaks to the pain and guilt. I acted impulsively when I suggested checking out Rotary Park instead of the bullshit under the bridge." His forehead creased in clinging remorse.

Connor cut a reeling look at McCruise, hastily arose, and sat on the corner of his desk, his glasses swinging from two fingers. "Cleavus, you have nothing to feel guilty about." His voice was guttural with outrage. "Rotary Park was part of your assignment. What's more, I have a devil of a gut feeling that did you not reacted immediately by diving into the available darkness for cover, you'd have been next. This hasn't exactly been a soirée for you. I can't even promise you'll ever forget the malice of it, but the pain goes away, and the guilt, and what's left is a measure of pride in how you handled an impossible situation." His emotional nakedness burned the words into the very air.

Pale and wobbly, Cleavus blinked with the promise of Connor's philosophy. Grasping the arms of the chair, he stared fixedly at the bubbly Berber carpeting.

McCruise empathized, but could eke small consolation from the kind words. Cleavus always felt formidable and indestructible while carrying his DEA identification. Now there was this. All the good stuff, all the pride and prestige he'd felt in his chosen profession disintegrated, along with Wally's head.

"You'll have a month off to scare up decent thoughts, a month to assimilate values," Connor consoled.

Thoughtfully, Cleavus steepled his fingers and tapped them rhythmically together. "Very often, when things become unsettled, I dwell on my home in Georgia and find peace of mind. The only thing tougher than Mama's ambition for me was the steak that I burned on the charcoal, but a guy doesn't have to be a good cook to be a good cop."

McCruise and Connor laughed—a raw, hoarse sound— at Cleavus's attempt at levity.

Again seated in his chair, McCruise moved uncomfortably, folding his hands over his lap, staring at his thumbs, speaking hard words into soft air, his tone guarded. "So it seems that within hours or days we can pin a murder rap on Shoney?" It was an unstable habit of his to be quickly analytical, drawing a bottom line. "That should earn him the sleeping needle," he said, his exhilaration difficult to contain.

"Yeah," Cleavus said, showing some awakening from his pathos.

"What bothers me," Connor said as he tapped his knee with a pencil, "is that Shoney's never been top dog; he's always been the gopher. Unsuccessful in actually connecting him with anything, I'd like to be able to nail him with the narc trafficking. Then, we can consider Laura's murder and Wally's murder. Add to that the murder of the poor construction worker who fell with the crumbled scaffolding, the murder by association of that pitiful child at the hotel, the slaughter of the elderly man and his dog at Cherry Tree Drive and God only knows, he may have killed Jaimie and made it look like a cartel knockoff." Connor did a quick take on McCruise.

"The pathology reports are in on Jaimie. He died of asphyxiation by choking, and his DNA matches the fingernail shreddings from the fourteen-year-old's body. He's unfortunate history; his body has been shipped back to his homeland." The words rolled ruthlessly unrepentant.

"He who lives by the sword." McCruise murmured.

Connor nodded. "We need to catch Shoney red-handed, and we'll do it. After putting fresh cheese in the trap last weekend, and the bait taken, it looks as if it's a safe bet they'll throw further caution to the wind and move big time this weekend. If not, we'll still have enough *prima facie* evidence to present to a grand jury."

Were they moving through the wrong maze? There counted six homicides—maybe seven, if he counted the identification of Valesano. A guy's mind can be up to some strange shit when doubt filters in, adding a new dimension of lateral concerns such as the analyzation of the traces of tea leaves found in the narc warehouse. They were highly refined Sri Lankan green tea.

Did the new thoughts meld with the old? Did they connect at all?

The trailings of this investigation didn't yet pass this smell test, and were as unwelcome as a diamondback rattler dozing on your doorstep.

CHAPTER SEVENTY-FIVE

Without a semblance of wind, this October Sunday morning was clear and cloudless. The sky, an inverted blue-glazed bowl, poured out hot but pleasant distils. The sounds of under-accelerated car mufflers drifted in the dry air as vehicles moved quietly from parking spots into the great circle driveway of the King's Retreat, small stones churning quietly under tires.

Sligh Ignatius Shoney rose smoothly from behind his desk, luxuriating in the flawless weather. Arrogantly, he glanced around his office and deeply breathed in the fragrance of the daisy and carnation arrangement Mallika Chilaw placed on the credenza.

The flowers were smart, just as he was smart—smarter than anyone else he'd ever known. He preened at the way he'd carried off the wasting of at least one of the nincompoop cops who'd interfered with his life. The gullible Tamil, Rama Adasa, and Chicken Valesano were a cinch, also. Killing killers was rewarding. An electric groin-tingle hit him.

Valesano and Adasa did a hell of a job on the wastewater treatment plants, resulting in positive and final negotiations with Global Technologies. He'd never have to worry again about supply, and demand grew every day, especially with kids. An amused chuckle escaped his skinned grin.

Still prominent on the television news were reports of the yet-growing death toll attributable to the unspeakable catastrophes in Sri Lanka, resultant of typhoid, burn victims, and chlorine poisoning. Who cared about a fuckin' bunch of third-world yahoos who couldn't as much as get along in their own country—killed each other off more often than not, okay?

Approaching a wall cabinet, Shoney removed a Heckler & Koch rifle. The weapon's long stock he broke down, leaving a pistol grip and a tall carrying handle on the top of which were sighting capabilities. He knew it as a comfortable companion, accurate within hundreds of yards. The rifle boasted a polymer cast made of numerous natural and synthetic compounds of unusually high molecular weight, consisting of up to millions of repeated linked units, each a relatively light and simple molecule. The shell injection and rejection component was lightweight metal, the barrel sleek and deadly looking.

The H & K was functional, portable, and accurate to a fault. It used twenty-round clips, and the clip that Shoney pushed into the rifle last night carried hollow-core bullets that mushroomed, even upon soft contact. With a felt cloth, he polished and stroked the firearm as if in a state of worship.

Ricki Rodriguez stood near the office door in abeyance, ensnared by the hypnotism of Shoney making love to his gun, while Vivaldi made love to his *Viola d'amour* on the Bose sound system. Ricki studied the fine piece of equipment in breathless silence, his coveting eyes darting from the gun to Shoney.

Observing how Shoney handled the gun as if it were a cherished woman, Rodriguez reflected the joy Shoney felt at the touch of it. He knew on good source that Shoney was *un gran enchilada* under the blankets with señoras—anyone's señora. Shoney liked possessions, power, money, and women, and didn't have any scruples about how he went about obtaining any of them.

Sometimes, the gleam in Shoney's cold, ice blue eyes sometimes turned to pewter, and *whap!* Someone caught hell, or worse. He would not complain about it, however; his paychecks were always ample and on time.

"What the hell is money for?" Shoney would say with a thin grin. "It's like after-shave splash, isn't it? Only does well when you spread it around."

Rodriguez's knowledge of Shoney's business dealings was a mere chip-off-the-iceberg. He didn't really care to know the darkness below the surface. Mexican-born, Rodriguez arrived in Havasu illegally. Under the shelter of the King's Retreat, he'd obtained a green card, and finally, his citizenship. He was nobody's fool and knew from whence his bread and butter came. He numbered a dozen illegal Mexican nationals working for him, all loyal cohorts, even if it took months to get their asses moving. Nonetheless, he found it more advisable to obtain green cards and get work permits for them, lending a soft façade to his hard activities. Ricki viewed things mostly in black and white, and garnered no colors in his landscape to confuse issues, which were already insurmountable in his non-intellectual world. Startled by Shoney's quick deviation from caressing the gun, Rodriguez quickly took two steps backwards when Shoney heaved the firearm at him.

"Smooth curves, right?" Shoney shot him a lascivious look, grinning at the innuendo and releasing a guttural laugh. "It's as fine a piece of work as a woman's body; it can be manipulated, lubricated, injected, and triggered. It's a Heckler & Koch automatic. Sight-in out the window at that roadrunner way the hell over there by the Queen's Bay condominiums. It's accurate from a country mile and has a selector button. You may use one, three, or continuous bursts."

Sligh bloated with chest-thumping satisfaction to wave such a prohibitively expensive firearm in Rodriguez's face. He waited an up beat, feeling Rodriguez's caution. He was a perfect specimen for Sligh's intentions—taller than most Mexican nationalists, used the workout room faithfully, a diminutive Hercules, wearing a swagger and suave mustache. Not much upstairs, of course, but that particular deficit fit the bill of requirements.

Rodriguez reflected the look of zany enthusiasm in Shoney's eyes. It was downright scary sometimes to admit that Shoney always played hardball. He was a powerful and conscienceless dictator. It was abundantly clear that if Shoney made a single concession, Rodriguez would repay, squared. He was a whole marketplace for trickery and deceit—a master, chilling and nerve stretching.

The silence in the room overcame Rodriguez. "Yeah," he murmured, one eye squinting through the crosshairs and adjusting for visibility through the skeletal limbs of an ocotillo. "I can see that cocky bird as if he were standing right in this room." He lowered the rifle to swing his attention back to Shoney, getting a roguish shock at the reels of information passing behind Shoney's eyes as if he were on fast-forward. If stealth was an asset, Shoney was wealthy.

Nodding, Shoney pointed toward the corner by the drapes. "Stand it butt-end in the corner." His hands extended and fluttered like hummingbird wings. "Careful, careful now..."

With his back turned, Rodriguez rolled his eyes toward heaven. *Dios mio!* Perhaps he was getting a little tired of kowtowing to a *jefe plastico*, but he opted for a wan smile so as not to ruffle the feathers of this peacock-like plastic boss.

Preening, Shoney sat behind his desk, patting it with both hands. Staring out of lifeless shark eyes, he signaled impatiently for Rodriguez to sit down. "So tell me, Ricki. What's your take on the sudden death of Jaime Hernandez last month? Huh?" Shoney's iceberg eyes drilled the minion.

Ricki's hands flew into the air, his shoulders shrugged guardedly. "Damned if I know what kind of shit flowed down to that *gabacho*." His voice rose in a condition of mental distress. "No one knows anything. The work assignment, in code, of course, that I placed in his time-card slot was to bag the bulk cocaine into smaller containers." He sat, pale, and accused.

Shoney held his patience for a month, staring and observing, waiting for someone to crack, someone to run to him with the completely sordid story, but nothing. It rocked like a kick in the kidneys, not knowing.

With startling suddenness and completely out of character, Rodriguez took the offensive. "Hey, what's up with you, *compadre*?" The hassled Ricki came near shouting. "You know all the rest! An endless line of fuckin' cops, shaking me down, muscling my Mexicans. It's a bunch of bullshit."

"What do you *think* happened?" Shoney's eyes were arduous with imperial judgment.

"Jaimie crossed us, set up his own sales network, didn't deliver as advertised, and met his just desserts in the desert. *That's* what I think happened." Ricki held his ground.

"My incoming quantities have been greater than my outgoing weights for some time, but I've been letting out the rope, waiting for whoever was dipping into the cookie jar to hang them. I will not countenance thievery or blowing smoke up my ass from anyone. You hear?"

The tension between the two men was palpable, vibrations coming off it, with Rodriguez ostensibly branded as a suspect or at least close enough to feel the heat. Rodriguez listened, barely breathing.

"You know you can trust me, *jefe*." His voice trailed away.

Shoney was aware of the absence of subtleties in Ricki's persona. His passions were as evident as a blasting Havasu monsoon. He'd keep his own counsel, however, on the Jaimie matter.

CHAPTER SEVENTY-SIX

Shoney continued his interrogation of Ricki, spreading his hands. "Have any trouble removing the dust from the warehouse?" His tone was ebullient, his interest Teflon.

Ricki didn't need to tell him about the trouble-free time he encountered removing the dust from the warehouse, but when Shoney shifted to a good mood such as this, Ricki's reserves were down. His body melded comfortably into the lush comfort of the leather chair.

Ricki shook his head, his heavy black mustache moving smoothly over gleaming teeth. Rodriguez, while not a big man, moved like a muscled panther. No one crossed him. He wielded his authority with an iron fist, exactly as the iron fist ruled him. Shit flows downhill, and he knew it. He'd been with Shoney for six years, and he'd seen a lot of flowing shit. Mentally, he adjusted his attitude to guard; his eyes whisked over Shoney skeptically.

"*No hay problema! Sí!*"

"Don't slip into Spanish," Shoney spat with intolerance. "*Habla ingles!*" He couldn't resist crunching on someone while he embarrassed him or her, and it always worked on Ricki. Once he rattled Rodriguez, he knew he could get anything out of him.

Ricki's eyes lowered, disconcerted. "*No hay calamidad* from the warehouse?"

"You experienced *no troubles, mishaps.*" Stark lines worked Shoney's mouth.

"No troubles, in and out. We went up the river to the Refuge, as you directed. *Sí*, yes." He stroked his busy mustache with a knuckle.

"How many people?" Shoney already knew the number. It didn't mean a tinker's damn to him how many people played on the boat; besides, he was getting restless with this game of Twenty Questions.

"*Ocho*—eight," Ricki corrected. "There were four of my best men and four of my wildest women!" Ricki's eyes danced with the memories, laughing so impetuously he lowered his head between his knees.

"*Gracias*," he said, regaining his composure. "*Fue una barco buena!*" Ricki found it impossible to sustain English when he became excited. His eyes fixed on Shoney with a gold mine of readability.

"Say, 'It's a good boat!' Did your women cooperate with the help of the matchless dust?" Shoney's eyes were excited with lust; it was unfortunate he couldn't have afforded himself of this opportunity to prey lewdly on the obsequious Latin women—the kind of women he liked—without minds of their own, their eyes black, hiding their dead brains. Shoney became bloated like a toad with the thoughts; sweat ran inside his Jockeys. He ached.

Nevertheless, back to the plan at hand. "Well, it appears it is indeed safe to remove materials from the warehouse." Shoney spread his hands positively.

Ricki nodded in agreement.

"So this weekend we'll move it all upriver." He stared at Rodriguez, his eyes turning beady blue. "You and two others will enter the warehouse, say 4:00 AM Saturday, and pack everything for transport: life preserver rings, buoys, and life jackets." Shoney paused as Vivaldi picked up the pace with *gusto allegro*, usurping his senses.

"At least half the nautical material will be hidden below deck; the lesser quantity above deck is logical, if observed." Shoney folded his arms on the desk, leaning forward.

Ricki studied closely the tensing of Shoney's muscles, the electricity he conveyed at seeing the light at the end of the tunnel.

It was at moments such as this that Ricki sealed the togetherness of his coalition with Shoney, the lifting of the barriers in a common need. Their oftentimes-bellicose resentment disappeared in a boding together like Aunt Jemima syrup.

"Here's the sticky part." Shoney made a glugging sound in his throat, tasting victory and revenge over one Miss Jacaranda Rose Remington. His was the theory that *might makes right*. For eons, one civilization or another was eternally crushing another into submission, just as he would smash Jacaranda Rose Remington into a big nothing.

"Make sure you leave the lab materials intact. You are to leave a small amount of crack and methamphetamine clearly visible on the shelves. I have other plans for them." He drummed his fingers on the massive oak and inlay desk top, a Diablo smile creasing his cheeks at the thought of incriminating Jacquie as a distributor. She'd never see anything but bars for the rest of her quality years.

"We take only the big-money stuff. Do you understand?" Shoney sternly stiffened his arms on the desk and squared his shoulders.

A rapid heartbeat was visible in Ricki's throat. "*Sí! Jas!*" Such elementary instructions! What was he, some kind of plowboy?

"About two thirty Sunday morning you and your team will float the Witch Craft, the Warlock, and the two pontoon boats up to the shoring space in front of the Golden Crest. From there, you'll rush out with all the prepared articles for transport, get them up and over the sides of the boats, and quickly move on." He went back to thrumming the desk, his eyes dancing. "I'll be there, but incognito, in the hull of the Warlock. I'll go up river with you to Bullhead City— orders from the Grand Poobah."

Ricki observed a pick-up in Shoney's respiration. He was sweating fiercely, his eyes darkening. Sweet Jesus! The *comandante* was getting off his jollies, mulling the escape at the Golden Crest! Big chunks of money did that to Shoney.

A building shudder shook Shoney, his voice strained. He was struggling with his breathing, but regaining control, much to Ricki's relief. He'd be the one to pay if Shoney exploded in his chair and embarrassed himself; the blame game would flow down on Ricki's shoulders.

"You'll have a crew of six on the Warlock and the Witch Craft, and four each on the party boats. I want you on the Warlock. Understand?" Shoney's voice was thready, but securely riding the edge after the comedown. "Don't get over-eager and race upstream. You hear? You're to act as if you're on another party-time cruise, but don't use your running lights. Our reconnaissance is superior; it appears there'll be no interference from the duped dicks, so relax—enjoy the trip."

Ricki nodded, glancing up at Shoney from under shaded lids.

"From the inventory I have in my computer, I figure you can manifest forty life-preservers, forty lifejackets, and a dozen seventy-five-foot buoy lines compacted with meth, ecstasy, and crack. The party boats will carry half the inventory." His voice was brittle with the industrial-sized task he was levying upon these pint-sized pissants, because, in spite of Norwood's instructions, he did *not* intend to be on the Warlock or the Witch Craft for the chase upriver.

Shoney vacated his chair of authority, walked around to the side of the desk, and leaned on it. He held Ricki prisoner in his glance. "You're to take the entire shipment to the River Rat Ferry Dock in Bullhead City and unload it immediately. Another crew will be waiting to load the cargo onto a Ryder truck for instant transport to the airport, where it'll be airlifted by private evac."

Ricki nodded, his eyes unreadable for self-preservation, the information magnetizing fast to his memory tapes.

"Listen closely," Shoney said quietly. "This is important. The Warlock and the Witch Craft were specially built with high density metal to withstand ordnance of any kind and can get speeds of up to sixty knots." He inhaled deeply through his nose, straightening at the side of the desk. Shoney's aggravation ran from mind to hand, to his beautifully coifed hair. As he eased into his soft leather chair, he was fraught with frustration—the element of a weak link in his effectuation chain.

"*No hay ningún problema*," Ricki said, underwriting the project as a done deal.

"Evasions are the best policy, but spare nothing." Focus reflected in Shoney's voice. "Violence is acceptable." A consuming restlessness ate at him. "Never underestimate the persistence of your opponent."

For chrissake, Ricki reflected. *Shoney must think I can't tell the difference between a handshake and an Act of War.*

"All four watercraft will be armed with two Russian AK-47 Kalashnikov automatic rifles. They're a parallel to the familiar American M-16, clip-fed shoulder weapon. In addition, in the event you run into a multiple-manned force, you'll have an Israeli Uzi on board both the Warlock and the Witch Craft. By the time you dispose of the lightweight law enforcement on the river you'll be in Bullhead City, unloaded, and found clean."

Ricki flexed his fists in a show of anticipation, while his toes cowered in apprehension. Yet, a firm swell of pride ran through him with the promise of rewards.

Standing, Shoney's voice turned automaton, as if coming from the Tin Man of Oz, words ringing over his tongue. "Not a word of this to anyone until the eleventh hour. You'll dole out information in a need-to-know mode. You hear?" He pointed, straightened his suit jacket, and brushed the sleeve.

"*Sí.*" Rodriguez pushed to his feet, recognizing the sign of dismissal.

"You meet me here Wednesday morning, 7:00 AM. We'll drive to Standard Wash together for target practice. On second thought, choose three of your best men to come along also, in case..." Shoney rubbed his upper lip thoughtfully, troubled to think that Ricki and his cohorts might see picked off in the event of a skirmish, leaving no one to use the Uzis.

"Take the H & K with you, Ricki. You can have it. You deserve a cut above for your personal use." Shoney squeezed his lips back, admiring his prowess by passing on the ownership of a murder weapon.

Rodriguez never saw Shoney so intent and bloodless, as if Freon hydrocarbons ran in his veins. An icy chill ran through him.

Was someone walking on his grave?

CHAPTER SEVENTY-SEVEN

Shoney's eyes became fixed hypnotically on the glistening palms outside his window-on-the-world; swaying shadows danced on the walls in the late morning light. With Ricki gone, he slid his hands into his trouser pockets assuming a gluttonous pose of self-satisfaction. He rocked with the cleverness of his choreographing power. Dancing to Norwood's tune to waltz up the river with the gauchos, however, was not going to happen.

Last night's shooting was his semi-semi *coup de gras* before transferring to a new hotel in Miami Beach. His eyes glittered. Everyone and everything played into his hands.

In this city, no one was more powerful, more clever than he was, or anywhere in the *world* as he'd proven. Who else would have so cleverly manipulated two men from polarizing backgrounds to do his bidding in Sri Lanka? The sewer-sodden mess they pulled from the wastewater treatment plant clarifier inlet was an unidentifiable mass of clothes, exposed bones, and hanging flesh—Lieutenant Anthony Valesano of the Lake Havasu City Police Department.

Pulling strings on people who pirouetted for him with complete unawareness struck him as bulletproof. He stayed a loner to be this effective, to be this powerful. A man couldn't get too close to anyone and have the same effect.

Awe was what he wanted, awe and respect—and he'd have it, buy it, or kill for it.

Kill! That fucking McCruise was still alive! He'd been so confident he'd wasted him last night. No one fools around with Shoney in his eight-hundred-dollar Italian suits—but no one. McCruise asked for an early demise from the time he interfered with his relationship with Ms. Remington. Today's paper withheld the name of the officer shot and killed until notification of... all that bullshit. His toadies already informed him that Officer Wallace Denton got whacked, not McCruise. It burned his ass.

Did McCruise really think he could get away with breaking his nose, his arm? The dupe suffered from delusions! He laughed aloud, soothed with his ingenuity. His eyes looked like a slice of December ice blue. The stupid ass wasn't as dead as yesterday's beef cut, but he was as good as gone—hopelessly, irrevocably, mindlessly dead. He wiped his fingerprints clean on the rifle, added Rodriguez's, then gave the gun away, assuring himself of complete exoneration of the Denton wipeout. McCruise would get his, soon.

Besides—and this one made him crack up—he'd been entertaining last night. Entertaining in his penthouse where he'd shown Mallika an exotic time in his private hideaway. It wasn't the first time he'd entertained her, wasn't the first time he'd supplied her with party-time highs. Mallika, the epitome of correctness and aplomb, was no lady when he removed her Sri Lankan chignon, allowing her hair to fall around her shoulders. His lust knew no limitations.

Shoney's rotating CD table moved to Vivaldi's "Guittara Del Sol," the notes picking mystically, punctuating his thoughts, mesmerizing. A slow smile crept over his face. Mallika! He'd played Mallika like a fine guitar, sipped her like a sarsaparilla, and dined her like a duchess. His footsteps echoed through her life like a savior.

In his chair, he leaned back, lifting his chin and entwining his fingers at the back of his head. There was something naïve about Mallika Chilaw, but he liked that. Her mouth was generous, her figure was a knockout, and she was putty in his hands. There was no doubt in his mind that she was madly in love with him, and why not?

He was a portrait of success. Look what he offered: money, prestige, success, and testosterone unlimited. Women invariably turned around to look at him twice, and Mallika carried a keen awareness of the existence of this condition. It planted a blatantly hungry look in her eyes. Her need of him was addictive, and he fed it generously. Involuntarily, his shoulders hitched at the thought of her captivity; a wry smile underwrote his state of mind.

In addition, what better as an alibi? He'd invited Mallika to his penthouse Saturday night, where they hung on a few hits. In the spa, he sat naked with her, setting the jets to run seductively between her legs, where he periscoped with the bubbles. Only a few times he'd left to mix more cocktails while she luxuriated in the blossom-scented water.

Recalling how he'd timed the progress of the two police officers patrolling the Channel area, his eyes clouded over. A wince captured him, remembering how it took him by surprise to find them walking toward Rotary Park when he expected them to stay affixed to the esplanade during the fireworks. The change of venue was an opportunity offered by the Mount Olympian gods. Minutes, only minutes it took to get off a shot from his lanai, the rifle in a cupboard and in readiness. The thunderous sound offended his ears, but was lost in the pandemonium of the fireworks. What the fuck! The end justified the tormented ears.

It yet annoyed him because he didn't get off the next shot, the second officer reacting with disconcerting speed, disappearing into the campus area. Add those foolish girls who walked into the line of fire. What the hell! It was okay; he'd picked off his prime target, McCruise, who wouldn't have a Chinaman's chance in hell to survive the H & K.

It amused him to no end, getting back into the spa to find Mallika with her eyes closed dreamily. Still and all, after a running debate with himself, he'd have to eliminate her before he transferred to Miami Beach, and he sure as hell wasn't taking *her* with him. For the time being, however, she'd be his alibi for the investigation of the downed officer.

It niggled at his mind that Mallika, Asian-wise, was getting tired of his philandering with other women. He needed to do something to assuage her—maybe another trip to Brazil. An unfortunate offshore drowning in the rolling ocean surf should lick his life into shape. He'd handle the accident before Miami, and that would be the end of the Sri Lankan intern.

Shoney knew Fayne could care less. He'd gotten what he wanted from Shoney: shipping contacts for the mountainous share of cocaine awaiting conversion for street sales in lieu of pharmaceuticals. Shoney provided special condominiums for two major shipping lines: The Royal Dutch Liners registered out of the Port of Amsterdam, The Netherlands, and one out of the Port of the Republic of Singapore: Majestic Lines. Loading at Trincomalee, Sri Lanka, these major lines manifested sugar, rubber, tea, textiles, and hemp.

His nebulous plans finally came into sharp focus; *Sunday* would be his final *coup de gras*. Norwood would be the key player in his final thrust at retaliation for Jacquie's rejection of him. Norwood would wheedle a dinner with her for old time's sake. The sedative Norwood would put into her wine, into her food—it would make no difference to Sligh. Whatever worked to move her out to the elevators and up to his penthouse.

CHAPTER SEVENTY-EIGHT

Reluctantly, McCruise opened his eyes and looked at the clock. The grip of the day's awareness tightened its hold, and he rolled onto his side in an effort to escape consciousness for a moment longer, but he was wide-awake. What he felt was over-the-top anger, some kind of severe, electrical overload between his ears. A consoling thought rolled over him: perhaps Wally was with his little brother, Jeff, and his hard-working mother.

He lay there listening to night sounds; crickets sang and coyotes yapped in the dry stillness. Their wailing reminded McCruise of Wally's tutoring. "Coyotes rarely shadowed children and never adults until recently. As our city meanders into their bailiwick, they're bolder, more aggressive. Within the past few years, several adults in Lake Havasu City have reported seeing stalking coyotes, and even incidents of coyotes attacking. One followed a woman into her house and picked up her two-year-old, right in her own living room. Luckily the mother frightened the critter off the child with no harm done."

Now their humanistic cries ground into him, sounding like lost souls tormented by demons, the sound eerie and hollow on this, the day of Wally's funeral. Wally! If McCruise lived to be a hundred, quips and adages would return to visit. Like a bursting bedspring, the thought kicked in that this could have been the day of *his* funeral, not Wally's demise. Cold shivers stole down his spine at the depth of the thought; his children would be parentless, Jacquie forsaken, with his child growing in her womb, Penny and Coulter would grow older—alone, and Tucker would lie at the door, awaiting his return.

He rolled onto his back, staring vacantly at the shadowy ceiling. His life was as empty as his bed, coldly impersonal for almost a year. The only woman he'd invited to share it turned him down. There was a part of Jacquie that no one would ever own, an impenetrable nuclear core. A ripping feeling tore through his chest. How was he going to survive this grieving? It was as if Jacquie died, as well as Wally and Laura, as if he was on resuscitation, but not yet dead. His mouth set grimly. He was less of a person and more of a robot.

Laura, he'd never get over. Never would he forget her innocence, her wholesomeness, and her warmth. He thought he possessed renewed life after knowing Jacquie. He mulled on Pygmalion, the mythical king of Cyprus who carved his wife, Galatea, out of wood, bringing her to life via Aphrodite. Did he want a wooden puppet for a wife, bending and bowing to his every command? He thought not, but nonetheless...

Jacquie took him a long way into the land of companionship that only two people in love can know, can respect. "Love is patient and kind," said Mark in his gospels. He would try a gentler approach; maybe she'd do a turn-around toward children. Children! My God! He threw an arm over his forehead in a morass of gray. *Murdering his child*! The thought was so appalling it made his heart thud. How consoling it was, however, when Tucker jumped on his bed, licked his face, and whined soulfully for his beleaguered master. McCruise wrestled a hug.

After what they shared together, it was apparent that Jacquie loved him. No one could shut love off and on like buying and selling on the commodities market. He'd seen it in her eyes, felt it in her remarkable revealing responses, read it in her expressions. McCruise swallowed, his mind reeling with the stark realism of abortion and all it entailed. *The child would be a boy; his name would be John.*

It waxed a dreaded moment when Marvel and Connor needed to know his engagement to their daughter was *kaput, nada.* He wished he could be in the blur of a prize ASU victory, ice water pouring over his head.

****

"I don't understand this engagement cancellation at all, McCruise," Marvel said in a whispering tone, taking Cleavus's chair upon his early departure the day after Wally's shooting. "I've never seen two people more suited to each other—in education, in background, in religion, in temperament. She speaks often of Mark and Luke, and thinks they're so smart, so beautiful," she reminisced, her eyes filled with pain.

McCruise used all his powers of discipline to tell these fine people, in broad strokes, what caused the rift. He stood up and paced. The air hung expectantly while he poured coffee from Marvel's urn. He didn't want to cause a rift in the family; they were very unpredictable things: rifts, not going according to any rules. They were worse than pains or wounds; they grew and festered like splits in the skin that wouldn't heal because there wasn't enough material, or so F. Scott Fitzgerald professed, and McCruise devoutly believed.

Facing Connor and Marvel from the sideboard, holding the steaming cup, McCruise slipped one hand into his trouser pocket, his jacket flipping back.

"I really don't know if it's my place to tell you this," he said in his fine soft baritone, glancing down at the coffee, "but Jacquie is pregnant with my child."

Marvel gasped.

Connor sat forward.

"I've been pushing her to set a wedding date, but she blows it off as if it's an exercise in Hassle 101. In addition," he paused, a lump in his throat the size of a football, "she's going to abort it, doesn't want it, doesn't want any part of motherhood, and doesn't want any part of my child." His voice turned hollow; he sipped the consoling coffee to clamp his emotions.

As if in powerful torque, his shoulders moved an unidentifiable shrugging gesture. "Of course, you both know how I feel about children and abortion." He was nauseated, felt as if he were in some kind of an outrageous comedy of errors. His muscled stance fought to message his prevailing command.

Somber eyes turned upon him, melding together disappointment and disillusionment, yet visibly struggling to kindle some hope in their disbelief.

"I can't believe she'd be so callused about the child, McCruise." Slipping a quick glance at Connor, Marvel breathed more easily, catching a reassuring nod of his head.

McCruise watched Connor's gaze settle on him for a fleeting moment; in that moment he felt marginalized to his basic character and every indiscretion in his past was clear to the gazer. It was an unnerving experience.

"I'm damn sorry about these differences, McCruise. Damn sorry." Connor's voice was soft and mystified, but taut cords worked in his neck. "So you've called off the wedding?" His body waxed taut.

McCruise nodded silently. What a load off his mind, and these people were handling the situation with graciousness. He walked back to sit near Marvel. "I told her no child, no wedding; abortion has no place in my life. Her response was to return my ring."

If he wanted to attain simplicity, he succeeded. If he wanted to leave animosity out of his voice, he did, but he couldn't hide the hurt and cynicism he was feeling. He sheltered his eyes by staring down at his coffee. A vast hurt constricted his throat... *kill a child... his child.* It left him bereft. His mind's jury never was out on this issue.

Connor searched his face acquisitively, a dichotomy of anxiety and empathy asserting in lines around his eyes. "You know," he said quietly, leaning back in his chair and taking a quick shot of the ceiling, "it's always been my contention that a man is never taller than when he bends to touch a child's life. I've never known that chance. So I bend to touch the lives of all you preppies in the department, but it's nowhere near as fulfilling as reaching out and," he paused, his voice growing thick, "touching your own child's life."

A deep sigh exuded from his large frame. "I would never have figured Jacquie for such a decision. I'll have a talk with her." Scrubbing his hand over his face, he turned his attention to Marvel, his eyes soft, but screaming with disappointment. A helpless gesture, he ran his fingers over his mustache.

Marvel leaned over with an angelic glow in her eyes and folded her hand over McCruise's wrist. "I know her refusal of marriage isn't because she doesn't love you, McCruise. She must be panicky, no longer having the luxury of time." An overriding fury seized her countenance as if suddenly conjuring up the image of her own grandchild torn into pieces—by choice, no less!

CHAPTER SEVENTY-NINE

McCruise roused himself from the reverie of last Sunday's memories by 5:00 AM, swung his legs reluctantly out of bed, pulled a pair of khaki shorts over his briefs and slipped his feet into a pair of thongs. Morning coffee was what he needed. Tucker tapped down the hall behind him.

It was the funeral home by 8:00 AM for honor guard. By nine, he'd walk alongside the hearse with five other officers, east on Swanson Avenue to Mulberry South, and later swing north on Daytona to Our Lady of the Lake Catholic Church.

****

Last night wiped out McCruise. He wore his Class A dress uniform, which he last wore at graduation from ALETA, but was required to maintain for occasions such as this. He'd forgotten what it was like to wear full regalia: long sleeved, blue-black shirt, trousers, duty belt complete with holster, handcuffs, come-along stick, black tie, gray Smoky Bear hat, gold buttons, and gold braid loops running though his epaulettes on the right sleeve, and white gloves. In as much as he held no rank, his lower sleeve knew decoration of only a gold star on the forearm, marking five years of service. His next stripe would be gold, also, awarded in increments of two years of service. Above his breast pocket sat his three-inch marksman ribbon—green with white and neutral stripes.

Sagging with burden, the two-hour wake was the longest penance McCruise ever experienced. Among the first six honor guards, he stood as part of a phalanx of three on either side of the bier. Two banks of burgundy votive lights flickered and dimmed like dancing souls in a room, holding a heady redolence of flowers.

The flag-draped closed casket sat at the front of a chapel-style room, divided by a center aisle, with seating running ten rows of pews each side, to the back of the room. Large windows faced Swanson Avenue, letting in the last of God's light at six p.m. High in the apex of the sky, complacent clouds caught the timorous rays of the sun, glowing baby pink, and purple, finally metamorphosing into a victorious magenta and wild rose. Finally, assertive graying shadows announced that day was done. *How ironic*, thought McCruise, *so was Wally's life.*

Over at Good Samaritan Hospital, another child was born to replace the old man who died in his sleep, which is the natural order of things. But to have a man cut down in the prime of his productive life, a child aborted from his mother's womb, they were inexplicable phenomena to McCruise. Tears burned at the backs of his eyelids. Still, life goes on like echoes rippling over the Mohave Mountains into infinity. His brown eyes softened with halting acquiescence.

****

There was no higher protocol event in any police department than a funeral for an officer killed in the line of duty. The route hung with American and Arizona flags, and closed to through-traffic on this, the final day of Wally's earthly travels—this day of beautiful sunshine, blooming bougainvillea, and calling birds.

The first vehicle in the procession, the hearse crawled along. Walking beside it the two miles to the church were McCruise and five other uniformed officers. Vanguard vehicles consisted of a sea of patrol cars and fire trucks with their light bars activated, afterwards came two motor division officers moving slowly, side by side, working at keeping their machines squared.

The small purple and white flag on the hearse's antenna hailed hypnotically, as if programmed. Lining the streets and intersections along the funeral route were hundreds of people, holding their hands over their hearts or saluting in the bright Mohave daylight.

McCruise looked back and watched the surging ocean of cars as they turned the corner onto Mulberry Avenue. Antennas displayed small rippling flags on funeral home limousines, private cars, and law enforcement vehicles from all over the state. In addition, they came from San Bernardino County, from the Las Vegas Metro Units in Laughlin, Nevada, the Utah Highway Patrol, New Mexico State Police, and the Colorado Public Safety Department.

Behind the limousine, bearing Karla and comforters, were limousines carrying state representatives, senators, county commissioners, police chiefs impressive in their gold braid and eagle-emblem hats. Mayor Hilderman and the city council personnel followed immediately in their own limo. Further cars showed dress uniforms with chevrons, gold stars, and shiny captain and lieutenant badges.

The hearse and honor guard stood in place at the front of the church as family, friends, and dignitaries arranged in standing sections. Hundreds of law enforcement officers in full uniform waited outside lining a walkway.

Flag bearers now snapped a healthy furl ahead of the bier, their colors respecting the stars and stripes of the USA Flag, the bursting sunrise of the state of Arizona flag, the bright red and black flag of the Knights of Columbus, and the post insignia flag of the Veterans of Foreign Wars.

Overhead could be heard the thrum, thrum, thrum of five Apache helicopters flying in "V" formation, with three copters on one side and only two on the other side, which was the standard missing-man symmetry.

McCruise held his breath, his vitals surging in grief, and his soul lifting to fill the empty position.

In full blue raiment, the high school band marched slowly, sandwiched in between the flag bearers and ahead of the honor guard, instruments glinting in the sun. Strains of "Onward Christian Soldiers" wafted across the parking lot to a heavy drum cadence. As the honor guard preceded the uniformed pallbearers in the narthex of the church, hundreds of white gloves tipped to the forehead and snapped a smart salute to one of their own, as closely united in a common struggle as blood brothers.

The church, filled to its capacity of seven hundred, found rows and rows of officers standing at attention, befitting the sedate occasion of Wally's bier as it moved to the front of the church. Outside, in numbers reaching many hundreds, supporters participated in the somber service via a public address system.

Our Lady of the Lake knew the design for one-hundred-eighty degree viewing of the altar, which situated at the apex of ninety degrees. Flowers bedecked every available space around the altar, save room for the movement of the three celebrants of the Solemn High Mass.

Upon Coulter's request and a long history of heavy donations, the Bishop of the Diocese of Phoenix was the celebrant. Resplendent in gold chasuble, worn over a white alb, an ornate miter sat sedately on his head; in his hand, he carried a crosier, the symbol of Christian leadership. The pastor and a monsignor in attendance came, garbed in white and silver capes, reflecting the subtle recessed lighting from the ceiling. Dressed in black cassocks and short lace-trimmed white albs, area priests paid their respects by their presence in the processional. The monsignor removed the bishop's miter, and mass began.

"Let us pray."

McCruise, sitting up front, scanned a brave Karla. A citizen of Bosnia, Herzegovina, Karla married Wally while he was serving in the military in Italy. Thus, there was no family present. Slumped in rejection, her dark blonde Dutch boy haircut screened part of her face. By fluke or by design, it offered her protection from probing eyes.

After communion was the designated time for the eulogy. Captain O'Shaughnessey kept his message short and dignified, in as much as Catholic funerals focus not on celebrating the life of the deceased, but on a reflection of faith in the resurrection, based on the scriptural readings

334

used at the Mass. McCruise was proud of the captain and felt he'd acquitted himself well on such a somber occasion, albeit his voice was raw with deep umbrage, his eyes darkly burdened.

Karla sobbed, sometimes the pain keened audibly in the still church. McCruise never saw her cry. Now she seemed dwarfed with devastation. Close friends, including Coulter, Penny, and Jacquie, stood to either side, as if shielding her from further pain.

McCruise felt lightheaded with immeasurable loss, yet he needed to get through this service—for Wally's sake.

CHAPTER EIGHTY

The pastor, a tall, dark young man sealed with the electricity of his vicarship, gave a homily that was surprisingly riveting, in view of the fact that it wasn't the day of the cop, but instead a time when law enforcement stood beat up and bruised. A cascade of searching questions punctuated his powerful delivery, and serious eyes made steady contact with all who attended.

"Today we bury the result of hatred, intolerance, and vindictiveness. Today we read a requiem to the ruthless waste of God's goodness, and the absence of sunlight on a good man's face." He paused, his face shadowed with frustration.

"Who among us has never needed the assistance of a law enforcement officer?" His stained glass blue eyes burned with intensity. "Who among us hasn't gone to bed at night and heard the wail of a siren drifting in the still night air? Who doesn't know our officers are sentries of our city, keeping us safe, giving the needy among us a helping hand?" He held the congregation to a fixed hush, losing no one, his eyes drilling.

"How many among us has ever thanked these dedicated men and women?" He spoke barely above a whisper, yet a whisper that reverberated throughout the church. Allowing his words to fall upon countenances reflecting the acid bitterness of the ghastly act committed amongst them, he paused. His glance penetrated with clarity to the last depths of his pastorate, searching, pleading, and asking.

"Bishop Fulton Sheen's television ministries in the seventies were hard-hitting and perceptive to human nature," he said. "I pass one on to you: 'Show me your hands. Do they have scars from giving?'"

"Wallace Denton's did," he said, his voice barely audible.

"'Show me your feet. Are they wounded in service?'"

"Wallace Denton's were." His voice grew softer, magically gathering his congregation to him.

"'Show me your heart. Have you left a place for God's divine love to shine through?'"

"Wallace Denton did. His goodness shined on everyone. I need to wonder, twenty years after Bishop Sheen's words, if violence would ever get a stronghold if these simple questions were asked of our own consciences."

After an effectively heavy pause, he said simply, "Let us pray."

McCruise's stomach weaved into solid knots. His long legs protested to his feet. Could he any longer walk in sponge-rubber-soled shoes to fight wickedness and catastrophes? In a swamp of negative energy, he struggled.

Sniffing was audible in the hushed silence of the church. Handkerchiefs whisked out. Wally did not die in vain. He'd live intimately in the hearts of all those who knew what it was to have a family member in the service of his city, county, state, or nation.

Upon arrival at the cemetery, the bishop led the mourners in prayers of the Final Commendation. Eighteen white doves saw release from cages, one for each year of Wally's service to the city. The thudding of their wings as they reached ever skyward did a slow decrescendo, as if lifting Wally's spirit to his God.

In meaningful finality, five representatives of the Veterans of Foreign Wars presented arms and shot a volley, which reverberated over the cemetery, raising the hackles on McCruise's neck. Gathering all his strength to breathe taps into his trumpet, McCruise stood beside the VFW flag bearer. The mournful, chilling notes floated off into the flawless morning. The instrument glistened in the sun, just as Wally gleamed at the same clear sounds of "I'm Always Chasing Rainbows" in their private times together.

In the intricate pattern of its recognizable perfect triangle, an American flag, which floated over the capitol building in Phoenix, presented to Karla, who accepted it with a courtesy and controlled calm McCruise could hardly muster for himself, encompassed in the sickening mystery of death. He examined her from under the brim of his Smoky Bear hat. Presently calm and unemotional, her endurance he admired — the epitome of a good law enforcement wife, one who lived with apprehensive thoughts of this tragedy as long as her husband wore the uniform. She'd go on to weep at another time and place.

Nearby, a humming bird's thrum whirred as it hovered over a brilliant orange Cape Cod honeysuckle, which nodded almost imperceptibly with the invasion of the slight bird, as if stirred by a heavenly spirit.

McCruise found all he could handle for the day, but there was yet more to endure. Getting a ride back to the funeral home in a patrol car, dispatch broadcast its last call for Wally: "After eighteen years of service and dedication to the Lake Havasu City Police Department, today, October 21, 1997, at eleven fifteen, Officer Wallace Lee Denton was laid to rest in the Havasu Gardens Cemetery. A hero lies in him. Goodnight, Sir."

****

Seeking the privacy of his home, McCruise sat on the patio, head in his hands, and wept at the futility of it all. His sorrow lay in no-man's land, his mind, and body being in total sync on an island of remorse.

Adjusting his trumpet lip, he played his dark and dismal sorrow on the instrument. The haunting climbs of "Once Upon A Time in the West" quietly conquered the stillness of the night, releasing his soul into the plangent vastness of the southwest in which he was but a small, small particle of blowing dust.

As was Wally.

338

CHAPTER EIGHTY-ONE

Keeping her mind intact was about all she could do. Wally's funeral yesterday washed Jacquie dry. Entering Fayne's conference room at Norwood Research & Development in Duluth, her legs were wobbly with apprehension. A report and update on the progress of the Golden Crest was the ruse, which brought her hurriedly back to Duluth, a place she'd always loved and called home. Why would the status of the Crest serve any purpose to the negotiations with the Sri Lankans?

The Crest was successful, yes, but Norwood's successes numbered in the greats and the manys. He wanted to lean on her, threaten her by association, while swirling her into the vortex of his clandestine operations. He was a runaway train, unstoppable, with total destruction and death at the end of the line.

The delegation from Sri Lanka sat around the conference table. Assistant Consulate J. R. Jayedene accompanied Singher Bandaranaike. As opposed to Bandaranaike's slight frame and fastidious carriage, Jayedene was a bear of a man with a burly chest, great pink jowls, and eyes bugging out as if he over-indulged at lunch.

Leaning into them from the head of the table, Fayne was pontificating upon the plight of the Sri Lankans, his sincerity and sympathy unquestioned. By his posture, he relayed complete and total dismay at the tragedy occurring in the homeland of Bandaranaike and Jayedene.

Across the table from the Sri Lankan entourage sat Mallika Chilaw, slim, beautiful, flowing brown eyes, skin of rich walnut. Her graceful neck was an artist's delight, her head resting slightly to the right. Intent upon the conversation, her hands rested gently in her lap.

Sligh sat closer than necessary to Mallika. An involuntary spasm pulsing through Mallika spoke to Jacquie, telling her that Sligh slipped his hand on Mallika's thigh. Why did this beautiful, educated hotel management intern suffer the disgraces visited upon her by Sligh Ignatius Shoney? A human leach, one-rung above a slug.

Charlie Grinne sat at the end of the table opposite Norwood, with Jacquie to his right. Grinne adjusted his small glasses, sighing in commiseration with Norwood's sucking grieving at the plight of the island people.

How could these good consulate people know the oily, sanctimonious words of this all-American icon were a sham? The man was an expert in deception. She always sensed materialism in his face. At this instant, it was positively powerful.

Jacquie knew as they spoke that more Sri Lankans were dead and dying. Although the substance of the contract met approval verbally, the skullduggery would renew itself if contracts for cocaine went unsigned today. After all, Norwood, God of all that is good and plenty, offered complete renewal of their wastewater systems.

Was her report to him on the status of the Golden Crest so important that it required her presence at this meeting? She didn't think so. She felt vacuumed into the Norwood cesspool and guilt-by-association, but was aware that her legitimate holdings lent credibility to Norwood's enterprises, his R & D accolades, and his altruistic nature.

Bile rose.

She felt as if she were going to be sick. She needed to excuse herself. Many eyes, wide in askance, followed her departure.

****

Norwood made available his R & D courtesy van for Jacquie's return to the Minneapolis International Airport, and he accompanied her. Arriving at the airport, the car leaned with curves on the parking ramps as they climbed upward. Conversation strained, the air hung heavy with tension.

Jacquie never was on such a wild goose chase, and was pressed with the realization that she was not in good graces, having left the meeting with the Sri Lankans without as much as a by your leave. If she bought tickets for a Shakespearean drama of high treason, she could not have observed a better-laid plot. It was sick, as sick as the motorized man who conducted the meeting. He'd have his sway at any cost; he lost any sense of fair play that may have at one time rolled off his tongue. She wondered if monsters owned minds, and suddenly saw Norwood as a vampire in pin stripes—one who daily dressed in impeccable suits to go out into the world and suck blood.

"What was the purpose of your meeting with Matthew Cruise at the Lake Havasu Community Center a few weeks ago?" Norwood inquired, his wary eyes scrutinizing for the smallest muscle twitch.

"We have a common interest in art, that's all." Jacquie wondered if her voice sounded as taut as her nerves were. Perhaps she came off as shook-up and frazzled. Norwood employed eyes all over creation—unidentifiable, unrecognizable cohorts.

"And did you share more than a common bed on your trip to Phoenix?" Norwood's lips pulled back with superiority and lust, intimating an aura of cheapness in her new relationship.

"Much more," she replied. She could tap dance around a subject as well as he could. Maybe given enough time, she, too, could become a monster and kill. "We have been friends since the day I arrived in Lake Havasu."

"Accordingly, you must have been distressed to learn that death hung near him when his partner was killed." He laughed in his throat; his chin dropped to his chest for a moment.

CHAPTER EIGHTY-TWO

Saturday morning, October 25, 1:00 AM.

The long white nine-passenger Dassault-Falcon 20 Jet set down on the glide path of the Lake Havasu City Municipal Airport, taxied to a hangar, and disappeared within the labyrinth. From the shadows of the enclosure appeared a Mission Linen van; it, too, was swallowed by the great cavity, the door of which quietly settled.

Without conversation or wasted moments, three individuals moved nautical accouterments from within the passenger-seat-gutted cabin into pillowcases, tablecloths, towels, and aprons, which were loaded into the Mission Linen van. The whole procedure consumed only seventy-five minutes including travel, the timing exacted weeks in advance.

In the same moments, a dually truck, speeding westbound over the London Bridge, crashed through the ornate concrete railing and splashed into the Channel only yards from where McCruise and Cleavus were ensconced in their nighttime lair of intrigue. Quickly, it sank to the bottom of the Channel, the headlights casting an eerie glow in the roiling water. The two knights of humanity reacted promptly with rescue efforts, which kept them occupied for hours.

The sinking truck a decoy, a Mission Linen van backed up to the Golden Crest, the three individuals moving as slickly as well-oiled pistons, unloaded the cargo, stored it in the narcotics warehouse, and returned with lifejackets, life-preservers, and strings of buoys wrapped in linens, then they loaded them into the van. Time lapsation counted seventy-five minutes, as planned, at fifty pounds per person for two of them, and thirty pounds per person for one of them, and five minutes per trip in and out. They moved in a ruse cargo and moved out 1,280 pounds of cocaine valued at $315,000,000.

Left behind were 480 pounds of cocaine, valued at $185,000,000. Also abandoned were three five-gallon gas tanks, filled with 40 pounds of cocaine each. A false top, holding ten percent of capacity, stood filled with gasoline, weighing four pounds each. The tanks were a cumbersome commodity, making them unwieldy, time consuming to move, and potentially hazardous in flight.

By 2:35 AM, five minutes over their calculated loading and route time, the Mission Linen van moved unobtrusively over the airport roads, entered the private hangar, loaded new cargo into the cavity of the Dassault-Falcon 20, locked plane, locked hangar. A party of three left, dropping one man off at the King's Retreat, a distinguished looking man with curiously tan eyes. It was 5:30 a.m.

"In one short week we're home free with $315,000,000. My informers assure me every tongue on the river transport will be squelched for eternity in a police sting; no traces of trafficking will remain, except for incidental paraphernalia left behind for arrestable evidence of the Golden Crest's owner." The man turned and quickly entered the Retreat.

In the darkness of a natural arroyo in the road leading from the King's Retreat, the Mission Linen label peeled from the van and stuffed inside before it drove off, with two occupants.

CHAPTER EIGHTY-THREE

At home on Bison Drive, the clock read 8:30 AM when Connor hung up in a seething rage, his brown eyes dancing around the den, his hand lingering on the phone.

Turning, he swiveled in his chair to face the window. Sadie! What a half-baked broad! His signature deep-frown lines appeared. What's this he remembered about human error being the weak link in the chain? It was true and flourishing right under his nose... Sadie!

At least she'd called.

"It doesn't matter anymore," she said. "I've made such a mess of things; breathing isn't even worth the effort." She sighed hopelessly. "Connor, I know you called off the weekend surveillance crews. That was a mistake. Sligh and Fayne are moving the entire warehouse of cocaine tonight, or rather tomorrow morning before dawn. Everything is packed and ready for loading." She paused, her words hanging frozen.

"Hold it, Sadie," Connor barked, offering no solace. "With your permission, I'll record this telephone conversation."

"Well, all right."

"So start from the beginning. I'll have a stenographer transcribe the recording, and you can sign the statement."

"I'll sign it Monday morning," she went on. "I'm willing to turn state's evidence, and I have a lot..."

Cutting her off, barely concealing his rage, Connor's voice was blistering. "Sadie, what the hell made you agent for those jackals? You know they're merciless, empty machines."

"Simply put—cocaine. It took over my life, enervating my intellect, my being. I need it more than daily bread." Her breath caught on a sob. "It's like pouring sand into a black hole."

"Sadie..."

"Hmmm?"

"Why are you forthcoming now? What's in it for you?"

"Because I'm going away, away so far no one will ever find me, and I wanted to do one thing right before I left this place." Her voice dwindled and died.

"Don't do anything irrational over the weekend. Talk to me Monday morning; come to work as usual. We'll go to the prosecutor together with your information sheet, and Sadie?" He paused, afraid too ask. "How did you know all the undercover plans when you were never privy to them?" Thoughts filtered through his mind in an accept-reject mode; he couldn't find a constant.

"Ticonderoga pencils."

The two words about knocked Connor on his ass.

"Fayne supplied me with fake ones, ones with recording devices in them. It was simple to get you to talk into them, because you were always toying with one. They were a stunning success."

He knew she was concealing a smile with tight-lipped humor.

"Damn!" he uttered in disgust as he hung up.

His eyebrows grew heavy as he pulled at his bottom lip. He needed temporarily to forget the pencils, set the gears in motion for tonight. He dialed Chalmers David of the San Bernardino Sheriff's Department. "No dry-run on Operation Water Lily tonight. All systems are Go: Plan A.

"My informant advises they'll be heavily armed, handpicked. I don't like what could happen. It's explosive. With the kind of money we're talking about here, nearly five hundred million, the sky's the limit on weaponry purchased to protect the Golden Egg. My guess would be a non-structured, just-in-case defense. The informant is uncertain of numbers, but nationality will be hand-chosen Mexicans in the employ of Shoney. One might anticipate a prescribed mode of defense from a trained mercenary, but not from these people.

"We'll strike where we're least expected, at the 1-40 bridge, instead of at the docks at Bullhead City. The narcs would expect us to set a trap there. Using the dark of night for cover, you, and Trehan will moor your boats under the bridge. I suspect, with a shipment such as this, there'll be counterintelligence at work somewhere along the route up-river. Terrorism isn't out of the question with these lunatics. They've taken high-risk gambles before. Look what they did to McCruise's wife—in broad daylight yet!"

O'Shaughnessey's eyes felt hot, stinging, as the past cart wheeled within recollection. There was a whole laundry list of unbelievable incidents, all spoking from the hub of hell.

He would be there in the DEA's new V-22 Osprey Aircraft. Boeing Helicopters of Philadelphia developed it for the military, along with Bell Helicopter Textron out of Fort Worth, and the Arizona DEA was its first civilian application. The new bird was capable of vertical or short take-offs and landings, with forward flight up to nearly three hundred mph, like a conventional fixed-wing aircraft. Graphite-epoxy composite materials comprised almost sixty percent of the weight of the airframe.

Connor leaned back in his chair, glad he was home where he could work without the interruption of any daily administrative responsibilities. The burdens of office hanging heavily upon him, he could feel pressure-exhaustion taking over. The lines at the corners of his eyes deepened as he called Tom Trehan of the Mohave County Sheriff's Department, reiterating what he'd advised Chalmers.

The Department of Public Service would provide a patrol car assignation on I-40 east for traffic control, while the California Highway Patrol would provide traffic direction on the west side of the bridge. The patrol cars were to remain incognito on side roads until dispatched.

The DPS helicopter, the Ranger, would give assistance to the DEA copter for overhead illumination on the river and on the outside chance that there may be emergency injuries, and would stand commandeered for air-evac.

"Everything sounds stabilized, except we have that little problem with the natural gas line strung out over the river." Trehan was not someone to overlook the slightest logistical blunder.

"I've been assured it's practically indestructible as well as automatically shut down when pressure suddenly drops." Connor started the wheel a-turning; he hoped it didn't spin too fast.

"Place your paramedics and ambulances on the north side of the bridge, south of Topock. We don't want to raise any questions in the minds of their reconnaissance people, and yet we need medical assistance in close proximity. God speed to us both."

He'd be at the Havasu Airport by midnight, waiting for a cue from McCruise and Cleavus, and fly upriver as if it were patrol duty as usual on a busy weekend. Connor got up and found a cup of coffee in the kitchen, his mind on fire with anger and activity. *Damn* Sadie for betrayals. *Thank* Sadie for her overriding allegiance. Back at his desk, he picked up a pencil. "Call McCruise," he wrote. "Cancel early reconnaissance shifts."

Was his life in order should he never come back? He struggled to maintain control. A long silence hung in the air. Marvel made his house into a home, morphing the word *home* into a completely new meaning. Thoughts of returning to her after the confrontation were precious.

He turned toward the window, catching a movement in the bottlebrush tree that cheered his days in the spring and early summer, with outrageous red blossoms. A small finch landed there, a male he knew, by the bright coral-colored breast; its song was as light as its stance on the branch. If he were a superstitious man, he'd find the visitation by the cheerful bird a good omen, maybe even a visit by Wally. He thumbed his chin in critical thought.

Although his plans lay in abeyance, could something send them awry? Did he leave any stones unturned? He slumped in his chair, emitting a mighty sigh, stared again at the finch as if he could find an answer there.

CHAPTER EIGHTY-FOUR

The brilliant Mohave day produced a mellow morning. Gone were the tongues-of-fire that the sun breathed in summer, when the very air itself seared like an inferno. Although, by speed of light, eight minutes from Earth, the sun's rays were serious enough to damage human skin and eyes.

With heavily tinted sunglasses, two individuals unlocked a hangar at the Lake Havasu Municipal airport and clambered aboard the sleek, Dassault-Falcon, corporate jet for an extended trip. It was 10:00 AM. Both licensed pilots checked the control panel, rolled out for a fuel stop, cleared for takeoff, and were airborne, headed north, northwest.

"First stop, Las Vegas; brokerage the same?" The deep male voice of Al Thompson was strong and confident, having been Fayne Norwood's pilot for six years. Sitting tall in the cockpit, the man was of intimidating size, his hands like hams, and his shoulders bursting at the seams of a white cotton pullover T-shirt messaging, "Play Later, Fly Now." His long black hair pulled neatly back into a ponytail of impressive length.

"Sure thing, Big Al. Same old brokerage in San Diego, too. The color of money is white; it matters not who's in possession of the white. God, how I've missed your steady company these past six years."

"No more, Sadie. It's you and I living on an estate in Trincomalee, Sri Lanka. We'll sip piña colatas for the rest of our lives on Mallika Chilaw's family estate. It's on paper; it's all ours. Mallika will have her own rewards in typical Tamil Tiger style. This Falcon 20 cruises at 419 knots with a range of 1900 nautical miles, meaning we can go on forever, if we wish," he said, his clearly chiseled features a complement to his aviator glasses.

"You 'n me," she said, smiling into the face of a cloudless blue sky.

CHAPTER EIGHTY-FIVE

McCruise was not surprised one iota by the call from Connor. He anticipated that Shoney would choose this weekend, when thousands of boaters would be using the lake and the river. Sligh surely inherited a genetic talent for getting lost in crowds like some kind of a Colonel Muammar al Qaddafi trained agent-in-pay.

What *did* surprise McCruise was Cleavus's agreement to work the assignment. Sometimes human nature amazed him at its recovery capabilities. Ostensibly, after rocking this baby for months, Cleavus felt a need to put it to bed. They'd be Water Lily One point men from midnight until the narcotic boats were loaded and headed upstream. Their vantage point was the grassy berm in front of the Island Shopping Mall, where there grew ample vegetation for concealment.

McCruise easily came to terms with police work and special assignments. He stayed incredibly professional in handling even unanticipated muckups, because Wally kept him straight. Wally seemed to have been imbued with correct ideology from birth—a people man, and a man of the people.

How he wished he could handle his personal life as well. The darkroom of his mind conjured up terrifying pictures of Laura's early demise, of Sligh Shoney seducing Jacquie. The man was capable of world chaos through flamboozle.

People took to him like kids to a carnival. His slickness found him in some of the highest offices in the world, with welcome. Paired with Norwood, they knew no bounds. They were a 20th century terror machine.

Every newspaper, every television broadcast brought new fatality figures from Sri Lanka. The horrors went on and on, the death toll climbing to mile-high 28,700 souls. Colombo, Kandy, and Jaffna authorities were doing their best to contend with the lack of sanitation, improvisation, and medical supplies. Help poured in from all over the world; infrastructure expertise appeared magically overnight from GETI.

After Jacquie's divulgence of her suspicions of the Sri Lankan new waste water systems at the Art Exhibit, McCruise questioned not how the multi-million dollar price tag was being covered nor by whom, but the entirety of the investment to be recouped in less than a year with the tradeoff negotiated. Negotiated? Power plus money equaled enormous advantage.

Would Sri Lankan authorities ever garner enough evidence to prove Norwood and Shoney's design in the sabotage? McCruise didn't think so. In the outmoded Package Wastewater Treatment facilities, anything could go wrong. He wondered if it were true that Jaffna actually used a holding lagoon for sewage because their treatment facility fell so far behind the demands of a growing city. If so, the alleged power-out at the Jaffna plant was all it took to have the city roaring like a diarrhea-bound bull elephant.

The chlorine gas release in Kandy was nothing short of Frankesteinish. Wastewater Treatment facilities all over the world used chlorine for disinfecting. The greenish-yellow gas was hideously corrosive, severely burning the mucous membranes in the nose, throat, and lungs. Carrying an extremely pungent odor, it was about two and one-half times heavier than air. Consequently, it flows downhill to the lowest point.

Kandy's Adam's Peak, standing at 7,359 feet, provided perfect valley topography for far-reaching devastation where the gas would seek no lower level. Leaked as liquid instead of a gas, it was especially dangerous because one volume of liquid yielded about 460 volumes of gas.

What kind of mind acrobatics did it take to spew fire throughout the Treatment Plant in Colombo? Would maniacs surface for the entirety of humankind's existence? McCruise wanted to throw up. Life was precious to cultures of all colors. What kind of worms crawled around in Norwood's mind to place such a low price on Sri Lankan humanity?

Was Jacquie's recent visit to Duluth getting her more deeply involved in the Sri Lankan affair, or was she seeing a physician for an abortion? The questions were both rhetorical and academic.

He revisited the times Jacquie said she loved him, her eyes speaking the words, too. Evidently, it didn't mean anything to her. Not the way it affected *his* life with the comfort and solace he'd enjoyed from their relationship. The magic was in her eyes, her clear-blue gentle eyes spoke of love for the boys, for him, played with Tucker, yet she wouldn't allow herself to have her own child—*his child*. More than once, he reminded himself of the strong Afro genes from his ancestors. Was this her problem?

Why did it always come back to the race card?

CHAPTER EIGHTY-SIX

By noon, Mallika paced. She opened her lanai doors, stepped onto the deck and lounged on a chaise. October days were pleasant, the monsoons gone, and only puffer-belly clouds dotted the sky.

The condominium provided by Shoney was luxurious, but she realized, it came with strings attached. She was queasy with the growing sense that she was adrift and isolated. At twenty-two years old, she found herself contemplating the direction of her life. Leaning back and closing her eyes, she allowed her past to wash over her like a lazy surge of evening tide.

When she was twelve years old, India sent soldiers to help enforce an accord between the Sinhalese and Northern Tamil, granting the Tamil minority limited autonomy. Her family plantation in Jaffna was burned when the agreement failed, her mother and father killed in 1989. This left her, at fourteen, to move with her Aunt Siri and Uncle Kotte to Trincomalee, a city situated within a beautiful harbor and removed from the northern Sri Lankan strife. Siri and Kotte lived as a laid-back couple, both old and retired, their races run, their passions spent.

The scars remained, however, and Mallika resolved to join the Tamil Tigers, when at sixteen, the Tamils' leading opposition figure saw extermination, gunned down mercilessly by the Sinhalese. The resultant assassination of

President Premadasa by a Tamil rebel who detonated explosives strapped to him was a coup of incalculable consideration.

Growing up with cousin Adasa was a love affair, as well as mind-bending to the Tamil cause. She'd grown close to Adasa, indeed, losing her virginity to him just one year after she'd come to live under the same roof of his family's home. She found it a fumbling, unenjoyable experience, which in time matured to experimentation and afternoon delights.

Adasa was a master of all he attempted. He'd always hold a special place in her heart, even more so because he was dead. The pictures of his death car rode the waves of the evening news in the Sri Lankan newspapers. How could he have been out-maneuvered? He stood a man of intense insight and street sense.

A heavy cloud of depression preyed on her mind. She'd introduced Adasa to Shoney and Norwood. They'd struck an agreement. Obviously, the accord struck between Adasa, Shoney, and Norwood was no gentlemen's agreement, because Adasa no longer walked this earth, and that left two.

Mallika's heart sank imagining Adasa dead. His wandering eye always held her transfixed and lent inquisitiveness to the plainness of his broad face. The eye moved in varying directions, leaving one with the feeling that Adasa enjoyed an inner sonar unit.

After he obtained his Masters Degree in Biochemistry, he provided Mallika with an American education. Hotel Management at the University of Arizona in Tucson was her concentration.

"Go to America. Get educated and sophisticated. Return to us with the expertise to move in upscale circles, gain vital information; we'll outsmart all of them, get our rightful land back, and be autonomous in the north once again.

Taking internship in Lake Havasu at a five-star resort condominium complex reeled out a boon, falling into her agenda of power wielding. By the time she returned to Trincomalee next year, she planned to live at her now-deceased aunt and uncle's plantation. A respectable position in hotel management would provide her with a cover for leading a contingent of Tamil Tigers. Overthrowing the government forced upon her people in northern Sri Lanka, rightful Tamil Territory was the be-all and end-all of her agenda.

Throughout her intimate association with Shoney, what a pleasure it was to be privy to negotiations with the Sinhalese powers-that-be, how transcending to dupe the very principals who denied her rightful title to her family's tea plantation. What an uplifting experience to provide Adasa's name as a Sri Lankan, government-employed biochemist. From across an ocean and through the mind bank of Norwood R & D, she could fight for the Tamil cause!

She stiffened with the reminder that Jaffna included in the unconscionable shutdown of its barely adequate wastewater treatment plant, her people dying of typhoid, enduring the hardships of finding contaminated water, living in makeshift accommodations, the indignities too numerous and too terrible to entertain. By gaining their confidence, she shuddered at the thought of how she and Adasa rolled over for Norwood and Shoney to divulge internal Sri Lankan information.

When Shoney invited her to meet him in Brazil, she covertly caught sight of his flight tickets from Colombo that he loosely left on the credenza. He'd been there—been there when Adasa was killed, been there when the Jaffna Plant was sabotaged, as well as when the other Plants were crippled.

Yet she loved Shoney beyond any rationale. Did Shoney think she didn't see the look of adoration and hunger when he looked at Jacquie? Mallika acknowledged that her color and culture stood far removed from Caucasian Americans, but the color of her skin did not reduce the culture of her mind. Her walnut skin tone and large watery dark eyes didn't make her less of a person; it didn't make her heart hurt less.

In the final analysis, Mallika realized her allegiance to her Tamil compatriots rose to a higher level of commitment than her love for the cunning American who entered her life quietly, but with great forte mucked up every burning aspiration she'd ever held for her country.

Her life and her estate were in order—all matters closed. She knew she must have the courage to act upon the canons, which pressed upon her since childhood. "Courage" was the willingness to take risks and evolve with the results. She allowed herself to walk blindly into risks, so she would handle the consequences. She would not sell her country short through personal gaffes.

For strength and endurance, she prayed to her Buddhist God.

CHAPTER EIGHTY-SEVEN

In the pre-dawn hours of Sunday morning, McCruise spoke softly to O'Shaughnessey on a courtesy phone he'd lined up at Shugrue's; a cell phone or dispatch was at risk of monitoring.

"Operation Water Lily One's prey is off and running."

"Okay. Let's roll."

McCruise and Cleavus boarded the Osprey to join Connor and three DEA officers from Phoenix for the eighteen-mile trip to the Interstate-40 Bridge. The transition from unrelenting reconnaissance to the final act of closure was a long, tenacious thread. Suddenly, the scars sustained across McCruise's back from the Troll seared, as if they came to life, anticipating reoccurrence.

The Osprey showed a low profile, with no surfaces reflecting radar directly back. The intensive substitution of radar-opaque composites of metals and an overall coating of a radar-absorbing material spelled a superior aircraft. Added into the modification was terrain-following-terrain avoidance radar, additional wing fuel tanks, and integrated civilian equipment.

Cleavus gave McCruise thumbs up.

In the cockpit were the captain and the flight engineer, who made a final check of the passengers, belted, counted — six with room for ten, and freighted necessities. In the forward cabin, the captain plugged his helmet into the intercom. No time was lost as the passengers heard the snarl and roar of the helicopter's two T406 turbo-shaft engines.

"All systems check," the captain commented over his headset. The DEA copter, dubbed the "Narcout," was in readiness. The Phoenix-based captain accessed his radio. "Tower, this is Narcout One-Niner-Niner-Seven requesting taxi time. Over."

"One-Niner-Niner-Seven, Tower. Request granted. Winds are minimal from the southeast at barely four knots."

"Roger on that. One-Niner-Niner-Seven is in motion. Out." The captain, who looked to McCruise to be on the thin side of sixteen, maneuvered the throttle grip on his collective control, and eased the cyclic stick forward.

The wands of the ground controller blended and pointed to the south. Bringing the throttle to full power and making another check of the instrument panel, the Osprey dipped forward as it began to move ahead. Leaving behind a small hurricane of desert dust, the copter started to climb. They were airborne, circling the city to the south before emerging on a course due north over the Colorado River.

The navigation system on line, McCruise was impressed with the futuristic technology of moving terrain on a map display. The Osprey navigated from a Doppler radar system, which interrogated the canyon walls, functioning from an inertial system using laser-gyroscopes, or from navigation satellites. McCruise's stomach flip-flopped with the harsh reality of their mission.

The DEA Narcout was state-of-the-art; it sounded like any other turbo-powered aircraft, but it was almost impossible to determine the direction from which the sounds were coming. Provided with night vision sets, any object projecting heat glowed infrared as far away as five-six miles upriver.

McCruise admired how Connor organized this *coup de gras*. His logistical expertise became legendary, his ability to negotiate admired, and his dedicated leadership unfailing. Every agency knew their assignations of responsibility. Was O'Shaughnessey having the same elation-deflation feelings that were writhing in McCruise's stomach? They were finally snipping the tangled strings in this covert-war damnable business.

Although the city placed their faith in O'Shaughnessey and he'd lived up to their every expectation, when layer after layer peeled away, there remained a wholesome man, an inch of façade from being scared, from being wrong, from being plagued with self-doubt, but he evinced no skepticism.

Consequently, Connor sat back, looking every day of his fifty-six years of age.

CHAPTER EIGHTY-EIGHT

Riding in the 1997 Narcout gave McCruise a feeling of being lost in time and space, like an experimental housefly on a spacecraft. His wits didn't shift into low gear, as they should have. It was hokey, this feeling: *the time is now.*

"The subject Watercraft is coming into view on the overhead readout," the Kid announced.

Still looking through his night goggles, McCruise was intrigued that he could see the four perpetrator boats ahead in the gray-green image, moving like spirits in the night.

Watching the Watercraft crews move in the eerie light, Cleavus exclaimed, "What the hell. They're loaded with arms like beasts of burden and drinking beer!"

"Beer!" McCruise cried. "They're dinking beer?"

Before the words landed on their ears, up the side of the canyon went a round of walking bullets. Poofing the red rock in a straight column, one of Shoney's "sailors" from a pontoon sprayed holes with his AK-47 set on automatic. Fellow hombres doubled over laughing. Another try. Another man. Glow of gunfire showed infrared in the night goggles as the bullets flew wild up the canyon walls. The boater ammo supply was limitless.

McCruise didn't know whether to laugh or fight fear. He balked at the bestiality of dispatching naïve neophytes on a mission requiring patience, intelligence and a large measure of self-discipline.

Shouting and gesturing from the crews of the Warlock and the Witch Craft halted the weaponry target tomfoolery. Sitting idle, the Chicanos stood around lighting cigarettes, the glowing tips generating heat, thus appearing red in the goggles.

Silently, Connor expelled a wilting sigh at the ineptitude of the crew compared to the size of the cache. He muttered to himself, remembering squid fed on the weakest among them, something like Shoney.

He hoped that they would all surrender peacefully. McCruise entertained no appetite for killing, especially when Shoney's Navy stood hoodwinked and disadvantaged by manipulating tyrants. Connor's ninja crew could take on formidable foes with their training and resources.

Firepower near the overhead natural gas line needed avoidance. Even though the gas company assured him it would practically take a direct hit by a nuke to invade the durability of the conduit, he, as well as Trehan, found it cause for considerable concern.

With further study, it became obvious to McCruise that the crews on all four boats stood bored to death and bullshitting, about their next hit, about their last jump, about the high they could have with the cargo they were carrying.

Although the scene played out on screen, McCruise knew the plot was volatile. The combined law enforcement agencies owned enough firepower to blow the unaware sailors into the next county.

The Witch Craft's crew gestured a challenge to pontoon personnel and proceeded to take the Blankenship Bend with daredevil audacity, skimming the canyon walls at the petroglyphics cliffs, cheering, and Skoling beer bottles.

McCruise's binoculars affixed to his eyes, his night vision glasses anchored to his shirt pocket. A copycat target practice sprung from the Witch Craft, while negotiating the Devil's Elbow at Topock Gorge. A brave *amigo* with a full bandoleer marched a series of bullets up the canyon wall, a cigar clenched in the side of his mouth.

"Dumb asses," McCruise muttered aloud from behind the binoculars.

"Connor," Cleavus stage-whispered. "Where's the heavy ammo?" He tried laughing for relief from the tension, but his throat made an awful choking sound.

"I have the Department Heckler & Koch MP-5's," Connor said and nodded. "Even if we never use them, they'll be good insurance." Reaching behind him on the floor, he slid out a Formfab weapon container that held two MP-Fives. Two identical containers sat on an empty seat. All ammo clips held twenty 40-caliber rounds. He motioned for Cleavus and McCruise to pass them around. The semi or fully automatic weapons postured incredible power, accuracy up to a half mile with scopes, and the selector switch optioned one burst, three burst, or rapid fire.

McCruise acknowledged the perfection of balance in the deadly instrument as he fed his clip into place. He never did like a long, cumbersome weapon, so he broke down the polymer stock, fitting the shorter element under his arm. He shifted gears, filled with the flow of adrenaline accompanying his moments of intense stress.

The DEA distributed weapon slings for steadying the rifles' excessive reaction to firing. Their skills and mind-sets running parallel, McCruise's and Cleavus's thumbs were on the selector switches. Each chose a three-round-burst setting as if it were pre-programmed. Glowing only enough for visibility in the darkened copter, the sights contained small traces of tritium.

As with all police officers, McCruise and Cleavus glued to a fraternity that united them, a bond by which they both recognized their capacity for endurance, their courage threshold, their intense revulsion of evil—the bonding never more pronounced.

Captain Kid's message came over the intercom, as well as keyed into Central Control. "As planned, we have overtaken and passed our quarry, leaving them unquestioning our presence. All stations alert and prepare. Only two miles to Point of Objective. I'm going to fly north over the I-40 Bridge, circle east and come in over the mountains at the great river bend south of the bridge. I'll hover there for shakedown."

If counter surveillance picked up the radio message, it was too late. *Too-late-too-late-too-late*, McCruise mulled, with a wave of sadness capturing him. He slid open the door of the helicopter, letting in a rush of mild night air and the sound of whining turbos. Returning over the mountains from the east, they faced the river scenario in a heartbeat; the 250-yard-wide curve leading up to the bridge looked panoramic in its dimension. The four perpetrator boats were closing the gap quickly, churning the river with a steady rhythm.

"Curtain time," went out over the keyed radio. McCruise didn't know how the Kid could be so calm; his own heart was hammering in his throat. Almost simultaneously, the million-kilowatt glare of spotlights and downlights illuminated the river, making every ripple dance dizzily. The smell of dampness from the river permeated McCruise's nostrils, as opposed to the dry air of the desert mountains. He reminded himself that there were only two rivers in the whole world flowing through deserts: the Nile and the Colorado. Goddamn! Why'd he think of trivia at a time such as this?

The river patrol boats, one to the east, and one to the west under the bridge, each flew its own set of flags and identification; their lights flared at full amperage. Hulls lay manned with MI-19's, with 70-mm shells exchangeable for incendiary rounds, fragmentary rounds, smoke rounds, gas rounds, or pepper rounds. Grenade launchers using 40-mm shells trained on the four approaching boats.

Simultaneously, Ranger One and Narcout One-Nine-Nine-Seven searched, with downlights glaring wattage. Although McCruise was privy to the Water Lily plan from day one, being there when the curtain went up on opening night was indescribable. This was no puny pissing match. His shirt streaked with sweat. Worry-water seeped from under his curly black hairline. In a glance, he could see the workforce on all the boats, ready and disciplined to deliver on order.

The scene was set.

The river was hot.

McCruise figured that the smart money was on a quick surrender and arrest.

Chalmers David, in a timely fashion, boomed out on his San Bernardino amplification system, "Hail and identify immediately!" The sound, as big as David's stature, spread over the suddenly frenzied river, with unquestioned authority.

Dazed in the glare of lights after the peaceful darkness of the river, the four cocaine-laden boats did not attempt to stop.

"*Detener!*"

No speed reduction.

"*Pare.*"

The cocaine deck crews offered the offensive bird gesture.

"*Pare, ya pronto!*"

Dumb shits, McCruise thought. Don't try anything cute.

"*Identifique al punto!*" Thee authoritative voice rung riddled with warning.

Christ, there it was!

A booming 40-mm grenade, launched from the San Bernardino patrol boat, passed light off the bow of the Warlock and exploded upon impact with the rocky riverbank.

McCruise heard the roar of the Warlock and Witch Craft firing up for a run. The pontoons, with non-competitive speed, increased their acceleration. They were going to run the blockade! Obviously the coke runners knew their orders, albeit seat-of-the-pants instructions. McCruise's stomach sank. He felt lightheaded.

Standing in the position they'd held when the lights glared on, the bandaleros opened AK-47 fire in a helter-skelter mode. Due to lack of control and inexperience with the unfamiliar weaponry, the bullets danced on the water like skipping stones, recklessly up in the air, pinging off the bridge.

A scanner light went out on the Narcout with an explosive crack; breaking glass crackled. The Osprey remained steady.

"Ranger One here. We've taken irreversible hits— rotors split, going down." The message was terrifying in its relay.

In horror, they watched as Ranger One hit the unforgiving, rapidly moving river water with a splash, crystallizing the brightly lighted air. Water droplets fanned out, jumping, and weaving as if the cataclysm staged for a water show. The night stood still and timeless, hanging breathlessly between action and disbelief.

It was then it happened.

CHAPTER EIGHTY-NINE

The holocaust from hell broke loose.

"Noooo" drifted eerily over the water above the din of gunfire as one nationalist's legs ripped apart by automatic fire. In an instant, a man standing next to him took a hit to the groin and arms, his body spinning, instantly becoming simply a torso hitting the deck as if it dropped from the sky. Coiled links of distended cherry-colored sausage spilled out of yet another man. They died in minutes.

Glass and wood splintered; the smell of cordite permeated the air.

McCruise, finding his position by the open door, wiped a sweaty lip, biding his time for a good shot at the spare gas tanks riding in the back of the Warlock and the Witch Craft. Stricken for a week over Wally's death did strange things to logic. His face was masked with selective outrage; sinews tightened in his shoulders, arms, and legs.

"*Take*..." McCruise pulled the first three rounds reaching his target.

"*No*..." moved his tritium bead to the strategic location of the Warlock's under-floor gas tanks, and released another round of three.

"*Fucking*..." moved to the Witch Craft and released another round of three into *its* gas tanks.

"*Prisoners*..." He said, gritting his teeth in a physical reaction to his mindset.

Cleavus poured his horrific recall of Wally's death into triple bursts into the pontoons.

In the melee, McCruise discovered that in perilous situations, the constants of any man's benchmarks are as fragile as puffballs. A man becomes a dragon.

Minimal movement stirred on the decks of the coke boats. Body parts lay strewn and ugly.

Yet to McCruise's amazement, there appeared Ricki and reinforcements coming out of the hulls of the Warlock and the Witch Craft with an Uzi and AK's, firing with greater dexterity than their unfortunate cohorts did.

McCruise froze.

Ricki's teeth clenched in deadly violence. His frenzied bullets sent red volleys of ordnance at the patrol boats, at the parapet of the I-40 Bridge, and at the helicopter. Firing at will, Ricki's crew spewed ordnance at random.

God forbid what McCruise saw in slow motion. His throat swelled to the point of constriction. His mind spiraled up into limitless space for timeless seconds.

The night sky filled with merciless white inferno as a small aperture struck in the natural gas line, and simultaneously, McCruise's goal-line bullets fired up the boats' gas tanks. The recruited, hapless Mexicans and Ricki stood silhouetted against the flames. Blowing into the air in flames like missiles, their legs ran for purchase, the flames licking around them. As the unfortunates hit the river, they spiraled like spirits on the water in a reflexive biological action, unaware that they were already dead.

Ammunition burned and exploded, sounding like crackling fireworks. The roaring gallons of gasoline sent great waves of black smoke into the clear Arizona night, lighted by pounds of pressure from the gas line. McCruise wondered if this was what it was like in Sri Lanka when the wastewater treatment plant went up in a ball of fire. Theoretically, anything could go wrong, and this was the devil's handiwork.

Staring in stupefied silence, scorched as the scene unfolded around him, McCruise denied himself oxygen while the Kid flew the Narcout out of harm's way.

"Release rescue drop basket for Ranger One," Captain Kid advised, retaining his calm throughout the fast-moving action. The Narcout dipped forward downriver for the survivors who were moving like cordwood in the river currents. Only three were accounted for—all deputies. The pilot never got out before the 'copter went to its Colorado River grave.

Tom Trehan's worrisome gas conduit shut down by programmed emergency measures. The fires diminished and cooled ever so slowly. What was left of the pontoon boats listed and sunk taking booty, bodies, and madness to the river bottom. The Warlock and the Witch Craft, veritable bastions of resistance, stayed afloat, albeit with a dying effort.

McCruise observed Connor putting his head in his hands at the synchronized terror, and he knew immediately that they'd never be able to block out the horror. This wasn't police work; this was a combat zone. Having avoided extremes all his life, what came down around him did not compute with his personal programming.

In the distance, Trehan's' ambulances wailed.

McCruise tried to regain the real world in the midst of the turmoiled silence. Wars didn't launch in Mohave County. Recreation sites grew—fishing holes, wildlife habitat, golf courses, and marinas.

What's more, although the plan asserted boldly and maintained plausibly, McCruise realized that he and Connor experienced a sharp slice of the truth. They'd been out-smarted once again. They still needed to pin down the brains behind this manic obsession. Capturing the menacing moneymakers was going to take some cunningness. He sat down, his knees shaking. They'd have salvage operations to implement immediately, bodies to count, to identify. It was going to be grisly.

"Needless to say," said Connor, drawn, but regaining his steel control, "not everything has gone according to plan." The deep lines in his forehead melded like convoluted tubing; his eyes bespoke of deeply felt burdens accompanying command.

In the presence of overwhelming reversals, Connor commandeered the key to Central Control: "Water Lily Two and Three, could I impose on your goodwill to cover the estuary south of Topock Gorge, locate bodies before daylight? We're picking up Ranger One survivors and flotation devices on the river. We need to arrange for salvage of the Warlock and Witch Craft immediately. We have over 20,000 visitors in the area for London Bridge Days. I guess that says it all. Over."

"Water Lily Two. Willco." Demurred. "No casualties here."

"Water Lily Three. Willco." Subdued. "Ditto."

McCruise watched as the nightmare of the last sinking debris quickly submerged in the twenty-knot, southern-flow river speed. He'd never seen people blown apart and burned to death before. The world was a better place. Wasn't it?

He was having doubts, then doubts about his doubts, but he wouldn't allow himself taken to task. Those unfortunate bastards were delivering cocaine to sell to kids next week—at schools, on playgrounds. Sold to his kids and thousands of other kids.

Shoney's minions knew what they were doing. They couldn't have been people. People don't do things like that to their fellow human beings for the sake of a buck. These people did, and for more than six years. McCruise comforted himself. Every trip they made up the river hooked another kid, another hundred kids, thousands of kids.

Kids as young as yours, McCruise.

The silent sky was a delusory fraud, containing a peaceful skinny moon and millions of stars. Twenty-one men killed in minutes. McCruise's shoulders sagged to his concave chest, the smell of residue burning fuel, flash burn, and seared metal violating the pure Arizona air.

Cleavus hunkered on the floor near the yet-open door, watching the rescue operation, his knees pulled up. "Too fucking bad," he mumbled, his head down. "The Mexican boat crews were at the wrong place, wrong time—like Wally."

Wally always lived as an honest man, an altruistic man, McCruise knew, a man deeply dedicated to law and order. Where does a guy find law and order anymore? The question mixed in his mind. Simmering in a state of rage,

McCruise determined that vigilante justice was what was needed here, *his* vigilante justice, metered out by a jury of one. His breathing was so shallow, his chest hardly moved.

The Ranger One crew rescued, Cleavus massaged his neck as some of the rescued life preservers, and life rings hauled on board.

"What the..." McCruise raised his eyebrows, speechless. "These aren't bogus containers! They're genuine nautical materials—the real McCoys?"

In muted silence, unchanged enroute from the scene of the holocaust to The English Village, the crew of the Narcout cast cutting searches of the warehouse and the converted boathouse at the Golden Crest. The gray dawn presented trailing horsetail clouds, smeared across the sky, a harbinger of a low front pushing in.

"It's almost all gone," said McCruise, sick at heart, devastated with the cleverness of the antipathy. "But where?"

"There's still enough physical evidence for an arrest," Connor adjudged.

Something was sticking in McCruise's throat. Arrest whom? Jacquie? He tasted bile, feeling like a small and inadequate schoolchild.

CHAPTER NINETY

By 10:00 AM, a swirling wave of immeasurable loss lay heavily in Shoney's office at the King's Retreat.

"It says here—right here, in the *River City News* in big headlines—'Drug Bust Yield Deadly and Disappointing.' Explain, Mr. Norwood," said Shoney, his eyes glittered like river-bottom pyrite. The back of his hand slapped the paper for effect.

Armored for the onslaught upon entering into Shoney's self-absorbed office, Norwood's defense was a good offense. "I know nothing. Nothing! Less than nothing!" His tan eyes prowled like a mountain lion's, his Kirk Douglas shoulders working as coil springs. "Perhaps if you were on the Warlock, and in command, none of this would have happened; you'd have aborted the objective." His thin lips creased.

"You son-of-a-bitch. You wanted to set me up to become history with the crews while you ran off with the cache. Where is it?" Shoney's voice shook.

"I have no idea. My Dassault-Falcon's gone, too, with Big Al and Sadie not locatable. It appears we've both been outsmarted," Norwood said stiffly. He edged toward the door in flat-out refusal to get involved in Shoney's tirade.

"A likely story. I get my twenty-percent or you're ruined. Ruined! I'll tell everything," he shouted. "I'll tell your routes from Sri Lanka, your contacts, your skullduggery at the Wastewater Plants, your takes..." Shoney's voice was as ragged as a pit bull, unwilling to release a bone.

The discerning Norwood stood his height. "I'm having dinner with Jacquie tonight. Afterwards, I'm out of your life forever; you've demonstrated what a bottom-mucker you are." Turning, he opened the door and dissolved into the hallway.

Shoney, still holding the Sunday paper, screwed it up, slammed the door, and flung the *River City News* across the room.

****

With the sky pelting a vengeful rain, range-style, raincoats were in order for the night shift. A cold front moved in and paralyzed the mercury at thirty-eight degrees.

"I'm glad to see you wore something sensible, old man." McCruise winked at Cleavus before briefing at the station.

"Hell, yes. It's easier to carry defensive weapons without scaring the hell out of hotel guests." Cleavus shot McCruise his widest grin, eyes laden with enthusiasm.

Sitting behind his desk, Connor was knuckling his mustache; the crinkle line at the top of his nose the deepest McCruise ever saw. "We take Norwood and Shoney tonight," he advised, excitement reined in tightly under the leather façade.

"In addition to the evidence we've already gathered, we have Sadie's statement safely tucked away." He rubbed the arms of his chair, as if working up momentum.

The chair squeaked as he leaned forward, elbows on the desk, hands folded. "At least we have meat on the bone to take to the prosecuting attorney," he said, tapping a thick file on his desk. "Here are narcotic trafficking, illegal possession of firearms, Jaimie's confession of following Shoney's orders with the jimson weed popcorn, and Wally's bullet casing from the same kind of gun Shoney harbored in his penthouse. In addition, there remains Laura's murder, which undoubtedly materialized out of Shoney's instructions. The evidence for some cases is circumstantial and heavily laced with implication, such as the appearance of Valesano's body in the works of a sewage plant in Sri Lanka, for chrissakes." He rested his chin on the ledge of his folded hands, gazing down at the pulp pile of repugnant justification.

"Nevertheless, there's suitable substantiation to take the cases for both men to the Grand Jury."

He paused, nodding to McCruise. "Since the speaking engagements for Norwood are completed for London Bridge Days, I anticipate Shoney and Norwood will attempt to clear out of here some time tonight."

Connor's pluses were the arrogance of the subjects, arrogance to feel they'd wiped out all traces of trafficking and witnesses. He conned the con men. Like Bankers, they'd never suspect anyone to cross them.

If Sri Lanka were their destination, Connor would never get extradition. The country was at odds with itself. Sri Lanka could harbor two fugitives for years, especially two of such needed resourcefulness: Norwood with his Ob/Gyn technology and global connections to the banking industry, construction industry, iron ore mining, and Shoney with his managerial prowess. They all added up to tremendous assistance for Sri Lanka.

Connor leaned back, resting his head gently against the high back of his chair. "Your hunch was right, McCruise, about Norwood being the super power."

McCruise could see the contempt for the perpetrators in Connor's eyes. It shook out a minor miracle that Connor held out this long for arrests without hyperventilating. He could have tagged them both back a while with enough circumstantial evidence to blow them away.

Running his pencil over his mustache as if it was itchy, Connor re-assigned the old code name of Wetland Watergate: McCruise, Wetland 300, Cleavus, 200, CRT's 100. He never met a well-oiled sleuth system he didn't like. There would be no attempt at subterfuge. The arrests needed to be immediate—on sight.

Suddenly, McCruise sat upright, his whole world tumbling down around him. "Christ!" He jumped to his feet. "I called Jacquie late this afternoon. She agreed to have dinner with Norwood tonight at 6:30 in the dining room of the King's Retreat. She said it was sort of a farewell to trash." He hurried a look at his watch: six thirty-five. "We don't want her in the middle of this!" His eyes scared up strength, cut around the group in quick glances.

Stark realization reflected on all faces.

Connor stood, putting both his hands on the desk, leaning forward. "McCruise, maintain your post on the third floor."

"Cleavus," he nodded to him for emphasis, "you wait until Jacquie and Norwood are leaving the dining room. Remove Jacquie quietly into the hands of the CRT, read Norwood his rights, and make an instant arrest. Where Norwood is, you'll find Shoney." Underlying his eyes was a depth of expression no one wanted to interpret.

McCruise groaned aloud. His chest felt the constriction of a hundred straps, as if he'd fallen out of a tree and the breath knocked out of him. "Holy Jesus, Mary, and Joseph! Connor, Norwood might try using her for a hostage. Desperate men do desperate deeds." His heart hammered; his mind ran wildly. "They might take her up to Shoney's penthouse without her consent. You know, a strong-arm threat or even a sedative in her wine." His breath choked in his throat.

Although their relationship never resumed after the trip to Phoenix two weeks before, McCruise observed Jacquie often, measuring how her jeans fit, her shirts; he noticed how her hips flared from their usual trimness.

She'd not yet aborted.

He dominated her with his eyes when they met by chance, and he knew it wasn't by chance. Sometimes he mentally undressed and caressed her, other times he tore her apart with furious vengeance for not succumbing to his values. As a tremor ran through him, he lowered his head into his hands. He only made that one phone call to her, when she informed him of dinner with Norwood. He'd found it such an incomprehensible gesture that he'd hung up.

Cleavus said, "C'mon, McCruise," his open palm smacking him across the back. "We're not going to allow

Jacquie out of our sight. Tonight's the night we take 'em, old buddy. This one's for Wally." McCruise felt a powerful infusion of reassurance from his partner's brown countenance.

Connor caught McCruise's eyes. "I share your apprehension, but I'd like to know that you are on board with us, with your head on straight." There was in his voice a hint of quiet desperation. The unspoken appeal bolstered McCruise's flagging courage. He'd always thought of Connor as a rock, but even rocks seated with cores.

McCruise swallowed. "I'm in." Dinner with Norwood slammed into him again. He sank down into the chair from which he'd arisen, groaning. If Norwood slipped a Mickey into the wine or in her dinner, what would the drug do to the child in her womb? Agonizingly, he ran his hand through his hair.

Connor nodded. "Let's get over to the hotel ASAP." Yet he continued holding a commanding stance. He was aware that unspeakable and nameless suffering lay locked inside McCruise's head, like toxic waste in a landfill.

His eyes cut around the room, covering everyone. "Cover your asses. You can go from hero to zero in seconds." Rising, he walked to the window and looked out over the city.

The slow-moving, low-pressure system gripped the area, bringing intermittent thunderstorms, some with hail, dropping the temperature fiercely. The weather matched the climactic night.

Volatile, turning, he folded his hands behind his back. "*Vaya con Dios*," he said. Shards of apprehension shredded through the softly spoken words.

CHAPTER NINETY-ONE

While Mallika observed the dining room activities, Fayne Norwood and Sligh Shoney escorted a bewildered Jacquie from what appeared to have been a pre-arranged dinner date in the dining room.

As Mallika swiftly closed the distance between the dining room and the west elevator shaft, it not too tricky to watch where the elevator light stopped — on the third floor: Norwood's condominium the destination. A soothsayer, she needed not to tell her what was going to happen. It sickened her.

Many deviled details she chose to ignore since her arrival in Havasu. The blatant ravagement of Jacquie Remington was damnably clear and near. Moreover, how much did *she* contribute to the bending-knee mortification of her island people? The negotiations were to be at-the-table compromises, not devastation, and death. Her heart shriveled with the eye-opening events transpiring at the Duluth conferences. Her fellow citizens bowing to the offerings of the Wall Street Bankers, but at what price? Thousands of people from her culture saw extinction, in addition to those maimed and marked for life.

How she longed for Sri Lanka and the impressive central mountain massif of gneiss rock, the highest point at Pidurutalagala at 8,290 feet. In addition, there was Jaffna, the home of her ancestors, lying in the broad coastal plains of the north and tapering off in the long low-lying Jaffna Peninsula. This was the month the monsoon season would start with its wild, furious wind and rain slashing the tea plantations, then lifting and moving on in a matter of minutes.

She thrilled at the memory of the long train rides to Kandy and Matale with her Aunt Siri, Uncle Kotte, and Cousin Adasa, where they toured ancient civilization ruins calculated at more than 100,000 years old, the Buddhist Temples, and farther south, the Mahaweli Ganga with great hydroelectric dams.

While Siri and Kotte were positively vitalizing guardians, Adasa was her constant companion and confidante. Her beloved Adasa, the top of his head blown off in ruthless waste.

Moisture-ridden clouds hung over the mountains where lightning played around the edges. Mallika drew a brightly woven sari out of her closet, the garment of her mother and her mother's mother before her. It was a garment consisting of a brightly printed length of lightweight cloth; one end she wrapped about her waist to form a skirt, and the other she draped over her shoulder. It was perfection in style, and draped for her mission.

A Tamil Tiger slotted vest fit very nicely under the loose-fitting garment, giving her the freedom of movement she needed and the concealment she required. It proved to be no problem getting components to accompany her on her final adventure. The Internet provided all the information and resource the explosives required.

She wanted to look her loveliest. Sligh told her many times that she looked like an angel — an island angel in the sari. How she thrilled at his slightest touch, responded to his slightest compliment, his private glance. She witnessed that private glance tonight, not for her but for tousle-haired Jacquie.

Sitting at her mirror, Mallika applied mascara to her long dark eyelashes, accenting her large eyes, eyes that bulged just slightly, so common to her culture. Apple-blossom white teeth flashed in a smile against her honey-smooth skin. She smiled into the mirror, but she did not recognize her eyes; they were frightening in their opaqueness. They spoke to her of remorse and deep pain, yet there remained strength — the strength to follow through with final payment for something owed, and then instant absolution.

Heart aching, she remembered the great pride she took in Sri Lankan history, the part when Sirimavo Bandaranaike in 1959 became the first woman prime minister in the world. Mallika recalled the wonder and excitement of her grandparents, mystifying the auspicious event. Thoughts of duplicating the effort herself some day — becoming the Prime Minister of Sri Lanka, through her education, her American contacts, her love for her people — exhilarated her every thought and ambition.

Less than two years ago, Sri Lankan government forces recaptured Jaffna, but the Tamil Tigers continued guerrilla warfare from the jungle. In January 1996, suicide bombers blew up the Central Bank in Colombo, and in July 1996, they succeeded in taking the Sri Lankan army's Mullatavu base in the east, with Adasa's covert help.

Mallika's dream was to roll into the city of Jaffna like a modern-day Joan of Arc, forcing government troops to retreat, thus marking a tenuous, but dramatic victory. The Liberation Tigers of Tamil Eelam, fighting for an independent state for minority Tamils since 1983, would enter their cultural capital and maybe even meet little resistance from government soldiers. She may have been able to get the job done with as few as two hundred Tigers moving into the city after crossing the shallow lagoon that separated the Jaffna peninsula from the rest of the island.

Sighing, she sat back. Now there would be no turning back, no forgiveness for the Liberation Tigers of Tamil Eelam, but she might find redemption in freeing them of jackals — the two-legged animals that preyed on the unaware. There were those who thought they needed to avoid the answerability of responsibility at all cost, as if it were epilepsy; they lived in an unconscionable world.

Since succumbing to Shoney's attentions, she carried an elevator key to the penthouse. The hour growing late this stormy evening, she knew she would put the key to good use. The penthouse would be Shoney's destination with Jacquie, and if she knew the lust hidden in Norwood, he would be there too. She could go to the bank on it. At once, she recognized that she was out of her depth with these two Satyrs, who passed themselves off as men. Within her, a belly fire grew.

CHAPTER NINETY-TWO

Lightning danced, and sporadic rain rode deep wind gusts.

McCruise stepped from the plain gray pickup truck he and Cleavus chose from the vehicle pool and parked at the Convention Center, away from the hotel. Through a break in the clouds, stars shone occasionally and the wind swirled dervishes of bougainvillea blossoms around their ankles with conversational clacking. Billowing range coats tugged at their sides, and two-inch-heeled boots sounded hollow on the parking lot cobblestones. Both tipped their Resistols into the cranky wind as they strode the hundred yards back to the hotel.

McCruise knew Cleavus noticed that he slipped his Spas inside his range coat. The short shotgun was better suited to a battlefield than a hotel. A semi-automatic twelve-gauge shotgun utilized in pistol fashion or stock and weighing only ten pounds, holding eight shells—ten with an extension. With a button to transform it from a single shot to semi-automatic, it was beyond description as noisy as hell.

Cleavus saw the firm set of McCruise's jaw, and he didn't like the way time was rushing headlong into the superiority of this offense. Sixth sense swirling told him that he and McCruise stood rendered merciless. In their last six months together they witnessed too much, dragged through too much. However, he knew McCruise needed someone to stand by him in this ocean populated by hungry sharks.

Small talk melded to a companionable silence.

Without preamble, McCruise headed directly to the third floor, nodding to Cleavus as he got off the elevator on the second floor. A shudder ran through McCruise as the elevator doors closed with a soft swish; fear and loathing gripped his guts. He never judged himself to be so scheming. He knew that in his mind, at least, he reduced the entirety of the investigation to one common denominator: the dragon with two heads. The two heads, spewing fire and evil with every breath entered his private life.

Fire.

Evil.

A picture of Laura's death speared his mind as fast and streaking as the malignant lightning outside. He winced with the pain. Ordinarily, he could make the most complicated enigma simple, could over-simplify most anything by paring to the heart of a matter, but not this time. He unwillingly smiled to himself, a raw tearing at his facial features. The man he was tonight was the culmination of nearly a year of grief and longing.

He reached saturation with the frustration of *handling it* until all returns were diminishing. Tired of the nightmarish epoxy memories, the harsh awakenings by disillusionment, the grief heaped upon him by people of lesser values, yet he faced a vacuum of uncertainty. The convoluted road of promises that tomorrow might bring, he derided. That was nothing but a blend of the smashed hopes of yesterday. He was prepared to act now, pay later.

McCruise found a quiet lanai on the third floor, extending over Kokomo's night entertainment. A light rain asserted itself in front of the distant thunder, and showoff lightning of rainbow colors bounced around on the rim of thunderheads hanging over the mountains from northeast, north, to northwest.

McCruise's mind turned on, he stared at the chairs and tables on the lanai in a self-inflicted hypnotic haze. What was he doing sitting here when Jacquie was in the presence of a certified monster? The possession of a few positive thoughts brightened his dreary spirit. The Spas 12 jabbed him in the ribs as he sat there, reminding him of his mission.

He wished that he physically removed Jacquie out of her condominium two weeks ago and tucked her away in his home on the mountain. The little bitch was driving him crazy. His thoughts deteriorated into a dilemma. His body adrenalized, McCruise dialed F-1 on his shoulder intercom.

"Wetland Watergate One Hundred... any action?"

"One Hundred. None. Subjects not in dining room, and haven't been since we arrived an hour ago."

"Copy. No action up here. Ten-four," said McCruise.

He dialed F-2. "Wetland Two Hundred. Any action?"

"Wetland Two Hundred. Nothing." Cleavus sighed.

"I'm going to check Jacquie's condo, three-zero-six. If she's not there, I'm up the back stairs to Shoney's penthouse. I have the ratchet key to his stairwell." McCruise abruptly clicked off before Cleavus could respond.

He was not about to engage in any dense debate over rights and wrongs—the plusses and minuses of his decision, his misgivings far too significant.

CHAPTER NINETY-THREE

Conventional wisdom would put the money on dinner at Norwood's condominium: stormy night, Norwood leans on Jacquie for cozy fireplace, dinner, a Mickey Finn, and Bingo. On stage, front, and center, Shoney appears. Across the hall from Norwood's condominium on the third floor is the elevator. A few steps into the elevator and Jacquie transports to Shoney's hideaway.

McCruise's gut churned with restless thoughts. A smothered groan erupted from his throat. *If they lay a hand on her, they'll be dead meat.*

"Dead meat," he said aloud, his senses sharpened to a hone. In this night of revelations, his body responded with the power of determination. The long corridor was deadly quiet, air heavy with the storm churning outside. He walked, long-legged, his respiration picking up with his strides, range coat flowing around him, Resistol hat low on his forehead. He was on defense for ASU and by means of an intercept, he was moving to the goal line.

His loping gait sent the Spas twelve rubbing robustly on his leg, holding great promise. He neither wanted nor hoped for a peaceful closure to this merry-go-round he rode on for the last ten months. Smash-mouth confrontation holds the greater appeal. Now that his taut thread of happiness saw threat by those who themselves were untouchable, he would defend his position to the end. However, thoughts that Shoney would burn him down for ten bucks never left his mind. *This American Tale* shook into Shakespeare 101, and McCruise was ass-deep in subterfuge.

He found carnal knowledge of Jacquie, known the intoxicating joy of her presence in his life, and the fulfillment of her companionship. Surely, she felt these things herself; her honesty was uncomplicated. She returned his affections, wanted him as badly as he wanted her. There was a soft sound deep in his throat.

Laura's death used to be the benchmark by which McCruise struck all time; everything fell either before that day or after. Last night, he went to bed and shed the sandpaper of self-infliction due to Laura's death. No matter how many times he re-ran that day, the result was the same: final and irreversible. He needed to live among the living. Only three things were important in his life now: God, his family and Lady Jacquie. Laura would always hold a large chunk of his heart, but a love deceased, no matter how treasured, is of no comfort when everything comes crashing down.

Cognizant that he was dealing with no kitchen-table conspiracy here, McCruise slipped his condominium card quietly into Jacquie's door. It opened readily. No chain attached indicated that she left and the door simply locked behind her. The condominium was eerily dark except for the lightning that flashed through the patio slidebys. He wished the high-octane stirring in his stomach would dissolve.

Listening at Norwood's condominium adjacent to Jacquie's served no further answers. No sounds of conversation, music, or laughter reached his ears.

Taking the stairs to the penthouse, he was frightened, and lonely. Was he skating to the edge of open water? Did he have probable cause for searching the private quarters without a warrant?

Mentally, he reviewed the Fourth Amendment of the U. S. Constitution. *Cause exists when facts and circumstances within an officer's knowledge and of which he has reasonable trustworthy information are sufficient to warrant a man of caution in believing that an offense has been or is being committed. Slate v, North Dakota.*

Hell, yes, he garnered more evidence *for* than *against*, and, in this case, exigency. This was no time to hassle with personal doubts. With probable cause, he could use the force necessary to make a valid arrest—in self-defense or *in defense of*. He was walking a thin line, filled with what-ifs. His breath came in hard rasps.

A police officer may have a specific duty to use the means necessary to prevent a crime in progress, including the use of deadly force, he reminded himself. *Arizona Revised Statues 13-411.*

How did he remember that shit? More information was stored on his hard drive than he was willing to admit. What's more, the courts held that: *police officers are entitled to a qualified immunity where they have acted with a good faith belief, and that reasonable grounds existed for this belief, based upon objective circumstances at the time they acted, and acted with prudence.*

Fuck prudence!

The octagon ratchet slipped into the aperture silently and turned like silk. Letting himself in, a heavy soundlessness surrounded him. The penthouse was incredibly quiet. What was that smell? *Ether*? Sure, Shoney used ether in his lab. The word compacted on his tongue.

The demand of the moment superseded all other thoughts. *Police officers need an arrest warrant to enter the suspect's own residence to affect his arrest, unless an emergency exists.*

Headquarters, we have an emergency, his mind called out.

McCruise's eyes scanned the long hall. Soft lights glowed in the living room at the end of the hall. Here, too, the night sky flashed in brilliant waves against the glass doors of the patio, yet there was no sound. Stalking toward Shoney's bedroom, the smell became stronger, but he found only darkness there.

His mind slowed down and nearly stopped working, and then froze when suddenly his good sense shifted into second gear. A moment, only for a moment did his mind stay in second when it shifted into high, remembering the Blue Boy rendering on the wall in the hall.

Stealth sat on a back burner. A loud crack of thunder rattled the walls as McCruise threw caution to the wind and pushed the penis point on the replication of *Blue Boy*, the sensitized area for admittance, the secret touch that opened onto a bizarre world of pleasure and pain.

It didn't open!

His chest constricted in a painful knot.

CHAPTER NINETY-FOUR

Drawing the S & W from his shoulder holster, he planted his size-twelve Justin immediately under the pressure point of the catch, springing the door open, the *Blue Boy* dangling in concert with the thunder rolling around heaven. One sweep of the room revealed Jacquie—alone. She lay colorless on the red velvet bedspread, her hands and feet tied to the bedposts, her light auburn hair curled in masses around her face. She lay anesthetized.

Jesus H. Christ!

If he could see inside her head, he imagined it would be a whorl networking of doubt and distrust. Everything within him stood galvanized. A nebulous ghost-fist squeezed his heart, turning his mood from dour to pissed.

Shoney had thrown a velour bathrobe over her to keep his "catch of the day" warm, undoubtedly. McCruise went half nuts, walked to the bed, reached out, and touched her hand as if he could infuse her quiet body with his strength. Her skin was soft to the roughness of his hand. On her cheeks, her lashes lay lightly, concealing the light of her topaz eyes; her breathing was barely perceptible.

She seemed at once an angel and a wood sprite. As a mixture of cold rain and hail lectured at the skylights, the reflective mirrors glowed in soft licks of yellow flame cast from scented candles. Memories of Wally waltzing around with a leather whip surged through his mind's tidal water. God in heaven, how he missed him, needed him. He closed his eyes and breathed hard with the vividness of the memory.

In the bathroom, water was running, hydro jets gargling. McCruise holstered his S & W and thumbed down automatic on the Spas 12. The hair on the back of his neck bristled, electrifying with the hunt. Silently, he entered the great bathroom where Shoney, clad only in a red terrycloth wraparound, was testing the water in the Jacuzzi, arranging the snorts on the corner. If that didn't work, there were some hypodermic needles on the shelf over the Jacuzzi.

Oblivious to McCruise's presence, Shoney adjusted the four jets, swiped his hand on a towel, and turned around with a sharp intake of breath. His face melded from self-satisfied to incredulous realization. Ice-blue eyes rounded with apprehension, darting from the giant of a man who materialized from nowhere, wearing desert-colored range wear, a western hat riding high on his head, tall in his boots and fire in his eyes.

In an instant, Shoney grabbed a needle and rushed with vehemence at McCruise. McCruise allowed the Spas to drop back to his hip and land a blow to Shoney's wrist. The plastic syringe flew across the room, smashed into a mirror and skittered to the floor.

"You interfering bastard, I'll kill you!" Shoney spit the words through his clenched teeth. "No one enters my private quarters. It's my home." The words waxed brave, the eyes weaved frightened.

McCruise held up a hand to silence him. "Your expectation of privacy is blown, jackass! In view of what I've found, I'd say I was correct."

"You're in luck, McCruise. I'll not kill you," Shoney's lips spoke in a face turned to ash. "I have something better: a payoff, say five hundred thousand, and the penthouse. I'll leave town tonight. We can close the deal right now." He skinned his lips past his teeth, his dead eyes assessing McCruise.

Mention of the God-almighty dollar curled anger like a hard fist in McCruise's gut. It was, of course, all disgusting bullshit. "Move!" McCruise ordered, slanting the Spas in the direction of the bedroom, moving the selector button on the Spas back to single shot.

Shoney stalled.

"Now!" McCruise thundered.

Shoney moved.

McCruise motioned to the bed where the unaware Jacquie lay in soporific bliss. "Untie her," he growled.

Shoney worked his way around the bed, untying the ropes, dawdling with a defiant slowness that was maddening. "I have a right to identification of you as a policeman, McCruise, yet you break and enter like some kind of a *Have-Gun-Will-Travel*." Delivering his message, he stopped untying the ropes.

"Don't test my patience, you son-of-a-bitch. Get those ropes off the bed now and tie them all together in one long piece. Your education in law enforcement has suffered along the way, old man. The use of undercover police officers does not violate the Fourth Amendment, and is essential to the enforcement of vice laws."

"Says who, smart ass?"

"Try the Supreme Court."

"Up yours."

"Them's fightin' words, Shoney. Another arrestable offense. Verbal attacks on an officer before an arrest are fighting words used to incite and are not constitutional speech. A conviction for disorderly conduct can result." McCruise shook his head in light of the microanalysis.

"Speed it up or you've heard your last raindrop," McCruise said in a voice so hoarse he scarcely recognized it as his own—maybe Clint Eastwood's, but not his own. While Shoney complied by tying the ropes together, McCruise adjusted the bathrobe that covered Jacquie only anemically.

As Shoney's gluttonous eyes drank in the whiteness of Jacquie's shoulders, her sprite-like face surrounded by Little Orphan Annie curls, McCruise shuddered. Bereft now of emotions, only primal instincts prevailed.

"Tie one end of the rope around your waist and come with me."

"Move!"

"What the hell... whaddaya think you're doing? Take the five hundred thousand and run." He laughed with a shallow sniveling sound.

"I have an anti-money mentality. Your offer sucks." McCruise felt ultra-high, which was a polarization from the bad case of the wobbles he wore upon entry.

At the end of the Spas, McCruise marched Shoney onto the patio. The wind blew with demented cold. Shadowboxing with low hanging clouds, brilliant streaks of lightning sliced the night. Blown and scattered were the patio wet-bar and cart; plastic glasses and pitchers strayed across the grumbling deck area.

"Over to the parapet," McCruise directed. It annoyed the hell out of him that if he did not shake Shoney down now, he would probably lose an arrest because some silver-tongued lawyer would claim the evidence was inadmissible, due to the manner in which he obtained it: *broke, entered, and searched.*

CHAPTER NINETY-FIVE

Shoney backed with slow belligerence to the three-foot wall.

"Now, affix the other end of the rope to the tie-down near the drain vent."

"Fuck you, McCruise! Have you lost you mind? It's cold out here. What did I do to bring this on?" Shoney's words were incisive, but the delivery lacked substance, the words splintering in a crumbling facade.

"Questions—I'll ask, and give *you* five minutes for straight answers or over the top you go to dangle and die of hypothermia or garroting, whichever comes first. You can hang there forever, as far as I'm concerned."

Mentally, McCruise added the word, "interrogated," to, "entered" and "searched," as menacingly, the smell of ozone drifted around them.

"The countdown starts now, Shoney. Why did you burn *Jaimie*?"

McCruise's mind ran to high velocity study of the facial reactions on Shoney. Knowing a truthful answer would go a long way to determining deceptiveness. The gaze that met McCruise's glittered with hate—hard, crystallized hate.

"What're you talking about, you crazy asshole? Instead of showing up at work, he showed up at the city morgue." Shoney was visibly shivering. McCruise liked the reading;

he saw the opaque shutters of Shoney's mind open for a count.

"A likely story. You imported him from Mexico and trained him to brandish damnation and disaster, made a predator out of him, and now you know nothing of him? Was he skimming off your profits? Is that why you killed him and dumped the poor galley slave in the desert for coyote feed?"

"No!" Shoney shook with cold. "If that's all you want to know, you have the wrong person; now let's move inside and I'll close the offer." The shutters came down with long practiced deftness.

"Four minutes, ten seconds. Now I suppose you're going to tell me that Jaimie poisoned the popcorn at the kiosk on his own volition—because he simply took a disliking to Wally and me." McCruise pulled his Resistol lower over his forehead.

"Hey, Copper," Shoney sneered, waiting for the derogatory word to mess up McCruise's mind. "You know kids now days; they do unexplainable things. Maybe he thought it was a joke." He tried on a derisive laugh that choked off as fast as it started. Sligh's eyes darted to a storage cabinet to his left, well out of reach.

Shoney's prattle did not distract McCruise's hyped senses from observing Shoney's glance to the cabinet. "Three minutes, eighteen seconds. How do you explain the brutal rape and death of the juvenile, right here, last July?" McCruise asked, the words shooting out as if launched.

"It was an accident, an investigated accident. The King's Retreat was not responsible. That accusation isn't worth a shit." Shoney folded his arms across his chest in defensiveness, shifted his eyes again, this time his feet moved subtly toward the storage cabinet.

A tight ball of fury formed in McCruise's gut at the audacity of this piece of shit. "It's macho manure, you speak; mega pounds of manure rolling off your tongue." He knew that the people who meted out judgment in courtrooms could not possibly assess the schmuck that law enforcement met in the real world.

If the law is to enjoy honor, those who enforce it must first exhibit honor. The end never justifies the means. Well, in this case, Shoney justified the means. McCruise suggestively adjusted the Spas under his range coat. "Time's fading fast: two minutes ten is all that remains. Who was responsible for filing thin the metal structure of the scaffolding at the Golden Crest in August? Hmmm? Think fast, Shoney."

"Christ, how should I know?" Shoney sucked air. His eyes shone like polished pyrite, but the glitter was as cold and hard as diamonds. "Accidents happen, you crazy bastard!"

"One minute, fifty seconds." McCruise stood at high alert under the extended overhang outside the patio doors, staring straight across the twelve-foot expanse of decking. "The warehouse under the Golden Crest, know anything about that setup, old man? Huh?"

"How the hell should I know what's under the Golden Crest?" His voice was thick; his whole body shook with the cold. This was the first time in his life that he was not the controller speaking silky words, but the controllee.

"One minute, ten seconds. When did you decide to take out Officer Denton? Was it right after the popcorn trick failed? On the other hand, was it after stalking both of us for weeks? Was it a spontaneous decision? Fifty seconds."

"You wouldn't send me over the edge of the building. We're four floors up and this rope was never meant to support much weight."

"Keep blubbering. The clock's ticking."

"Who knows who shot Denton? Anyone could have gotten to the roof and whacked him. I can't keep tabs on every fruitcake that checks in here."

"Thirty seconds to hell. This is the jackpot question: you get it right, and you stay. Who rammed and exploded my wife's Jeep vehicle?" McCruise started forward, his hand menacingly creeping into his range coat.

"Jesus Christ! You're crazy-nuts. Your wife's demise was as much news to me as it was to you. It's long ago. Forget it, man," he said in a creaky voice.

McCruise's face came into relief as a searing flash of jagged lightning rent the roof from end to end, eerily illuminating the patio. Reasonable, burning anger flared.

"You're smart-assing me, Shoney." Explanations such as Shoney's would have been specious coming from anyone, but double deceptive coming from him.

"Time's up. Over the wall. If you don't repel down now, you know there is an alternative." *Courts would consider this reasonable and prudent?*

"You can't get away with this. It's against your training, against everything in your cultured lifestyle. You couldn't do it," Shoney said testily.

"Over the side," McCruise growled, moving to Shoney's position near the parapet; from under the range coat, the barrel of the Spas bulged at Shoney's groin.

Sometimes courts were not judicial at deciphering what was reasonable and judicial.

CHAPTER NINETY-SIX

Shoney jumped over the ledge, a strident scream tearing from his throat. He caught, the knots held, the fibers pinging over the brick abutment. The shivering rope hung down the wall and swayed with a sudden wind gust, needles of hard hail hitting a soft target.

"This is coercion," he shouted hollowly. "You can't let me die like this. I've been good for the community, employing hundreds of people, bringing in tourists, and boosting the economy." The puppetry recitation came through blue lips and spilled out between convulsions of chills.

"You're breaking my heart. Maybe I should light a candle," McCruise said. "My wife and Wally were good for the community, too. The young girl who died without ever living will never know her potential for community contributions. The death of the construction worker left a wife and three children without a provider. The innocent man walking a neighborhood street of the city was good for the community when death dealt him out. Thousands, hundreds of thousands of unsuspecting young people, our country's future, have been hooked by your trading, selling, and dealing narcotics."

The advantage of taking Shoney by surprise knew offset by his choice of sites for the job. McCruise shivered with the bone-chilling cold, his lips compressed into two straight lines. "You can hang there until the rope gives out and you cross over the River Styx, where the devil will look after you. You're lucky it's raining; the rope will tighten around your waist and makes it less likely for you to slip through when you lose consciousness." McCruise sat on the parapet ledge, an awesome sight in the night, figuratively powerful and realistically deadly. The Spas rested safely inside his range coat.

"Where is Norwood? Where's all the cocaine?" He paused.

"How the hell should I know? He's a double-crossing nightmare." The guttural sound that ensued made his mouth open and shut like a fish's.

"Would you like me to read you your rights, you bastard?"

McCruise didn't care anymore. He became as cynical as a corner tavern Madame. "You have the right to remain silent."

"You'll pay big time for this, flatfoot."

"We're going to lose you to the elements like a super nova, Shoney. Telling me the truth will get you a nice warm bed in the city jail before you transfer to a warm bed in the county jail, then yet to another warm bed at Florence before you transfer to the white chamber, screaming, and dragging the full distance—a dead man walking. You're going to die either way. At least you'd get half a chance with a jury." McCruise allowed his voice to fade to allow for sinking-in time.

Be professional, they taught him at the academy. The thought made his chest rise and fall in an expulsion of air that blew off the vast separation between the two-pronged argument of "by-the-book" and "get real."

"Anything you say can be used against you in a court of law." McCruise dragged the words out slowly.

"All right. All right." Shoney's voice was weak. His eyes blinked to wash off the raindrops and haze of the hypothermia. "The warehouse is mine, and Norwood's." He paused. "That's it. That's all."

397

"You have a right to the presence of an attorney."
Looking down at the great eyes staring up at him, McCruise
made an excessive gesture at rubbing the rope on the bricks,
creating a grating sound, and snapping fibers.

Shoney's mouth gaped in a rictus of startled alarm at
McCruise's ruthlessness. Lightning popped around him,
followed by cracking thunder. Shoney's eyes glazed over.

"If you cannot afford an attorney, one will be appointed
for you prior to any action." McCruise snapped, impatience
overcoming professionalism. The kindergarten of Miranda
Rights was nothing but debilitation to an arresting officer.

"It was all me," he squeaked in acquiescence. "Just get
me the hell off this building," his voice pleaded sickly. "I
don't want to hear any more rights. I can buy and sell every
attorney in town."

"My wife's vehicle t-boned to hell?"

"Yesss." The word lingered on Shoney's chilled tongue.

"Officer Denton shot and killed?"

"Yeah." No more than a grunt.

"The construction worker fiasco?"

"Jaimie. I ordered Jaimie to do it," he chattered.

"The popcorn?"

"Jaimie."

"Who directed him, paid the kiosk?"

"My orders, my money."

"What did you give Jacquie to sedate her?"

"Darvon."

"What else?"

"Ether," the words were paling now.

"You shall enjoy the right to a speedy and public trial by
an impartial jury of the State of Arizona and County of
Mohave. Excessive bail shall not be required, nor fines
imposed, nor cruel and unusual punishments inflicted."
Words! Stupid! What an ineffectual pain in the ass, in light
of Shoney's crimes.

McCruise stabilized himself against the parapet with his
foot and slowly pulled the weighty body to the top, grabbing
Shoney's now imperfect coiffure and tugging until his
shoulders came abreast of the wall, sliding him over the
ledge like a hooked marlin, leaving him flopping on the floor

of the deck. As he unfastened the rope from the tie-down, he wondered what kind of heyday a defense attorney was going to have with that confession.

Turning to the patio doors, McCruise moved to re-enter the penthouse. The least he could do was seek the pathetic pig a blanket. That's when his heightened senses heard it.

CHAPTER NINETY-SEVEN

The storage cabinet door slicked open. The click of a hammer pulled back sounded like an escape hatch clanking shut, with McCruise on the outside. Every nerve in his body responded.

In the time it took Shoney to apply three pounds of pressure on the trigger and the time it took McCruise to turn and shoot the Spas 12 from his hip, the time lapse was minutia, but the difference was survival. Shoney's frozen fingers were no match for McCruise's vengeance. Time stood immeasurable as the two men faced each other in a split second of final commitment.

The Spas blast shook the deck and reverberated with thunder from overhead as simultaneously, lightning found Shoney's wet body and metal gun. With sheer blue-white light, the night ripped open with outward spirals of high-tensity undulations starkly silhouetting Shoney's levitated body. His eyes popped with dead dismay, his mouth formed in a soundless wail, his flesh tearing into fragments.

Although McCruise was jolted backwards against the patio doors, he got off one more shot, disintegrating the genetic misfit, lifting what was left of Shoney's body up and over the parapet into the nothingness of the night, straight to hell, the rope trailing over the edge in mockery of what small security it gave him. It was as if he cut away from an umbilical cord. Lightning again licked out and pierced the indescribable descending mass. If this was a world without justice, here, at least was proportionality.

McCruise stared. Inner turmoil burned his stomach. His teeth ached from inadvertent clenching, his nose repulsed at the acrid smell of cordite, ozone and scorching flesh. In an adrenaline decline, he melded unsteadily. His heart adjusted pace, sweat turned cold on his back, and he slid to a squat on the deck, his chest heaving, his head bent in torment, incoherent as cold, blowing rain mingled with the onslaught of his tears.

He didn't know why he wept, and he was past applying logic.

He wept alone, sitting propped against the patio door for an exhaustive eternity, when the door slid open behind him. His whole body bolted, feeling the unmistakable steel of a gun on his bowed head.

"I say, that was awfully decent of you. Nice show! I couldn't have done better myself." Fayne Norwood stood just within, stripping McCruise bare with his gaze, making sure McCruise knew what was coming next. There was a deep loathsomeness about him, revealing no soul.

"Drop the gun and march over to the wall," Norwood demanded. "This is the finest fortune I've ever stumbled upon. I came to kill the intolerable toad myself." In the few moments during which he spoke, Norwood stationed himself in the warm recesses of the penthouse, while consigning McCruise to the deepest pits of hell.

"Right now, McCruise. I have no qualms about dropping you right here and throwing you over the side. It's perfect. You and Shoney quarreled, and you both rode the lightning to hell." He gave a disdainful sniff. "This is hardly a challenge." He laughed, but a steely light overrode any amusement in his tan eyes. His overlying condescension was worse than his words.

McCruise rose, his knees objecting to the unfolding, his mind rejecting to the undoing of his *coup de gras*. So, was this to be it? From below, a gaunt coyote howled, sniffing at the dinner from heaven that was lying in front of him. In the distance, another coyote answered, and yet another.

He braved the sins of humanity; put himself through a ten-month tapestry of pain and grief, to end like this. He un-holstered the Spas, dropping it to the wet patio. This was not a favorable time to match his ungainly weapon with the rapid fire of a small handgun. McCruise's earlier cool control leaked away; the staunch resolve appeared to ease out of him. His world was falling apart.

Hidden and forgotten memories flooded his psyche, memories buried deep within his sub-consciousness surfaced: the childhood fear of the dark, the gripping apprehension of his first confession, his pride at making his First Holy Communion. His very own cocker spaniel puppy, Pesky, rode the memory train along with his T-ball team enthusiasm. On the train sped the elation of the first time he ever rode a two-wheeler, the masterful feeling of winning the third-grade spelldown, his hard-won high school, and college football trophies. Another coach sped by, carrying the fitful doubts resultant from the first time he made love to a woman. The halcyon years with the ASU Sun Devils came to full bloom as his memory train tore down the tracks.

The London Bridge granite lump was in his throat again. Would his Creator understand his motives for tonight's actions?

A gentle, robotic voice permeated the demonic storm. "Mr. Cruise, move down the patio and enter the den door." The soft words lay thickly laced with lethal arsenic; McCruise's skin prickled all over. He spun around.

Holding a small caliber gun in her hand, the Asian woman's face drew tight, her eyes unreadable. Mallika stood like a specter behind a rigid Fayne Norwood. Her immobile expression never flickered as her gaze made a study of McCruise's frozen reaction.

"You must have faith," she said, nodding to McCruise. "Move away."

Although she possessed a coveted combination of exotic beauty and intelligence, McCruise stood forewarned by the controlled violence in her voice. With a mixture of gratitude and unconcealed admiration, McCruise edged to the right along the patio. If he could get as far as the den sliders, he'd make a last desperate move to re-enter the penthouse.

He faced west into the shrieking torrent that was lashing the granite walls of the Retreat. The wind howled down the expanse of decking and moaned against the den's slidebys.

"Don't make a move, Mr. Norwood," Mallika ordered, her voice an evil cup of hatred pouring from a dulled mind, her words dripping slowly, as if practiced, but delivered from the stupor of a self-induced hypnotic trance. "Drop the gun and don't try anything heroic." She broke off as Norwood's body tensed, his backward glance darkening.

"You can no longer intimidate me." Mallika's eyes glittered warningly. "Wog!" He called her a "wog," a disparaging term, and the dubbing struck with all the force of a ninety-mile-an-hour pitch at a Diamond Backs baseball game. Bastard! He'd sucked her brain and stripped her soul of sustenance. Her dream of leaving her footprints indelibly etched across the width and breadth of Sri Lanka now laid deleted forever, irretrievably dust. The self-acknowledgment worked on her nerves, which were already teetering on the brink.

"Let's cut a deal, Mallika," Norwood shouted with an anxiety factor registering above the shriek of the icy winds. "I'll make you the most powerful woman in Sri Lanka. I can do it." His words hastened. "I'll credit you for the completed negotiations, the new waste water treatment plants, and more—much more." The largesse of the offer thinly disguised his desperation.

"Drop the gun, Mr. Norwood." Mallika was almost shrieking, the high hysterical note in her voice cutting through McCruise like a machete—venomous and cold. She wasn't crying, but her eyes were magnified and shiny-wet with unshed tears, her dark skin beatified with the zealousness of the task.

McCruise's eyebrows cocked with the challenge in her words, heard the sound of Norwood's gun hitting the deck, observed the slow motion upward unbending of Norwood's body, as if he were calculating his advantages of wrestling with the fragile woman. Nothing cut ground from under Norwood quicker than a woman's advantage.

"Don't even think about it, Fayne. You're all done with your earthly challenges of power and might, riches and women. You were bored with every woman you ever courted; no one was a big enough challenge. Well, I'm not your usual run of fluff and stuff. You'll not use me anymore, or my people, or countless other innocents," Mallika recited as if doing third-grade timetables.

"You're the most important to me." Norwood's voice quavered as Mallika slowly nudged him to the parapet. The outline of her chest pressed against his back was rock-hard tubular—the small gun pressed to his gonads, daunting.

"No one is important to you, Mr. Norwood." Mallika spoke with vacancy in her tone. "You're all done preening for the public at the expense of others. I'm going to melt your ass."

CHAPTER NINETY-EIGHT

The words were enough for McCruise. He made it to the den doors, slid one open, and moved inside.

"I know you are safely inside, Mr. Cruise." McCruise stiffened at the astuteness of this Sri Lankan enigma. His eyes grew round with surprise and indecision.

"Close all the doors tightly. Go to Jacquie. Take her out of here. Quickly! You have only minutes."

The mystery of Mallika's appearance, the heart-thudding presence of Norwood, the electrifying disintegration of Shoney shot through McCruise's mind with indescribable dread and horror.

With heightened sense, he hastened to remove Jacquie from the bed wrapped in Shoney's robe, and then he pressed the "down" arrow on the elevator. Seconds were an eternity, the elevator never before so slow. Finally, it opened. He was grateful that Jacquie lacked consciousness; he didn't want to watch the pain of embarrassment steal into her eyes as it did the night Shoney attacked her.

As long as he'd known Mallika, he'd never figured her for his savior; he'd never gotten a peek within her soul. Although they'd become friends over the investigative period, they never lived in each other's pockets or heads.

He could feel his heart pounding furiously. The rush of thoughts teased and touched him; one could not forget the grim unfolding of the price paid for his rescue, and that of Jacquie. On the third floor, McCruise rushed Jacquie into her condominium, closed the door behind him, encouraging it with his foot.

The explosion rocked the building.

CHAPTER NINETY-NINE

Filled with the violence of Mallika's suicide justice, yet grateful to be alive, McCruise's trial was not yet over. He yet needed Jacquie to pull through. Explanations were due O'Shaughnessey. An apology to Cleavus hung in abeyance for leaving him. The re-wind of hellfire he'd just walked through unscathed brought on a violent attack of tremors. He laid the deeply sleeping Jacquie on her bed. Her coloring was a wipeout, a waif without dignity, as she lay oblivious to what took place around her.

The wail of sirens assailed McCruise's ears.

The clambering of footsteps in the hall brought relief in the form of Cleavus and Connor, lead by the Crisis Response Team. Cleavus put a hand on McCruise's shoulder in empathy, squeezed with unspoken message.

How long was he in this torture chamber? A lifetime, equating to less than twenty minutes by his watch. Nausea washed over McCruise, cautioning him to beat a path to the bathroom, where he threw up. Mind-over-matter didn't work, unless it didn't matter. Thus, no one minded. However, he minded. He minded; he minded terribly. Gathering his hijacked brain together, he walked back to the bed and pulled Jacquie into his arms, rocking her gently, still tasting the acidity of his own vomit.

The Crisis Response Team was setting up shop in Jacquie's condominium, taping off the hallways and instructing the ground crew below, all hustling with quiet conversations.

"What the hell?" Connor put things together as he scanned the room, which looked as if it existed in a war zone. While the penthouse disintegrated completely, the blast created huge ceiling and window damage to Jacquie's condominium.

The Emergency Medical Technicians, sent straight from heaven, worked on Jacquie, administering oxygen, applying a blood pressure cuff and starting an IV. McCruise messaged *thanks* to Cleavus for second-guessing his needs.

"This woman must be transported." The EMT Captain cut a quick glance to McCruise. Jacquie's pulse was increasing as her blood pressure decreased. Shock. The Emergency Medical Team, moving in unison, slid Jacquie smoothly onto the gurney. McCruise stood helplessly by, holding her limp hand. It was damned tough to uphold your reputation as the department hardass when a loved one was involved in a crime scene.

The weather was insistently wicked when McCruise arrived at the hospital; snarling rain spattered at his turned up collar, pelting his Resistol with savagery. Glaring parking lot lights reflected dizzily on the pavement.

Charged with activity, the emergency room was hectic as McCruise entered the cubicle where Jacquie lay in treatment. Connor nodded a silent greeting. Marvel was enroute. A multiple intravenous plug lay taped to Jacquie's wrist where glucose and nutrients flowed into her inert body. Oxygen was leading to her nostrils in minute transparent tubes, and catheterization commenced.

Dr. Ron Nettlesum, an OB-Gyn called in by O'Shaughnessey, issued orders. "Blood tests for sedatives, drugs, any foreign bodies. STAT."

Jacquie lay white and unresponsive.

McCruise's gut chattered, his personal life in some kind of a limbo.

"I'd guess nine, ten weeks pregnant," Doc said, pressure-measuring Jacquie's abdomen. He cast a quick glance at McCruise. "She's holding on, all right." His voice was low and intense. "Let's hope this trauma doesn't bring on an early abort."

A sound—part sigh and part groan—came from McCruise's throat, riding the edge of emotional extinction. He said nothing; words were beyond him.

"She needs observation. I'm going to keep her here for at least another day. She'll be weak. We need to consider the onslaughts to her body—the trauma, the psychological bearing this incident will impose on her well-being."

Doc shook his head, puzzled. "Vicissitudes," he said, peeking over his bifocals. "It won't be long before she surfaces." He sighed. "She's one damn lucky woman. I'll have lab results later." His words echoed over his shoulder as the short, amiable man breezed out of the emergency cubicle.

****

With Connor and Marvel keeping the first watch, McCruise went home, showered, and shaved. Pulling his mouth into strange contortions, he razored every nook and cranny. In the stillness of the house, the scratch of the razor sounded like scraping bushes on stucco, but a new image emerged.

A man needed goals in life, something to show for the time he'd spent on earth. He created Mark and Luke—his blessed Boticelli Angels. He wanted more: more joy, more fulfillments, more of Jacquie, more of what she could bring into his life. He didn't want to go back to the half-life in which he floundered. He didn't. He didn't. Tucker weaved in and out between his legs in a show of friendship, tongue lolling, and eyes empathetic.

He wanted another child to bring greater continuity between himself and the future. He'd slain the dragon. She must come around after this night of demented terror. Worn thin with this balancing act, he looked into the mirror at a face that was set with determination.

Admittedly, however, McCruise knew Jacquie to be a self-possessed woman who seldom needed anyone to bolster or abet her.

CHAPTER ONE HUNDRED

It was close to 10:00 PM before McCruise re-entered the hospital, looking as worn as an old book, but with a new cover. Connor and Marvel were managing a struggling conversation with Jacquie. The lowered lights of the hospital bed lamps on the wall threw warm pools of light on the stark whiteness of the sheets and the patient.

"Jacquie." Connor's voice was resonant. "The first thing you need to know is that McCruise saved your life. If he didn't show up when he did, God only knows what would have transpired. It's terrifying." His voice broke, drawing her hand in between his and leaning over to look more closely into her eyes, eyes fighting to stay awake.

Marvel smiled wanly, her left incisor a smidgen offset, as Jacquie's identical tooth grew offset. She nodded in appreciation of Connor's message, twisting a tissue around her index finger repeatedly, sniffling.

A tremor ran through Jacquie as she applied a small amount of pressure on Connor's hands. "I can remember almost nothing—having coffee after dinner—great feeling of peacefulness." Her voice was tiny, almost childlike in its timbre.

Dr. Nettlesum returned. "Well, young lady, your blood work shows the sedatives Shoney chose were no more than strong tranquillizers, but they were ample enough to put you into a layer below consciousness until he anesthetized and really took you out of it." He busied himself with checking blood pressure, respiration, and pulse again.

Putting his stethoscope to Jacquie's belly, his head bobbed, his mouth smiled widely. Removing it and adjusting it around his neck, he said lightly, "That fella in there has a picking-up heartbeat as strong as a grandfather clock. Congratulations." He included McCruise, Connor, and Marvel in his good news, his perfect teeth glistening in the softly lighted room.

"I'll leave you with your family," he addressed Jacquie, "and return in the morning to do a progress check." A hearty laugh of levity enveloped his privileged belly, breaking the gloom in the room.

Connor and Marvel gave Jacquie a caring kiss goodnight, Marvel cupping her face, and promising to be back in the morning.

McCruise could stand there forever. The Irish texture of her flesh seemed drawn and luminous, as if she were living in skin too small. He bent over and held her closely, the love in his chest making breathing difficult for him. "I love you, Jacaranda Rose Remington," he whispered. "I intend to love you and our child forever and ever, and that's a long, long time." His warm breath flooded her ear.

"I love you, too, Matthew Cameron Cruise," she said brokenly, covering her face with trembling hands at the thought of coming so close to losing him and her child for the sake of success, for the sake of staving herself from the ravages of an imagined man-hurt. "Can you ever forgive me?" She cried, her voice shaking with the temerity of her previous views.

"Yes," he said quickly, placing a chair near her and lifting a hand from her face to stem her self-condemnation. "Don't, Jacquie. We've both been through a lifetime of trauma tonight. We'll be married as soon as you can stand up and say, 'I do'." Quietly, he kissed her palm.

Her eyelids battled to stay open.

"But you must come as a matched set: you, and the child." He searched her face, her crayon blue eyes overflowing with a dichotomy of pride and repentance, but perhaps he saw a flicker of healing there, too. He moved his strong hand to her cheek.

She breathed softly, "Yes, to all the above."

Ever since she spun upward from the anesthesia, she'd hoped he'd come. Never did she need him more, needed his love, his strength, his protection, his acceptance, the lifestyle he'd offered her repeatedly. She even loved his stiff-necked arrogance.

An overwhelming flow of happiness shot through him as if he'd been infused. "I have a nervous engagement ring needing the confidence of a home," he said, his voice deep. Slipping it into his mouth, he swirled it around his tongue, and slipped it onto her finger. "Look how it smiles at you, Jacquie; it's home again." He felt tears burning the backs of his eyes; she seemed so small and shaken.

She smiled and nodded.

His posture before her was princely. He was an undefeatable conqueror, starkly primitive and barbarous, but he was as proud as ever of any victory in his life.

Wordlessly, he recalled *all gold, in view of her, is but Havasu heated sand.*

He was going to concentrate on how very right that was.

About Peggy DePuydt

Peggy was born in Nahma, Michigan and graduated high school as valedictorian. While successfully raising four children, (a registered nurse, a para-legal, a speech therapist and a policeman), she spent 13 years as a legal secretary, and an additional 13 years as executive secretary to the plant manager for American Motors Corporation.

She then returned to college and completed a lifetime aspiration of a degree in Liberal Arts. It was during this time that she developed a zest for creative writing, taking three semesters.

Successes have been counted along her path to creativity. The political arena has been an activity in which she has taken an active part. She was a Precinct Committeeman, then County Chairman of the Iron County, Michigan Republican Party. She ran for County Commissioner and was elected handily to that position.

In 1988, Peggy moved to Lake Havasu City, Arizona with her husband, Richard, a retired Michigan State Police officer. Since that time she has been Vice President of the Lake Havasu Republican Women, and Second Vice President of the Arizona Federation of Republican Women.

Peggy joined the Keep Havasu Beautiful Committee, (KHBC) an environmentally driven organization. She has been chairman of this committee, overseeing fifteen sub-committees each having a chairmanship of its own. Peggy and her committee received the coveted Hammer Award from Vice President Al Gore's office for Re-inventing Government. Her committee retrofitted the Lake Havasu City U.S. Post Office with new irrigation and landscaping vegetation at a cost of 10% of that which it would have cost had it been let out on bids.

Through Peggy's efforts, a multi-agency, lakeshore anti-litter and anti-pollution body, Buddies on the River (BOTR), was formed. Their success was so tremendous that the program received the Governor's Pride in Arizona Award, a once-a-year recognition for innovative ways and means of litter and pollution control. Subsequently, Peggy was named Volunteer of the Year by the Lake Havasu Area Chamber of Commerce for the extra-mile service to her community as Chairman of the Keep Havasu Beautiful Committee.

The author of four books, Peggy is now relaxing and authoring, much to her content.

Printed in the United States
83800LV00004BA/3/A